# THE BINDING CHAIR

KATHRYN HARRISON is the
author of the novels *Thicker Than
Water*, *Exposure*, and *A Thousand
Orange Trees*. She has also written
a memoir, *The Kiss*. Her personal
essays have appeared in *The New
Yorker*, *Harper's Magazine*, and
other publications. She lives in
New York with her husband, the
novelist Colin Harrison, and their
children.

# The Binding Chair

*A Novel*

## Kathryn Harrison

TED SMART

This edition produced for The Book People Ltd,
Hall Wood Avenue, Haydock, St Helens WA11 9UL in 2003

This paperback edition first published in 2001
First published in Great Britain in 2000 by
Fourth Estate
A Division of HarperCollins *Publishers*
77-85 Fulham Palace Road
London W6 8JB
www. thestate.co.uk

10

A catalogue record for this book is available from the British Library.

ISBN 0-00768-036-8

Printed and bound in China by Imago

*Book design by Barbara M. Bachman*

*You'll always arrive at this same city.*

*Don't hope for somewhere else;*

*no ship for you exists,*

*no road exists.*

FROM "THE CITY," BY CONSTANTINE CAVAFY, 1894

# CONTENTS

APPRENTICESHIP                                      3

THE CZAR'S CLOCK                                   10

THE BINDING CHAIR                                  22

CONSTRUCTION TRAIN                                 29

TWICE THWARTED                                     39

APPARITIONS                                        51

THE VIEW FROM THE
    GARDENER'S BACK                                56

THE SHORT HISTORY OF
    A PRODIGY                                      66

A LONG-HANDLED SPOON                               73

SÉANCE                                             84

A WEAKNESS FOR
    RUSSIAN OFFICERS                               91

A VISIT FROM THE FOOT
    EMANCIPATION SOCIETY                          105

| | |
|---|---|
| ADVENTURE AND ARREST | 116 |
| A SEARCH UNDERTAKEN | 124 |
| BRIGHT, WORTHLESS COINS | 128 |
| THE YEAR OF THE FOOT TAX | 139 |
| THE CURE FOR LISPING | 153 |
| DISCIPLINE FOR GIRLS | 161 |
| TEN-IN-ONE | 172 |
| JUSTICE SERVED | 176 |
| DOLLY CLEANS HOUSE | 182 |
| CIRCUMNAVIGATION | 190 |
| HEROES OF THE GREAT WAR | 197 |
| SYNTAX AND SYMMETRY | 210 |
| SPANISH INFLUENZA | 218 |
| DRINK THE WATER | 226 |
| THE PIPE DREAMS OF A RAT | 233 |

THE HEAD OF THE FAMILY                241

HOSPITALITY                           254

A FACILITY WITH LANGUAGE              265

THE SUNNY COAST OF FRANCE             270

SHOES FOR WALKING                     278

PROPOSAL                              285

PROMENADE                             291

BIRTHDAY CELEBRATION                  300

THE BAY OF ANGELS                     303

THE BINDING CHAIR

# APPRENTICESHIP

THE GATEPOST, STUCCOED PINK TO MATCH THE villa, bore a glazed tile painted with a blue number, the same as that in the advertisement. *Please inquire in person. Avenue des Fleurs, 72.*

A hot day, and so bright. Sun flared off windowpanes and wrung sparks from freshly watered shrubs. One after another, applicants paused at the locked gate, considered its wrought-iron flourishes and the distinctly self-satisfied hue of the residence glimpsed through its bars. They checked the number twice, as if lost, hesitated before pushing the black button in its burnished ring of brass.

When the houseboy appeared with a ring of keys, his severely combed hair shining with petroleum jelly, they ducked in response to his bow and followed him through the silently swinging gate with their heads still lowered, squinting dizzily at the glittering crushed white quartz that lined the rose beds along the path.

"Won't you sit down?"

May received them in the sunroom. Behind her chair, glass doors offered a view of terraced back gardens, an avalanche of extravagantly bright blooms, a long, blue-tiled swimming pool that splattered its reflection over the white walls and ceiling.

Of the eleven men and women who answered her notice, four did not resist staring at May outright, and she dismissed them immediately.

Whatever the name Mrs. Arthur Cohen might suggest to someone answering an ad, May would not have been it. To begin with, wasn't Cohen a Jewish name? And there she was, unmistakably Chinese. Now who in 1927 had encountered such an intermarriage, even among the Riviera's population of gamblers and gigolos, its yachtsmen and consumptives and inexhaustible reserves of deposed, transient countesses living off pawned tiaras? In the summer months, when sun worshippers overtook the city of Nice—women walking bare-legged on the boulevards, and bare-lipped, too, tennis skirts no lower than the knee and not a smudge of lipstick, their hair bobbed, their necks brown and muscular, canine—May Cohen looked not so much out of style as otherworldly.

Despite the heat, she received her eleven candidates in traditional dress: a mandarin coat of pink silk embroidered with a pattern of cranes and fastened with red frogs, matching pink trousers, and tiny silk shoes that stuck out from under their hems like two pointed red tongues.

Her abundant and absolutely black hair was coiled in a chignon. Pulled back, it accentuated a pretty widow's peak, a forehead as pale and smooth as paper. Her eyes were black and long, each brow a calligraphic slash; her full lips were painted red. She had a narrow nose with nervous, delicate nostrils—imperious, excitable nostrils that seemed to have been formed with fanatical attention. But each part of May, her cuticles and wristbones and earlobes, the blue-white luminous hollow between her clavicles, inspired the same conclusion: that to assemble her had required more than the usual workaday genius of biology. At fifty, her beauty was still so extreme as to be an affront to any sensible soul. Her French, like her English, was impeccable.

Of the remaining seven applicants (those who did not disqualify themselves by staring), the first offered references from a local sanitarium. Perhaps this explained his solicitousness, his tender careful moist gaze, as if she were moribund. "Please accept my apologies," she said. "You won't do."

The second was, she decided, an idiot. "You have had—it was an accident?" he asked, and she smiled, but not kindly.

The third, a narrow, ascetic Swiss with an inexpertly sewn harelip and a carefully mended coat, looked as if she needed employment. But she wrinkled her nose with fastidious disapproval, and May rang for the houseboy to see her out.

The fourth's excitement as he glimpsed the tightly bound arch of May's right foot, his damp hands and posture of unrestrained anticipation: these presaged trouble. May uncrossed her legs, she stood and bid him a good afternoon.

The fifth and sixth changed their minds.

The seventh, who was the last, would have to do. He was taciturn; and that, anyway, she approved.

"When do I start?" was his longest utterance.

"Today," May said. "Now." And the houseboy provided him with bathing costume, towel, and robe, a room in which to change.

May, using her jade cane, slowly climbed the stairs to her suite of rooms, where she took off all her clothes except the white binding cloths and red shoes—for without them she couldn't walk at all—and put on her new black bathing costume. She pulled the pins from her hair, brushed and braided it, and, wearing a white robe so long that it trailed, began her long walk down the stairs. On the way she met Alice, her niece, breathless and ascending two at a time.

"I'm late," Alice explained, unnecessarily. And then, "Please!" as May blocked her way with her cane.

"For what?" May asked. "For whom?"

"I'm meeting him at the Negresco. We're having tea, that's all, so don't let's quarrel." Alice tried to push past, but May held the cane firmly across the banister. "Look, he'll think I'm not coming!"

"Just remember." May pointed the tip of her cane at Alice's heart. "We all die alone."

"*Please!* I haven't time for this now!" Alice made an exasperated lunge for the cane, which May abruptly lowered so that Alice lost her balance; she ended sitting on the step below her aunt's feet.

May looked down at her. "I'm more fortunate than you."

"And why is that?" The words came out tartly, and Alice scowled, she stuck her chin out belligerently; still, she considered her aunt remarkable for the tragedies she'd survived.

"Because," May said. "Opium is a better drug."

"Well," Alice said, after an amplified sigh. She stood up. "Any advice?" she asked, sarcastic.

May shrugged. She raised her perfectly symmetrical eyebrows and turned up an empty white palm. "Avoid marriage," she said. "Obviously." She continued down the stairs, Alice watching as she navigated the foyer, her white robe trailing over the parquet, her abbreviated steps invisible, disguised. Through the salon and out to the pool: who could guess how she hobbled?

In the garden, on a chaise he'd pulled from the shade of an umbrella into the afternoon sun, the young man was waiting. Sprawled long-legged on its yellow cushion, the robe folded, unused, at its foot, he opened his eyes at the sound of the patio door; he stood as May approached. A low stool had been placed just at the very lip of tile that overhung the stairs descending to the shallow end of the long blue pool, and May sat on it. The young man watched in silence as she untied the sash of her robe and pulled her white arms from its white sleeves, let it fall back from her shoulders before bending to unbind her feet.

Because she was so graceful in all her movements, the clumsiness with which she entered the pool surprised him. Still, the young man said nothing, he made no move to help May as she used her arms to maneuver herself from the low seat to the edge of the pool and from there onto the steps.

For a moment she rested on the highest one, submerged only as far as her waist and looking into the water. Under the pool's refracting surface her feet appeared no more foreshortened than any other woman's.

She turned to him, her hand on the side. "Well?" she said, and he nodded. He hopped onto the diving board, executed a conceited dive and came up gleaming, grinning, as relaxed and easy in the water as a Shanghai boatman.

SHANGHAI. What city could be farther from the pristine and clear, the enviably sparkling coast of southern France than dirty, seething Shanghai, her filthy waterways? The other side of the world, and yet as immediate and implacable as the underside of consciousness: flowing, undammed. Undammable. May carried it with her, the fetid Whangpoo hung with haze, busy with ferries and junks, the occasional body of a dead addict or whore bobbing between hulls. Barges sinking low under the weight of coal and cabbages, steamers along the jetties exchanging cases of biscuits for crates of tea, wines for silks. Mail boats disgorging their sacks of correspondence and journals, wedding banns, death notices, the occasional love letter smothered among missionary reports and month-old European newspapers.

"TAKE A DEEP BREATH. Keep your mouth closed."

May hesitated, and he put his hands on her shoulders and pushed her slowly down, under the water's surface. She watched silver streams of bubbles escape her nose, then came quickly up with her eyes burning, grabbed for the side, his shoulder, anything to keep from sinking. Drowning.

"Not bad," he said. And again, after she'd stopped gasping, he pushed her gently under. They did this for an hour.

"You have to be comfortable with your head underwater," he said. "Holding your breath."

Not once did he mention her feet—not on the first day, not subsequently—and the fact that he didn't earned him her respect.

If she came downstairs late for her lesson, she found him doing chin-ups on the end of the diving board, easily pulling his torso up out of the deep end. Through the trees, the sun scattered the surface of the pool with bright shards. Over and over, he lifted himself out, disturbing the water just enough to make them dance.

After breathing came kicking. He brought a life preserver and told her to hold it and kick hard enough to travel the length of the pool and back. She made slow progress and stayed close to the side. Three times she stopped to catch her breath. He swam next to her, propelling his big body as if it were weightless, turning from stomach to side to back. A gap separated his front teeth; through it he sent up silver arcs of water when he did the backstroke.

"If you don't get so you don't need to rest, you won't make any progress." He made the comment noncommittally, as if he didn't care much, either way. His eyelashes, bleached white by the sun, clumped together into wet, starry points, and his tanned face conveyed the benign condescension of an animal trainer. She liked it, his detachment; she preferred it. Her successes, her failures: these were not his but hers. They belonged to her.

IN THE NEXT WORLD, May had been warned, she would find a lake under whose surface swam those women who had borne children. The lake was a lake of blood. Blood lost each month and lost in childbirth. The blood of stained cloths washed in the rivers.

To ease the sufferings of the dead, the temple bell, as wide and as clamorous as that in the firehouse, was lined with their hair, a few strands taken from each and stuck to the cold metal with a dab of wax or a smear of rice syrup. With every strike of its clapper, one swimmer could come up for a gasp of air. Or so May's mother explained, many years before—a lifetime ago—when Chu'en took her past the joss house and May asked why it was that tangled drifts of dark, shining hair blew through its dusty forecourt.

May and her mother had stared past the sedan chair's curtains. "I'm never going there," May said, shaking her head. "Not to that lake." Her mother didn't answer. Instead, "Hurry! Hurry!" she called out to the boys carrying the chair. They were late returning home; May's grandmother would be angry.

...

ARMS WERE HARDER than legs. She tried holding the life preserver with one arm while stroking with the other, but in the end he had to support her while she practiced. He stood in the shallow end and held her up on the surface of the water with his broad palms. The feel of his hands against her ribs, his frown of youthful concentration, their formal yet physical intimacy—these reminded her of a time when she was as young as he, and working as a prostitute in Shanghai.

"No. No. Your timing is off. You turn your face up out of the water when you lift your arm. You take a breath as you lift."

WHEN SHE WAS HOME, Alice watched the lessons from the balcony outside her bedroom, her vigil silhouetted by the white curtain behind her.

May didn't do things casually. She wouldn't pursue swimming for the pleasure of it. Certainly not for the exercise, never on the advice of a physician. She must have some sort of a . . . a plan.

Crawl, back, breast, side: Alice tracked May's progress through the strokes, her own arms folded, her dark head dipped apprehensively.

# The Czar's Clock

ALICE BENJAMIN HAD BEEN SEPARATED FROM May only once, in 1913, when she was twelve years old and was discovered in her aunt's dressing room, rolling up sticky balls of opium for May to smoke in her long ivory-and-silver pipe. Alice had made a dozen or more of them, the size of marbles, and had lined them up on the vanity table among perfumes and creams, when her mother walked in. Was that the moment that everything changed?

Until then, all the family had lived together in the same big house on Bubbling Well Road in Shanghai: Aunt May and Alice and Alice's sister, Cecily; the girls' father, Dick Benjamin, and their mother, Dolly, and their mother's brother, Uncle Arthur, who had fallen in love with a Chinese prostitute and then indulged the bad taste or poor judgment or whatever it took to induce an otherwise intelligent white man to marry a native—a whore!—even so beautiful and cultured a one as May.

"Now that," Dolly said, looking at the dark crescents of opium under Alice's fingernails. "That is the final final straw."

"It's not as if anything were happening," May said. "You know I love Alice as if she were my own. I'd never smoke in her presence." But May's declarations of love were no comfort to Dolly. In the inevitable alignments of familial sympathies, Cecily belonged to Dolly, Alice to May, and Dolly had long worried about her sister-in-law's influence over her younger daughter.

"Anyway, Alice prepares her pipe all the time," Cecily said, eager to tattle. "She's been doing it for years."

"She most certainly has not!" the girls' governess protested.

"Yes I have!" Alice said, for how could she resist arguing with the know-it-all Miss Waters, with her face that looked as if it would shatter if dropped? The governess was as vain as a debutante about her pale skin and swallowed arsenic tablets to maintain its china-like luster.

"You see," May said, when Alice told her about the little white pills, "I was right when I said she was poisonous. I wouldn't kiss her if I were you."

But Abelard's Complexion Tablets were one thing, and opium was quite another. Just like that, Alice and Cecily were taken out of day school and enrolled in a London boarding school, far far away. "Seven thousand, eight hundred and forty-some-odd miles," calculated Uncle Arthur, who had an amateur's delight in geography.

"High time, too," said their father, and he made the usual observations about Shanghai's climate, the malarias and miasmas and Whangpoo River gases.

To get to London, the sisters and their mother and governess and amah went by train. First to Harbin on the Chinese Eastern Railway, its cars dusty and black, and then all the way west to Moscow on the beautiful blue Great Siberian Express, and then on to Paris via the Nord-Express, and from Paris to Calais and on across the Channel. A very long trip and one that would convince Alice's mother that it was too late, Alice ought to have been separated from her aunt years before. For when she at last arrived in London at Miss Robeson's Academy for Young Ladies, Alice Benjamin was immediately famous.

Infamous: stared at and whispered about, as the girl who had gotten off a train with a strange man. And admitted it!

Yes, Alice had stepped off the express into a city in Siberia, a place she'd never been, holding the hand of a man she didn't know, an army captain. Only twelve years old, but not so young that she didn't know better than to go willingly off with a stranger. The police had come, of course, a *gorodovoi* in his shining boots. And for three days the family was delayed in Kuybyshev, a place that wasn't even a place, as no one had ever heard of it. But Alice wouldn't say any more. She did answer questions about the express. Yes, it was luxurious, if a bit stuffy. The windows didn't open.

As insurance against claustrophobia—to which her mother particularly was susceptible—Alice's father had reserved three train compartments for the five of them, enough room, according to the booking agent, for twelve persons.

May went with them to the railway station, and at the prospect of separation from her aunt, Alice cried all the way along North Honan Road, right up to the unfailingly overwhelming sight of the station's crowds of beggars and peddlers and lepers and thieves, a smattering of addicts lying insensate underfoot.

"The whole damn *danse macabre*," Alice's father said, and he took his handkerchief from his pocket, rubbed it between his palms. He was irritable, as he always was on those days he took off from his brokerage, leaving his fortunes—the future!—even briefly in the hands of his partners.

May kissed Alice and said, "Now you must stop crying, really you must, darling," and Alice did. For as her mother feared, Alice was entirely in thrall to her aunt; she did anything to please her.

Because of a mishap with the brougham (a broken axle as they turned out of their private drive), the family disembarked at the station from a convoy of rickshaws: Alice and May in the vanguard, followed by Alice's mother and father, then Cecily and Miss Waters and at last the amah, squeezed between two precariously swaying towers of luggage.

"It says," Miss Waters said once again, "that the dining-car attendants speak English, German, French, and Russian. And that the bathrooms have marble tile." She had a brochure from the Wagon-lits company and, when not afflicted with migraine, consulted its pages frequently, reading over and over of the comforts it promised. "A stateroom with lounges, armchairs, and writing tables. Private toilet rooms with porcelain bathing tubs. Hot water, and fresh linen daily.

"Since the completion, in 1904, of the Circumbaikal Loop," she announced, "a train can cross Siberia in eight days."

"You read that already," said Cecily, sitting down on a trunk, watching as their father disappeared into the crowds in pursuit of a porter.

"We have our own food," their mother said.

"Yes," said the governess.

"So we don't need waiters who speak four languages."

"No," Miss Waters conceded.

They did have food: three hampers full. Fifty bottles of Vichy water, twenty packages of Lu biscuits, jars of peaches and pears, apples and apricots, all canned by Dah Su and his slavish staff of cookboys. Packets of tea and cocoa, imported oranges, each wrapped in pink tissue paper printed with a honeycomb design, sixteen tins of Portuguese sardines, four jars of lemon curd, four tubes of anchovy paste (looking like toothcream, only brown), two dozen eggs (laid by their own chickens and hard cooked in their own kitchen), five pounds of chocolates filled with liqueurs (a gift from May, who eschewed the purely practical), a bottle of L'Angoustin bitters, eight tins of potted meat, twelve tins of Bear Brand Swiss condensed milk, and two Dutch cheeses sealed up in black wax—all packaged items imported at considerable expense only to journey back toward Europe. But who in his or her right mind would buy Chinese staples?

Besides the food, they carried towels and linens, a rubber lining to put between them and the train's bathtub, books, stationery, pens, ink, decks of playing cards, and boxes of stereopticon cards, as well as the viewer, needlework, toys, and of course clothes and toilet articles, everything packed into three leather-bound trunks with brass fittings, a set of matching train cases, and one hatbox.

Two larger, dark blue trunks, filled with what the sisters needed for school, would travel in the express train's luggage car at a surcharge of twenty-one rubles, forty kopecks. Nothing was inspected by the Chinese Eastern, but at Harbin and innumerable stops along the way west, each piece of luggage would have to be carried off the train by Russian porters (who would have to be tipped generously if they weren't to mishandle and drop them), opened, and examined on the platform.

As usual when under the care of their father, the family arrived at the station early and were forced to fill time. In the crowded first-class lounge, Dick read the *North China Daily News,* and Dolly walked around and around the hampers, mentally reviewing their contents: servings that had been added up, divided by five, added up again, and then doubled in case of disasters or delays, so that the traveling party could last for weeks without using the dining cars, whose fare the Wagon-lits company declared equal to that of the best restaurants in Europe.

Dolly Benjamin was convinced that cholera and typhus and hepatitis—every imaginable tragedy—were waiting for her to relax her vigilance. Disease would enter the bodies of her family through the indulgence of a suspect ice cream, an unwrapped sweet. Who knew what went on in the train's kitchen, or in the kitchens of the best restaurants of Europe, for that matter?

BUT THE GRAND express *was* grand, especially after two days on a dirty Chinese train. Its compartments contained all the promised amenities, seats upholstered in a dark blue brocade, walls covered with embossed leather. A large mirror tilted out from the wall above the divan, and Cecily stood on the cushion and looked in it. She smoothed her eyebrows with her finger, licking its tip and then applying a sheen of saliva to the fine dark hairs. The large windows were of double panes of thick glass to protect against the cold, their tops etched with a design of urns and garlands. The writing desk was stocked with paper and envelopes bearing the words *Compagnie Internationale des Wagon-lits,* just as in a hotel. On the wall was a framed print of the ice-breaker *Baikal*, its three stacks belching black smoke. The ship was moving across the frozen lake, cutting a dark trench through the surface. In its wake, great white slabs of ice floated on black water. To the left of the ship, on unbroken ice, rested huge sledges, three reindeer harnessed to each; and between them stood a small group of men, shapeless in layers of furs.

Alice sucked the end of her brown braid as she looked at the photograph. Her braid was as thick as her mother's arm and long enough to sit on. She wasn't a pretty child when compared, as she inevitably was, with her older sister, Cecily, with her serene eyes and pink cheeks, her smooth curls. Alice was dark and fierce, with lips too full, too hungry, for a little girl.

She brought her eyes close to the glass covering the picture. Beneath his fur hat, each man had a beard and a mustache like her father's. The print was dated 1900 and there was a copy of it in each of the three compartments they had booked, side by side in the long blue coach with the number 578 painted in white on the side. Miss Waters and the amah were to share the compartment closest to the front of the train; after them came Alice and Cecily; and last their mother, who had an entire compartment to herself in order to prevent anxiousness brought on by sleeping too close to another person, or in case of headache or stomachache, or whatever might keep the shades drawn, the sleeping berth down, and the door locked, as it sometimes was at home.

After a guard came to check their passports, another man, in a belted black blouse and voluminous trousers tucked into shining black boots, knocked at each compartment door and introduced himself as the *provodnik*, or porter, who would come back at nine o'clock with their linen and make up the berths.

"What time is it now, if you please," Cecily said.

And the man took off his hat to answer. "Half past noon," he said, in his good English.

"But how can that be?" said Cecily. "We've already had lunch and tea."

"Yes," said Alice. "It must be time for supper."

The *provodnik* withdrew a leather folder from under his arm and from it a printed table of local times throughout Russia. He handed this to their mother, and another copy to the governess, evidently lumping the diminutive amah in with the children and deciding, as might a waiter who needs to economize on menus, that such a document would be wasted on her. As the women looked at the table, printed both in Russian and in French, he explained that these real times were irrelevant in that between Harbin and Moscow meals would be served and beds made up according to imperial time, and that arrival and departure times as well were always based on the czar's clock. He paused, audibly inhaling and then releasing air through his nostrils, then handed them another long folded paper, the timetable of the International Express stops. Were they to get off the train, he cautioned, they must lock their compartments, they must carry their passports, and they must remember that three bells would announce each station departure: one a quarter of an hour before, another five minutes before, and the last immediately before. At Irkutsk, they would be changing carriages, as the imperial Russian track that lay west of that city was of a narrower gauge than the one to the east.

"The dining car?" Miss Waters asked, her voice rising an octave, a function of hope despite Mrs. Benjamin's insistence that they wouldn't be using it.

"Open from seven in the morning, imperial time, until nine at night."

"But," said the governess, noting from the table of local times that Harbin was six hours and twenty-five minutes ahead of St. Petersburg, "Doesn't that mean that breakfast will be served in the middle of the . . . That is to say, when it's . . . well, lunchtime?"

The *provodnik* looked at her. "Seven, imperial time, until nine."

"Yes," said the governess, moving quickly on to the other object of her devoted interest. "The bathtub, it is—"

"Porcelain. In the lavatory to the rear of the carriage."

The amah made a sour face. "No washee train tub! No belong clean! Belong dirty! Dirty!" She turned on the governess. "What you belong fooloo woman! Make too much care for porcelain! Who know who go tub before! Porcelain no count for no matter."

The *provodnik* looked witheringly down at the old Chinese woman in her blue tunic and trousers and flat black shoes, and then turned back to the governess. Clearly he felt she was the only one of the party of travelers who had any real appreciation of the marvels of this train, which would carry them thousands of miles westward, toward Europe, toward the czar and civilization. And away from the ignorant Chinese, this one in their midst no more than a generation's distance from savages who defecated in their own rice paddies and washed their armpits with urine. What could such a person—a person who wasn't even a person—understand about hygiene?

He bowed slightly, so slightly that the motion might almost have been mistaken for a shudder, as if he were suddenly aware how cold it was in the corridor of the coach, and said that he must attend now to other business.

It wasn't until after the third and last warning bell, when they were pulling slowly away from the brick terminal, that they saw the other passenger in their car, a Russian officer in white tunic and blue trousers. He paced twice up and down the corridor, stroking his gray mustache with his right thumb and forefinger in a nervous, sweeping motion, and then stopped outside the compartment in which Alice, Cecily, their mother and governess were still trying to decipher the timetable, and knocked. Miss Waters retracted the lead into her silver mechanical pencil and folded her page of calculations; their mother stood and opened the door.

"Captain Litovsky," the officer said, and he bowed deeply from the waist, removing his white-and-black hat and then replacing it before he was quite upright. "Engineer with the Imperial Command."

"Mrs. Benjamin," their mother said. "And my daughters, Cecily and Alice. Their governess, Miss Waters."

The adults exchanged politenesses; the girls stared at the officer, ignoring Miss Waters's grimace of disapproval. He had a fascinating habit of touching first the brim of his hat, then his mustache and his collar, his pockets, and at last what seemed to be the stock of a phantom pistol holstered at his hip—either that or the hilt of an equally invisible sword.

"Why do you speak English?" Alice interrupted.

"Alice!" said her mother.

"That's all right," said the captain, staring at Alice and looking almost frightened, as if he'd seen a ghost. "I . . . I . . . I have children, myself," he stammered.

"Tell me," said their mother. "Is it usual that the train should follow so eccentric a schedule? The, uh, *pov—provodnik* said that meals would follow St. Petersburg time even here, in Eastern Siberia, and . . ."

"Lunch is served at dinner!" said Miss Waters.

"I'm sorry?" said the captain.

The governess handed him the tables along with the equations she'd made on the Wagon-lits stationery. "Look for yourself," she said.

He held them under the reading lamp's fringed shade, bending over to see them clearly.

"Not that it really matters in relation to meals, as we won't be using the dining car, but if the beds aren't turned down until dawn—"

"By why shouldn't you use the dining—" he said, interrupting first Miss Waters and then himself and looking out the window as if at something that surprised him.

"Captain?" said their mother after a minute. "Sir?" For he was standing very still, rigidly erect even for an officer, and he dropped the timetables and Miss Waters's calculations and began once again the mysterious series of motions from hat brim to mustache and so forth. His face was immobile, his eyes wide and unmoving. Behind his pupils, though, Alice thought she saw a terrible velocity, as if he were dropping through space. And then, suddenly, he did fall, right onto the floor.

For a minute, no one moved, no one attempted to help him. He lay on his back, his feet projecting out of the compartment door and into the corridor, and he spoke in three languages at once, Russian words mixed up with French and English. "*Nitchevo,*" he muttered. "*Nitchevo.*" The expression was one he would use again later, and translate for them: *It doesn't matter.*

Tears squeezed from his shut eyes, saliva from the corners of his mouth. He said a name, too, several times. *Olga! Olga!* He said it loudly, as if calling to the woman from far away, as if he were afraid she might not be able to hear him. And then he was still, his body relaxed as though asleep.

"He's taken a fit," Miss Waters concluded.

"Go," their mother said. "No. You stay, and I'll go with the girls to get the, the porter, whatever he's called."

But by the time they had returned with the *provodnik*, the governess was in the corridor and the captain inside their compartment, with the door shut and the curtain drawn.

"What's happened?" said their mother. The *provodnik* tried the door handle.

"It's locked," he said, knocking. "Sir!" he said. "*Zdrastvuyti!* Hello! Captain, I must ask you to open the door. This is not your compartment!"

"Perhaps he's dead," Cecily said.

"No, I can hear something," said their mother. "Why on earth did you leave him!" she asked the governess.

"I don't know," said the governess. "What I mean is . . . Here," she said. "I took your bag and the passports."

The amah made a snorting sound.

"Captain!" the *provodnik* said. "*Pazhalsta!* Please! I must insist that you open the door immediately."

And he did. "Can I help you?" He bowed, an expression of aggrieved suspicion on his face. Perspiration stood out in large drops on his forehead; he removed his hat and wiped his face with a large pink silk handkerchief.

"Sir!" said the *provodnik*. "What do you . . . Are you all right?"

"Why shouldn't I be? I was just . . . I was writing a report."

"He's mad," the governess said. "He's intoxicated."

"This is not your compartment," said the *provodnik*.

"What do you mean by that?"

"I mean," said the *provodnik*, "that this compartment, number one-sixteen, is the compartment of Mrs. Benjamin, and that yours is three doors to the rear, number one-nineteen.

"One, one, nine," he added when the man did not respond. Captain Litovsky stared silently at them all. He twisted his beautiful handkerchief into a pink rope and bound it nervously around his knuckles.

"See," Alice said. "That is my doll on the seat, and Cecily's cards are there on the writing desk."

The captain turned and looked at the doll. He touched the brim of his hat, his mustache, collar and pockets and the missing weapon at his hip. "Yes," he said at last. "You must please forgive me. I haven't been entirely well since . . . I'm not myself.

"I'm going to take the waters at Sergievsk. At the springs, the springs near Kuybyshev. It is on the advice of my physician. I have a cottage reserved for the fifteenth of the month." He slipped his hand inside his tunic, as if searching for some confirmation of what he was saying, and handed the porter a worn leather billfold inside of which were two creased banknotes, an envelope with a broken wax seal and his *propiska*.

"This is your pass. I need your ticket." The *provodnik* sounded irritable. "If you have your ticket on your person, I'll show you that one-nineteen is—"

"Yes, yes. I remember now." Litovsky turned to Mrs. Benjamin and her daughters. "Forgive me," he said. "I . . . I . . . I am . . . I am honorab—I am discharged. I am returning to my home and taking the waters en route."

"Of course," said Alice's mother. "Please, let's not talk of it anymore. We were concerned only for your health."

"Yes. It is . . . I am . . ."

"Shall I take you to your compartment?" the *provodnik* said.

The captain followed the porter meekly down the corridor, swaying slightly with the motion of the train.

"What happened to him?" Alice asked.

"An attack of some sort. A kind of—"

"He may be a drunkard," the governess said.

"He's an engineer, an officer of the Russian army!" said Alice's mother.

"Well that certainly wouldn't prevent him from drinking. It may even be a requirement." Miss Waters allowed herself a small, malicious smile.

"Who do you suppose Olga is?" Cecily said.

Miss Waters was counting the envelopes in the writing desk. "His wife, probably."

# THE BINDING CHAIR

ONCE A YEAR, IN SEPTEMBER, MAY'S FEET BE-
came infected. It was humid at that time of the year, the
time when, in 1913, her nieces departed for boarding
school. The house smelled of mildew; the edges of the
wallpaper curled away from the damp plaster below;
the wrappers of Alice's father's cigars, if left outside of
the humidor, unrolled and disgorged lumps of sticky, fragrant Cuban tobacco. Bedclothes were heavy with moisture, and the bleached linen bandages around May's feet
were saturated with perspiration. She slept deeply, the
dark, dream-soaked sleep following a pipe of opium, and
as she did, her foot bindings seemed to grow tighter and
tighter. Perhaps it was that which made her dreams so
claustrophobic. In one, which recurred, May was lost in
the Shanghai bird market. As she tried to find her way
out of the maze of stalls, she grew smaller and then
smaller still, until one merchant, mistaking her for an
escaped bird, grabbed her, tied her feet together with

twine, and sold her for three silver coins. She'd start awake just as the man who bought her was replacing the twine with hairs taken from his long mustache.

It wasn't good for her to sleep so late; it encouraged nightmares. But the house was so quiet, so dreary and dispiriting and dull without the sisters—especially Alice. May missed Alice coming in to wake her, the sudden jar as she landed on the bed, the frankness with which she grabbed her aunt's toes, shook them.

A bound foot is not, as Alice's uncle Arthur assumed before seeing his wife's, a foot whose growth has been arrested. A bound foot is a foot broken: a foot folded in the middle, toes forced down toward the heel.

Were an admirer to consult Fang Hsun's *Classifications of the Qualities of Fragrant Lotuses*, he would find May's feet plump, soft, and fine in the classic style of the Harmonious Bow. They were perfect with regard to all nine criteria of excellence, and she cared for them with the respect due objects purchased at great price.

May was five when her grandmother devoted herself to May's feet, and to her future. May's name, at the time, was Chao-tsing. It is the duty of a girl's mother to bind her feet, but May's mother, Chu'en, was too tenderhearted and remembered too well the pain when her own feet were bound. Chu'en consulted an astrologer for the most propitious days on which to begin but allowed one and then another of these to pass without taking May to the family foot-binding chair. This procrastination became foremost among Chu'en's differences with her mother-in-law, Yu-ying. As soon as their husbands left the house in the morning, Yu-ying would come to Chu'en's quarters and harangue her.

"Do you love your daughter," Yu-ying would say, "or do you love her feet?"

Chu'en wept; she covered her face with her hands. "I can't. Not now. Wait another year. Chao-tsing is so small. Her feet won't grow much in a year."

"The choice is this," Yu-ying said. "Either Chao-tsing will grow up to be the bride of a prosperous merchant, or she will be as large-footed as a barbarian and find no husband at all!"

But Chu'en shook her head. She wept, she begged for more time, she made promises she couldn't bear to keep.

At last, on the morning of the nineteenth day of the second month, the goddess Kuanyin's birthday, Yu-ying came to Chu'en's room, where she and May were playing, building a little village of mah-jongg tiles among the bedclothes. Yu-ying held out her hand. "Grandmother will do it," she said, and Chu'en nodded and bowed low to her mother-in-law. She thanked her for relieving her of an honor and an obligation she could not fulfill.

As an indulgence, Yu-ying allowed Chu'en to prepare a dish of clay, in which May stood, leaving for her mother a sentimental impression of her feet, and of girlhood. Then Yu-ying took May into her bed-chamber, where she sat her on a red chair decorated with characters for obedience, prosperity, and longevity. She took May's shoes and threw them in the fire, and when they had burned away to ash she brought a bowl of warm water perfumed with jasmine and set it under May's feet. The water just covered her ankles. "Do you like the smell?" Yu-ying asked her granddaughter.

"Yes." The water made May sleepy, and she closed her eyes. When she opened them, her grandmother was standing before her with a pair of yellow silk slippers with butterflies embroidered on the toes.

"Do you like them?" Yu-ying asked.

"Oh, yes!" May reached for the shoes. They were the most beautiful she had ever seen, but they were several sizes too small. Already May's feet were as much as an inch longer than her grandmother's.

"These slippers are yours," Yu-ying said. "I will help you to wear them."

Yu-ying kneeled at May's feet. Next to her was a black lacquer tray on which was a roll of white binding cloth, a knife, a jar of alum, a needle and thread, a paintbrush, and a water chestnut. Yu-ying said a prayer to Kuanyin and gave May the water chestnut to hold in her left hand and the paintbrush to hold in her right. The chestnut, Yu-ying explained, would help May's feet to grow tender, the brush would make them narrow.

"See the white cloth," she said, unrolling one end of it. "This is the fragrant white path you will travel. This is the journey from girl to woman." She walked backward from the bowl, pulling the linen out into an undulating, hypnotic banner.

May nodded, slowly.

Yu-ying took May's left foot in her hand and dried it. She cut the toenails and sprinkled the sole with alum, and then she took one end of the white bandage and held it on the inside of the instep and from there pulled the strip of cloth over the arch of May's foot and on over her four smaller toes, so that they curled under, into the sole. Then Yu-ying pulled the bandage tightly around the heel, and then over the arch and the toes again, making layers of deft figure eights. When she was finished, only May's big toe was left unfolded. From under its nail she could feel the thrumming of blood.

"Oh!" May said, surprised. She opened her hands and the chestnut and brush fell to the floor. Her father's mother had never before hurt her. "Please, Grandmother!" May tried to pull her foot away, but Yu-ying held it tightly and looked into her eyes.

"Did I not make the offerings to your patron god on the day of your birth and for every year after that?"

May nodded.

"And when you were a baby and could not sleep, was I not the one who fetched your soul back?"

May nodded again.

"Well, I am telling you that you may not speak now," Yu-ying said. "You must be quiet while I do this." And she sewed the end of the bandage in place with a needle and strong thread. When she had finished with the left, she began with the right. It was astonishing that so small a woman had such strength.

May, obedient, said nothing while her grandmother bound her feet, but when Yu-ying put on the first pair of training shoes and told May to stand and to walk back to her mother's quarters, she refused.

"I can't," she said. "I won't."

"You will," said Yu-ying. And she pulled May to her feet; she kicked the red and gold chair out from under her.

May sat down hard on the floor. The pain in her feet was sharp, like teeth. Dizzy, she closed her eyes and saw her grandmother's hand pulling the long needle right through the flesh of her toes.

"Walk," Yu-ying said. "It will not work unless you walk."

"I feel sick. I want my mother."

"Then get up and go to her."

"I can't," May said.

Yu-ying shrugged. She collected the bowl and the towel, the knife with which she'd pared May's nails. She picked up the water chestnut and the paintbrush from where May had dropped them.

"Please," May said.

"What?"

"Help me."

"I am," Yu-ying said, and she walked out of the room.

IT TOOK MAY an hour to reach her mother's wing of the house. She began by crawling, but her grandmother caught her and made her stand. "No woman in my family, no daughter of my son, goes on four legs like a turtle!" Yu-ying watched as her granddaughter pulled herself up by the edge of a small table. Then, when May still did not walk, Yu-ying got on the other side of the table and began dragging it away, out from May's hands, so that in order to remain upright she had to follow.

"Don't you dare let go," Yu-ying said. "If you let go, I'll bind them tighter. And don't make a sound, just walk. Just walk toward me." She looked at May, looked into her eyes and kept them locked in her gaze as she walked slowly backward on her own tiny feet. The table legs whined and wept against the wood floor, but May made no noise as she cried. Yu-ying's binding technique was so skillful that with each tread the bandages tightened, crushing May's toes.

"It hurts you now, Chao-tsing, and it will hurt you tomorrow and the day after that. This month and the following. All this year you will have pain, but the next year will be better, and by the time your feet fit the butterfly shoes, they will feel nothing." Yu-ying continued to walk backward as she spoke, and on the other side of the table May followed, not daring to drop her gaze from her grandmother's eyes.

"When you are grown," Yu-ying said, "you will be very beautiful. Your feet will be the smallest and the most perfectly formed lotuses.

Your walk will be the walk of beauty, and we will tell your suitors that you never cried out when your feet were bound." They reached the door, and Yu-ying pulled the table over the sill and into the courtyard that divided her wing from that of her daughter-in-law.

"Tell me how you never cried out," Yu-ying said. "Say the words, I never cried out."

"I never cried out," May whispered, her face wet.

"Again."

"I never cried out."

"Louder!"

*"I never cried out."*

"Do you hear that?" Yu-ying said to Chu'en, who was standing at the threshold of her room, watching the slow progress of the old woman and the child across the slab-paved courtyard, each holding tight to the sides of the little black table. "Here is your daughter, Chao-tsing, who is telling you that she has had her feet bound and she did not cry out."

Chu'en, arms folded, stared. She stood on her own bound feet and willed herself not to cry lest she distract May and cause her to falter or to moan.

At last they reached the doorway. Yu-ying took May's hands from the table's edge—she had to pull them off—and transferred them to Chu'en's hips. She called for a servant to take the table back to her room, and as he retreated with it she looked at her daughter-in-law and granddaughter. "So," she said. "It is begun."

Chu'en forced herself to bow. "Thank you, Mother," she said.

Yu-ying nodded. "Perhaps a rest before it is time to eat."

In Chu'en's bedroom, May and her mother lay on the bed and held one another and wept, their faces hot and wet and pressed into each other's necks. The bed shook, but they made no sound. Outside, a dog barked; the cook lowered a bucket into the well and the rope squealed against the pulley.

That night, the evening of the birthday of the Goddess of Mercy, May's father did not return home from work. Instead he stayed out, playing poker and *ma chiang* at the home of the local police detective. It was another day before May had the opportunity to speak with him and to discover him unmoved by her tears, the look on his face one of ill-concealed exasperation. "Whimpering is for a mother's ears," he said, and he turned away.

Who, or what, could have inspired such impertinent hopes in a daughter? Was not suffering the lot of females? After all, he himself enjoyed marriage to a nimble and delicate woman—a woman whose whole foot he could take into his rectum, even as her left hand cupped his testicles, her right squeezed the shaft of his penis, and her mouth wet his glans. There was a price for luxury, for a house with servants. Every daughter must arrive at that time when life as a child, petted, carefree, is over.

EVERY THREE DAYS, May's feet were washed and rebound. Every month she wore a smaller shoe. Yu-ying had a carved ivory ruler with which she measured May's feet. The ivory was marked not in inches but in the gradations of pleasure May's feet might one day arouse. Titillation. Solace. Satisfaction. Delight. Bliss. Ecstasy. As May progressed through measures of bewitchment the bones in her toes were slowly, inexorably broken. The skin on her feet rotted away and reformed. The once strong muscles in her calves withered; the flesh of her thighs loosened and spread.

It required a dozen pairs of successively smaller shoes for May to achieve the satin butterfly slippers, and every afternoon, while Yu-ying slept, Chu'en and May held each other and wept, and so the years of childhood passed away.

# CONSTRUCTION TRAIN

"A DRILL, OLGA!" CAPTAIN LITOVSKY CRIED. "A drill will pass the time!"

He'd met the sisters and their governess on his way from the dining car to his compartment, and he was carrying a glass of hot tea in a silver-plate holder. "I shall teach you how to march like a good Russian soldier, with a straight back and level head."

"Yes!" Alice said.

"I don't think—" said Miss Waters. But already he had removed his hat, replaced it with the steaming glass. "Please!" the governess said. "The train is lurching."

"Watch now, Olga!" he said, looking at Alice. He'd made the mistake several times, calling Alice Olga, and it was a mistake he'd made only in reference to Alice, never Cecily or their mother or Miss Waters. He let go of the tea glass's handle and began marching, legs held straight, knees unbending, through the empty corridor. Despite the train's rocking on the tracks, he kept his head perfectly level; the tea did not spill. He made an about-face at the end of the car, and saluted. "Shall I teach you?" he asked, his face moist with exertion.

"Please!" Alice said.

"You'll be burned." Cecily folded her arms.

"Well, an empty glass to start—"

"No, thank you." Miss Waters caught Alice's shoulder in an attempt to redirect her toward the library car.

But she gave in—"Oh all right"—when Alice begged to return with the captain to his compartment.

They were approaching Chita, the train pressing forward through a white landscape dusted in places with soot from locomotives. As they had been on the train together for three days, the captain's engaging, essentially harmless demeanor had convinced the girls' mother that he was perhaps not a drunk or a madman but a diversion.

"Who *is* Olga?" Alice asked him. Cecily was across the corridor with Miss Waters, reciting a French exercise. Through the open door came the sound of her bored, perfected accent.

"Did you expect there to be this much snow?" the captain asked, not answering her question. It wasn't the first time she'd asked it.

"Oh, yes," Alice said. "At night, in Shanghai, I'd close my eyes and see all the silent miles of snow. Everything white and clean."

At home, when she'd thought of the great train trip across Siberia, she pictured a land that was silver-white and splotched with lakes that gleamed like mercury, like burst thermometers. Before her brother died, the nurse had dropped a thermometer in the hall, and the shiny bright beads of the stuff bounced along the floor and into the cracks between the floorboards. Alice chased some with her fingers, and they skidded away from the heat of her flesh.

"What's the part they're going to cut off?" Alice had asked Cecily. Together they'd undressed David; they'd looked at his penis, touched it. Because their mother was afraid of the Shanghai rabbi's grimy fingernails, their little brother had not been circumcised. The family was waiting to take him to London, to a clean rabbi in clean London, when he was older.

"What part?" Alice asked, standing on a stool and leaning over the crib rail.

"The end," Cecily said.

"Why?"

"Because it's dirty to leave it on."

But as it happened, David succumbed to meningitis subsequent to a teething infection and died just days before his second birthday, and before he had been circumcised. The rabbi with the gray fingernails buried him in the Jewish cemetery off Bubbling Well Road. The following week his grave was desecrated.

"If you had circumcised the body . . ." Alice had overheard a man talking to her father in the parlor. A noise of a teacup against its saucer. It was four in the afternoon. Already her mother had gone to bed. Or perhaps she hadn't gotten up.

Her father's voice, almost too low to hear: "Dolly didn't want it."

"Well—"

"To break up a baby's gravestone!"

"People feel strongly about certain things. There are . . . Some things are not . . ." A loud sigh. The noise, like the hiss of a snake's tongue, of feet on the thick carpet. "You must, for your own peace of mind, find it in yourself to forgive."

Alice watched the man depart. His rickshaw had a long red fringe on its canopy.

THE CAPTAIN LOOKED out the window. "Often there isn't so much snow, sometimes just bare ground. A lot has fallen for the past month." As he spoke, he rehearsed the familiar motions of touching his hat brim, mustache, and pockets. "This enterprise," he said excitedly, "will have a more important influence on the progress of man than any other undertaking." His voice grew loud, as if he were making an announcement to a crowd. "On the progress of civilization!"

Alice watched the empty landscape. "What enterprise?"

"Why, the train! The great Siberian railroad, of course!"

"Oh." Alice had never considered a land so impoverished that it lacked trains.

"I helped in its construction," the captain said.

"Did you?"

"Yes. That is to say, as engineer . . . And the army . . . What I mean to say is, the people who are indigenous, the . . . they were savages. They threw rocks and knives. Bones. Anything they could. They threw themselves at the workers to prevent them from laying the tracks."

Litovsky described the construction process. A train filled with men and equipment moved across the frozen landscape, every tree and rock and hill rendered white, a veritable tabula rasa—that was how they had understood it, Litovsky and the others. It was the ready page: the eager, empty future upon which the team of engineers would inscribe their extraordinary gift to posterity. According to the plans they drew, the construction train proceeded, laying track in front of itself, some days progressing no farther than a half a mile, creating the steel road that would offer to the far eastern reaches of Siberia things of which her people hadn't yet dreamed: Coffee and vanilla from South America! Books from Paris! Glass from Venice! Medicines from New York! Seventeen-jewel watches from Geneva! Whatever Siberia lacked, whatever she desired, would come to her.

"Picture this train, this train that invents itself, that chooses its own direction. It can happen only the one time." Litovsky put his hand up to the window. "If only . . . if only I could convey the majesty of it," he said. "The impossible, grand audacity. It was beautiful. Even after . . . No one could deny its beauty." He fell silent, staring out at the fields of snow. On cloudless days, the setting sun had lit up the new steel rails; it made them into a burning path, at the end of which some saw a light that was heaven, some an inferno. The native people had been frightened. They possessed instincts he lacked.

"Were they really savages?" Alice had looked carefully at the people at the last station. As they stood together in silent groups, their faces had possessed a squashed look, flattened as if by fatigue. Their eyes were narrow, like Chinese eyes. Except for a few gypsies, begging to tell the passengers' fortunes for a kopeck or two, the Mongol people on the platform stared in wordless awe at the towering blue train, its locomotive shuddering dyspeptically on its great grinding wheels while belching black clouds. The station house was filled with men dragging huge bundles of skins, the air heavy with the smell of tanneries, acrid and nauseating.

"Savages?" Alice asked the captain again. "Are you sure?" The people on the platform had seemed incapable of the energy required for violence.

"Certainly! They thought the train was a beast! An apparition! They attacked it. And the workers, some of them, were not much better. Being convicts." He stopped, remembering the gaunt, expressionless men chained to their wheelbarrows by day and to their bunks at night. It was misery that had made those men dangerous. One had to assume that having lost everything, they were capable of anything.

He'd had to use convict labor on the battlefields of Mukden as well, to supplement his forces, an infantry corps so battle-fatigued that the only bullets the men were deemed responsible to handle were those that had already been fired. An insulting appointment—punitive—the judgment against him still pending. Soldiers and convicts worked side by side, ragged, silent, the former distinguished only by their uniforms, their unfettered ankles. Under his command, the men began at one end of a scorched plain and made their way slowly across it, using hoes to harvest the abandoned lumps of lead, some of which were twisted into fantastically sinister shapes.

Sometimes at night, when Captain Litovsky closed his eyes, the brown plain of Mukden stretched out before him forever; and if he slept, he dreamed of having to rake through the hard earth with his bare fingers. In one such dream, which he could not dismiss even when awake, he suffered an enchantment by the czar, who severed his hands from his wrists and his feet from his ankles and switched them around. Hands sewn to the ends of his legs with black wires, he was compelled by the czar to go on digging.

"How many wives do you have?" Alice asked, interrupting his thoughts.

"Well! What a question! One, to be sure!" Captain Litovsky touched his mustache and collar.

"Are you not a Mohammedan?"

"Most certainly not! Here, look." And he pulled a little round circle of gold metal from his pocket, a coin bearing an image of the Virgin, and held the icon out to Alice. The Virgin's face was worn as smooth and as flat as one of the savage's, so often did the captain, his hand hidden in his pocket, rub his thumb over her features.

"I am an understanding man," he said. "Particularly with young persons. But you mustn't ask such questions. I am as Orthodox as the day is long!"

"I'm sorry," Alice said. "Your wife—is she named Olga?"

"No," he said. "My wife is named Tamara. After her mother."

"But then who is Olga?" Alice asked.

"Why don't you tell me about living in China?"

"What do you want to know?"

"Whatever you would like to tell me."

Alice looked assessingly at the captain as she sorted through her Westerner's repertoire of the alien and picturesque. Walking with her amah past a Chinese dentist's stall? Extracted teeth were arranged in tidy rows on a piece of black cloth, as if the rotten brown lumps were jewels. Amah had pointed proudly to one of the lumps. "That one belong mine," she'd said, and opened her mouth to indicate a red gap where the tooth had been just a week before.

Men smaller than her father carrying whole tea shops on their backs, bamboo frames bearing braziers, pots, cups. Native children with slits in their trousers squatting to defecate in the gutters. Streets boiling with life. The only thing Alice could compare to the sight of a Shanghai street was what she'd seen once when she'd turned over the body of a dead raccoon with a stick; seeing the maggots, the packed, churning crowd of them, she'd thought: *Shanghai.*

Every morning Alice held up her arms for her amah to dress her. She watched the woman's back bend as she got down on her knees to button all twelve buttons on each of Alice's white kid shoes. When David died, Amah had wept, she'd struck her fists into her eyes, she'd beat her head against the wall and the floor. But apart from that day, how quiet she was, and how silently Chinese servants moved, wearing felt slippers. They picked up what had been dropped, cleaned what had been dirtied, wiped up whatever had spilled. They never saw nakedness or indisposition. Nameless, ageless. Cook Boy, Rickshaw Boy. Boy Number Six. Number Seven. Eight. Old men with gray hair, eyes blue with cataracts: *Boy.*

Litovsky asked Alice what it was like, China, and she rehearsed a few of these emblematic encounters with the East, but when she opened her mouth what she said was "Did you know that the Chinese are expert torturers? One of the things they do is slice open missionaries' wives from here to here." She pointed to her breastbone, then her lap. "They grab one end of a woman's intestines and thread it on a spool, turn a crank and wind up her insides like a garden hose. If she's brave and doesn't faint, she gets to watch it happen. I once saw a girl cut in half, but she wasn't a missionary."

"Who has allowed you to know of such shocking things!" the captain spluttered.

"Why, my aunt," Alice said. "Her father—he cranked the spool. And the cut-up girl was in the Old City. We went to see her ourselves."

"IT'S A PLAN with that one," Miss Waters had reported darkly, after she caught Alice and May coming home. "A campaign."

"What sort of plan?" Dolly asked.

The governess narrowed her eyes, she looked past Alice's mother as if seeing into the future. *"Indoctrination."*

"Into what?"

"The woman undermines me! Tries to teach her just what life isn't!"

And Miss Waters hadn't even known about the trip to the Old City. Her objection was to the book of Russian folktales May had bought Alice at Kelley and Walsh. Stories about Baba Yaga in her hut that walked about on the legs of a chicken, tall and yellow and scaly, with knees that bent backwards. In one night, the hut could travel great distances. Baba Yaga had sharp teeth and ate children. Jewish children especially. After reading about Baba Yaga, Alice looked warily at the chickens they kept at home in Shanghai. White Orpingtons, shipped across the Pacific on the SS *Tacoma*. Their eyes were gold and cruel, the color of poison. Their beaks looked dipped in blood.

It was a sparkling day; as they left the bookstore the sky seemed unusually clear and high, and Alice imagined she could see all the way to the Yangtze. "Please please," she begged. "Let's go to the Old City." She expected a refusal—she knew how her aunt hated the Chinese Quarter—but May indulged Alice. The fine weather, perhaps, or her awareness of their imminent separation. She asked the rickshaw man to take them to the North Gate.

Once inside the wall that divided old from new, Chinese from European, the wide street splintered into alleys overhung with signboards and banners, dark, squalid passages that Alice found mysterious, even romantic. Every so often a finger of light revealed freshly bleached binding cloths trailing from a washpole and stirring in the faint breeze.

May poured perfume on a handkerchief and held it to her face as the rickshaw man pulled them through the markets, but Alice drew the air deep into her nose, trying to sort out smells. The rickshaw threaded through alley after alley clotted with pedestrians until it came to a standstill by the Yu Yuan Garden wall. "No farther," the rickshaw man said to May, who translated. Alice stood up to see what was blocking their passage. Ahead, in the courtyard of the Temple of the City God, a throng had gathered around a platform in the center of which was something that looked like a flagpole.

"Is it a holiday?" Alice asked May, who rose to her feet, slowly. The rickshaw man sat, his narrow buttocks balanced on one of the shafts between which he spent his days running, his feet on the other. Few things could induce him to waste an opportunity for rest.

"No." May's voice was strangely flat, uninflected. She spread her arms wide. "Not a holiday. Just an ordinary one. You said you wanted to see the Old City. China. Here she is. In all her . . ." Alice waited for the word *glory*, but May had stopped speaking.

The two of them watched an officer lead and then push a native girl, her hands tied behind her back, up a flight of wood stairs to the platform. As the crowd heckled, she fell to her knees, keening.

"What is she saying! What's happening to her?" Alice shook May's arm up and down, as if trying to pump a reply out of her.

"Look," May said finally. "Watch."

A second officer, dressed identically to the one who had forcibly escorted the girl, dragged a bale of wire up the steps of the platform. He began unwinding it as the first read aloud from a paper. Alice watched the shining loops fall from the bale as the officer made one end of the wire fast around the weeping girl's waist with a slipknot that he tested and tightened. Then he climbed a stepladder in order to thread the other end through a pulley, creating a primitive tackle attached to the top of the pole. When he let go, the wire dropped; its tip fell like a bright needle and swayed, glinting in the sunshine. The officer stepped carefully down from the ladder. He stood still, saying nothing, surveying all the faces turned toward him. A few words to the crowd, and a basket was passed forward over the heads of the onlookers. Woven from stout sticks, it was the kind of basket used for carting firewood, and the officer in charge of the wire lashed its dangling end to the basket's thick handles, so that it hung just at the height of his shoulders.

While he worked, the crowd remained quiet, as if engrossed by the performance of an especially adept magician. At last even the rickshaw man stood up on his shafts, pulling cold dumplings from his pocket and chewing them with a circular, ungulate motion of his sinewy jaws. Every third bite or so, he used one finger to extract a bit of gristle from his mouth, examined it minutely before flicking it into the crowd.

The officer who had read aloud from the paper made a further announcement, and the onlookers began mounting the steps in single file, more orderly than any group of Chinese Alice had yet seen. It remained quiet enough for her to hear the girl's cries.

"What's she saying! What are they doing to her!" Alice kept asking her aunt, but May said nothing. She appeared as transfixed as the rest of the crowd.

Alice saw that each person who climbed up to the platform carried a stone and reached up to drop it in the basket. As the basket grew heavier and was pulled progressively downward by the weight of the stones, the girl stopped screaming. For as long as she could, she stood on her toes. Then she tried to climb the pole, perhaps hoping to lower the basket all the way to the platform and thus relieve the wire's constriction; but if this had been her plan, she'd waited too long, she no longer had the freedom of movement or the strength it required. Her forehead against the pole, she coughed, and blood came out of her mouth.

"Why," Alice said. "They'll . . . They will . . . It's going to cut her in half!"

May nodded, expressionless. She looked at the tears running from Alice's eyes.

"But why!"

"Adultery. She ran away and was caught. She brought disgrace to a powerful family. She didn't understand, perhaps, what marriage . . . What it demanded of her."

"But can't anyone—"

"No," May said. "They can't."

## TWICE THWARTED

WHEN MAY WAS TWELVE, HER FATHER DIED. According to the European calendar, this happened in 1889, in October, as May would calculate years later, consumed with the task of translating such dates—and anything else of importance—from Chinese to English. The district necromancer was consulted for the most propitious day on which to bury him, and as that day was two months after his death, the rigors of mourning seemed to May interminable. Her father, only forty-six, had died unexpectedly and had no coffin waiting, no suit of clothes in which to meet the rulers of the next world; everything had yet to be prepared. The household shivered with activity.

On the third day after his death—when his spirit would have reached the bridge between worlds—a phalanx of priests arrived to read scripture through the night. During these rites, May yawned, she swooned; in the morning she awoke on the floor, sleeping at the feet of her dead father.

On the seventh day after his death, and on the fourteenth and the twenty-first—each week for seven weeks—May and her mother and grandmother chanted May's father on his way through the next world; they urged him toward reincarnation. He was a famous man, her father. A spirit like his was one for whose return China waited. After all, had he not defended their town from foreign devils? With his brothers he had burned the homes of missionaries, he had rid the countryside of their corrupt texts, their pale-eyed wives and daughters, and their disgraceful, impoverished, and downtrodden god. Of course May's father might, it must be acknowledged, not be reincarnated at all. He might become a god himself, with a local shrine, a day of observance.

For weeks, his body lay in state, receiving homage. Around him tables overflowed with his favorite foods and servants squatted to burn incense and spirit money. An artist, fingers black, tunic and trousers immaculate, labored over a last portrait. Every so often, he climbed onto a chair to look from above at the body's blind, silent face. As it was expected that she wail, May did. And at the encoffining ceremony, she kneeled with her mother and grandmother. With them she bowed so obsequiously low that she bumped and bruised her head on the floor.

To initiate the funeral procession, in unison the three women—mother, wife, and daughter—unbound their hair and swept it over the lacquered wood of the casket, relieving May's father's corpse of the corruption of death. Then the shining black box was carried from the courtyard while firecrackers burst, driving off jealous spirits. Ghosts without homes, without family to love and care for them.

Wearing white, May followed her father's new and flattering portrait through the winding streets and into the ancestral graveyard. Next to May, as was the duty of a new widow, Chu'en wept and tore the hair from her head. In the graveyard, family and mourners were shocked to discover May's father's tomb already filled by the remains of some bold scoundrel eager to share in the blessings heaped upon so illustrious a resting place. The interloper was exhumed and dragged outside the cemetery wall as May, Chu'en, and Yu-ying looked on.

...

THOUGH NO ONE else in the family had died, the necromancer returned when May was fourteen. It was time for her betrothal, and in order to make an auspicious match, Yu-ying said the concerns of May's departed father must be addressed. At a table reserved for only the most honored guests, the necromancer dipped his fingers in a bowl and wiped them dry. Offered wine, he drank, and he ate all the morsels of meat and fish and every cake set before him. When May's grandmother had paid for his expensive advice, she contracted with a matchmaker, confident that May's feet were as beguiling as her face. Yu-ying was almost sorry that propriety dictated that they remain bound and unseen. Left and right, each had a big toe that curled up, four that folded down, and a plantar crease so deep that several coins could be hidden inside it. Under her grandmother's tutelage, May had learned how to care for her feet in privacy, how to wash them and to cut the corns and calluses with a sharp knife, how to stop infections with borax and odors with alum. She'd learned never to move her skirt while sitting, never to move her legs while lying down, and never to wash her feet in the same basin as her face—otherwise she would be reborn as a pig.

Following Yu-ying's instructions, May had sewn a dowry of sixteen satin slippers, four for each season, and had embroidered their toes with peonies for spring, lotus flowers for summer, chrysanthemums for autumn, and plum blossoms for winter. She had made the red sleeping shoes that would contrast so startlingly with her white legs that they would tempt the most surly husband into bed. Advised that for the first eleven nights as a bride she should surreptitiously slip her tiny feet into her husband's big boots, May hoped by this ruse to gain power over him. She was prepared for a future as a dutiful wife to the rich silk dealer selected for her.

A diviner was summoned to examine the prospective match by studying the Eight Characters. His blind eyes, lacking both pupils and tear ducts, shone; they spilled over down his cheeks. Sitting across the table, unaccountably May found she wanted to press her thumbs into them. "Auspicious," the diviner pronounced. "It could not be more so." He pulled himself to his feet, catching hold of the wall-hanging with fingers still greasy from the offerings he had gobbled.

As he left, May told herself how lucky she was. She was thinking of her cousin, married off to a hunchbacked tin peddler. Among May's suitors, the silk dealer was certainly the most handsome and polite. Twice he had sent his manservant with gifts: ten expensive bolts in ten jewel-like colors, along with a seamstress to sew the goods into gowns, a pair of jade bracelets, two gold hairpins, a butchered pig, and a chest filled with tea and spices and wine.

ON THE MORNING of the wedding, fixed upon the first day of the second month, a large marriage sedan with red silk curtains came to collect May, dressed for the ceremony, from her home. The sedan was not accompanied, as May and her mother and grandmother expected, by a blue chair bearing the groom, but came instead with a note explaining that the silk dealer's presence had been required that morning to avert a business emergency. The wedding would nonetheless take place at the divined hour, and May's future husband awaited his bride eagerly.

May read the missive, shrugged. As there was no one before whom to wail and carry on, lamenting separation from her mother and grandmother, she got into the fancy red chair quietly. She had not closed her eyes the previous night, and during the rocking ride from one town to the next she fell asleep and dreamed what seemed a not unpropitious dream of lanterns. She woke only slightly perturbed by the fact that the dream lanterns had been decorated with symbols she could not read.

The sedan had stopped moving; she parted the curtains to discover herself parked before the closed main portals of a large and prosperous looking household. Over the lintel hung varnished plaques painted with gold announcements—past honors awarded the silk merchant's family by the emperor. "Highly favored ... lavishly bestowed . . ." and so forth. Between gate and gutter were stacked May's few trunks and furnishings, which had been picked up from her grandmother's home the previous day.

She yawned. "Are we early?" she asked one of the men who had carried the sedan. "Why are the doors closed?" But the man didn't answer. Beyond the walls she could see the roofs of west and east wings, each enclosing a separate courtyard. May sat back against the cushions in her itching, cumbersome skirts. Her ornate hair combs, of red enamel the same shade as that of her dress, bit into her scalp. It couldn't be that she'd come on the wrong day—after all, it was the silk dealer's servants who had come to fetch her.

An hour passed, then another. She was hungry, thirsty and needed to relieve her bladder. But now the sedan was surrounded by meddle-some neighbors, eager to inspect its occupant, who sat, still unre-ceived, in the street.

"You'd better go home," an old woman said, pulling the curtains wide open with the hooked end of her furled black umbrella, and May agreed.

But the bearers wouldn't take her. The sun began to set, the four men drew cloaks over their heads and leaned their backs against the wall around the courtyard. May sat shivering and willed herself not to cry. "Don't worry," said one. "This happened with the third."

She looked at him. "The third what?"

He rolled his eyes. "What are you? Simple? The third wife. The one before you."

May said nothing. She widened her eyes, she drew in her breath sharply, but her mouth she kept closed. She was not so young that she would betray her shock to a servant and thereby widen the net of her own vulnerability. Instead, she shrugged. She sat back against the cushions; she yawned and unfolded her arms as if she'd known all along, of course, that she was not to be the silk dealer's first wife but his fourth.

The sedan chair man watched her. "It could be all night," he said. "There's a pot under the seat if you want to go."

May didn't answer. She forced herself to wait until all four of the bearers were asleep, and then she drew the curtains and fastened them before clumsily squatting to urinate, her wedding dress bunched up under her arms.

Outside, from beyond the wall, came a high, shrill wailing. Had the

sedan chair offered any room for May, in her awkward crouch, to star-
tle and upset the contents of the pot, she would have. But as it was,
jammed tight between the wooden front of the vehicle and its upholstered seat, motionless she listened to what sounded like the screams
of not one but many women. Though the howls were not intelligible
words, they conveyed a quality of conversation, as if one answered another.

May got to her feet and, having no place to empty it, replaced the
pot carefully. She peered out of a crack between the curtains at the
bearers. Eyes still closed, they slept through the racket undisturbed,
and how could this be? Was she hallucinating the howls? Were they a
message from the gods of matrimony, a message sent only to her, a
woman on her wedding day?

The wind picked up, and in the dark behind the trembling red fabric around her, May smoothed her skirts, she felt to see if her hair was
still in place, she sat—she couldn't have said for how long—as if hyp-
notized. When the curtains blew apart, she made no move to refasten
them but watched as the clouds fled, revealing stars, remote and immaculate, a moon wasted thin as an eyelash.

Just before midnight—it was still the first day of the second
month—the door in the wall opened, and four women appeared, one
considerably older than the others. May knew orthodox customs of
marriage required that a new wife could not step over the threshold
unless escorted by an established woman of the house, either the master's mother or one of his wives, preferably the first; but having waited
all night, the last thing she expected to see was a full entourage. The
expressions on the four women's faces implied that they had at last decided to share the burden of their distasteful duty.

May stood and bowed. Seeing the women, she understood that she
had come to a place where beauty would be no guarantee of favor. She
felt the first wife's hand burn with jealousy as she helped her to step
down from the sedan.

ONCE INSIDE THE gracious, well-tended garden, May looked for
nuptial preparations, but there was no awning set up, no tables with

food or drinks. No lanterns, no guests, no offerings. **Nothing.** Could it be that no celebration was expected? Without walking, May stumbled, as if what she saw—what she didn't see—had literally jarred her. A servant brought a chair, and she sat, silently, feeling as though she had fallen out of gravity or some equally powerful force, whatever kept her securely placed in the world.

To her predicament May applied whatever of Yu-ying's proverbs she could, but, like small bandages on a large wound, they fell away, useless. Worse, the disillusion that began at the front gate intensified with each successive doorway through which she passed. No sooner had May stepped inside the courtyard of the residence's east wing than her soon-to-be mother-in-law refused her gift of black silk shoes decorated with seed pearls, saying she wasn't that old yet and threatening to be more trouble to May than Yu-ying had been to Chu'en.

The marriage ceremony was performed by a single priest, who stood before the ancestor tablets in the silk merchant's family shrine on the drafty second floor of the east wing. It proceeded without music, without applause, without bells, and resembled no wedding May had ever witnessed. In fact, this occasion for which she had long waited—for which her whole life thus far was mere preparation—was so perfunctory as to leave May with only one memory, that of her new husband's freshly shaven cheek, cut in two places, as if he had flinched under his manservant's hand.

Within minutes it was over, she was in her new room, not chased there with the groom by a laughing crowd making merriment and yelling unnecessary instruction. No, May was accompanied by one person only, a coolly quiet maid who helped her to undress and to climb under her cold covers. Then she was alone. She lay in bed thinking of the two cuts on the silk merchant's cheek. Perhaps it wasn't her husband who had moved; it could have been his valet's hand. Which one of them, listening to the screams, had been, like her, alarmed? Which, like the sleeping sedan-chair men, accepted such protest as part of the household?

. . .

THE RIVALRIES ENGENDERED by May's arrival were so acrimonious that the silk dealer spent two nights with each of his previous wives before once visiting May, and so her first week set the course of married life: one of tedium colored by nervous apprehension. Each day she waited in her room or the tiny garden adjoining it, trying to occupy herself with the comely arts she'd been taught, needlework or painting or singing. In the morning she ate by herself, seated before her own small table; at noon she ate in a dining room with the other women, none of whom spoke to her, but who watched the movements of her chopsticks so intently, she wondered if they might not be waiting for a poison to take effect; and at night she ate alone again, as did whichever wives were not honored by the master's company.

Bored, she crept off to explore, tiptoeing painfully through room after unused room. The house was dark, the damp and poorly ventilated ground floor decorated with European-style paintings of pink, fleshy woman whose bodies overflowed from tight dresses. May found the pictures sad and pretentious; the rooms in which they were displayed smelled of mildew. The second floor was not so dark as the one below, but it was poorly insulated, the floorboards so cold that her feet ached all the more. Looking for an unobtrusive place to sit and rest them, May came upon her two fragrant cedarwood trunks and vanity table, her paper and brushes and bottles of ink, her black lacquer chest of cosmetics, and her set of red lacquer stools, all the things she'd seen stacked by the gutter. She knelt before the trunks and table, stroked the smooth surface of the black lacquer box. Why were none of these taken to the rooms where she had been exiled, a spartan suite not overfilled with furnishings?

At the sound of approaching steps, she hid behind some dusty draperies and then, when it was silent, returned to the chair by her bed. So now May had two images on which to dwell: a freshly shaven, cut cheek; and her belongings, still packed and piled, without any place allowed them.

On the seventh night, the silk dealer came to his fourth wife. Far from being eager to at last hold his youngest and most lovely, he was enraged by the trouble May had caused him. First wife had spent the week sulking, second vomiting, third weeping. He ordered May to take off everything except her foot bindings and to get on her hands and knees on top of her bed. Anticipating an inaugural beating to remind her that she had been born a woman in payment for evil deeds in a past life, May cowered. Not that she was afraid—she wasn't—but she'd been advised more than once not to reveal her pride, lest its reward be rage and punishment, perhaps more than she was ready to accept. But her new husband did not beat her that night. Instead, he lashed her feet to the bedposts by their cloths. And there he left her.

The next night was the same. It was the same for her, but not for her maid, whom he took on the floor as May looked on from the bed. As he exerted himself, a vein stood out on his forehead, marring its handsomeness. Dispassionately, May catalogued her husband's features: wide-set eyes, broad nose, strong chin. There was a statue of Ho Toy in the temple she used to visit with her mother, and he looked like that, except not so fat. The young woman, pinned down, layers of skirts pushed up over her face, thrashed her head from side to side as if suffocating. When the master left, she lay on her back, motionless. She wasn't dead, though; she sat up when one of the other servants called her to return May's dinner bowls to the kitchen.

On the following evening, the silk dealer arrived earlier. "Sing the songs you sang when I visited you at the home of your father's mother," he demanded, and May did. Afterwards, he dined with her, he poured her wine. Then he lashed her by the bindings to the bedposts, lashed her kneeling with her face down, her hips in the air. He was silent as he unfastened his clothes, silent as he rubbed himself stiff with oil, and silent as she bit the bedclothes to avoid crying out when he thrust and discharged himself into her rectum.

"HAVE IT ANNULLED," she said to her grandmother and mother, home for the traditional visit one month after the wedding. "I'm still a virgin."

Chu'en, her face as white and expressionless as spilled candle wax, said nothing.

"You must get a lock of hair from each wife's head and with them line your shoes," said Yu-ying.

"Mother! Holy Mother of Mercy!" May howled. She picked up a dish and hurled it across the room so that it broke against the wall and showered the hearth, the table, and cushions with white splinters of porcelain. "I never had a chance to do the other stupid trick! He doesn't even take his boots off! He comes to my room and puts himself inside my . . . my . . . with his boots still on!"

May threw herself on her knees before her grandmother. "Did the matchmaker tell you I was to be the fourth? Why why why didn't you tell me?"

"What you must do," Yu-ying said. "Is to expel his seed into your chamber pot. Then, Chao-tsing, you can put it yourself into the right place." And she gave May some powders that she said would help her to do this.

As May was leaving, Yu-ying followed her out into the courtyard. "Do not displease your father," she warned. "We have consulted with the necromancer and his medium and your honored father wishes this marriage to succeed. He bids you to obey your husband."

May looked at her grandmother. She opened her mouth but no words came out.

Back in her sedan chair, she left the curtains open, watched the spring landscape wither under her gaze, so scorched with anger were her eyes, so poisoned her heart. The chair pitched and jolted past the shrine of Ah Tai, and she remembered her mother's telling her that years before, when Chu'en had failed to become pregnant, Yu-ying had taken her mother to that shrine, where Ah Tai's supplicants provide her with more tiny shoes than she can possibly wear. From the pile at the goddess's bound feet, Chu'en had selected one. At home Yu-ying burned its laces; with the ashes she brewed tea for May's mother to swallow. The shoelace tea made Chu'en pregnant, and then Yu-ying sewed a new pair of shoes for Ah Tai, and embroidered them with gold threads. Then she carried the shoes all the way back to the shrine on her own bound feet.

Of course, it hadn't been worth such effort. May hadn't been born a boy.

. . .

RETURNED TO THE silk merchant, May brooded. Her anger shrank and cooled into sullenness, punctuated by fits of agitation and despair. How could it be that marriage, for which she had sacrificed all the pleasures and comforts of childhood, was to be nothing more than wretched servitude? How could she have been such a fool? How was it that she had looked every day at her mother, at beautiful, miserable Chu'en, without concluding the obvious: that her own fate would be no less unhappy?

Still, May was young, and youth invents optimism. Even as she suffered her new and uncomfortable clarity of vision, May waited to become a mother herself. To obtain what she needed to accomplish this end, she ate as little as she could and used the cathartics her grandmother had given her. She might be the last wife, but with luck she could yet be favored, she could grab hold of the legs of a son and pull herself up. She wasn't afraid of childbirth. After all, she could stand pain, and what was death? For her it would mean release from insult, and from loneliness. And if the old stories contained any truth, were May to die and leave a son, then when he was grown he could make offerings on her death day, he could perform rites that a daughter could not.

He could free her from the underworld's lake of blood, from the company of the drowned.

But as if in keeping with a curse, months passed and May still waited, while the silk dealer's two older wives, long barren, became pregnant. In their excitement and confidence they consulted with diviners, they bestowed grand and propitious names on their unborn children to guard them against harm and evil spirits—against the ill luck May would not have hesitated to summon, had she only known how.

May paced. She abandoned herself to impatience, to acts of desperation. In the privacy of her room, she threw muffled tantrums, burying herself in the bedclothes, gagging her screams with her fists. One fall afternoon, when the sun sank and left dark hours to be filled before dinner, she lit a lamp and sat on the floor to tend her feet. But instead of removing her bindings, she found herself staring at the flame. After a minute, she snuffed it and lit a candle so that she could see into the lamp's reservoir of oil. Not enough—she slipped down the corridor to a supply room and found more.

Once back behind her door, she locked it, understanding that what she was about to do was an act of vandalism, just as surely as had been her furtively scratching the finish of one of the silk merchant's valuable tables, puncturing his wine casks, breaking a slender finger from one of his ivories. But these and all other amusements had lost their power to distract her; she was weary with her lot, tired out by monotony and cruelty. Now it would all be over. How calm she felt, having made a decision.

She took a deep breath. She poured and drank one, and then another, brimming cup of lamp oil, but this, after a few uncertain days, failed to kill her. Although it did make her sick enough to see death, to learn what it looked like. Death is a master of change; it has many guises: the death May saw was a white buck with silver antlers, a bridle set with jewels, a saddle of jade. As she recovered, the buck retreated, he danced over a hill, the saddle still empty.

After this disappointment, and the savagery of a punitive beating that dislocated her left shoulder—the silk merchant was calculating in his viciousness; he never left a mark on her face or her neck, her white hands and forearms—May hung herself from a beam in her room, but a servant found her and the merchant had her cut down. The buck had just reappeared, dipping his beautiful head and teasing her, his antlers bright, when she hit the floor.

This time, her husband made her kneel in the courtyard like a disobedient servant. No child, but a heavy stone in her arms.

# APPARITIONS

Litovsky was sleeping when Alice knocked at his compartment door. As was often the case in his dreams, he had returned to the year 1895, to the Doks Expedition. Though he and the other four engineers had in fact been stationed near Sludjanka during a mild and forgiving April, the ground thawing and creaking beneath their boots, Litovsky's dream transported him to a tent constructed of untanned hides and pitched on the frozen surface of Lake Baikal. It was night; he worked at a drafting table as the others slept in their sealskin bags. In a golden circle cast by a kerosene lamp, he drew plans for a viaduct, one that could not fail, as the actual one had. Flying buttresses—these were the key. Buttresses such as those that supported the roofs of cathedrals. He drew them in as supports for the piers that rose from the gorge.

Spread before the captain were equations, elementary formulas he had learned as a cadet for calculating the force of compression on a rigid structure in which mass

$m$ is supported by symmetric members, each forming an angle $\theta$ with the horizontal, all the while bearing in mind the train, the train moving forward on the track, and thus the coefficient of friction, horizontal force $F$ applied to body of weight $W$ resting on a surface at an angle of $\theta$, and so forth. It was straightforward, it was simple, a child could figure it out. But then Ashmentov, one of the other engineers, woke; he drew a folded paper out from under the sealskin and handed it to Litovsky. On the paper was written the number 168.

*What am I to do with this?* Litovsky asked, recognizing the number as the count of fatalities.

Ashmentov blinked. *Why, you must apply it,* he said. *You must figure it in.*

*But how?* Litovsky wanted to know. Ashmentov lifted his shoulders. *That's your affair,* he said.

Outside the tent, the lake's frozen surface broke with an explosive noise. Litovsky pushed aside the flaps and saw black rivers divide the ice, bodies float up from below. "Olga!" he cried aloud. "Olga!"

Alice watched as Litovsky brought his hands up to shield his sleeping eyes. She didn't think to wake him; instead, she stared from the doorway. She counted the worn books arranged on the reading table beside him: a dozen, their titles indecipherable; they included those inspirational texts issued to every soldier, Skobelev's *Gift to Comrades* and Lebedev's *The Truth of the Russian Soldier,* as well as outdated manuals of strategy by Goremykin, Barons Medem and Jomini, a topographical survey of Russia, some of its pages missing, others loose; and two of the shorter novels of Dostoyevsky: *The Gambler* and *The Possessed.* It was between pages of this last that Litovsky had tucked a newspaper clipping dated 12 June 1899. Of course, even had she known to look there, Alice would not have been able to read the Russian words.

### 168 PERISH IN MOST RECENT OF TRAGEDIES TO BLIGHT RAIL EFFORT.

Difficulties connected with the construction of track around the southern perimeter of Lake Baikal have thwarted the realization of His Majesty's plans for uninterrupted rail service across Siberia by the year 1900. A locomotive and three cars were derailed during Saturday last's opening of the elevated viaduct traversing the Olkhana tributary. Among those who perished were Prince Kordenky-Novgorod, third cousin to Her Majesty the Czarina, and family members of engineers Doks, Litovsky, and Ashmentov, all gathered for opening celebrations. The viaduct's failure is assumed to have resulted from design flaws. Investigations are pending.

The paper on which the article was printed had been folded and unfolded and refolded so many times that in places it was perforated, unreadable even to a Russian.

A large traveling clock ticked on top of Litovsky's pile of books, its brass case engraved with the maxim *Prayer to God and Service to the Czar Are Never in Vain.* Against the table leaned a walking stick with a head that screwed off to reveal the mouth of a secret drinking flask. The other end unscrewed, too. Inside was a long, sharp saber.

Litovsky sighed in his sleep, a cadet again and back in school outside St. Petersburg, where his regiment was preparing for a review of the troops by the czar. *You must make it smooth, smooth, smooth,* the commander was saying in the captain's dream, and he swept his hand back and forth through the air. *Not a rock. Not a molehill. Not a weed or a crease.* It had been the cadets' duty, in the weeks before review, to prepare the parade grounds, to make the packed dirt as even as a ballroom floor.

Alice, growing restless, rattled the compartment door. "Smooth!" Captain Litovsky cried aloud. He opened his eyes, looked around in confusion.

"I'm sorry. Did I wake you?"

"No. Not at all." Litovsky straightened his rumpled tunic. "What *is* the matter, Olga?" he asked in response to Alice's stare. She opened her mouth to correct him, but stopped herself. "You don't want to go off to school?" he asked. Alice shook her head. She sat beside Litovsky. The light coming in the window had a faint pink cast, the light that presages a snowfall.

Litovsky patted Alice's knee with an absent, fatherly benevolence. "When I was a cadet, the czar and his sons came to our summer encampment. And the czarevitch gave each of us a cake and a packet of nuts and two silver rubles. I have one still." From inside his tunic he pulled a dingy gray silk cord on the end of which was a red embroidered pouch. He teased open the string that held the pouch closed and shook the coin into her palm. "And there were oranges. Baskets and baskets of oranges." Alice handed back the coin.

"I don't care about oranges."

"Still," said the captain. "You may like school." He looked at his ruble in the pink light. "Perhaps you will." But he was thinking, suddenly, of Ismailikov, the top-form student who had forced him, his first year, to drink his own urine. "Boys are cruel." He put the coin away. "I like girls better."

Alice scratched her nose.

"You are in heaven!" the captain cried suddenly. "Tell me it is so!" Beneath his hat his face was flushed, his forehead shone with perspiration. "You've just come to visit your old papa! To comfort him on his journey!" With surprising force Litovsky pulled Alice into an embrace, holding her so tightly that the buttons on his tunic grazed her cheek. "Olga! Olga! Forgive me!"

Alice shoved her hands against Litovsky and kept her eyes closed, afraid to see his face. As she struggled to get away, his chest heaved with violent soundless sobs; she felt her own squeezed by panic. Alice had seen a man cry only once, at David's death, when her father had gone down on his knees holding the bedroom curtains. Gone down so slowly that whenever she thought of that morning it was the slowness she remembered. Slowness which taught her that death had the power to suspend lesser laws of nature, to interrupt gravity, to stop the earth in its transit around the sun. Shutters closed and curtains drawn, for weeks the house blazed with light; no one could stand for even one lamp to be extinguished, no one knew the hour. But this was a different kind of crying. Naked, jarring.

"A perfect child! As innocent as an angel!" Alice shoved again, and Litovsky fell against the table, upsetting the books, the clock. "Why! Why!" He rocked back and forth, hands clasped before his chest. "Why could I not have traded my life for yours!" Litovsky picked up his walking stick and banged its tip on the floor.

Before she knew what she was doing, before she heard another word, Alice was hurtling down the corridor, she was bumping into other passengers, grating her knuckles on a window frame. She didn't stop until she had reached the frigid passage between the last two cars, her breath gusting out in clouds of vapor. The sound of Litovsky's stick echoed in her head like the report of a gavel on a judge's bench, as if the captain's wish—that lives could be traded—had been mandated into law.

# THE VIEW FROM
# THE GARDENER'S BACK

MAY SPENT MANY HOURS IN THE COURTYARD, but rather than contemplating the disobedience that had brought her to her knees, embracing a stone, she looked around herself and plotted her escape. At suicide she'd been a failure. Perhaps, for the time being anyway, she'd have to make her way in this world. If she couldn't die, she'd have to live; what she was doing now was neither. The silk merchant's grounds were kept by three gardeners: one was old and wizened; one was burdened by a wife and twin daughters; and one was a huge strapping lout named Ahng-wah. On this last one's broad back May rested her plans.

After a month of decorous, almost imbecile docility—the purpose of which was to blend in, smiling and bowing, with the silk drapes and cloisonné vases, transformed from troublesome concubine to pretty possession—May gathered all her jewels into a purse and hid them under her mattresses. A simple swoon after the midday meal rewarded her with an afternoon undisturbed in her bed; after allowing curtains to be drawn and cool compresses applied, she dismissed her maid.

Then, once the household had settled into the usual postprandial stupor, May sat up; she threw off covers and compresses, and retrieved her jewels. Ignoring the pain in her feet occasioned by haste, she slipped past the kitchen and into the back garden, where she found Ahng-wah alone, asleep and snoring in the shade of a maple tree, sitting with his back to its trunk, his head lolling and his bottom lip falling forward in a loose pout. Having made certain that no witnesses were lurking, she poked him awake. He opened his eyes to see a soft white palm filled with pearls and jade, around which delicate fingers slowly closed. "I am going to Shanghai," May whispered. "If you help me, these will be yours."

Ahng-wah sucked in his lower lip and nodded, and so at nightfall, as they had planned in the scattered shade of the maple leaves, May ran away on the big feet and strong legs of the gardener. En route from Ch'ang-shu to Shanghai she made one stop, in the town where she had grown up.

May knew her grandmother's habits as well as her own and arrived at Yu-ying's gate before dawn of the second Tuesday of the month, the day when her grandmother was sure to go out to play mah-jongg and gossip with her sisters. She hid herself and the big-footed gardener where neighbors and servants wouldn't see them, inside the small shed where the spare rickshaw was stored alongside baskets of apples and onions and crates of eggs, which Ahng-wah broke into his mouth and swallowed, one after another, while they waited. It was nearly dusk before Yu-ying's sedan chair departed, and May could creep through the courtyard to the house. She resisted her mother's door, from under which beckoned a blue finger of opium smoke. At the family ancestor shrine she paused only as long as it took to spit on the soul tablet of her father.

In a special chest in her grandmother's boudoir, in a perfumed drawer lined with black silk, Yu-ying kept her sleeping shoes. Having secretly explored its contents many times, May knew where to find the key; and the brass lock turned with well-oiled ease. May had barely to touch the drawer's handle for it to slide out toward her like a thing enchanted, a fairy-tale casket inside which were pair upon pair of red silk shoes: favorites saved from all the years of her grandmother's marriage. Shoes decorated with birds and flowers, with symbols for life and health and fecundity. Shoes embroidered with gold thread and pearls. Shoes bearing little bells on their pointed toes. Shoes Yu-ying had worn when May's father and his brothers were conceived. Shoes in which Yu-ying had kicked and writhed and curled into the damp wall of her husband's lust.

Shoes that had been squeezed and bitten and licked, whose linings had been wet with tears and with wine and with semen. Shoes that had been wiped and mended and perfumed and carefully put away.

From the small purse hanging around her neck, May withdrew the knife she used to groom her feet, and with it she cut up all of her grandmother's sleeping shoes. She used its sharp point to rip out characters for life and for happiness. She ground little pearls under her own wooden heels, crushed bells until they were silent. When she was through cutting and destroying, she squatted over the heap of torn fabric and glinting gold threads and urinated on it. Then she refastened her trousers, picked up the wet red silk and replaced it in the drawer, feeling how heavy and warm her defilement had made it, like something recently killed. May closed the drawer, crying as she did so without noise, because it was long ago that she had forgotten how to cry out loud.

On her way back through the courtyard, she paused again at Chu'en's door, but she reminded herself that she couldn't stand the sight of her mother after she had been smoking, the terrible stupidity in her eyes, and she returned to Ahng-wah, now eating onions in the shed. She climbed on his back, wrapped her legs around his waist, and tucked her feet into his belt. Reaching over his shoulder, she held her jade beads out and let them swing before his eyes on their string.

"It's fourteen miles more to Shanghai," May said. "We must continue to travel by night, but I'll give you all of these and more if we arrive safely." As they left, she tore down the military citation that hung on the outer door, the one proclaiming her father's home that of a man of glorious deeds.

AHNG-WAH, WHO WAS three times the size of May, had a large, irregularly shaped mole on the back of his thick neck. As they made their uncomfortable way toward the city, creeping not along roads but on paths near roads, all of May's distaste for him centered on that blemish. The gardener was a coarse man, and the mole, too, was coarse. He smelled of onions and of perspiration, and it seemed to May's nose, just inches from the mole, that it was this brown and black blot which released the unpleasant odor. With her arms and legs aching, stretched across Ahng-wah's broad back, the mole too seemed to stretch wider and wider; it made her eyes ache as well.

Peering around the gardener's shoulder, May looked everywhere for a wheelbarrow they might steal, chastising herself for running away too quickly to plan, but all the houses and farms they passed in the dark were guarded by dogs, and Ahng-wah was frightened of dogs; May could feel his body stiffen under her as they came within earshot of barking. In fact, the gardener was frightened of all animals, and of the noises they made. The whinny of a horse or the rustle of a nocturnal rodent moving through the grass would make him quicken his lumbering pace.

On the third night, made even more clumsy than usual by the sounds of some local skirmish, the eye-smarting smell of campfires, Ahng-wah fell as he was carrying May. He tripped on a root and plunged heavily forward on to his hands, pitching her over his head. As May reached out to break her own fall, the string of the purse in which she had safeguarded her jewels and her knife broke, and the little silk bag fell out of her reach. Ahng-wah snatched it up.

"That's it," he said, scowling at her maliciously. For, naturally, just as she detested him, so did he detest her. As he walked, Ahng-wah had come to regard May as the literal burden of his greed, a chafing weight not only on his sullen back but on his soul. And just as she thought he stank and mentally recoiled from the body that she was forced to hold, so did May offend Ahng-wah's nose. With her legs open against his damp, filthy shirt, she smelled to him like a whore: a confusing mixture of sickening rich woman's perfume and the sharp, briny odor of her sex. Ahng-wah spat, calling May an ugly bitch in heat.

In his twenty years, the gardener had had two women, his village chief's cretin daughter, whom everyone had had, including the chief (all of them considering this barely just compensation for the village's supporting so otherwise useless a being), and the girl he'd allowed to sleep in the shed where his uncles stored chilies. She, too, was running away from someone or something.

"Give me my purse," May said.

Ahng-wah looked at May. Why shouldn't she be the third? Having carried her this far, feet and knees and back aching, he considered a handful of jade inadequate payment.

"Wait," May said, seeing that he was unfastening the belt in which for eleven miles she had tucked her feet. If she convinced him that rape was too risky, that she would turn him in, perhaps he'd decide to murder her. And if anyone was going to take May's life, it would be May herself, not this bone-headed lummox. Fury more than danger hastened May's thoughts. Ahng-wah was strong, but he was stupid and his fears were the fears of a stupid person.

"Careful!" May said, suddenly inspired. "Careful of the foxes!" Ahng-wah looked around wildly.

"What fox!" he said. May willed any expression of triumph from her face. What a blessing that he was frightened of animals.

"Surely you know about the fox girls," she went on, alluding to local legends that told of bands of female grave-robbers, able to transform themselves into foxes who dug swift, deep holes in which they hid themselves and their loot. "How do you think I came to own so many necklaces?" she asked. "You don't think I'd run away from a husband who gave me so many jewels?"

Ahng-wah said nothing, but he studied her face, the exaggerated widow's peak and long eyeteeth that had always encouraged May herself to believe that she looked a little more like an animal than a woman should.

"Well," she said. "Shall I call my sisters? Shall I show you my tail? The hair on my hands?" She thrust them forward.

"No!" he cried. This was not the chief's cretin daughter.

"Then give me my purse!"

But Ahng-wah was running, running, and May was sitting, dirty, in a ditch, watching her jewels vanish. She touched the one necklace she still wore to make sure it was there, around her throat.

Five miles to Shanghai—not even a night's walk, but that was for someone like Ahng-wah, a person with feet, real feet. May sat and listened to the sound of her own heart, cursing her luck. The cruelty of the silk merchant, it seemed to her, lay in not allowing her to die. If he had, she wouldn't be hiding from him in a ditch, she wouldn't be bruised and hungry and frightened, forced to draw bitter solace from the one comforting thought available to her: that of the shoes she'd ruined. May fell asleep watching silk divide under the blade of her knife, an image she would resurrect on subsequent bleak nights of her life.

WHEN THE SUN came up, the road filled with traffic heading toward the city: carts of peppers and leeks and eggs, men staggering under yokes to which forty chickens were bound upside down by their feet, flapping, squawking, shitting. Afraid to beg a ride, sure that her husband was hunting her, May stayed in the ditch, listening and waiting, hidden by high weeds. Another night passed, another day.

On the third night, as she was falling asleep, aching head filled with visions of torn wet silk, a strange, howling clatter raked the calm. May startled. She got to her feet, dizzy with hunger, and peered over the edge of the ditch at a boisterous crowd approaching under the light of torches, shadows leaping ahead with the flames. It was the clamorous dance of a local bandit-king's triumphant all-night parade, his dusty, grinning cohorts dragging devices of war of every conceivable vintage: cannons and crossbows and catapults; a string of stolen, filthy donkeys stumbling under equestrian battle gear; the carapace of a rusted, armored carriage pulled by twisted, fraying ropes. The bandit-king, immensely fat and nearly naked, sat atop this astonishing conveyance in a loincloth and an untied robe that fell open to reveal a gleaming, greasy belly from the center of which popped a strangely protuberant, almost childlike nipple-navel, which gave all of him the aspect of an enormous breast, one with limbs and a head, larger than life, male and female at once. Here, May thought, was someone who would not be afraid of her husband. The intoxicated parade moved forward so slowly that she had time to shake out her clothes and smooth her hair before scrambling out of her ditch.

At the sudden sight of a woman in the road before them—a beautiful one if torches and moonlight could be trusted—the rabble came to a halt. "What are you?" the bandit-king said, as if addressing a ghost. His voice was slurred; his eyes strained for drunken focus. At his feet, one of the men pulling the carriage dropped his rope, put his hands on his knees and vomited an extravagant quantity of wine in the road.

"I am . . ." Given the confused state of the men before her (and still proud of her success with Ahng-wah; apparently old stories were good for something), May considered announcing herself as a messenger from the god of prosperity, but decided not to test what appeared to be a glimmer of good fortune. "I am on my way to Shanghai," she said, "and if that is your destination, I humbly inquire if I might accompany you in your victorious march." She bowed, very low and not at all obsequiously.

The bandit-king contemplated her. Beautiful girls were a feature of his celebration that he'd saved for Shanghai, but when a sylph stepped into the road, was there sense in saying no? Could harm follow from arriving in the city with one bird already in hand? It might even be advantageous in luring others.

For a slow five miles, punctuated by innumerable stops and detours in order to seize every opportunity for further drinking and revelry, May sat next to the bandit-king; and the bandit-king required nothing of her but that she listen to the details of his recent triumphs, a matter of forcibly seizing control of a network of roads by routing out their formidable (if not so formidable as he) ruler. According to the fat king—whose name she didn't ask for fear of seeming impolite, and which he didn't tell, assuming she knew it already—his recent battles had required great cunning and courage, and May quickly learned which of his pauses she should answer with an amazed *ahhhh*, and which should elicit *And then what?* In this way, she so satisfied his desire for an awestruck audience that he forgot to take further advantage of her, and the jolting slow hours passed in an almost companionable tedium. By the time the parade had reached the outskirts of Shanghai, May was leaning drowsily against the bandit-king's flank, but at the sight of so many houses all crowded together, she sat up. Was this at last the infamous city of danger and opportunity? The familiar architecture of the Chinese countryside had given way to avenues of immense structures bearing mansards and gables and cupolas and balconies, each brazenly tall and visible—no high walls around these houses, for apparently their occupants didn't need such protection. They were favored by the gods; either that or they were unafraid, they were untouched by celestial plots. May stared as a woman with hair as yellow as the yolk of an egg came out of a black door with a shining brass knob and knocker. The parade hesitated to let an ox cart cross, and she slipped down from the armored carriage, to be fully awakened by her feet.

"Hey!" the bandit-king cried. But she waved and hurried determinedly away, stiffening her back with false courage, willing herself to ignore what felt like broken glass and molten lead, spikes, salt, boiling oil—any and every torment imaginable—devouring her broken feet. She walked away, and the king made no move to stop her, perhaps realizing that the amount of wine he had drunk would have unmanned and embarrassed him.

MAY SAT ON a curb, feeling the ache in legs that for two nights had been spread across a gardener's broad back, then folded in a ditch and jounced on an armored carriage. She had crept as far as she was able—barely a quarter of a mile—and so she broke the string of her last necklace. A triple strand of pearls, it had been a wedding gift from her mother, and she'd never yet taken it from her throat, not even on the day she'd tried to hang herself. The pearls were large and of obvious value, and for one of them she hired a spot on a wheelbarrow, wedged between two girls heading for work in a cotton mill.

As they drew nearer to the center of the city, the houses grew larger and grander and then abruptly disappeared. Now everything was commerce, and commerce of every description. On the corner of Ningpo and Honan roads, May saw a large red sign offering her the opportunity to pawn the remains of her necklace, and she called for the barrow to stop. She got off stiffly, ducked under the banner, and went inside, watched two transactions before stepping up to where the broker sat. The shop's counter was five and a half feet tall; May had to reach over her head to lay all but two of the pearls on its sticky surface, two that she'd hastily unknotted from the string in a spasm of sentiment. Then she backed up several feet to see the broker behind his cage. With one eye he peered through a magnifying glass at what she offered, tested several of the pearls against his stained teeth, and gave her a receipt and less money than she had hoped. She counted it twice, folded it, and hid it in her clothes before going outside.

Using a discarded laundry pole as a cane, she limped slowly toward the river, clotted with barges and ferries and junks. A ship was moored at every jetty; customs houses larger than temples, and banks far more grand, looked down as goods were unloaded. May had never seen so many people, nor so many different kinds of people. Tall people, from the tall buildings, with hair that was brown, red, yellow. And people with skin burnt black. All of them walked through and past the crowds of natives, Chinese who seemed busier than those May had left behind in the villages. Squatting and washing clothes in the creek, eating as they walked, quarreling as they worked, beating dogs, plucking chickens, hurrying, hurrying. The nervous trill of Shanghai, its frantic restlessness, as if a wind of desire passed through all its denizens, making them itch and jig with anticipation—although May was tired, the city made her stand at attention.

With her money she bought one week at the Astor House Hotel, a smug and substantial pile of stone and mortar that overlooked the Whangpoo just north of the point where the Soochow Creek poured its silt into the river's clouded yellow waters. She considered the expense of her small room not so much an extravagance as the necessary cost for a period of consecration. What good would come to her from a month in a cheap inn? Her plans required a good hotel, a perch from which she could watch the kind of people from whom she could learn what she needed to know.

Upstairs, resting with her elbows on her windowsill, she could see the Garden Bridge, and on it a coolie hurrying over the creek with a harp on his back—a gilt harp six feet tall. May watched the man jog on under his fantastic burden and understood that she had come to a place where anything was possible.

# THE SHORT HISTORY
## OF A PRODIGY

As THE TRAIN CONTINUED WESTWARD, EVEN THE
elements conspired toward elegance. Storms sheathed
the coaches' external fittings in bright ice and hung
silver stalactites from the window frames. To the solitary
auburn-haired woman writing letters at her table in the
dining car, the engine appeared like a horse in a funeral
cortege, except that in such case the white plumes of
steam would have been a respectful black. The woman,
thirty-nine years old and unmarried, was returning to
Paris after settling her recently dead brother's affairs in
Vladivostok, and her mind, which had always suffered
from morbid imaginings, now found images of death
everywhere. Still, she kept these to herself and wrote the
kind of glib and cheerful letters her mother had taught
her to write when she was a girl. *Chère Lisette,* she began
to a friend in New York, *The coffee on the famous Russian
train is as good as the vodka! For dinner last night I had toast
points with caviar, two glasses of champagne!*

She did not mention her brother's bankruptcy (he'd been an exporter of furs, but the extravagance of his mistress had outstripped the profit in sable skins), nor that he'd poisoned himself with prussic acid. (Had the poison imparted to his skin an unnaturally white smoothness recalling the cheap celluloid collars worn by gendarmes on their evenings off? Or was this an effect of the climate?) Nor did she say that she had been the one to wash his corpse, which until her arrival had lain untended in his apartments overlooking the steep, twisting Znamensky Road, the rooms of which (fortunately, under such circumstances) had remained unheated since his failure to pay the coal bill the previous month. In the letter to her childhood friend, the woman from Paris referred to her younger and only brother's demise as a *departure*, a *passage*, invoking travel and literature. Diversion rather than death.

In fact, when she reached his home, summoned by a cable from his business partner (who described Sergei as dying, not dead), she had been shocked to find his body frozen to the rug, which was now cleaned, dried, rolled, tagged with her address, and wedged into the baggage compartment between the door and two blue trunks with brass hardware belonging, as an abundance of tags and labels proclaimed, to Alice and Cecily Benjamin of Shanghai, China.

The red and blue and black wool rug, hand loomed in Bokhara and as good as new save for two silverfish holes, was bound for Paris along with its former owner's still-frozen corpse (in a pitiably inexpensive pine casket—she'd spent all her savings on the express ticket), a mahogany armoire, a set of lamps with solid malachite stands, and a silver christening cup engraved with the initials S.S.P., all that the woman from Paris had managed to secure from creditors, partner, and mistress—equally greedy forces. At the last moment she'd taken a muff, so large that at first she'd thought it an obese cat curled on the shelf. Whose it was she didn't know; she hoped it belonged to the mistress. She'd found it in her brother's pantry, between two canisters of stale tea, and as each passenger on the train was allowed a full set of furs without paying a coat tax, she'd carried it on board with her and for the past four nights had slept hugging it to her stomach in the cramped berth. *I bought a sable muff*, she lied in her letter, *quite exquisitely supple and soft, the kind you can find only in Russia. But where else would you have need of such a thing? I've been using it at night, to keep my hands warm in bed. The cushions in my compartment are of green brocade. A writing table with a lamp and an inkwell that does not spill no matter how the train lurches. And the library car has embossed leather walls.*

The woman from Paris dipped her pen into the exemplary inkwell and finished her letter, signing it with a flourish that betrayed her love of pens, ink, fine paper. Her name was Suzanne Petrovna, and she and Alice Benjamin would meet again, fourteen years later, on Avenue des Fleurs, 72, in Nice, where, failing to recognize each other, the two of them would reminisce about the express train's generous supplies of writing materials. Suzanne would have forgotten the scandal of the girl abducted from the train by an army engineer; and Alice wouldn't remember the woman whose hands had almost always been hidden in a muff. Even though she had spied on Suzanne, Alice's memory of the French woman would be obscured by the trip's subsequent, more forceful impressions.

Upstairs, in the pink villa behind the black wrought-iron gate, on the same night she and Alice had idly discussed stationery, Suzanne would take one of Alice's aunt's red silk sleeping shoes from the high shelf on which they were kept and ask May to use the pointed slipper on her.

The Suzanne in the dining car of the train would probably not recognize her older self, a self who had torn off her clothes, who was pacing naked and ranting in a room whose every light was lit. This Suzanne had lost all calm; she wasn't careful or reflective, nor was she self-possessed. She threw things, and some of them broke. She didn't bother to fetch a step-stool to reach the high shelf; but in the throes of a destructive, irreversible passion, she yanked open a drawer and stepped inside it, her feet sinking into piles of carefully folded lingerie.

*Enleve-moi!* Suzanne demanded that May force the red shoe between her legs.

*Enleve-moi:* not the vulgar *Baise-moi,* nor the angrier *Saute-moi. Enlever* was a literary choice, a verb that even the bookish Suzanne might not have used if she had been thinking clearly. If, in her usual deliberate fashion, she'd rehearsed her lines before daring to speak them.

A calmer, more familiar Suzanne would have considered *enlever* and its suggestion of plunder. She'd have remembered that the word can mean *peel*, as with an orange. Was that what she was asking for?

By that time—if not already, on the train, and even during the years before her brother's death—innocence was no longer clarity; it was confusion. It wasn't freedom but entrapment. And at last, in 1927, on Avenue des Fleurs, 72, Suzanne had found her deliverance. In a rash, furious, spluttering, and exultant instant, she recognized the one person who might change everything. May.

So perhaps she was asking for plunder. After all, *enlever* suggests transformation, and what Suzanne wanted—it wasn't sex, exactly, but a different life. The chance to start over, from the beginning, under other circumstances.

SUZANNE FOLDED HER letter and looked up to find the Benjamin girls' governess taking a break from her charges and approaching the seat opposite her own. For several days Miss Waters had had the idea of cultivating the woman from Paris as a means of improving her French. Another week and she'd be back in London without employment.

"Do you mind if I join you?" Miss Waters sat down without waiting for an answer.

Suzanne shook her head and soon found herself entertaining the usual questions about the Ile de la Cité, the Place Vendôme, the Musée du Louvre, the Jardin du Luxembourg, and all the other landmarks of her celebrated home.

"Tell me about la Tour Eiffel." Miss Waters's grammar was correct but her accent thickly Scots. It took Suzanne a moment to decipher the request.

"I haven't seen it, actually. Not close. From a distance, yes."

"But, but it's been—well, the exposition was more than twenty years ago!" The governess looked at Suzanne as if she'd admitted to a serious lapse in hygiene, as if, for example, she'd said she never cleaned her teeth.

Suzanne nodded. "You are right, I'm sure." But, she explained, she lived far from such places, and far from the Seine, in the shabby fifteenth arrondissement, where she made her living as a translator of Russian texts. Both she and her brother had grown up speaking Russian because their father had been an acrobat from Kiev. "My father, he came to France with a troupe of performers and never left. My mother was the daughter of the concierge across the street from the room he rented. And so now my father is—he is gone, my brother is dead, and my mother, she died, too. I am alone." Unconsciously, she brought the muff up to her face as she spoke, hiding her mouth but not her eyes.

"Ah," Miss Waters stammered, flustered by so naked and absolute a bereavement.

Suzanne began to cry, surprised to find herself, after the cheery performance of her letter, so suddenly and publicly stricken. She did that sometimes—it wasn't intentional, but what Suzanne hid from her few friends she shared with strangers. "My brother," she began, by way of explanation. "My brother learned to play the piano with astonishing speed. We had no money, no piano, but the father of one of his companions was a musician who played in a restaurant. Not a *boîte*, it was a respectable establishment. It had linen on the tables. Sergei spent many afternoons at the home of his friend, and one day the father reported that Sergei sat at the piano and played. He played perfectly a sonata he had heard the father practicing.

"The father came to our home and he told us that Sergei was a prodigy. What were we going to do, he asked." Suzanne stared at the window, the curling fronds of ice on its pane. She used the muff to blot her wet cheeks.

The governess was a person who grew impatient during any silence. "What happened then?" she asked.

Suzanne spoke without looking at Miss Waters. "My father beat

Sergei. After the musician left, my father hit my brother. Sergei tried to defend himself; he did not cry, but finally he went down onto his hands and his knees. And then my father stepped on my brother's fingers." Suzanne turned from the frozen window back to the governess; she searched Miss Waters's face as if she expected some explanation of her unhappy story. "This was the first act of violence I had witnessed from my father," she added. "Never before had he struck me, my mother, or my brother. Never once, before that evening. Although . . ."

"Although?" Miss Waters prompted.

Suzanne shook her head. "Ours was a family in which the mother loved her children too dearly. It would have been better to hide it, to appear to be wife first, mother second. But she was not clever, and our father understood her devotion and was envious, especially of Sergei. Mother would touch the back of Sergei's neck sometimes when he was at the table eating, and a look would come into my father's eyes. Ugly, worse than anger. Hatred.

"When the musician told us of Sergei's brilliance, I think my father saw some pride or hope in my mother's face, and it must have been that which inspired such rage. He never recovered, my father. From that night forward, he was a violent man. One day, mercifully, he left. Without a word."

Miss Waters examined her left hand. With her thumbnail she pushed back the fingers' cuticles. "What happened with your brother, his talent?"

"Nothing," Suzanne said.

"Nothing at all?"

"He moved away, from our home and from Paris and finally from France. He moved out as soon as he could support himself. He would do any odd job. Shoe-blacking. Brick-laying. Menial jobs that degraded his brilliant hands. He never played the piano. I had hoped to see one, when I came to his apartments. So far away from home, so many miles, I imagined that I would. I pictured it. In my mind, it had a red fringed cloth over the lid, and on the cloth were a vase and a lamp. A photograph of our mother. Odd, how clearly I could see it, because this piano, it didn't exist. It was only in my mind. And Sergei never did a thing except love the wrong women and lose all his money."

Once again Suzanne fell silent, and the sadness cast by her story smothered every comment Miss Waters thought to make.

# A Long-Handled Spoon

Contemplating her future from the gardener's back, May had not been unrealistic. She knew that she possessed more beauty than skill, more courage than stamina. Having experienced a husband, she would now adopt a clientele; and so, on each of the seven days she spent at the Astor House Hotel, she got up late, breakfasted at noon, lunched at dinner, and hired a rickshaw to take her slowly up and down Kiangse Road, where she could observe the traffic outside the brothels. She wanted to discover which among them attracted men whose rickshaw boys looked well fed, men whose clothing was elegant, whose faces were open, and whose eyes were raised and honest rather than downcast and ashamed.

Returned to the hotel, she sat in the lounge and watched the Europeans as they came in and out of the lobby's wide doors: men, mostly, with dark suits and glittering watch chains, exotically barbered faces. But there were a few women as well, dressed in punitive blues and grays. What long strides they took, though. May listened to their heels strike the floor with the force of horses' hooves. With her eyes closed she let her head rest on the chair back and listened. Despite their drab clothes, the Western women fascinated her, as might birds whose plumage was dull from one vantage, luminous from another.

May told herself that these were dangerous activities: brazen, bare-headed rides through the streets, leisurely long spells in the lobby. What if the silk merchant had had her followed? What if he'd contacted the *chen chang*, set police and spies on her trail? But try as she did, she couldn't feel afraid; and she couldn't forbid herself to sit in the lobby. She couldn't not look at the women, and especially she couldn't not hear the beautiful sound of them walking. And any-way, the silk merchant wasn't a fool, and he wasn't young. Probably he was grateful for the peace that returned once May had gone.

Upstairs in her room, May stood at the window, watching the dirty water of Soochow Creek spill into the Whangpoo. Light from the street touched on its surface, beckoning like lantern flashes. It wasn't until long past midnight, when traffic on the Bund and the river slowed, that she could hear the water, the slapping and sucking of the current.

*Jump!* she thought each time she crossed the Garden Bridge, sur-prising herself with the idea. After all, the creek was so filled with boats that even though she couldn't swim, someone would certainly pull her out before the water could close over her head. Besides, she wasn't the type. She wasn't a jumper.

On her last night in the hotel, in order to exorcise such thoughts, May held a funeral. For fear of setting her room on fire, she did it on the roof, to which she'd gained access by means of a bribe. The cham-bermaid who unlocked the attic door squatted and watched in silence as May, freshly bathed, wearing white, laid out what she had bought. As a compromise between mourner and mourned, she loosed her hair, she tucked her two pearls into her cheek.

"Do you want to help me?" she asked.

"Who has died?" the girl asked.

"I have."

The chambermaid shook her head. "I'm from Hangchow," she said. "We don't do such things there."

May shrugged. She kneeled by the plate of rice and pork she'd carried back from a street vendor. On a thick page of hotel stationery she wrote the name her mother had given her, Chao-tsing, or Morning Star, for she had been born just at dawn. Then she burned that name, along with a thick stack of spirit money, a bundle of joss sticks, a gold paper sedan chair, seven gold paper dresses, and seven pairs of gold paper shoes: all she could think of that her old self might need in its journey through the next world.

The sedan chair was not small, and she'd worried on her way through the hotel's lobby that the concierge might stop her from taking it upstairs. But he'd barely looked up from his newspaper. He was a European; the idea of her setting it on fire must not have occurred to him.

On the hotel roof, the blaze lit May's face. The characters of her name, painted large, the black ink not yet dry, hissed and burned green; then the page curled like a drying leaf. She watched the paper dresses, the shoes, and the chair ignite and collapse into ash. How quickly it was accomplished, the passage from one world to the next. She didn't provide herself a paper house in which to live, a place for Chao-tsing to settle and shelter, but—never considering the possibility of her return—sent that girl traveling among the ghosts, ever away and away.

*Sa. Pai. Jer. Sa pai jer. Sapaijer.* May couldn't stop the syllables from repeating in her head. One of the last rituals she'd performed with her mother was the spreading of porridge, or *sa pai jer,* on the night set aside for feeding hungry ghosts. All the household observed the seventh-month festivities, and each member, down to the lowliest servant, had taken a turn stirring the cauldron in the courtyard. They'd all walked through town with a steaming bowl in one hand and a spoon in the other, and when they reached the outskirts of the cemetery they ladled porridge onto the ground. The townsmen lit incense and burned spirit money, and everyone called out to the ghosts to eat and to fill their pockets and then be gone for another year. Now Chao-tsing would be among them, separated from her father by a graveyard wall, he lying cosseted and splendid among ancestors, and she prowling alone in the dark.

As May had no flute, no funeral drum, she made her own music. Pursing her lips, she whistled and felt her last two pearls click against her teeth. The girl from Hangchow watched her. She'd seen many peculiar things at the Astor House Hotel; here was another.

The new name was the one May would use from now on: May-li. *May-li* meant *beautiful*, and she'd chosen it while still smarting from the gardener's telling her she was ugly. What it lacked in imagination it would make up for in suitability. Could there be a better name with which to begin her new life? *May:* In English, she'd discover, May was the warmest month of spring. The word meant possibility, if not exactly hope. It meant permission to go ahead.

When the sun rose over the river, she was at her open window, watching. She hadn't slept but had sat there, waiting for the light. She washed and bound her feet, put on her best shoes, not those in which she had run away, but the only other pair she'd brought, those in which she'd been hastily married. Dressed in a new embroidered silk blouse and matching trousers, she breakfasted in the second-floor lounge, at a small table set for one person, and at eleven o'clock she took not a rickshaw but a carriage to Madame Grace's. The only brothel in Shanghai to employ girls of any nationality, Grace's was a cooperative venture between two madams, one English, the other Chinese. It was the one place, May imagined, where she might make a life among Europeans, among women who walked with strides as long as men's.

"SHE HAS A BEAUTIFUL FACE, but an unlucky one," cautioned Grace's Chinese partner, who had interviewed and examined May.

"Beauty makes luck," Grace said.

The partner snorted. "I hope you are right. She's intact, anyway. That's worth something."

"It's worth quite a lot. Who's that Beardsly or Bromly—the one from the customs office? He wanted a native girl. 'An untouched one,' as he put it."

The partner nodded, silent, her eyebrows drawn. There was something peculiar about a virgin who didn't disrobe with a virgin's timidity. This May-li had a haughty look, the look of a girl who'd come from wealthy circumstances, and yet she had unbuttoned her blouse as efficiently as if she'd never relied on a maidservant. And she did it with practiced vacancy. "These too?" she'd asked, indicating her foot bindings.

"No," the partner said, shocked. What Chinese woman, even a paid woman, ever offered to show her feet?

Without hesitating, May lay on the couch and opened her legs. Most novices to the trade, despite—or because of—their vulgar ambition, covered their faces with their hands. One young Cantonese had closed her eyes and stuck her fingers in her ears, as if expecting an explosion rather than a quick exam.

"What are you running from?" the partner wanted to know when May was dressed.

"Fate," May said, after a silence.

The partner raised her eyebrows. "Good luck," she said. "No one before you has escaped."

May smiled, said nothing. Silence didn't seem to make her uncomfortable—nothing did—and this, too, worried the partner. Just how inexperienced was the heart hidden inside that cool silk bodice?

The partner called down the stairs for a kitchen maid to bring a tray with teapot and cups. Watching May, she poured two and offered May one. May set the vessel down without drinking from it.

"A third of what you bring in is yours. Out of it you must pay a room tax, a laundry fee. 'Accidents,' visits from the physician, these also are your responsibility. Board is provided, but you must buy your own clothes, or receive them as gifts—if you inspire such affection." The partner paused. She licked her lower lip. "One day off each week, and one afternoon. If after a year you're still with us, you get half of what you earn."

After a calculated silence—she didn't want to appear eager—May nodded.

"Do you have any questions?"

"A provision," May answered.

The partner raised her eyebrows. "What is that?"

"I won't ... I'll do anything for *na guo ning*"—a foreigner—"English, French, Russian. A black African, for all I care. But"—May reached forward, as if to pick up her tea, withdrew her hand before her fingers were around the cup—"Chinese I won't touch."

"Well," said the partner after a pause, a frown. "If you can afford it, that is your business." They stood, the table and the steaming cups between them, and bowed.

FOR THE FIRST WEEK, May watched. This was Grace's established means of educating a prostitute, and at no loss of revenue; there were always customers who paid extra for an audience, especially one so beautiful, so seemingly rapt. As her exemplar, May was given an American woman, Helen, from San Francisco. Until she'd earned enough in her capacity as voyeur to pay the tax for a room of her own, she would sleep on the other side of a yellow curtain strung across a corner of Helen's.

Accustomed to servants, to lacquered tables, silk-hung walls, and cloisonné dishes, now May had only her one new blouse and trousers, a silk tunic and shawl, and the stained clothes in which she'd traveled. Her shoes. Two pearls. A borrowed blanket. The wall beside her bed was clean but unadorned. In the morning, a crack of sun came through the curtain and crept across its plaster surface. When the angle grew sufficiently extreme, the light picked out and shadowed imperfections. Awake but not up, May touched the wall; with her fingertips she felt the otherwise invisible blemishes.

Helen knew enough Mandarin that she and her apprentice could converse, if simply; and May learned English. She learned it with the speed of a prodigy. When the older woman entertained a client, it was her mouth that May watched attentively, more interested in the forms of language than of copulation. Sitting on her cot, the curtain open, she listened to the foreign words as they emerged from Helen's lips, short ones like *arm* and *take* and longer ones, *absolutelydarling*. Silently, May formed the sounds with her own mouth, ignoring the rest. She'd seen enough of the silk merchant with her maid to understand what intercourse would demand of her. As her employer suspected, her virtue was only technical.

Helen told May that afterwards men sometimes asked if she had been praying, if prayers were what she mouthed, and May smiled. How stupid men could be, how bullying. Prayers. They would like to inspire such fear.

At the end of a night, Helen wanted to sleep, but May cajoled until she agreed to sit at her table under the window and name all the objects at which May pointed: shutter and sill and doorknob, water and soap, hairbrush, bust bodice, shoe, slip, buttonhook, playing card, ribbon. May put a pen in Helen's hand and Helen wrote English words on a paper until, too tired to keep her eyes open, she shoved the page aside and went to bed, burying her head under her pillow to block out the early light, the noise of Shanghai streets waking. While Helen slept, May sat on a creaking chair and copied the words out, ten times each. As she wrote, she tried quietly to say them.

If she was to capture what already she understood was the prostitute's dream, a wealthy patron who would set her up for himself in an apartment with servants, kitchen, clothes, and jewels; and if that man was to be English (French would do, or German, but the English seemed to have all the money in Shanghai), then May would have to learn to speak his language. *But-ton-hook. Play-ing-card.* She whispered the words and imagined the place she would live—high above the street in rooms painted blue, a low lacquer table set with white cups, porcelain so thin the light shone through.

In return for the English lessons, May offered to teach Helen Chinese characters, but the American woman shook her head and gave May's shoulder a nudge as if to say *Come on!*

"No," May agreed soberly. "Not, uh . . . Not, um . . ." She didn't have the word.

"Useful," Helen said. "Not useful."

May nodded. "Not useful," she repeated.

. . .

MAY GOT HER place high above the street. Grace and her partner moved her to a room five flights up. It wasn't blue, but it was her own, for as long as she earned its tariff, anyway; and in it she worked every night except Thursday. Eight hours after moving upstairs she sold her virginity to Mr. Barnes from the customs office, grinding shyly against him and mewing in a way calibrated to suggest innocence, pain, and the awakening of pleasure—whimpers privately inspired by visions many times retrieved and refined: visions of bitten, gashed, and fouled red shoes.

On top of the surcharge for an unspoiled maidenhead, Mr. Barnes rewarded May's diligently manufactured responses by tipping her generously. The next morning, banknotes hidden between shoe and bindings, May pulled the linen from her bed, considered the smear of blood, no longer red but an abashed, almost apologetic shade of brown, and concluded that she had arrived somewhere that offered if not justice, then recompense. In a few days, she'd have the afternoon off, and she knew already where to go to buy a dictionary.

Each day she got out of bed by noon and used whatever time she could to read. She taught herself English grammar, she taught herself French and European history. If she remained as "native" as her profession encouraged, a seemingly traditional singsong girl, still she forsook the traditions and even the memory of her family. When Chinese intruded, May pushed it aside with English or French. When thoughts of Chu'en or Yu-ying beckoned, she banished them with another chapter of *The Middle Kingdom*. She traded dumplings for toast, green tea for black, bean paste for marmalade. She taught herself to forget her star god and the festival days marked by her mother and grandmother. Of her father's death day she made no observance; her ancestors she declined to worship. And when the New Year arrived, she hid from the fireworks and the lion dancers; she didn't light so much as one stick of incense to celebrate it.

Her dreams, though, remained stubbornly Chinese, filled with all the old superstitions. In them, the Emperor of Hell made frequent appearances, sitting on a throne, a pile of books in his lap. He looked benign, avuncular, and he tweaked her rouged cheek with such relish that she knew his desire for her. Consulting a text, he explained that the laws of the next world ordained that in death a woman be divided among the men who were her earthly partners. He showed May the passage and the sword he used to effect its directive. *But what*, he asked, *am I to do with you?*

*Well*, she said, shrugging, *you'll just have to chop me into bits.* He nodded.

*Such a shame to defile your beauty*, he lamented playfully, and he stroked the cheek he'd pinched.

*Who is doing the defiling?* she thought. *You or I?* But she said nothing.

May felt no fear in the dream, no regret. It was as if the two of them, she and the Emperor of Hell, were considering a plucked chicken and how best to dismember it.

FOR SEVEN YEARS May worked without finding her benefactor. "It's your own fault," Helen told her. "It's because you won't go with a Chinese."

The problem, of course, was *Chineseness*, May's own. For Westerners, she was an exotic dish, one they weren't sorry they'd tasted, but why choose her for a steady diet? Not that May didn't have loyal clients, men who were happy to visit her once or twice a month, to sit with her afterward and help her with her English or her French, to make her gifts of books instead of bonbons—but even those men didn't want a Chinese woman for a mistress. Not any more than they wanted to eat braised eel every night, or noodles slippery with hot pepper oil.

And now what could May do? She'd traveled even farther from herself.

Seven years. Seven Shanghai winters, raw and gray with dreary, dirty snowfalls. Seven damp springs and oppressive summers. Seven falls. One year, a painful rash on her thighs and a case of the grippe that hung on and on. The next, a pregnancy and a visit from the doctor—so expensive she wouldn't have any new clothes that season.

May lay in bed for a week, then two, three, no longer in pain. Not exactly. "For pity's sake, it's happened to us all," Helen said, sitting on the end of her bed. "A little miscalculation." She moved to squeeze May's foot through the bedclothes, a friendly gesture, but feeling the bandaged lump, she stopped herself. "You'll get up tomorrow?" she said. "Promise?"

May nodded.

How to dismiss the long, efficient spoon, horribly like the instruments with which they ate? *They*? She. *She* was almost one of them now. Year by year she was becoming a foreigner, stranger even than they.

With what chilling swiftness it had been accomplished, the "procedure." A little morphine, then, as the doctor said, "a nice, nice nap." The only problem was waking up, swimming to the surface of the dark lake of sleep. Taking a breath. Unable to drown the memory of Yuying's prescription for motherhood, to surface without humiliation scraped newly raw by the long curette. How had she borne it—so ignominious, so pathetic—her attempts to harvest the silk merchant's seed?

"It's not so horrible a thing as all that." Helen was perplexed, watching May retch into a basin. Knowing nothing of May's previous life, she shook her head. "With most girls, they're sick before and it cures them."

May looked up, face as white as the bandages on her feet. "You'll lose your looks if you go on like this," Helen said.

But she didn't. Somehow she summoned her talent for transforming despair into rage. And rage was good, it was tonic, it picked a person up. Besides, the whole wretched thing, the "miscalculation," presented what Helen would call a silver lining: two new forms of solace and escape. Opium, May discovered, was almost as good as morphine, although the first time she smoked the drug, it provoked a fit of weeping, so pungently did it remind her of her mother.

Novels were more reliable. Especially one, *Madame Bovary*, which seized hold of May with a force equal to that of a narcotic. Not so much on account of Emma, who didn't interest her after the heroine's own spell of infatuated reading gave way to more reckless passions, but because of Charles: the botched foot surgery. Many nights, aching for

THE BINDING CHAIR · 83

sleep but stubbornly conscious, May imagined herself married to a doctor such as Bovary; and in her dreams (the kind, when at last they came, characterized by the dreamer's sense of paralysis, suffocation) she endured his ill-advised attempts to repair her as Bovary had the hapless clubfoot Hippolyte. May's doctor-husband boxed her deformities in little wood and metal caskets; he tightened the screws, sending her toward delirium and death. A death that only amputation might spare her.

It was, May knew, her feet that held her between one world and the next. On her red shoes she balanced between East and West, China and Europe, misery, happiness. Even her regulars, men who licked her face with the sloppy enthusiasm of dogs, who kissed her eyelids and murmured as they made love, and who after years of assignations still arrived bone hard with lust—even they refused to acknowledge a matter so troubling as May's feet. In her company, their eyes avoided the floor, the end of the bed. And if ever she suggested unbinding, they changed the topic, or they left.

# SÉANCE

WESTERN SIBERIA. OUTSIDE THE WINDOW, A
land of yellow lakes, black mud. The track, when Alice
could see it, converged into a silver line through the
muck and grass. Camels moved through the slush,
shaggy and stoic, completely unexpected, looking lost
and chilled. The towns they passed reeked of tallow boi-
leries.

Alice slept during the day and found herself awake at
night. In the dark, the lights from the train were reflected by the greasy surface of yet another river. The locomotive's whistle made a keening noise, carrying an
animate pitch of grief; and the vibration of the wheels on
the track affected her as it didn't during the day. Weeks,
even months, later, lying in the dormitory at Miss Robeson's Academy for Young Ladies, Alice felt the rattle
under her back. She'd sit up, her blood beating in her
temples, and pull back the curtain around her narrow
bed, expecting to see out of a window to an empty blue

expanse of frozen swamps. At school Alice slept the way one does on a narrow berth, as if expecting, at the blast of a whistle, to bolt, fully dressed, into a new station.

*Tomsk! Omsk! Toboltz!*
*Ilka, Shilka. Chichma, Ufa.*
*Zagladino, Abdulino! Ust-Katav!*

The Trans-Siberian Express did carry souls between worlds. It pulled them past reason and into rhyme.

The train was crowded now, all the compartments filled. At Toboltz embarked Madame Veronica, a spiritualist, who announced that she would organize a séance in the library car, following dinner that very night. She promised Suzanne Petrovna that she could summon the ghost of her dead brother. The recently departed were very helpful; the proximity of his corpse was a definite enticement, as was the movement of the train itself.

"Spirits like carriages. Ships. Trains. Anything that isn't tied down," she explained.

The captain, listening, pushed aside his untouched plate of lamb. "May I, if you would be so kind, have a word with you?" he said to Madame Veronica, and drew her aside.

There was a piano in the dining car of the Express, but no one played it. Over it hung a blue-gray pall. Russians smoked a great deal, even the women: thick cigars, thin cigars, and long, black cigarettes in holders. The smoke rose to the ceiling and stayed there. The waiters stacked dirty dishes on the piano's black lid. Madame Veronica sat on its bench; Litovsky fingered the untouched music on its stand. "I have . . ." He cleared his throat. "I have had a daughter," he said, emotion scrambling syntax.

"Yes." Madame Veronica nodded. "I know. She died."

"Yes!" he said. "That's remarkable! It is . . . I've . . . Do you know I believe I have seen her on this train!" Litovsky took off his officer's hat. He turned it over and held it so Madame Veronica could see that inside the crown, protected by a circle of clear celluloid, was a photograph of a girl of perhaps fourteen. The girl had long, dark hair held back with a broad white ribbon. Her deep-set eyes were dark and her mouth full; over its left corner was a beauty mark like Alice Benjamin's, one that imparted to her lips a strangely knowing and sexual air—as if even then, sitting poised and still before the camera, she anticipated the consummation of her death.

Madame Veronica looked at Litovsky with professional kindliness. She had not removed her own hat for dinner; its long black plumes gave her the aspect of a disorganized stag beetle.

"Do you, that is to say, what I mean is . . . She died in the . . . on a train."

"Of course!" Madame Veronica said. She grasped both his hands. "Tonight. In the library car."

"A DISGRACE! An absolute mountebank!" Miss Waters said to the girls' mother as they were preparing for bed.

"Yes," Dolly Benjamin said, nodding. "She's holding it in the library car?"

"This very night! And the captain hasn't the sense to stay away from such chicanery. If this is what the Russian army is coming to, it's no wonder the country is going to rack and ruin. I read that several hundred people were trampled at the czar's recent public address. The army couldn't contain them. It's—"

"I'm surprised that officious *provod, prov*— I always forget the name of that porter person."

"*Provodnik.*"

"Yes, him. Why is he allowing it?" Dolly asked.

Miss Waters made a snorting noise.

In their berths, the sisters lay still, listening to the sounds of their mother pacing in the neighboring compartment. The snap of the latch on her traveling case, the sound of pills being shaken from a bottle. To swallow them, Dolly didn't trust the water from the train's electric samovar. "Damn!" Alice heard her say, struggling with the seal on the cap of a liter of imported water.

It wasn't just living in China that had done it. Dolly's own mother had died of puerperal fever after the birth of her sister, and she'd always worried about illness. As a prospective bride, among the concerns she had voiced through her father and the office of the Sydney marriage broker were whether Mr. Solomon Benjamin had a water closet in his home and an American milk boiler in the kitchen. And would he agree to yearly travel, particularly during the feverish month of July, and at least as far away as the mountains of Japan—Lake Chusenji would be fine. And surely Shanghai had a kosher slaughterhouse, a proper fire brigade, and European hospitals and *accoucheuses*? Was smallpox absolutely controlled? Did the Chinese servants live on Mr. Benjamin's own property? Was the water from a well or from the river? Put as delicately as possible, wasn't the Whangpoo afflicted with overly high levels of human excreta? And, really, she couldn't think of boarding a ship from Australia unless Mr. Benjamin assured her that he would tolerate visits from her relatives. She hoped he understood, she had lived all her life in Sydney, where it was dry and healthful, and if her poor widowed father was to let her go, he must know that she was going to be safe and happy.

"Say that, Daddy. It's the truth. And put in that I'd like to call him by some other name. Anything will do—Tom, Dick, or Harry—but Solomon is, well, impossible. It's too, I hope he's not the type to take offense, but it's too fat and grizzled and biblical, and he doesn't look like a Solomon. At least not from his photograph."

Mr. Benjamin wrote in reply that all of Miss Cohen's fears were those reflecting life as it had been lived a generation ago in Shanghai. The new water purification plant was unparalleled. Sewers were installed throughout the settlement, and the plumbing in his house was better than what she would find in London, Paris, or even New York. Midwives were certainly either Swiss or English. If, God forbid, there was need of a hospital, Miss Cohen would go, as did all foreign residents, to Kobe or Tokyo. The milk boiler was on order, and could the broker forward a notarized copy of her birth certificate? Here was proof of his British citizenship, and the year-end report of his banking firm, Benjamin, Kelly, and Potts, on Jinkee Road, just off the famous Bund.

In sum, as the broker said, here was a lonely, eligible bachelor whose financial security was more than sufficient to offset his geographic limitations. Miss Cohen would have no trouble with in-laws, as Mr. Benjamin's father was dead, his blind mother in Baghdad, his siblings all in Bombay. His house was large and had a staff of three Europeans and thirty Chinese, including a laundress, a hairdresser, and a tailor so clever he could copy any Paris gown without a pattern—he had only to look at it or see a drawing. All the servants lived on the premises and bathed regularly. Her sister, her brother, her cousins: they would be welcome and comfortable; and, all other concerns being satisfied, he would accept the name Dick.

The marriage broker in Sydney leaned back in his chair and looked at Miss Dolly Cohen and her doddering father. He raised his eyebrows. "Really," he said. "You won't do better."

In Australia's frontier days, money was to be made in the importing of wives. That was when the broker's father had established a business in providing Australian men with London girls whose noses were large, whose eyes were small, whose bloom was off. Now there were rather too many of these women's daughters, even pretty ones like Dolly, and so he sent them off to Singapore or Hong Kong or Shanghai, places where clever nomadic Jews were making a lot—a disgraceful lot—of money. The broker felt no compunction about taking them for all they were worth.

AT TEN O'CLOCK, Alice, still awake, heard her mother open and then quietly shut her door. Alice slipped from under her covers and peered down the corridor just in time to see her mother's skirts disappearing through the exit at the end of the coach.

"Ces?" she whispered, but her sister didn't answer.

Miss Waters's door was closed, and Alice slid silently past it, through the rattling corridor, its lights dimmed by nine, Petersburg time. She hurried after her mother.

In the library car were assembled Captain Litovsky, Suzanne Petrovna, a whispering Polish couple, and, to the surprise of Alice, hidden in the shadowy draperies behind the club chairs, the austere *provodnik*, recently widowed. He laid a photograph of a fat, blond woman on a table that had a chessboard inlaid on its surface. Without speaking, Suzanne and Captain Litovsky produced photographs and laid them down beside the *provodnik*'s. Dolly removed a locket from around her white throat and opened it to reveal a little boy's round face, his lips open in laughter. As her mother's finger's undid the tiny gold catch, Alice felt a twist of jealousy, so familiar she barely noted it.

Madame Veronica looked at all these and hummed to herself in concentration, releasing more of a buzz than a tune, as if she were a small motor. "All right," she said. "Yes, yes," she said. "Shall we sit?" And everyone took a chair pulled up to the inlaid table. Around it, they were seven, and uncomfortably crowded, shoulders hunched and touching.

"Mlle. Petrovna?" Madame Veronica turned to the woman from Paris, who withdrew a signet ring from the depths of her muff and set it in the center of an ebony square.

"Mr. Borodi?" Madame Veronica said, and the *provodnik* turned out all but one small light on the wall. Alice, taking advantage of the dark, crept forward into the shadow between two of the big club chairs.

Madame closed her eyes. No one spoke. Minutes passed. The noise of the track passing under the wheels of the train grew and grew, ticking and ticking like a great clock grinding forward, pressing the breath from their lungs. Dolly Benjamin began to weep.

"What will he say?" she asked, as if to herself. "What can he say?" She stood, jarring the table. "He only knows a few words," she said. "Dog. Moon. Mama.

"Oh!" she said, turning to Madame Veronica. "Don't you let him say Mama! If you let him call me, I shall die! I shall!"

Alice hugged herself. What sympathy she felt for her mother was drowned out by the undignified sound of Dolly's grief. That David, in death, commanded attention withheld from his living sisters was not a thought Alice permitted longer than an instant. At twelve, her outrage found a more comfortable target in her mother's noisy weeping. *Shut up. Shut up.* She tried to obliterate the tears with the force of her silent will.

"Mrs. Benjamin," began Madame Veronica. But just then, as she began to reach her plump hand toward Dolly, the captain stood as well. He fell face-forward on the table, rigid, his eyes open and fixed, unseeing.

"A medium!" Madame Veronica cried. "He must be!"

The *provodnik* turned on the lights and snatched up the photograph of his fat wife.

"The man has been taken ill," he said. "He's subject to apoplexies. Not apparitions." He turned the captain's rigid body over; he laid him on the floor and loosened his collar and his belt. He began to mop at the shining puddle of saliva Litovsky's open mouth had left on the table.

Alice, forgetting that her presence was uninvited, came out from between the chairs and stood among the grown-ups, who were so absorbed by the disastrous culmination of their séance that it was a minute or more before anyone noticed her.

"Why, what is this?" Madame Veronica said, as if Alice might be a supernatural manifestation, the lost child summoned by her father's faint.

*"Alice Benjamin—"* Dolly began.

"You can't punish me," Alice interrupted. "I'll tell Father." She crossed her arms. "See if I won't. I'll cable him at the next station and tell him you were talking to spirits and spiritualists on a Russian train. That you tried to contact David." Dolly covered her face with her hands, and Alice felt the cool thrill of power.

*"Alice,"* her mother whispered. "Not in front of—"

But it was too late. Having emerged from the shadows, Alice discovered suddenly, with intoxicated surprise, that she didn't care, no, not at all, what any of these people might think of her.

# A WEAKNESS FOR

# RUSSIAN OFFICERS

NINETEEN TWENTY-SIX.

Thirteen years and three months after her journey across Siberia, in a cramped apartment over the fashionable Promenade des Anglais in Nice, France, once again in thrall to a Russian officer—his name was Michael Evlanoff—Alice Benjamin remembered the old captain's paroxysm and its unanticipated result: her disembarking from the train with him into a dusk so blue and cold that their breath glittered. They exhaled and the moisture froze in the air before their eyes. He can't still be living, she thought to herself. He must be dead by now.

(Yes, in fact, of influenza contracted while on holiday with his wife. They had taken a trip to Venice to celebrate their golden jubilee: fifty years of marriage. It was the epidemic of 1918, and the captain died in a pink palazzo with green shutters on the Grand Canal, just east of the Rialto Bridge. He dreamed, as he died, of drowning, a dream inspired—it must have been—by the sound of water lapping at the foundations of the building where he slept. And even as he struggled for breath, the trains of which he had been so proud, and so ashamed, the majestic blue cars of the Trans-Siberian Railway, were taken over by Bolsheviks, who confiscated all locomotives save those used to transport troops and the one to which they attached ten cars full of diplomats. From Manchuli to Vladivostok, the revolutionaries shipped the American and Japanese ambassadors from Petrograd, as well as the Siamese and the Brazilian ministers, along with all their suites, a total of 145 persons, each of whom, at some point during the journey east, stopped to consider the framed print of the icebreaker *Baikal* that hung in every compartment. "Ah, Olga!" the captain said to his wife before he died. He reached for her, and his wife drew his cold hand to her lips and kissed his fingers, which were slightly blue at the tips. "Olga!" he whispered. "There you are!")

Not that Alice had forgotten Litovsky. She'd been thinking of the trip just that morning. Rummaging through lingerie, looking for what Evlanoff might admire, she'd held a white lace camisole up before her face. Light came through the fabric. Fantastic in its delicacy. Where have I seen this before? she thought. When? *A window with ice.* But where? And then she'd remembered Litovsky's arm around her shoulder, the astringent smell of the 4711 cologne he poured onto his pink handkerchief. Waiting outside the station for a trap, their breath falling from their lips, a sparkling shower.

Now the camisole lay on the floor of Evlanoff's room, a melting white puddle in the light cast by a candle on the nightstand. (Any stronger illumination would have revealed how shabby were the furnishings, how dingy the paint.) The flame made shadows of their heads on the wall opposite the bed, shadows as big as pumpkins.

"What's funny?" Evlanoff asked. "Why are you laughing?" He touched her cheek, found it wet. "You're not crying?"

"No," she said. "Don't stop."

"Keep your left hand in your lap, dear," her mother had said on the train. "And, Alice, not such big bites!" She must have said this at every meal—at least she had until the night of the séance, when the only spirit summoned was that of Alice's defiance, a spirit that proved impossible to exorcise, and the responsibility for which was always given to her aunt. An imputation that May interpreted as credit, although eventually she, too, would curse Alice's unashamed disregard for authority.

"He could be a Mohammedan!" May had said of the Russian in whose bed Alice lay, echoing Alice's long-forgotten insult to the captain. It had been a common Shanghai prejudice, the assumption that displaced Russians, of which there were thousands, might espouse not only foreign religions but extra wives.

"You know nothing of this man!" she'd said. "Not his family. *Nothing!*"

"He's a prince." Alice was surprised by how small the word sounded, how suddenly unlikely.

"Goddess of Mercy! He *says* he's a prince. Do you have any idea how many refugees calling themselves nobles there are in Nice? Men looking for a young woman like you?"

"What does that mean, *like me*?"

"With money! That's what it means." May set the teapot down so hard that its contents leapt up and sloshed out of the spout.

"He's not like that," Alice said. She considered saying *He loves me* but stopped herself. May was even more dismissive of love than of titles.

"He may be married. He may have a wife and children in Russia."

"He does not."

"How would you know?" May said the words slowly, as if speaking to an idiot. How. Would. You. Know. "You don't think he'd tell *you*, do you?"

Alice opened her mouth to argue but couldn't think of the words that might convince her aunt of Evlanoff's sincerity. "Can I tell you something about Mohammedans?" May went on. "They marry as often as they please. A man of thirty-five, why he could have ten wives!"

"I won't listen to this!"

"They don't believe women have souls!" May cried. "Do you hear me! Do you hear what I'm saying!" She wiped up her spilled tea with the doily and then crumpled it, wet, and dropped it on the tray.

"How will a man treat you if he doesn't believe in your soul!"

Alice left the room.

"Like a dog!" May cried after her. "That's how!" But Alice was running down the stairs; she left the house without her wrap.

"Promenade des Anglais," she said to the chauffeur.

"Yes, miss," he said.

A BREEZE DISTURBED the hot night, and the candle went out. "Are you crying?" Evlanoff said. "Or laughing?"

"Both." Alice used her hands, one on either side of his head, to guide him back between her legs. "Don't stop. *Please.*" What did she know about him? The stories he told her. The body he gave her. He'd been a sickly child, he'd spent months confined to bed. But with barbells and spartan regimes, with military training, he'd remade himself. When she caught him in profile, his posture straight, his chest full, she ached, an actual ache, as with the onset of an illness, fever. Her wrists, her elbows, her neck. Her knees and feet and ankles and back—in such moments love made even her head throb, so that she had to shut her eyes. Was this because his shoulders appeared not so much square as squared? The first time she touched him, she found every muscle tensed, as if for a blow.

"You have a weakness for suffering," May had said accusingly. "You appropriate tragedies. It isn't a virtue."

"What if I care for him?"

"What if you do! He has no money! Nothing!"

"His family was destroyed."

"Does that make him more attractive?"

"No," Alice lied.

"You're lying," May said. "A displaced, depressed Russian pretender. What could be worse?"

"He's a *doctor.*" Alice pronounced the word with more force than she had said *prince.* "And who said he was depressed? You wouldn't be so angry if . . ." She didn't finish.

"If what?"

*If I were still in love with your tragedies,* Alice was thinking. But instead, "How can you judge a person you don't know, a person who's lost everything?" she asked.

"By having been one myself. People who have nothing— they're . . ."

"What?"

"The ones who stop at nothing."

"Does that include you?"

"Yes," May said. "It does. And what kind of doctor is he! A charlatan!"

"You only say that because he told you to stop smoking opium."

"No." May crossed her legs, swung her foot angrily. Its pointed, silk-sheathed toe jabbed back and forth at Alice: a poison dart. "You meddle. You meddle in people's affairs. It's as with the shoes. All that orthopedic nonsense you're trying to foist on me. You think you can fix things."

"Perhaps I'm one, too," Alice said.

"One what?"

"One of the people who stops at nothing." May was looking at her silently. "Isn't that what—isn't that who you wanted me to be? A woman free of all the—" *Crippling rules*, Alice had been going to say, but as it turned out, neither of them finished the conversation. The argument.

"Saved by the bell," May quipped, acidly, for someone was ringing at the front gate.

Alice smiled, an ironic little twist of her lips. "It must be your . . . swimming master."

May uncrossed her arms and legs. "I wonder, was it I who instructed you so successfully in sarcasm?" She felt her hair, making sure it was smooth, used her cane to stand. "Or perhaps it's organic. Perhaps, by chance, we share that . . . attribute." The houseboy led the swimming teacher through the foyer. Alice gave him a cold look.

"How is your student progressing?" she asked disingenuously, her attention still fixed on May. Alice knew her aunt would refrain from continuing a dialogue that might appear contentious to someone she considered outside the family. A little test: just how friendly *was* May with this smugly tanned and muscular young man?

"I think," he said, "that Mrs. Cohen has nearly outgrown me." It was a long sentence for him, and he spoke his words carefully, as if he considered them fragile, easily broken.

May smiled a tiny and, Alice decided, purposefully enigmatic smile, before turning to ascend the stairs. The young man dipped his head in an abbreviated bow and excused himself to change for the lesson.

FROM THE FIRST, Alice had known: here was the one she wanted. The men who'd come before, she didn't regret them, not really. How could she, when she didn't even remember their names? Not while in his arms.

They'd undressed in his room and looked at each other. *Stared* was a better word. "Turn around." They said the words at the same time.

Evlanoff smiled. "I feel as I did when I gave my cousin all my Easter candy to take off her clothes."

Self-conscious, Alice folded her arms over her chest. "Not worth it?" she asked, and he took her wrists, gently pulled them away from her body.

"Very worth it. You, I mean. My cousin was just a little girl, scraped knees and no front teeth. What I meant was that I felt foolish."

He turned out the light, and they found their way to the bed, explored each line, curve and cranny by touch: his finger tracing the part in her hair, her tongue tasting his forehead and nose, a loitering kiss on the lips, lengthy detours around nipples and navels. Discovery and cataloging of moles, scars, those few divergences from the expected. He had well-formed, fleshy earlobes; she didn't. "Not even enough for earrings," he lamented, and Alice bit the examining hand. "You'll think of other presents," she predicted. She took the hand back, kissed its palm, put it back on her ear so he could feel her prowess at wiggling it. "The other as well?" he asked. She moved the hand to demonstrate. Also, she could roll her tongue, he could not. "What do they call the biscuits that come in that shape?" he asked.

"Profiteroles?" she suggested.

"No, those are round Italian cakes, not cookies. I mean the French ones."

She couldn't remember.

"*Tuiles*, that's the name."

She shrugged. "Quiz me on chocolates," she said. "The rest I can't be bothered with."

His longest toe was the first one, the big toe; hers was the second. Both of them were ticklish; neither revealed exactly where. So much to do, and how long it took before he at last arrived at the destination of her, going to elaborate efforts to part the hair away from that wrinkled pink nub. She was eager, but didn't want to hurry what felt like reverence. Then, when at last he'd settled in, it was as if he couldn't end it. He was lost in the wet rhythm of her, Alice's thighs tight on either side of his head, deafening him to her begging, *I want you inside me, I want you inside me.* She had to pull him up by the hair, drag his dripping face to her lips. Kissing the taste of herself on his mouth, *Please don't make me come again without you inside me. Please oh please please.*

"I want. I want . . . *Yes*," she said. *Yes. Yesyesyes.* And as this was all the conversation she provided when he was in her, moving, it became a game with them: he set her the task of every time saying the word in another tongue.

"Surely not *every* time?"

"Well, there are five—or is it six?—thousand. Distinct languages, I mean. Not dialects. That should last us a while."

"Not forever," Alice said. "Not if you let me have my way with you."

He laughed. "Are you the one who's having your way?"

Alice, eyes closed, nodded yes into his beard. Funny, she'd never liked beards, not on other men, but his, neatly barbered, the way it framed his ruddy lips; and it smelled so good. Soap and cologne and under the gentlemanly hygiene, his own smell. Musky and hard, salty, that faint tang of metal—it made her want him, and this surprised her, too. She'd never before cared or even thought much about how a man smelled. Unobjectionable or not: until Evlanoff, these were the only criteria. But now Alice pushed her face into his chest, his beard, nuzzled her nose into his armpits, the nape of his neck, tasted his skin through the hair. If he rose early, she woke up embracing his empty pajamas, still inhaling what she could of him.

"At least I can say the one word," she murmured. "You, you don't even—" He smothered her sentence.

"Don't even what?" he asked, but the kiss had been long enough to obliterate thought.

"Don't even speak," she answered when she remembered, at breakfast.

What he did do was howl, growl, yowl, groan. Arched his back, pointed his muzzle up like a wolf's. "For what you do," she said, "we need a new word entirely. Something like . . ."

"What?"

"I don't know."

He'd scared her the first time, the second as well. Was this rage? Could he be in pain? The expression on his face suggested otherwise. Now it would be silence that frightened her.

The candle, relit, blew out again, and instead of groping for matches, he lay next to her, singing in Russian.

"What do they mean?" she asked. "The words."

But he wouldn't translate. "It's not good, to answer every question."

"Isn't it?"

He shook his head. "Not conducive to love."

Alice wheedled; he didn't relent; she offered certain payments for information, fingers hinting as to what these might be; he was obdurate; she flounced out of bed. "Where are you going?" he asked. "Don't." But she'd stalked over to the window and to its view of the sea. He got up as well, pulled on a dressing gown.

Alice was leaning naked out of the open window, and the moonlight fell on her back, made it luminous, so white it was blue. Evlanoff put his left hand on her waist; with his right he guided himself back inside her. She drew in her breath, and for a moment, neither of them moved, they stared out into the night. It was late enough that the city slept, they could hear the waves as they turned over on the beach. The wind had unknotted one end of the tobacconist's awning, and it flapped furiously, dropped, and then sailed up again, a striped wing.

On a bench overlooking the beach was the solitary figure of a woman, next to her a bag or a bundle. Brave to be out alone in the dark, Alice was thinking. To be a woman sitting alone in the cool air. Contemplating the light on the water, or perhaps just listening to the noise of it, eyes closed.

"What are you looking at?" Evlanoff asked. "What do you see?" Slowly, he began moving inside her.

Alice held on to the sill. "Nothing." She moved against him, off tempo for a moment before finding the stroke. A picture of herself at eight or ten, trying to skip into the turning rope, catching it between her knees, clumsy. One end tied to the plane tree's trunk, the other in Uncle Arthur's hand, May watching from her chair. *Try again. There, you've got it, just don't lose the* . . . Alice put her forehead on the windowsill. "See what you've done," she said, in answer to Evlanoff's moan. "I've forgotten the word."

He paused, breathing. "What . . . word?"

"The yes word. Swahili for yes."

Passersby could see them, if they looked up. But there were so few, and they looked straight ahead, intent on a late destination. Even at the nearby Negresco, pouring yellow light onto the pavement, the doormen were looking at each other rather than out into the street. The one on the right chopped the air with his hand, making a point. Evlanoff pulled back too far and slipped out of her. When he thrust forward again, the tip of his penis had moved, ascended. It bumped against the tightly furled muscle of her anus.

"Oh," she said. "You've lost your way."

He stepped back. "I'm sorry."

"Why?" She reached back, felt for him. "Why are you?"

"I don't want . . . it might hurt." He held his hands on her hips, not moving.

"Try. See. If it does, I'll tell you."

Once inside her, he stayed still, still and hard, growing harder. She could feel his pulse. It quickened her own, to feel his heart beating there. He didn't start to move until after she did, her fingers exploring herself and him, too: the angles of this new geometry.

"*Ndio,*" she said.

"You . . . remembered."

"*Nnnn. Diiii. Ohhhh. Ndio.*" Alice laughed; she did sometimes, after she came, a little something for him to get used to. Evlanoff tried, unsuccessfully, to restrain his growls. Afterwards, he was barely more articulate. "Did you . . . ? Was it . . ." He faltered. "You liked it? That."

She turned around. "I mightn't with anyone else. With you, whatever you do just makes me love you more."

"But," he said, "that was something you did."

"Was it?"

"Yes."

"All right, then, whatever I do just makes me love you more." She retied the sash on his robe, lay her cheek on its slippery lapel. "If your family were still living, they'd disapprove of me." Evlanoff said nothing. "They would, wouldn't they?"

"Perhaps."

"Because I'm a Jew?"

He put his lips to her hair. "They would think you wanted to buy a title." Alice was silent. "Aren't you cold?" He offered his pajama shirt to her, and she took it, buttoning it unevenly, so that the two sides of the collar didn't align. She frowned; her eyes had their narrow, stubborn look.

"Does she need to get an X ray first?" she asked, as he undid the shirt and rebuttoned it.

"You're speaking of the shoes? Your aunt?"

"Yes."

Evlanoff drew his fingers through the dust on the windowsill. On it were imprints of Alice's flank, her hands and forehead. "Why is it that . . . that woman is forever finding her way into my bedroom?" He turned away.

"Don't be insulted. Please."

"Why not?"

"Because." Alice hesitated. "Aren't there always more than two people in a bedroom?"

He looked back at her. "I don't think so." Scratched his chin through his beard. "I didn't invite any."

"But surely I remind you . . . I . . . Other people must come into your mind."

"Never." He laughed, a low laugh, the kind he laughed at himself when choosing to be amused rather than angry. Hurt. "You don't put me in mind of anyone. I've never met anyone like you."

"Really?" Alice said the word again: "Really?" She frowned, and now her eyebrows were drawn together and upward; the expression conveyed both wariness and surprise. "I always seem to be reminding people of someone. I've grown resigned to being the kind of woman people mistake for—"

"For what?"

"For someone else."

"What do you mean?"

"Nothing." Alice put her hand on his chest. "I'm sorry. Please don't be insulted."

He nodded slowly. "All right. I think." Then he sighed, loudly enough that it wasn't just a sigh but also a reconciliation: he was making fun of himself, his sensitivity. When he spoke again, it was about May.

"It would be better, of course, to have X rays. But Dumonteil can work from impressions alone."

"I'll take her." Alice pressed her lips together, truculent in advance of any contest. "I'll get her to go. She will if I insist."

"But why? Why insist? If she's not willing . . ."

"She doesn't understand." Alice shook her head. "Half the trouble with her is her feet. If she could walk more easily. If she could *walk*. Life wouldn't seem so . . . impossible. She'd—She'd be less bad-tempered. With me."

Evlanoff took Alice in his arms. "And what happens," he said, "if this doesn't work? If she still rages and despairs? Comes uninvited into your head, and my bedroom?"

"Then I'll have been proved wrong." Alice looked up at Evlanoff, the clean margin of cheek above his beard. What a naturally distinct line it drew, the angles of his face as sharp and tidy as if he shaved. But he didn't. Once or twice a week, a judicious trim, using whatever scissors came first to hand—nail scissors would do. The small sink over which he barbered himself was sprinkled with dark hairs that inevitably escaped the bowl's confines, insinuated themselves into Alice's lipsticks and powders and creams. She complained about this; she came to him petulantly when a hair got into her eye. "Can't you be more careful? Why won't you rinse them down?" But she liked any reminder of their intimacy, even sharp little itching ones. Once he'd used his tongue to retrieve from under her red lid what turned out to be an eyelash. Delicately, he transferred it from tongue's to finger's tip. "Unjustly accused," he said, holding it out for her to see.

Alice put her cheek back against his chest, stared out the window. "Shoes would have to help," she said, as much to herself as to him. "How could they not?"

OUTSIDE, hunched on the black wrought-iron bench, the small, eccentrically dressed figure held her arms before her chest as if fending off an attack. She was counting backwards in an attempt to slow down her anxious breaths. *Seventeen, sixteen, fifteen,* when I get to *one,* I will be calm. I will think clearly. I will make a decision.

It was a warm, dry night, but Suzanne Petrovna was wearing high boots and two sweaters, a wool coat. In her head, she subtracted and resubtracted one number from another. Not that there was any point in it; she hadn't enough money for even a third-class ticket back to Paris.

She'd arrived in Nice the previous month, on the advice of her physician. She'd had pneumonia that spring, and had not regained her strength. Even on the sunny coast, she wheezed as she walked. The round pebbles of the beach seemed as big as boulders as she picked her way toward the water; she barely had the energy to bathe in the blue sea. And on top of everything, she'd been a fool and left her money in her room at the pension and come back upstairs from breakfast to find it missing. A stupid mishap. She'd moved the bills from one hiding place to another so many times—from her purse to beneath her bed's mattress, from there to behind a picture frame, then into the toe of her boot—she'd lost track; she'd gone down to breakfast thinking she had her money with her, back in the pocket of her purse. All she'd brought with her, all the money she had in the world, was gone. The owner of the pension had been no help; he'd berated her for implying that the chambermaids were dishonest.

Since ten o'clock this morning, Suzanne had been without any-place to go or to stay, wearing as many of her clothes as possible, so that she wouldn't have to carry them. She'd pawned her mother's amethyst necklace and received fifty-five francs, which so far had af-forded her a glass of orangeade and several hours of useless calcula-tions. Then, at teatime, sitting on the same bench she occupied now, she'd been approached by a very astonishing woman, an Oriental in a sort of a litter carried by two old men. The woman had introduced her-self as May-li Cohen, an unlikely-sounding name, but there it was on the calling card she'd given to Suzanne. The woman had written her telephone number and address on the other side. "In case you should need it," she said. *Odd. What an odd person,* Suzanne had commented to herself after she departed.

But then, *I suppose I am odd,* she thought. *I suppose that I am.* She was nearly fifty-four years old. Her hair was still auburn, but it was thinning. She had never been in love. She looked at her feet. The only conclusion that could be drawn from shoes such as her own was that the woman who wore them had given up on romance. Before her, the sea opened endlessly. This wasn't so bad during the day, when the faintly curved line of the horizon implied a boundary, however illu-sory, but it was horrible at night, when the licking black waves merged into the black sky.

A gendarme stopped before her. "Madame?" he inquired. "It's past the hour for a lady to be out unaccompanied. Perhaps—"

"I'm just taking a breath of air," Suzanne said, her lie made the more obvious by the worn tapestry bag at her side.

"Yes," the gendarme said, as if humoring a child. "Can I be of as-sistance?"

Inside her pocket, Suzanne felt the edges of the card on which the Oriental had written her address. It was after eleven o'clock, too late to arrive unexpectedly, even at the house of a friend. And May-li Cohen was not a friend of Suzanne's. Still, where could she go?

"*Les voyoux. Les voleurs.*" Hoodlums and pickpockets. "The casinos, they attract all sorts. You will, I'm afraid, be prey to unsavory characters."

Silently, she withdrew the card and handed it to the gendarme.

"Mme. Cohen's?" he said, with what sounded to Suzanne like amusement. And then he sat down on the bench next to her and laughed, not unkindly.

"Well, yes," he said. "*Bien sûr.* Why not? Come along then." He picked up her bag, and she got up to follow him.

# A VISIT FROM THE FOOT
# EMANCIPATION SOCIETY

ARTHUR AND MAY MET ONE EVENING IN 1899.
Afterwards, he was sure it was a Monday, the twelfth of
June; May thought the fourteenth, a Wednesday. Expecting an overnight guest, she received him in her room on
the fifth floor. What light there was came from under a
dark shade. There was a smell of gardenias; an amah offered Arthur two trays, one with an opium pipe, the
other with a teapot. He declined both.

"Are you difficult to please?" May asked.

"I beg your pardon." Arthur took hold of his left earlobe and gave it a series of impatient tugs. "I'm a little
hard of hearing."

At Chiverly House School, in Melbourne, Australia,
Dolly's brother had been whipped. He'd been strapped,
caned, and flogged. His ears were boxed so often and so
violently that he developed tinnitus, a ringing in his ears
that had never subsided.

Of course, many people hear what others can't. They

pray and hear answers; they sing and hear music; they hear their names called out in warning or whispered in secret messages. But what Arthur heard was a relentless, shrill whistle, like the noise of an approaching siren—except that it never arrived but trilled on, on, on, growing sometimes louder, sometimes softer, according to its own illogic and to certain aggravations. Fever made it worse; so did headache powders, as well as coffee, tobacco, chocolate, and drinking cold drinks too quickly. If he managed not to pay attention, it receded; but if he was listening for something, a bell or a signal, a song or a voice, it drew near, it blocked out whole registers of sound.

He was twenty-six. He hadn't been able to read law, hated literature, was hopeless at mathematics. Pressed by his father, he had pursued architecture, and it fled from him. His drawings all listed, each line leaning off the page as if refusing to be fixed in the company of that vexatious, ringing, buzzing jangle of a noise. Since disembarking in the city of Shanghai—for a protracted visit with his sister, Dolly, and her new husband, one that had lasted, so far, nearly a year—Arthur had spent hours going for long walks, up and down the streets and even into the countryside, where the natives regarded him, not incorrectly, as just another British eccentric pursued by his demons.

"I asked if you were difficult to please," May repeated.

Arthur answered by telling May that what had happened to her—he indicated her feet with a pained gesture—was immoral.

May looked at him sharply, blew air from her nose in an exasperated gust. "Immoral?" she said.

Arthur nodded, vehement. "Wrong." He explained himself as a member of the Foot Emancipation Society, his first philanthropic association since having arrived in China. "You've been badly used," he told May.

May smiled. "Really?" she said.

"Yes. Look at you. You're lame."

May leaned back into the cushion of her velvet chaise longue. She looked at the red-haired man standing before her, at his wide, round blue eyes, his black coat with its too-short sleeves that revealed wrists also sprouting red hair. She had encountered them before, the Foot Emancipationists; they hosted tea dances in the big hotels. During the orchestra's breaks, they delivered homilies and passed a gleaming silver collection plate. Shouldn't every woman waltz? Shouldn't she, if she felt so inclined, leap, pirouette, even skip? The Chinese women in attendance, those few cosmopolitans who mingled with the Europeans, tucked their feet further under their chairs.

"What need have I to walk?" May asked. "I have boys who walk for me." And before Arthur could answer, she called her amah back and asked for her pipe.

Oh, dear, a zealot, a reformer, a do-gooder: one of the inevitable drawbacks of her profession, and of Shanghai, crawling as it was with missionaries. Arthur sat with his hands on his knees, looking at May. His earnestness, his coat that looked as if he'd inherited it from someone else: both of these irritated her. Once again, here was a useless sort of foreigner, a man with big ideas and little money. She'd have to get rid of him; then she could go to bed and read.

"Unwrap them!" she said, suddenly and frantically angry, as she hadn't been for years. Her voice shook with rage.

"I beg your pardon?" Arthur stammered.

"Unwrap my feet! Or one! Unwrap one!" May pulled up the hem of her blue cheongsam, a garment that had confused Arthur when he entered her room: its color matched that of her chaise so perfectly he couldn't tell where woman ended and furniture began. She unfastened her left shoe and thrust her foot out at him, the end of its white bandage untucked, dangling.

Arthur hesitated for a moment, and then he kneeled. He took the end of the linen and began to unwind. It seemed to go on endlessly, dizzyingly. He was astonished to find that with every layer he removed he grew that much more eager to see beneath the next. Having missed the Emancipation Society's indoctrination meeting and the lecture by Dr. Fallow, the surgeon who explained the crippling fractures of the binding process, handing around radiographs of ankles balanced on grotesquely folded arches, Arthur pictured May's foot like that of a doll: Tiny. Perfect. It would fit in the palm of his hand. Absurdly—*What am I thinking?* he asked himself—he saw the two of them by the bandstand in the public garden, May dancing on fence posts and flower stalks.

The last loop of cloth fell away from May's foot and revealed a warm claw of flesh, luminous and slick and folded in upon itself. It wriggled slightly, and he let it go, then grasped it again.

"You were saying?" May said.

"What?" Arthur spoke slowly, as if hit on the head. "I was saying what?"

The tiny foot in his hand shape-shifted. One minute it repelled him, the next it seemed suddenly to express the beauty of the whole female body. Wasn't it all there, in May's foot? The smooth white of her neck, the curve of her breast and hip, the crook of her smallest finger, the delicate, mauve folds of her most intimate places.

Arthur's head felt hot inside. The thought sickened him, but he wanted to take the misshapen foot in his mouth. To swallow it, *her*, whole.

"That I am wronged and crippled and immoral?" May withdrew the foot from his grasp, her voice still shaking. She felt strangely capable of striking or even biting the man kneeling before her. "And if I am, what advice do you have for me? Is this something that can be straightened out? Fixed? *Undone?*"

"Oh, no. No. Don't!" Arthur said.

"What!"

"I don't want you to." He looked at her, each black nostril dilated round with fury, her red-painted mouth closed over clenched teeth. A muscle in her cheek ticked.

Arthur groaned and sat back on his heels. He closed his eyes and dropped his face in his hands. *Those lips,* he thought. *What a color. So unnatural.* But determined as he was to dismiss them, their bright image hung before him as if burned into the backs of his eyelids. He felt intoxicated, lost. Inspired, bewildered. Perhaps opium induced amnesia, perhaps he'd smoked the pipe he'd been offered and then forgotten he'd done so. He had an erection of bewildering, almost insistent rigidity—what if she were to see it?

Arthur opened his eyes and stood clumsily, holding his coat closed. "Please," he said, "I apologize." And before May had a chance to respond, he'd backed out of the door to her room, he'd knocked into her amah and upset the tray and pipe she was carrying.

May lay back on her chaise and abandoned herself to a fit of silent tears. "Oh, what's the matter with me," she said to the amah, who, having picked herself and the tray up, held out her mistress's pipe.

What was the matter? After all, Arthur Cohen was hardly the first man to have left in a hurry after seeing one of May's feet. The amah, no more than fifteen, her cheeks pitted by smallpox, lifted her narrow shoulders in a gesture of muddled solidarity. She brushed a strand of hair from May's white forehead.

"Tired. I'm awfully tired. That's it." May dried her face, and the girl nodded. Although she wasn't mute, she might just as well have been.

"It's just that I can't do this all my life. Be insulted." May watched dully as the girl lit her pipe for her. "It will make me ill." She exhaled smoke as the girl pulled the combs from her thick hair, brushed it so that it hung in a mass over the chair back, so long it coiled on the floor. May transferred her pipe from one hand to the other as the amah unbuttoned and undressed her, brought her a long red-and-gold robe.

DOWNSTAIRS, OFF MADAME Grace's parlor, was the water closet Arthur had used on the way up, and he slipped back behind its blue door, slid the latch into place, and unfastened his trousers. He held himself for a moment before setting to the task of dispatching lust with the hasty, pragmatic strokes of an habitual onanist—one who rarely indulged in fantasy, who had only enough experience to supply him with the most meager repertoire of worn, thin, homely images: the suggestion, while at the shore, of his cousin Amelia's nipples, dark and erect and suddenly visible through the wet wool of her white bathing costume, and two stolen flashes of a housekeeper's naked lower back, the set of nicely matched dimples over her less interesting buttocks. In the looking glass over the washbasin, Arthur's reflection gazed mournfully back at him. Water dripped with dysphoric rhythm from the cold-water tap onto the roses painted inside the basin. No. He was not going to bring the lonesome act to its usual graceless conclusion.

With some trouble Arthur rebuttoned himself into his clothes and made his way back up the stairs. He stopped, four times—once on each flight—to reconsider the impulsive extravagance of losing his virginity to a Chinese temptress. What if he were to catch an exotic disease, or even a prosaic, domestic one? What if—but what was the point in trying to think when he was entirely and irredeemably overcome by desire?

Pausing outside May's door, Arthur readjusted his coat so that it fully obscured the front of his trousers. He wondered if perhaps the other foot might be naked now as well. At his knock, the little amah opened and then looked back at May, who sat up and put her long pipe on the table by her chair. "Have you forgotten something?" she said, and now her voice sounded not so much angry as languidly sarcastic. "Some pamphlets, perhaps? A tract?"

Arthur, his thoughts newly disorganized by the sight of her hair falling down the front of her opulent dressing gown, shook his head.

"Well?"

"May I come in?" he asked, when he had regained the use of his larynx.

May shrugged.

"I'm sorry." Arthur emptied his pockets, spilling coins on the floor, incidentally parting the front of his jacket to reveal the outline of his unmistakably erect penis. "I'm sorry. I'm very terribly sorry. Please, will you please, please, please undress?"

May looked at this strange white man, at the ginger-colored foreign-devil hair that sprouted not only from his head and face but from his arms and, if experience could be trusted, his everything else. She quoted a price five times the usual and watched him nod eagerly. "Anything to touch you," he said. "If you would please just let me."

"I may be lame," she said. "You, however, are a fool."

PERHAPS A FOOL, but then, what virgin isn't? It would be the same all his life: each time Arthur entered May it seemed to him that he was about to understand something, an important something—about himself, about her. About life or even about God. Of course, in the sudden glare of his orgasm this truth eluded him, but only just. He was always sure that the next time he would last a little longer, everything would become a little clearer.

It would because there was silence inside May—not just inside her, but inside his head when he was in her. For the first time since he was a child, since he was a child in his mother's lap, Arthur heard what he'd been waiting to hear for all those years: nothing.

He tried to be patient, polite. The first dozen times he visited May, he tried to make conversation, to arrive and casually deliver anecdotes he'd rehearsed as he walked through the city and perfected on the way up the stairs to her room. But once the door closed, once he saw her, all he managed was to fall on the floor before her feet and beg her once again to unwrap them. How smooth she was. How absolutely smooth and hairless were her arms and her thighs and the nape of her neck, that sweet curve of leg just below her groin. He brushed his lips against her, pressed them wherever she would allow his touch, anointing his mouth with her taste.

Arthur had a horror of body hair. Once, at five or six, unable to sleep, he'd felt his way down dark halls to his mother's room and as she got out of bed at the sound of his footsteps he collided with her, naked, reaching too late for a nightgown. He dove forward to bury his face where he always did and his mouth found his mother's crotch, bristling with hair, rank and scratchy and wild. In his panic he thought first that an animal had attacked him, then—more horrible!—that under her clothes his mother was entirely hirsute. Though he later believed the incident a nightmare, he grew up repelled by women with body hair. He liked them smooth all over, with no more than three tidy triangles, in the right places. The sight of hair straying down legs or dusting forearms made him ill. A cousin's collection of stereopticon cards included a Greek dancer whose navel was ringed with hair, and just looking at it, the saliva welled up under his tongue.

Arthur returned and returned to May. He quit the Foot Emancipation Society—How could he, under the circumstances, hope to convince any woman to unbind?—and devoted himself to May instead. He brought silk, he brought sweets. He borrowed from his sister and brought flowers, furs, perfumes. Each week he went to Kelly and Walsh, searching for new books.

May's friend and mentor, Helen, watched him run up the stairs with his purchases. "Not that one," she said after he'd left, arms empty. "He's all wrong."

"He can't have *no* money," May said.

"Nothing except what he gets from his brother-in-law." Helen yawned without covering her mouth. Her teeth were small and even; like a child's, they had spaces between them. "I know Shanghai," she said. "I've lived here for fifteen years, and I know who lives in every house on Bubbling Well, and on Weihaiwei and Avenue Foch. His sister is married to a taipan, to Dick Benjamin, and Arthur Cohen has nothing apart from what he wheedles out of his sister's husband."

May lit a taper from the flame of her spirit lamp, and its glowing end broke off and fell on the rug so that she had to step on it. She said nothing, lit it again.

"Fine," Helen said. "All right. I've noticed it's always the clever people who do stupid things." She flapped her hand at the smoke coming from May's pipe. "Didn't you know—every opium den is crowded with geniuses."

"The problem is—"

"Don't talk about love. It's not something you can afford. Not you or anyone else in this—"

"I wasn't going to." May wasn't as naive and romantic as that. She'd listened to all the lectures. She'd learned that love was nothing more than a calculus, an equation whose variables could be manipulated.

But how was she to remain unmoved by a man who unbound and kissed her feet, who bathed them and then washed himself in dirty water from the basin? All the rest—gifts, tender words, the eager expression on his face when she opened the door, how tall he was and how good-natured—May was not lacking in discipline, and all these she could deny herself.

But not his desire for what she had to hide from everyone else.

AS FOR ARTHUR, he knew he was in love, he didn't hesitate to say so. He told everyone he met how perfect May was and how much he wanted her. She was beautiful, but anyone could see that. How many women of any nationality were as cultured, as educated? May spoke four languages, and just ask her who was Robespierre, or Diderot, or to list the Stuart monarchs and the dates they ascended the throne. Or why not challenge her to a game of chess, because it wasn't rote memorization—she was smart. A person had to be, to have so keen a sense of humor.

Arthur dined out with May. He introduced her to his friends and saw how they enjoyed her high-spirited company. Quick-witted, she got the best of them, but who could object to her teasing? To the source of such brilliant, intoxicating smiles? Who couldn't May bewitch, sitting with her feet tucked under a table or folded under her silk skirt, hidden, as Arthur preferred them to be. Hidden, because they belonged to him alone.

Arthur didn't tell even one soul how he worshipped May's violated, broken, and sometimes pungent feet. He kept them a secret, and he cautioned himself that if he shared this secret with even one person, then the mysterious revelations they promised would be denied him. As soon as he uttered a word, the silence of sex would be shattered; in would rush ceaseless shrill chatter, the siren of tinnitus.

And when she put her feet on his shoulders he moved slowly, so slowly, and tried his best to last. "Open your eyes!" he said, the first man who had ever asked her such a thing. The others, they wanted their privacy. "Please. I want to look in them. I want to see them when you . . . When you . . ."

"When I come?"

"Yes!"

So she left her eyes open, and he looked into them for words she didn't say, noises she didn't make. May soundless beneath him: this excited him more than any moan or cry. No matter if all the lights blazed, her silence made her every touch mysterious, unknowable. The hot sun of a lunchtime tryst grew as dark as midnight. Inside Arthur's head a thick scroll unrolled. On it, he knew, was written the past and the future. On it was explained every hidden truth. On it was a map to salvation. But then he came, the scroll burned up before he had a chance to read it.

Privately, in the hours he spent alone, apart from May, Arthur paced and chewed the skin around his lips. Why couldn't he despise her feet? Why didn't he recoil from them, as he should? Not because they were unnatural, but because they caused her such pain.

In years to come, Arthur would catch May doubled over, weeping, holding her feet in her hands. This didn't happen often—only a handful of times in their life together—but each time it seared him, and all the more so when he tried to comfort her, and she straightened up and said he was mistaken. She hadn't been crying at all.

What was the matter with him that he could love not just her, but her disfigurement? A Chinese could blame the attraction on ignorance or custom, but Arthur was not Chinese. Arthur would spend his life in quixotic pursuit of utopias, of societies cleansed of folly and affliction. Devoting himself to an ill he could not cure: that would be romantic. What Arthur felt was not romance; it was lust. And though he scourged himself for the thought—a thought he would never confess, never speak aloud—he was glad they couldn't be straightened. For then how could he resolve the conflict? How could he choose between the woman and her anguish, between May and her feet?

Arthur proposed thirty-seven times before May consented to marry him. "You can't refuse me!" he would cry. "You cannot when I want you so!"

May looked at him, considering. "My first husband seemed kind, too, before the wedding," she teased, trying not to be a fool, trying not to succumb to love, which, as everyone knew, was either evanescent or fatal.

"I will be kind to you forever. For as long as I live. And after. I will leave you all my money."

"You haven't any money."

"I'll make some. If you would only just marry me, I'd be able to settle down. To think about something else."

"So you say. But perhaps you are no better than the others. Perhaps you think—"

"Just let me prove myself to you. If you are unhappy, I will release you."

"If I am unhappy I will run away."

Arthur fell to his knees and embraced May's legs. "So, you consent! You are saying—At last, you are saying *yes*."

May stroked the rough curls on his head. "Yes," she agreed. For, in the one essential way, he had already proved himself to her.

# ADVENTURE AND ARREST

THE DAY AFTER THE SÉANCE, ALICE VISITED THE captain in his compartment. It was the first time she'd been alone with him since the day he'd frightened her with his tears, his hot, shuddering embrace. "I'm . . . I've brought you some Sanaphos. It's for nerves," she explained.

Litovsky patted the side of the berth. He was dressed, but evidently had not risen, not completely; his bed had not yet been made up.

"Sit with me," he said. Through the window beside him, the flat, open steppes organized themselves into small hills and then larger ones as the track cut through the somber woods of the Ural Mountains. Everything was dripping and gray. A freight train passed on the opposite track, loaded with logs, their ends raw, yellow circles, stacked up and bleeding sap.

Litovsky put his hand on Alice's knee. "Russians," he said, as if by way of explaining his indisposition, "are prey to homesickness. They suffer homesickness everywhere and at all times."

"Even when they are at home?" Alice asked.

"Yes. Even in their own beds!" The captain nodded, vehement. "Especially in their own beds," he said. Against the white linen pillow slip his face looked smudged; his cheeks were not—as they usually were—freshly shaven.

"Yes," Alice nodded. "I understand."

"Do you?" He searched her brown eyes. "Yes, I think you do, even though you are still young. I am sorry for that." He fell silent. Then, "Shall I tell you how they make kopecks?" he asked, as if he were talking to a girl much younger than she.

"All right."

Litovsky sat up a little. "Copper bars from copper works in the Urals are melted down into bands about this thick." He put his thumb and forefinger together so that no more than a sliver of light shone between them.

"The bands are fed like ribbon into a cutting machine that makes blank coins. Some are good," he said. "Some not so good." He made a so-so gesture with his hand, let it drop heavily to his side. "They throw the bad ones back into the pot, polish the good ones. Stamp a coat of arms on one side, a likeness of the czar on the other, and polish again." He paused, sighed. "There are a few more steps, but that's the idea. The coppers in your purse come right out of the mountain."

The train passed a frozen river, as dull and gray as a road. On it stood sheep. Alice said nothing and Litovsky, too, was silent. After some minutes there was an announcement that the train was approaching Kuybyshev.

"Be quick and get your cloak," Litovsky said, pulling himself to his feet. "Your hat and muff."

Alice did as he told her. She walked back to her own compartment where her coat was hanging.

"Where are you going?" Miss Waters asked.

"The platform. Some air."

And perhaps that was what she had thought in the moment. That she would go no farther than a few steps beyond the train's blue door.

Afterwards, when she asked herself, when others asked her, if she knew then what she was going to do, Alice couldn't remember. Later, much later, it would seem to her that after the séance, after Litovsky's faint and her mother's hysterics, after her own "shocking meanness," as Dolly would forever put it, she had at last gone to sleep and dreamed of going to the Old City with May, a familiar dream, and one that often ended badly. But this time the execution turned out to be a conjurer's trick. A blink of the eye, a billowing scarf passed over the platform, the pole, and the Chinese girl stepped whole from the basket where the stones had been. She pulled up her tunic and showed the crowd her smooth white midriff, without even a scratch.

But it couldn't have been as tidy as that. Alice rarely remembered her dreams past breakfast. Like all of us, she raveled the dramas of childhood, made of them a fabric more seamless than fate allows. After all, how could the punishment of a girl in China have any bearing, really, on Alice's detour from the long journey to Miss Robeson's Academy?

No one followed Alice and the captain; no one stopped them. She put her hand in his, and together they disembarked. They didn't see the *provodnik;* he must have been otherwise occupied. A guard checked Litovsky's pass and waved Alice on through. Once outside the station house, she saw a town that bristled with church spires.

Litovsky used his walking stick to hail a troika, and after a terse negotiation, its driver took them to a hotel eleven blocks from the station. Alice counted as they passed the street lamps on the corners, standing black, solemn, waiting for the lamp-lighter's flame. When they dismounted from the trap they found a sidewalk made of boards. Immediately the tip of Litovsky's stick got caught between two of them.

What were you thinking! people always said to Alice. Did you imagine that you could just step off into another land? Another life?

Her mother and father, her sister, governess, friends, teachers, and, later, lovers: all of them expected answers. And Alice would discover that the less she said, the more they thought they understood. If she let them, they told the whole story for her; they furnished whatever justifications they wanted.

You were infatuated with him, a girlish crush. The uniform, the boots and cap and military posture—such things have their effects. And the confinement of such a long trip! That would of course be disorienting.

A change in schedule, in diet, and sleeping on those hard narrow berths—it doesn't take much to disturb the equilibrium of certain constitutions. Something to consider when you travel, Alice.

The snow. The ice. The threat of boarding school. How irrational young persons can be! Angry with your mother for sending you away from home, away from your aunt May. You never got on with your mother. Or your sister, for that matter.

There are individuals—did you know?—who are affected by coal gas leaking from the engine. You didn't know that? Such people can't take trains; train travel makes them absolutely mad.

Whatever theories were offered, Alice accepted. After all, she didn't have any better explanation, not the kind that would satisfy people. What could she say—that it was the warmth of the captain's gaze, the *heat* of it? She'd been frightened two days before; she'd hated his embrace, so desperate, claustrophobic. She'd run, but then she'd had to return. Unaccountably, she wanted to feel it again. As for being angry with her mother—when hadn't that been true?

The tip of the captain's cane came out from between the planks with a squeal. He held her by the shoulders. "Another chance," he said. "I've one more chance. I won't be . . . this time I won't be . . . I only wanted—you know that I only wanted you to be proud."

He had a room booked and asked for another. "I didn't know I'd have the pleasure of my daughter's company," he explained to the concierge, touching his mustache, smoothing it. The sallow man nodded and wrote something in a ledger. He handed Litovsky two keys. Upstairs the rooms were papered with a pattern of yellow flowers; the windows had double glass to keep out the cold.

Alice sat in an armchair upholstered in horsehide. The seat's corners were worn, exposing a pale, dry skin pocked with dark, empty follicles. It was impossible to resist worrying more hair from those places, making the bald patches bigger. From his suitcase Litovsky withdrew a few neatly folded shirts and some clean linen, a pair of gray trousers and two pairs of socks, his books, his clock, and his toiletries, which he arranged on the top of the dresser. He turned to Alice.

"Unpacked so quickly, Olga?" She nodded. "Then take off your cloak. Your room—it isn't too cold?"

Alice shook her head.

Litovsky looked around, rubbed his palms together. "A long while yet before dinner. Perhaps I should order tea?"

"Please."

"I'll just talk to the concierge, then."

When he left the room, Alice jumped up. She counted his shirts: four. She picked up his toothbrush and smelled it, examined the varnished wooden backs of his two hairbrushes, set together with their bristles interlocking. From between them she pulled one silver hair and let it fall to the floor. A pocketknife whose blade folded into a sheath set with a lozenge of amber—when she picked it up she found it warm to the touch. It must have been in his trouser pocket rather than his valise. She held it to the window to see the stone's gold flecks and what looked like lace, the membrane of an ancient insect's wing. At the sound of Litovsky's footfall, Alice slipped the knife into her jersey pocket and returned to her place on the worn horsehide chair.

"What?" He touched her cheek, chiding her gently. "Still sitting here? It grows dark, Olga, and you haven't lit one light." He pulled a table out from the wall and set it before her, placed the desk chair on the opposite side. "I ordered a jam cake; however I'm not sure it will be any good." The table was spotless, but he dusted it with his handkerchief.

"There are usually tragedies on the Moscow stage." Litovsky looked out the window as he spoke, watching snowflakes spiral down into the cone of light coming from a street lamp. "The people of that city have a penchant for moral entertainments. They want punishments. In Petersburg . . . In Petersburg we want. Solace."

They heard a knock at the door, and he stood, expecting a waiter with tea. Instead, it was the police.

. . .

WEREN'T YOU FRIGHTENED? Not even a little? Didn't you think the train would go on without you?

But no, Alice wasn't, she hadn't been thinking about the train or her mother or anyone else. She'd slipped—it was possible to do this for an afternoon—into another skin. She wasn't gone very long. Only two hours and forty-one minutes from the sounding of the station's bell to the policeman's knock.

Of course, the train did go on, it went on without all of them. They had to wait three days and take the local. Bad beds in a bad hotel, and they missed their Paris connection; it was a mess and all Alice's fault. Each afternoon, Miss Waters took the sisters out in the frigid air for exercise.

"Girls," she said, "I want you to run around the hotel fifteen times each." And a Russian soldier in a uniform of blue and black, carrying a long-barreled gun with a bayonet attached, watched as the two sisters obediently circled the brick building, Cecily loping with the languid, pale ennui that would characterize her every movement for all her life, and Alice running in earnest, as if pursued.

Afterwards, they walked alongside a pond that had frozen, thawed enough to crack, and frozen again. The ice was smooth, but beneath its surface, black fractures reached toward them like bony fingers.

"A girl," Miss Waters said on their inaugural trip outside, "a girl who would do a thing like that is a girl who would do anything." Alice didn't reply. "It's all the fault of your aunt," she went on. "Of that I am certain."

Cecily, smugly innocent, said nothing. What more could she add to Alice's torment?

Back at the hotel, Dolly suffered palpitations, attended by a physician who spoke neither English nor French. The amah, unsurprised by yet another complication, scolded perfunctorily over lost luggage and squatted for hours in the drafty hall, thinking how good it was that Chinese children never dared behave in so dishonorable a manner.

But it was worst of all for the captain: taken to the police station and asked repeatedly who he was and who Olga had been and exactly what had happened to the cars derailed from the viaduct over the Olkhana Gorge. What could any of it have to do with mistaking someone else's child for his own? Litovsky's explanations made no sense and perfect sense and ended with equations drawn on the backs of envelopes. He handed his hat around; everyone peered at the photograph. A policeman cut it out from under the celluloid and put it in a file. As he watched, Litovsky's heart felt suddenly empty, as if it had pumped itself dry.

To be sure, the girl in the hat did resemble Alice, who was questioned twice: once in front of all the others; and once privately in a room the size of a coat closet, by an enormous wheezing clerk whose Russian was translated by his niece, a schoolteacher summoned to the police station to serve as interpreter. *Did he touch you, did he touch you anywhere?*

"No, he just looked at me," Alice told her. "He said that was all he wanted to do, and that was all he did do."

"Looked you? Only looked?"

Alice nodded. It had all taken place so quickly, it hardly qualified as an abduction. And yet, thinking of dusk in that quiet room, it seemed that the sun, as white as the moon against the cold, slate-blue sky, had taken a very long time to set. She couldn't make sense of the time that had or hadn't elapsed. They had faced each other across the empty table and he had reached across it once as if to touch her cheek or her chin, but then he pulled his hand back. He said nothing, and she said nothing as well. The chairs were not comfortable, and she fidgeted. She remembered that when she blinked her eyes had felt dry, as they did when she was feverish or in need of sleep. That twice Litovsky put his hands before his face and then replaced them on the table, sweeping them over and over its surface as if to be sure it was clean. She remembered that she had sat as ladies ought not to sit, with her chin on the heels of her hand, both elbows resting on the table.

In the end, Litovsky was remanded to the armed services. A military attaché came to collect him. Someone cabled his wife.

"May I speak to the captain before he leaves?" Alice ignored Miss Waters's protests. The *gorodovoi* nodded. Litovsky stood as she approached. "I wanted something . . . I wanted," she began, but then stopped. She found she didn't want to confess about the knife.

Litovsky gave Alice a crushed, puzzled look, then nodded excitedly.

"Yes. Yes, of course." He touched the cord around his neck, withdrew the pouch containing the last of the czar's rubles, but before he had teased it open, he thought of a truer gift, one he was more likely to miss. He reached into his pocket for the little worn icon. "Here," he said. "For you." Alice took the coin bearing the Virgin's benign and somnolent face, her golden eyes and mouth rubbed clean of expression.

"Oh," Alice said, immediately conflating the image with one of May, seeing her aunt as she reclined on her dressing-room chaise, languid, lids half-closed, the musk of her pipe lingering. "Thank you!"

The next day, she was on the local train to Moscow, which departed at two from the station at Kuybyshev. It picked up speed and went around a bend, and Alice watched everything disappear: the station, the town, the women selling boiled potatoes and onions. She ran her thumb over the icon in her pocket. Probably there were no berths on a local train. No berths and no porters to turn down the covers.

Staring out the compartment window, Alice found she didn't mind being in disgrace. After so much talking, it was restful.

# A SEARCH UNDERTAKEN

THE SOLICITOR'S OFFICE WAS ON MUSEUM ROAD, just off the corner of Peking. Outside the black door with its polished brass knocker and name plate, May sat in her sedan chair without moving. "You want me to wait?" one of the boys asked, and she spoke back sharply.

She had a headache and the indigestion to which she was prey; it radiated into her chest and sent sharp pains under her right shoulder blade. All of Shanghai was limp under an oppressive autumn heat wave. May felt as if she couldn't draw a breath. The previous night she and Arthur had sat nearly undressed on the verandah outside their bedroom, but the air was without a breeze. They kept their eyes on the drooping branches of the plane tree; not one leaf moved.

"What is it?" he'd said at last.

"What is what?"

"Why are you so glum? Is it because Alice is off to boarding school?"

"I'm not glum. It's the weather."

He looked at her. It was impossible to lie to him successfully.

And now, here she was at the solicitor's. On a fool's errand. How often had she asserted to Arthur, and to herself, that mistakes—those of any import—could not be undone; the past could not be revised. At breakfast, when she'd told Arthur she was going out shopping, he'd lifted his eyebrows suspiciously. "In this heat?" he asked.

May called to the boy. "I'll be here an hour at least," she said. "You needn't wait. Come back at four." He nodded. She gave him a little money. "Get something to drink. For your brother, too."

A secretary greeted her inside the office door. Clearly May was not who the name "Mrs. Cohen" had suggested to him over the telephone.

"Won't you please sit down?" he said, speaking slowly and loudly, succumbing to the temptation to stare. May was wearing one of her favorite jackets, of red silk brocade. It was fabric underneath which a person felt substantial, even brave, and she wore the jacket over silk trousers of a matching red. Her shoes were red and black, her hair lacquered and high.

"Mr. Barrett will be with you in a moment," the secretary said to her. "May I offer you tea?"

"No, thank you." May sat.

Mr. Barrett, when he appeared, was a man of fifty, not more. His thick gray hair, parted in the center, was held in place with fragrant pomade. The rich smell of it struck May as somewhat unlawyerly, but she liked his face. The mouth was businesslike, the eyes kind.

"How old would the girl be?" he asked, after they were seated behind the closed door to his office.

"Sixteen," May said.

"And it was through the Door of Hope? You are sure?"

"No, not sure at all. I was not ... I wasn't able ... I didn't pay adequate attention at the time."

Mr. Barrett nodded.

The Door of Hope was a charity organized by European and American missionary ladies. Its objective was the reform of young prostitutes, the rescue of the unfortunate children they bore. May cleared her throat. On the solicitor's desk was a photograph of his family, himself posed in the midst of a wife, a son, three daughters.

"I think I have the correct date," May said. "I've . . . I contacted a person I used to know. A woman who kept . . . it was a kind of journal. The child would have been picked up, well, it would have been in March, the second week of March."

"In ninety-five?"

"No. Ninety-six."

"She was how old?" Mr. Barrett put his elbows on his desk and brought his hands together, fingertips touching like a peaked roof. He peered at her over them.

"Not quite two."

"I see." Mr. Barrett sighed. "Some organizations keep meticulous records," he said. "Some not so meticulous. The Door of Hope works closely with a number of mission homes. Holy Trinity, the American Church Mission—that's the Protestant asylum out at Jessfield. And Siccawei, of course." He picked up his pen, tapped it on the blotter, a thoughtful rather than nervous gesture. "Her age does complicate matters," he said. "What was her name?"

"She didn't have one."

"Oh, I didn't mean a surname."

May looked at him. "She didn't have a given name, either."

"She was almost two years old and had no given name?"

May nodded.

"Well, Mrs. Cohen," said Mr. Barrett. "You need a detective, not a solicitor."

"I see," May said. "Can you recommend one?"

"No, no." He shook his head. "What I mean is, there isn't anyone who does this kind of work."

"No one? No one at all?"

"Look," he said. "I'm not trying to discourage you. I'll do what I can. I was just expressing my, my feeling that this will be, well, a bit of a challenge. I don't have much to go on."

"Yes. I know."

"If the child went to mission school, then she learned a trade. Needlework, most likely. Spinning. Sewing. How to use an industrial loom. That way, she could find work at a cotton filature. She probably learned English. She may—" Mr. Barrett interrupted himself.

"If I find her." He paused to look pointedly at May. "What is it that you want?" He raised his hands in a gesture of inquiry, palms up and empty, then dropped them. "With regard to domestic situations," he explained, "it's always for the best if all parties are clear about what it is they want."

"Yes," May said. "Of course. For now, what I want is just to know."

"To know?"

"Yes. Where she is. How she is. That's all."

# BRIGHT, WORTHLESS
# COINS

JULY OF 1898, AND THE SUMMER SKY OVER Shanghai glowed yellow, as it did nowhere else. The Whangpoo slopped and simmered around the jutting breast of Pootung; among the hulls of steamers slipped crowds of junks, their prows painted with vigilant, unblinking black eyes. The river stank of birth and death and every seething stage between. Sun gilded the cornices of the buildings along the Bund and made the spire of the German Club into a bright needle. Bolts in the girders of the Garden Bridge glittered seductively, like the earrings of a harlot, under the fierce midsummer heat, the famous *fu-tiens*, which sent the English running to the mountain resorts of Japan.

On the sweltering July morning when he disembarked from the *Mathilda*, Arthur Cohen thought he had never seen any place so lovely. Even the destitute river families, eight or ten people living aboard each narrow boat, even this floating slum seemed to him exotic rather than debased. His visit to his sister, Dolly, and her wealthy new husband had rescued him from their neurasthenic second cousin, Amelia, and her mute, pathetically patient expectation of his never-coming proposal. The Monday he departed, in exchange for his cowardly lie, a promise to return soon, Amelia had given him a locket bearing one of her lusterless curls; and although en route he was filled with rueful self-recriminations, upon arrival all unpleasant feelings were burned away by the heat, pushed aside by the smell, drowned out by the noise. He leaned over the rail and dropped the locket into the harbor.

It was the fourteenth of July, 1898, and the French Concession was preparing for its grandest Bastille Day celebration yet. On the south end of the Bund, members of a marching band had assembled, their horns and cymbals glowing in the haze, all of them adjusting their costumes, oblivious to a black cart pulled by a skeletal ox, its legs splattered with filth. The driver turned off the Bund onto a dilapidated jetty from which he dumped the previous night's dead or comatose opium addicts collected from the gutters. As the bodies fell, the player holding the cymbals brought them together with a crash, and then did it again, over and over, as if to test their timbre.

Was there any place as loud as Shanghai? Frenetic native weddings. Cacophonous funeral processions. Markets. Military parades. Holidays. Fire brigades. The clanging of the post office clock. The unnervingly human-sounding scream of a pony burned by lamp oil. The dull, tuneless voices of wharf coolies, singing as they staggered under crates. Arthur heard all of these within hours of his arrival; that night there was a display in which firecrackers discharged thousands of pieces of colored paper that floated down onto his head like blossoms. Never had he felt happier, more alive. He decided he would make himself indispensable to Dolly's husband. Dick Benjamin would have to keep him forever.

BUT "GOD IN HEAVEN!" Dick was yelling fifteen years later. "Arthur, Arthur, Arthur," he was saying, and while he said it he held his head in his hands. Unfair as this was, irrational as it was—a matter of coincidence, of having received the cable from Kuybyshev only minutes before coming upon evidence of Arthur's most recent lapse in judgment—it seemed to Dick that of course Arthur was to blame for Alice's having gotten off a train with a deranged captain. Because Arthur had allowed himself to be seduced by May, and May had corrupted Alice, which was, after all, why his wife and daughters were on a train to London in the first place. Though Arthur had not proven himself indispensable, certainly he was ineradicable, as permanently fixed in the household as any successful parasite, as the gall worm that had gnarled up the tree in the back garden, twisting and swelling its limbs.

"I know," said Arthur. "I know, I know, I know."

"What do you know!"

"I know that this is . . . that I am . . . insupportable. But it's only until next week. Next week they'll be gone," he promised, referring to the undernourished rickshaw boy whose infected leg he was treating with mercury salve in Dolly's dressing room and the boy's half-dead addict of a sister, both of them eaten alive by syphilis.

And who could Dick blame but himself, his own indulgent nature? "No," he used to tell the gardener, "don't cut so many branches." And "What can we do?" he would answer Dolly's complaints about her brother.

"I'll give you the money." Already Dick was reaching into pockets, patting his trouser legs to locate his billfold. "I'll pay to keep them in a suite at, at the Astor House. If Dolly ever knows—" he broke off, shaking his head. That awful, grating Australian accent. So harsh on his ears. Could his wife ever have sounded like that? All day he endured the shrill cries of native brokers, the endless clacking of their abacuses. The rise and the fall of the tael, the dollar, the pound. The strange febrile jumps and dips of the yen. The collapse of rice, the resurgence of tea. And then to leave his office and make his way home through the clamorous streets to news of Alice's adventure, followed by Arthur: Arthur and his latest project.

Dick rang the bell for the boy. "Brandy and soda," he said, and the boy bowed. "And try to find a bit of that Stilton cheese, if there's any, with toast. A biscuit. Something. Anything. Dash it all, I've missed tea again."

He sat in one of his study's two dark-green leather chairs and stared at Arthur, who nervously pulled at his earlobe. Any kind of strain was likely to drive the volume up inside his head.

"D'you, um . . . ," Arthur said. "What I mean is, shall I have a drink with you, or do you want me to work on this, uh, problem now?"

Dick glared at his brother-in-law.

"Of course," Arthur said. "I'll just call Boy and have him, or Amah, yes, Amah, get them dressed and then take them myself to the, uh, somewhere."

Dick counted out a few notes and handed them over without speaking. He had transcended his volatile ancestry. He had cultivated a stiff upper lip. Born in Baghdad, raised in Bombay, schooled in England: by sheer force of will, Dick Benjamin had made himself as British as a person could. Being British meant being stoic, of course, as well as rational, condescending, civilized. It meant regarding the Chinese with contempt. Not disliking them, exactly, but counting them of little value.

The capacity of his wife's brother to love the Chinese, to find them mysterious and exciting and redeemable—no, not redeemable, but worthy, not needing redemption!—astonished Dick Benjamin, who cringed each day en route to Jinkee Road, his pony cart threading its way through filth and misery of every description. The Chinese were a people—well, it wasn't just that they were heathens, and not kosher. It was fair, yes, it was fair to say that they were aggressively anti-kosher. They would put anything, *anything*, into their mouths. Considered the hairless bodies of newly born mice a delicacy. Dropped them in sauce and ate them still wriggling. Ate monkey brains and pigs' ears. Ate eels and leeches. Drank the blood of dogs and heaven knew what else. Dick Benjamin may not have remained orthodox, as his mother would have wished, but the idea of clean and unclean retained a firm hold on his head and his heart, and the Chinese—the Chinese were emphatically not a clean people.

Naturally, Dick understood that on some people the forbidden exerts an irresistible pull. Arthur's problem was one of erotic fixation. Dick would not say this to his wife about her brother, but it is what he had concluded. Arthur was ... he seemed simple, but he might be complicated. Almost as soon as he'd arrived, fourteen years ago, he'd fallen in love with a famously dexterous prostitute who had, beneath a banquet table at a singsong house, removed Arthur's penis from his trousers with a set of priceless jade chopsticks. Or so gossip went. It was the kind of story you heard from someone else, not your suspect brother-in-law. Of course Dolly and the girls knew nothing of this, and they never would. Not about the chopsticks, nor about the new disaster, of which Dick had only just that morning learned, from a solicitor friend of a friend. Before she met Arthur, May had apparently had a child, a girl, who got lost and whom she was now trying surreptitiously to find. Well, even a hyena would make a better mother than May. Less dangerous. And who on earth could have predicted that the extraordinary denouement of the jade chopsticks would be that Arthur would marry the woman who wielded them and father a child by her? Another doomed child.

Not that everyone in the family hadn't pointed out to Arthur that he was mad, and asked for the millionth time why it was he hadn't kept his promise to that poor Amelia, who had wasted away out of despair. Her death was on his head, wrote Amelia's mother to Dick Benjamin, as if he'd had any influence in the matter. Why, any idiot knows there's no point in trying to talk sense into a lovesick fool. Not that Dick had replied so rudely; he was, after all, a gentleman. But really.

And Arthur's marrying May was just the beginning of the trouble. After relentless, and useless, weeping from Dolly, who couldn't see how the little brother she'd helped to raise could lose his reason and marry a Chinese, the newlyweds had moved into the west wing of the house.

"They have no money," Dick had said to his wife. "Not a sou." For ironically—that was the meaning of *irony*, wasn't it?—it was he who'd argued for their living all together. "What *are* we to do?" he'd said to Dolly. "Turn them out into the street? That would be even more of a scandal."

Predictably, Arthur had long ago abandoned all pretense of ever returning home. The notion of a creature like May in the outback was hardly more absurd than the idea of her in Sydney. Australia was an outpost and always would be. Not that China was any great shakes. Although Arthur seemed genuinely not to share the European regard of Shanghai as a way station; he remained untroubled by the conceit that civilization was necessarily West, even for those who'd been born in the East.

No one knew better than Dick Benjamin that Settlement life was one of comfort and complaint. Disappointment in the present. Enduring the minutes and the days and the weeks in anticipation of the future—which most Shanghailanders imagined as a resort: Biarritz, Monte Carlo, Lake Como. Dick planned to take his family to Nice. Another ten years and they'd be basking in the Mediterranean sun. Already he had a French agent investigating available waterfront properties. It was a disease of empire—this plundering the present to favor other tenses: future, future perfect. It afflicted all colonials, Australians as well. But Arthur—who could avoid concluding that Arthur was different? He was immune, a free spirit. He took a Mandarin tutor, espoused Buddhism, and followed this conversion with a series of intensely unfashionable interests, studying local arts, visiting pestilential temples, as large and conspicuously red-haired a pilgrim as could be imagined. At five feet eleven inches, Arthur towered above diminutive May, so besotted with his Chinese wife that he'd been seen more than once on Stone Bridge Road, cold sober and sweeping the ground before her sedan chair.

It wasn't that May was a bad sort. She didn't speak pidgin; no, she was far too proud for that. (A prostitute and a polyglot! What next!) Not that anyone asked him, but May's clear, eccentrically accented queen's English was a little oddly musical for Dick's taste. It rose and fell in pitch like Mandarin, with an occasional syntactical slip, which she managed to make charming. And everything would be fine if ever one could get used to the unremitting sound of her long jade-sheathed nails at table, against tea cups, on mah-jongg tiles—which of course one couldn't if one had even one nerve in one's body—but then they had to go and have a baby. Now Dick admitted that Rose, even if a half-caste, had been the most beguiling and delightful of children. Her eyes sparkled, her cheeks were pink and round, her surprisingly fair hair was as shiny as that of a polished brass god. But, being the sort of people who suffered a propensity for mishaps and tragedies—this was what came of bohemianism; free spirits did have a way of colliding with hard truths—Arthur and May had to go off on a houseboat and somehow manage to let the child drown, so that he went mad and she went madder.

IN HIS MIND, Arthur had returned to the river countless times. He saw them all onboard the boat, May reclining by the tea tray and, to amuse him, drinking from the spout of the green porcelain pot. "What a vulgar girl you are," he'd said, laughing, and he'd kissed her on her painted red lips, still wet with tea. Beyond the river, rice was just sprouting in the paddies; a delicate green haze shimmered over the surface of the water. Rose, four years old, squatted at her mother's feet, playing with the silk cherries dangling from May's absurdly tiny shoes. Arthur read aloud from a guide to Soochow's Garden of the Humble Administrator. It was nearly dusk; the boat passed under a stone bridge whose span, a perfect semicircle, met its reflection to form a luminous whole. Inside the boat, the boy was preparing a turtle to stew over the brazier.

The picture Arthur held in memory was useless, though, because Rose was suddenly, silently, and inexplicably gone. Arthur, May, and the boy searched all night and all day and then all night again. Round, white lantern circles reflected by the bobbing mirror of the water burned into Arthur's head, so that forever after when he closed his eyes he would see them, like bright, worthless coins scattered at his feet.

May sat on the boat, shivering. The blanket Arthur had wrapped around her shoulders lay crumpled at her feet. She didn't eat or sleep; she didn't move except to shake. "I didn't deserve her. I didn't deserve her," she said over and over, her voice low and entirely without inflection.

"Stop it!" Arthur yelled. "Who deserves anything! None of us!"

She turned to him. "You don't understand," she said. "You don't know. You don't know what I'm talking about."

"What! What are you taking about! Because of your past? Because you weren't a . . . a chaste mother?" Arthur felt he could dash his ringing head on the deck, stop its noise like that of an alarm clock.

"No," May said. "Not that."

"What then! What!" He shook her shoulders.

May looked at Arthur. She opened her mouth but said nothing. The delicate skin under her eyes trembled and contracted, as if in a wince of fear.

"What!" Arthur cried.

"I'm not talking about anything," she said at last.

"You are," he said.

"Yes," she said. "But not anything that has anything to do with . . . anything." And she began to cry. He'd seen her cry before, of course, but never as she did on that day. Before, May had always cried silently, but this time she made an awful, low moaning that he tried not to hear, a sound that defied his deafness, penetrated tinnitus, a sound that opened a hole beneath his feet, the boat, the water. He resisted putting his hands over his ears. The boy, afraid, hid himself in the boat's little galley.

Rose washed up, five days later, on the south shore of the creek, just a mile upriver from Shanghai. Her body was perhaps hastened toward land by the activity of the Dragon Boat Festival, just coming to a close. Their daughter was pulled onto the bank by a leek farmer who had seen her necklace glint from the mud and recognized by the color of her hair that she wasn't Chinese—at least not all Chinese. She wore a gold lock on a chain around her neck, in accordance with a native superstition which held that they bound the wearer to life. Although May was embarrassed by quaint Chinese customs, Arthur had prevailed upon her to accept this gift from Rose's amah. If only it had worked a little better, Arthur sometimes found himself thinking; for it did call attention to her body, it had returned Rose to them. But too late.

Out of respect for the dead, especially the wealthy dead, the farmer left the necklace on the corpse and took it to the police, who restored

Rose to her parents, so water-logged that were it not for her untarnished hair, her dress and necklace, she would have been unrecognizable. Dick rewarded the farmer's self-interested honesty with enough money to afford him the kind of coffin of which he'd long dreamed, and which he could be sure his lazy sons would never provide.

So it was upon two very different households that Dick Benjamin bestowed a white lacquer casket with brass hinges and handles, silk pillow and fringe: one six feet long—it would remain empty for many years; the other only three, filled and closed within an hour of its delivery.

IT MUST HAVE been Rose's riverine destiny that provoked Arthur's obsession with charting the flow of Soochow Creek. While May descended into one and then two and sometimes even three pipes of opium a day—whatever it took to blunt the memory of little fingers swelled almost as wide as they were long—he sent the empty houseboat up-country, with only the boy on board, and cases of empty Aquarius table-water bottles. He gave the boy his own pocket watch, taught him how to read it and transcribe what he'd read, and then had him drop a bottle each hour from the side of the houseboat, moored in the same lazy eddy where they'd anchored when Rose went overboard. Inside each bottle was a slip of paper on which the hour had been inscribed by the boy's graceful hand. Arthur waited on the bank where Rose was found to catch them, however many made the five-mile journey. It worked out to about 28 percent, but it wasn't a consistent 28. Almost three-fourths of the bottles dropped between midnight and dawn traveled the five miles, whereas far fewer survived the daytime traffic.

"How can you!" Dolly said. "How can you spend even a minute on that lugubrious stretch of horrible, dirty water!"

But Arthur just shook his head. He couldn't explain his need to observe flow and flux and current, crossflow and crosscurrent, conflux and drift—a dreary, diverting obsession punctuated by exhausted, helpless dreams that visited him as he slept on the greasy lip of the creek, dreams of fairy-tale rescues of Rose, of savior fishermen with enchanted nets, of frog princes, and of oystermen whose knives cut out not pearls but little girls who lay sleeping on the salty, pale, labial flesh of the plundered shells.

As for May, his beautiful May, she spoke hardly at all. Mute, she appeared blind as well; opium made her pupils disappear into the deep brown irises around them. By nightfall, the eyes he loved were rendered as soulless, as flat and desperate as a shark's.

Based on the results of his research, Arthur wrote a report, which he donated to the Siccawei meteorological society, one which he felt the missionaries at the observatory underappreciated, but they did publish it in their year-end report of local phenomena. Seeing the result of his labors—a year of grief-soaked pilgrimages—reduced to three cramped pages rife with typographical errors cured Arthur's romance with Soochow. He forsook the creek for a plan to regulate the treatment of corpses at the Ningpo Joss House (insufficiently limed), a cause that provided him an education in Chinese bureaucracy before it gave way to a campaign to replace Settlement water closets with "earth closets." These, Arthur assured anyone who would listen, "return excrement to the soil, where it belongs, by means of coal ash," and thus would protect the waterways and the population's health. To promote more responsible waste management, Arthur wrote a tract explaining in detail how to construct an earth closet, and convinced his sister's long-suffering husband to pay for a thousand copies to be printed. But he gave away less than half before he took up the anti-streetside-cauterization banner and stood on the corner of Peking and Kiangse roads collecting signatures on a petition to prevent Chinese doctors from performing minor surgeries outside.

Aside from his being pursued by the specter of a child with sparkling brown eyes and bright curls—for, after all, ghosts prey on all of us—what made people regard Arthur as peculiar among Settlement residents was his assumption that the graceless, money-mad city was worth improving not only for Westerners but for the indigenous population. For five years now, he had agitated while May smoked. His nephew David's death had the effect of increasing the speed with which Arthur tired of causes, and in one season he had supported the registration, taxation, and periodic examination of prostitutes; crusaded against the installation of pornographic Western picture boxes in the old city; demonstrated in favor of weekly moxibustion clinics to combat tuberculosis (coolies laid out like cadavers, with smoking brown lumps on the ends of long, dirty needles projecting from their limbs and chests and ears); and exhorted the English to give up cured tea leaves in favor of green.

Since he'd arrived, Dick liked to point out, the one job for which Arthur had been paid was coffin-counting, a service he undertook for the municipal council's native census efforts; the number of living Chinese was extrapolated from the rate of their death, a tally that had formerly been calculated incorrectly (owing to graft) by the number of gate passes issued to funeral processions, and even less correctly by means of a mathematical formula based on the number of bodies of addicts, drunks, and suicides found floating each March off the Bund.

The only thing that might save them—not just him, but all of them, May and Dolly and Dick and his nieces and their friends, and everyone, everyone, all the world mysteriously and irrefutably bound together in Arthur's mind, his soul, his grief—was another Rose, another child. But May was not as young as she had been, or perhaps organs other than her heart had been damaged, for although she became pregnant, she lost each baby in the fourth or fifth month, always trying to hide the fetus from Arthur, to protect him from seeing it where it lay vividly red in a basin—hopeless, raw, curled in silent accusation.

# THE YEAR OF THE
# FOOT TAX

WHITE ICE CAME APART LIKE UNDERCLOTHES
ripping. Slips and underskirts ripping from the hem upwards to the bodice. Alice closed her eyes and saw it like
that. Black and dark beneath the white. And cold. She
didn't know why, but every time she thought of the ice
she saw undergarments tearing, she saw the dark place
between her aunt's legs.

She saw what she wasn't supposed to have seen.
Amah caught her but said nothing. Her aunt sat at her
vanity table. On the outside Aunt May was white, not
pink like red-haired Uncle Arthur, not dark like her father or creamy like her mother, but white, as white as ice,
but then she cracked wide open and inside she was dark.

Every night, in her bed in the dormitory at Robeson
Academy, Alice thought of the train going through the
ice on top of Lake Baikal. *Think of something pleasant,*
May used to say when Alice couldn't sleep, *Think of something you like,* and while the idea of a train wreck wasn't

pleasant—no more than May's own recipe for calm, the vision of a knife rending red slippers—it had become the surest vehicle toward sleep. The locomotive plunged, the ice opened like her aunt's underclothes, and after it came all the cars full of people.

She never imagined them dying.

Some had been in their berths and had to wake up to change out of their nightgowns. They had to brush their long hair, which had tangled among the bed linens; they had to put it up again with combs and pins. They had to look among all the bottles and jars in their train cases to find their headache powders, their complexion creams, their nail buffers and corn plasters. Only when they were dressed and had had their good breakfasts, their cups of tea, their coffees and *pain au chocolat*, all warm and sweet and sticky in the middle, only then did she give them last embraces and farewell speeches.

Those who had quarreled she reunited. Those who traveled by themselves she allowed to write letters home, to say good-bye to family and friends left above, in the world. She allowed them to tidy their compartments, to set their belongings in order, to fold their clothes and to tuck their jewels away.

All of this took a long time, of course. Now thirteen years old, Alice was not so young that she imagined resolution to be uncomplicated. The train would have been resting at the bottom for hours before she was ready to let them go, and by that time there seemed little point in killing them—not when they'd survived the wreck, not when they'd learned how to live in the cold, dark water.

They didn't breathe. How could they? But they spoke; they mouthed the words. They sat in the dining car, now rinsed clean of smoke from cigars that could no longer be lit. They played cards and charades; they read books and bought bicarbonate from the concession car, and they looked out the window at nothing. At the dark water pressing on the glass. They slept in their berths under sodden blankets, and the smell of wet wool didn't bother them. Not underwater. Not when they were holding their breath for the rest of their lives.

...

ON THE SISTERS' first night in the dormitory, Alice had felt her way to the room where the older girls slept, gently touching each curtain drawn around each bed, counting seventeen of them, just as she'd counted carefully when the lights were on. At the eighteenth curtain she'd run her hand over the linen until she found the opening, then pushed her head through.

"Ces?" she said.

"Mmm?"

She'd crawled into bed with her sister, fit herself exactly against her sister's back the way she had on the train, her arms around Cecily, her knees bent into the backs of Cecily's knees. They were lying together when the curtain parted and faces peered in: one, two, three of them, stacked like a totem and all talking at once.

"You don't look Chinese. Are you sure you're from China?"

"What's it like?"

"Does your father have a pigtail? Is he yellow?"

"Let's see your feet. Why, they're not small at all! I thought they'd be pinched off, you know, like hounds' tails."

"What's an S.T.? D'you know? Stands for sanitary towel. Well, do you or don't you know?"

"If you're not Chinese, what are you then? You don't look English."

"D'you sleep together in China, too? The whole lot of you in bed together? Your mother and father, as well?"

Alice said nothing in response. She sat silently up on her elbows, looking at the round pink faces.

As for Cecily, "How dare you even think we might be Chinese!" she'd said, and she leaned forward and twitched the curtains shut.

"THE LAKE OF Baikal is as deep as the deepest ocean." Alice said this to the nurse, and the nurse said, "You're studying geography, then?"

"No," Alice said. "I'm not talking about that."

"What, no geography?" said the nurse.

"No," said Alice. "I mean yes. Yes."

Geography, maths, spelling, general knowledge, deportment. And something else. What? She couldn't think properly. Oh, French with Mlle. Vailard.

There was something the matter with her head, and she had to go over and over the things she knew. What were they? She knew that at home in China Mah Foo was taking care of her dapple pony, thirteen hands high and a cross between the native Mongol and a Shetland, pouring potassium permanganate into the crack of his right forehoof so that it hissed and produced a wisp of purple smoke (a pretty trick but one with limited curative properties, just the kind of thing to which the Chinese were prey). She knew that even though the climate in China was considered unhealthful for children, it was all right for horses and for Tony, her dog, a Boston bull bred in Seattle, Washington, purchased in Banff, Canada, and shipped on the *Princess Christina* from San Francisco to Hong Kong and on to Shanghai in time for her birthday. She was resigned to Tony's staying home in Shanghai because, as everyone knew, England had no rabies and a six-month quarantine for all pets made sure she never would. Ireland had no snakes because Saint Patrick drove them over a cliff into the sea, but that was a fairy story for Catholics, and she was a Jew. Chinese children had their own stories. Aunt May said that once the rivers of Fukien were filled with crocodiles, but Han Yü wrote them an obituary so convincing that when the literate reptiles encountered his words they rolled over onto their green backs and stopped breathing.

She had been carried from the dormitory rolled up in her mattress. Someone had come into the room. She was hot and thirsty and thought Ma Robey was bringing the water she'd wanted. Miss Robeson's mother had been in and out of the little infirmary on the top floor. She'd tied up Alice's throat in cheese cloth wrapped around a sachet of asafetida, so vile-smelling that even though she couldn't get any air up her nose, the foulness of it penetrated her consciousness; it went right through her skull and into her head and made her retch violently.

"I'd call the doctor tonight, if I were you," someone said, and someone else sighed loudly in exasperation and said, "Yes, I'd better." And then they'd made an astonishing noise on the stairs, as if they were jumping down in hobnailed boots.

And Arthur, her uncle Arthur, he was on the other side of the wall washing his coins. On the advice of his sister, Dolly, he disinfected his money with carbolic soap; through the wall she could her them clinking against the enamel basin. In the morning they would be stacked, bright and shining, and there would be wet bills pinned to a string drawn across his dressing room. It was so humid in Shanghai that it took days for them to dry sufficiently to use.

But the doctor didn't come. Another man came instead, and he leaned down and she could see only his eyes because a cloth was tied around his nose and mouth, and *Well, he's a bandit*, she'd thought, banditry being a commonplace in Shanghai. Words came out of the criminal-looking cloth: "Easy now, miss." And then the bandit had bundled her up and she'd kicked and cried and called for her father.

Alone in the Fever Hospital's children's ward, Alice knew that already the school had burned her clothes, her dolls, her books. The linens on her dormitory bed and the white curtain pulled around it would have been stripped off by the charwoman, just as they were when Elizabeth fell ill, the woman's mouth and nose protected by a handkerchief knotted at the back of her neck. Everything was stuffed into the furnace; the mattress, too expensive to discard, dragged onto the roof to air. But if Elizabeth's mattress had been taken to the roof, why was hers taken with her to the hospital?

"Is this my mattress?" she asked the nurse.

"Well, who else's, I'd like to know."

"I only meant was it the school's or the hospital's."

"It's the fever talking now, is it?" said the nurse. She dipped the flannel into the bowl, then wrung it out and sponged Alice's other arm.

Alice felt on the pillow for her hair, but it was gone. Someone had cut off her braid and sent it to be incinerated as well. *In-cin-er-a-ted.* The sounds added up to something hotter than a regular fire.

The first Friday of every month, the hairdresser came to wash their hair. He started with the youngest girl and worked his way up to the eldest, and after all their hair was dry, he brushed it out and sometimes then he singed the ends with a red iron. He never used scissors. He said it was bad for a girl's hair, to cut it with a blade. In the winter, when the windows stayed shut, the smell of burned hair lingered for days.

At home, just the previous summer, Alice had measured her braid against that of one of the boys who carried May's chair. "Velly velly long!" he'd said. "Just as!" But he wouldn't leave his braid down; he'd rolled it back up and tucked it under his hat so that when he went out revolutionaries wouldn't harangue him. Along with bound feet, the queue, as it was called, was regarded as a sign of oppression and backwardness.

"Look here," Alice remembered Aunt May saying to her uncle at the breakfast table. She pushed the paper toward Arthur. "I'm everything that's wrong with China."

"What is it?" Alice had said, reading the editorial over her uncle's shoulder as he kissed her aunt's white knuckles. Another diatribe from K'ang, the reformer, against opium and foot binding, against sedan chairs carried by boys with long braids.

"Oh, dear," Arthur sighed. "They'll bring the foot tax back, it looks like."

And in August May had bought herself a pair of Western women's shoes in which she might disguise her suddenly illegal feet, and so avoid being forced to provide revenues to maintain the empress dowager's flower gardens—an aesthetic that had fallen into disfavor supporting sanctioned beauty.

"So, so unfortunate and infelicitous!" May tried them on before the family, laughing and crying at once. "Have you ever seen anything to beat them for ugliness!"

"I rather like them," Dick said carefully.

"Yes." Dolly's voice went up in enthusiasm. "Elegant!"

"You'll have to stuff the toes with cotton wool." Arthur shook his head with distaste at the shiny, dark leather laced up over his wife's ankles.

Alice had seen May put on the Western shoes at times other than when she was going out. She caught her when her only witness was herself, or so May thought. Alice found her aunt in her dressing room, taking off her tiny Chinese slippers. She pulled on one and then another layer of Arthur's thickest wool socks and slipped her feet into the high-lacing leather. Stood for whole minutes before the mirror, turning first to the left, then to the right. Looking glass in hand, May turned her back to the full-length mirror and walked two wobbling steps to see what she might look like from behind.

"Insufferable," she whispered, "insufferable." She could still hear Yu-ying: *We will tell them that you never cried out. Say the words: I never cried out.*

"What are you doing!" May gasped, her voice strangled, so startled to see Alice that she almost fell.

"Nothing," Alice said. "What are *you* doing?"

May dropped the hand mirror to her side. "Practicing." How could a person compose herself so quickly? If anything, her voice was even more lilting than usual. "Pretending to be modern in readiness for the foot tax." May smiled. "You know how I feel about the empress dowager—you don't think I intend to buy even one daisy for that old bitch!"

SCARLET FEVER WITH rheumatic complications. Alice's knees and elbows and finger joints throbbed. Her dreams tried to explain the terrible burning of her hands and included upset kettles and overturned spirit lamps. A birthday cake ignited by candles so the icing melted and poured off. Reaching for a piece, she caught her white gloves on fire.

Then suddenly Alice was walking down a road and her aunt was walking before her, walking swiftly, walking as she never did in life. It was foggy, dusk. A black dog pursued May, its head down, its tail down as well. The fur on its neck bristled. Alice was frightened by the look of it. When the dog sprang at her aunt's back, May turned her head in surprise. The dog plunged its teeth into May's throat, she sank to her knees.

*Rabid*, Alice thought, a rabid dog. But her aunt wasn't dead, she was weeping. She was holding a curtain that hung magically in the road, hung from nothing: no pole, no rings. The curtain was red velvet, as red as blood, and then blood was dripping onto May's hands, her clothes, her shoes. Alice screamed and screamed, and when the nurse came, she caught her hand and cried, "I know why she wears so many underclothes! So many slips and skirts and garters. The layers of white bindings!"

"Who?" said the nurse. "What?"

"They're bandages! Don't you see? Real bandages! To stop the blood!"

"Who?"

"Why, May, of course, Aunt May."

The nurse was angry because she'd cried out, she would wake the other sick children. But she was the only one there, the other beds were empty, they'd all gone home, they were dead or recovered. The ward was hot, or was it cold? Wrapped in a wet linen sheet, she shivered and her hands itched. *Crying only makes it worse,* the nurse said, and the obedient tears began to burn as they fell.

A hundred times the train derailed, and Alice plunged after the locomotive, down and oddly through her aunt's underclothes, through bandages and blood, down through cold water, so cold. A smooth glide to the bottom of the lake, where fish with eyes like dinner plates swam up to the glass windows of the coaches. Litovsky held out his arms, and he and Alice danced in the dining car, around and around the piano stacked with dirty dishes, and the solemn staring fish stared and stared, and he bent her back over the lid of the closed piano, among the greasy plates, and kissed her deeply.

May had come to see her. Alice was sure that she had. It couldn't have been a dream, because here was the proof: a tin of biscuits tied with a pink ribbon. Alice was imprisoned in a dreary London hospital, but May had come and May would rescue her. If she could bite just one biscuit, it would work like a spell: her aunt would appear by her side. But the nurse wouldn't allow it.

"Nothing. Not a thing but beef tea." And, no, she wouldn't take the biscuits and let Alice have the tin, because "What do you want with it? Just a picture of a dog. Now don't make a fuss, a big girl like you. Aren't you ashamed?"

...

"YOU MUST NOT be frightened of marriage, girls," lisped Miss Clusburtson. *Girlth.*

On Thursdays, Miss Clusburtson taught laws of health instead of maths, a supplementary course whose text was a book of drawings that made a body look like the cutaway of a passenger ship. A Deck. B Deck. C Deck. Steerage. *Lower abdomen,* pronounced by Miss Clusburtson as *ab-doe-man,* was the means of referring to the locus of any indelicate function. She handed out pamphlets for the girls to keep. Folded inside was a picture of an upside down woman, either that or a tree. It was both: the woman's ashamed face was hidden under the grass, her trunk diverged into two thick limbs topped by leafy feet. Between them, in the tree's crotch, was a nest of curly hair, and inside the nest an indistinct, vulval egg. Alice hid the pamphlet in her underclothes drawer. The picture had a distressing power, the way it buried the woman's head and left her private parts in the light.

"One of the teachers keeps telling us not to be afraid of marriage," Alice said to May.

"Does she really?"

"Yes. But I think she means *consummation.*" Alice whispered the word.

"Do you?" May said. She put her hand on Alice's hot head. Her voice was like water trickling. Alice touched her smooth silk knee.

"She took us on a trip to the cast courts." Halls filled with plaster casts of renowned statuary. There the *lower abdomens* of naked males were dressed in paper underclothes. "And some of the girls were terribly mean to her," Alice wept. What was it about a fever that made a person cry all the time?

"Oh, Lord," Claire had said. "Save us. It is deadly deadly beastly beastly deadly bloody dull in here. And there's no air. I'll die if we don't leave."

"Watch your pen, Claire. You're getting ink on my jumper," Alice had said.

"Bloody bloody beastly bloody dull!"

"Girls! Please!" *Pleathe!*

"There's dirty bas-reliefs in India," Claire said. "My father's seen them. It's disgraceful pictures of people lighting the lamp, all of them at once, men's things out of their trousers and the women with their knickers off." The class was dispersed around the cast of Trajan's Column: Roman soldiers marching wearily up and around in stripes, as on a barber's pole.

"What's lighting a lamp have to do with it?" Alice asked.

"What are you, the village idiot? It means *doing it.* Hindus think that if you get expert at copulation it's religious. That's why me and my sisters were sent home." A missionary's daughter, Claire was full of contempt for Christ and an astonishing authority on all things immoral. She wasn't supposed to be friends with unrepentant Jews. "But I don't care," she said.

"What do you mean, unrepentant?" Alice wanted to know.

"It means it doesn't matter to you whether or not you go to hell."

"But," Alice protested, "it does."

The girls walked double file, each holding a partner's hand, through plaster reproductions so faithful as to make the actual redundant, to ruin the real places later. Ghiberti's Gates of Paradise from the Baptistry of the Florence cathedral. A pulpit from Pisa, and a set of stairs ascending to nothing.

For whole long minutes they stood before the Pórtico de la Gloria from Santiago de Compostela, to which men in nightshirts were glued by their backs, all of them gripping musical instruments. None of their eyes were open, their faces were tipped heavenwards in sightless ecstasy. It looked like a music class for the blind or the backward. Below them, Christ held up his hands in a gesture of shock and dismay, just the way Mr. Samuel did when he heard Alice's faltering attacks on Ma Robey's old piano. Other men displaying scrolls and open books wore a look of malicious delight, as if anticipating all the poor marks on next week's history examination.

"This floor," said Miss Clusburtson suddenly. "I want you to look at this mosaic floor, girls. *Opus feminae.* Work of women. It was made by women inmates from the Woking prison."

"Thi*th* mo*th*aic opu*th* wa*th* ma*the* by inma*the*," Claire said, not so low that the teacher couldn't hear.

"*Don't,*" whispered Alice. "She can't help it."

Above them, Michelangelo's *David* towered, his groin obscured by brown paper, like something from the butcher shop. Claire thrust her chin forward in a manner that presaged aggression. "Mi*th* Cluth-ber*th*on," she said.

"Yes, Claire." *Yeth.*

"Why if you're always telling us not to be frightened of marriage aren't you married?"

Miss Clusburtson looked at Claire for a long moment before managing to speak. "You're speaking of my private life, Claire. It's not—"

"It's because of that, isn't it?" Claire jerked her head toward David's modestly wrapped genitalia. "You don't want relation*th* with men. I*th* you who*th* frightened."

Eleanor Clusburtson went pale and then flushed a deep red.

"You might," Claire said with a worldly, superior tilt of her head, "be an invert. A lizzie." The fourteen girls standing hand in hand around the statue began to laugh, most of them out of nerves more than amusement. Still, having begun they couldn't stop. They clung to one another, gasping.

Enflamed by the hysteria, Claire climbed onto the pedestal and pulled the paper from David's loins. "Well," she said, touching the un-circumcised tip of his plaster penis, "I thought it would be a bit more—well, just a bit more."

In the midst of what Miss Robeson called the most disgraceful chaos with which Robeson Academy had ever had the misfortune to be associated, Miss Clusburtson stood silent, unmoving, her hands at her sides.

Alice broke away from the group and grabbed Miss Clusburtson's frozen arm. "Please," she said. "I need you to take me to the W.C." She pulled, but it was as if Miss Clusburtson were cemented into the very mosaic she'd pointed out. "It's an emergency!" Alice pulled harder, and Miss Clusburtson came free and allowed herself to be dragged away from the rest of the class, still reeling under Claire on the pedestal.

Alice towed Miss Clusburtson around a cast of the Virgin drawing back from Gabriel in fastidious alarm, as if the angel had made a lewd suggestion, and tore past lesser saints and personages, all white white white, as if with shock, and none paler than Eleanor Clusburtson. Inside the washroom, Alice bolted the door and Miss Clusburtson fell against the sink, her hands covering her eyes, tears leaking out from below.

"Wash your face." Alice turned on the faucet. "Use cold water. Then we'll go back and you'll tell Claire she's to be expelled." But Miss Clusburtson didn't move, she went on weeping silently.

"Now," said Alice. "I hope you're not crying for Claire. She won't give a fig. She's been thrown out of dozens of schools." Alice tried to pry the thin hands from her teacher's eyes but gave up. "All right," she said, after a few more minutes. "You stay here. I'll check on the rest of them."

But when Alice returned to the statue of David she found him quite alone, his paper pants rumpled but restored. The hall was empty except for an ancient-looking scholar standing before Trajan's Column and making notes on a bit of parcel paper. "Pardon me, please," Alice said. "Have you seen a lot of girls?"

"Girls?" the man asked. "What sort?"

"Schoolgirls. About my size." The man shook his head.


"WELL, THEY'VE GONE," she reported to Miss Clusburtson, news that at last inspired the woman to remove her hands from her face.

"*Gone?* What can—What do you mean, *gone?*"

"I mean they aren't there, not one of them. They've . . . They must have left."

"Oh. Oh no no no." Miss Clusburtson swayed as she moaned. "No no no. She'll have me out on my ear. I've lost them, thirteen boarders. I'll go to prison."

"You'll make mosaics," Alice tried to joke. "Much nicer than school-teaching."

But Miss Clusburtson only shook her head. "What shall I do? Whatever shall I do?" she said over and over, wringing her hands and pacing and giving every sign of impending hysterics.

"Please don't," Alice begged. "It won't help a bit, crying won't. What we need to do is think. Tell you what, we'll have tea in that shop at the corner, the one we went past on the way." Miss Clusburtson stopped pacing and stared at Alice as if she were speaking another language. "It's all right," Alice said. "I'll pay. I always bring a bit of money, just in case. Something my aunt taught me." She patted the teacher's cold hand. "That and separate bank accounts. When you're married, I mean." Alice hooked her arm through Miss Clusburtson's, noting the sharpness of the elbow hidden by the gray sleeve. "We'll have a big tea," she said. "Food helps a person think."

But at the tearoom, Miss Clusburtson wilted over the steaming cups. "Now we've run away. We've run away. Away from the scene." Her scone grew cold; she didn't touch her tea.

"Don't be ridiculous. We've had an accident," Alice said.

"We have?"

"Definitely. We've . . ." Alice took the spoon from the jam jar and put it in her mouth, licked it clean, and replaced it. "I know." She leaned forward over the table, exhaling sweet fumes. "We'll tell Miss Robeson that I began to menstruate. Just today. For the first time. In the cast court."

Miss Clusburtson opened her eyes wide. "Did you?" she asked, looking newly terrified.

"No! That's what we're going to say. We'll tell her I was frightened and that I needed your help. The girls will back us up. They heard me say *emergency*, they saw us going to the water closet."

Miss Clusburtson shook her head. "She'll find out. She'll know we're lying."

"How?"

"She'll ask for proof, and we haven't any."

Alice folded her arms belligerently. "She'll demand bloody drawers? I'd like to see her try."

"You don't know Miss Robeson."

"We'll tell her I threw them away and came home without."

"Then she'll absolutely know we're lying."

"No! Listen! This is—I'm telling you, I mightn't be good at maths but I'm brilliantly clever at this sort of thing!"

Miss Clusburtson opened her mouth but nothing came out, so Alice had to accept astonishment in lieu of congratulation.

# THE CURE FOR LISPING

MOST OF ELEANOR CLUSBURTSON'S STUDENTS called her Miss Cluthburthon, not to be mean, but after her own example, and Eleanor never tried to correct anyone's pronunciation. How could she when her lisp was so pronounced, her mouth so uncooperative that she couldn't enunciate even the name her mother and father gave her?

She did have a brilliant, an exceptionally brilliant, mind, but wasn't this also a liability? Everyone knows intelligence is no guarantee of success, and why suffer more than a normally acute awareness of injustice? In 1887, when Eleanor was twenty years old, she was accepted to Oxford University, the only woman admitted to the study of higher mathematics. Her school examination results were so remarkable that, in the opinion of the dons, they excused Eleanor from her gender. The occasion was not one of celebration.

"How can I go!" she cried, and she threw herself into

her father's arms and just as quickly pulled out of them. "As soon as they hear me speak, they'll think me stupid!"

She wept, she tore up the letter of acceptance; she slammed the door to her bedroom and locked it when he tried to follow.

Isaac Clusburtson, widower and second violinist for the Philharmonic Society, sat at his desk in the drawing room of their small house on Cheyne Road. He held his head in his hands; he drank gin with bitters; he spoke solemnly to the tintype of his deceased wife, petitioning her advice for their daughter; and then composed a letter to Dr. Andrew Scott, whose notice he had seen in the December 8, 1885, issue of *Harper's Weekly*. Eleanor's father subscribed to a number of American publications, among them *Appleton's Journal, Popular Science Monthly,* and *Christian Union*. A man who considered America a land of reason, hygiene, and promise, Isaac Clusburtson often cut out advertisements that illustrated these virtues and saved them in the cabinet where he kept the gin.

Dr. Andrew Scott cured abnormalities of speech. *Don't allow a lisp or stutter to obstruct the course of fortune! Of profession! Of love!* read the message below a drawing of a beaming groom and shyly smiling bride. An address was printed at the bottom of the notice: 848 Broadway, New York City.

Isaac Clusburtson's penmanship was precise and anguished and sloped downwards on the page. It was his habit to include a narrow line underneath his signature. In writing the letter to Dr. Scott he added this emphasis with such force that twice he tore the page with his nib and had to begin again.

Within a month, Eleanor's matriculation had been postponed, a consultation with Dr. Scott of New York arranged, passage by steamship booked. Eleanor would travel with her father's older sister, the aunt who had often stepped in as surrogate mother and chaperone.

Delayed once, twice, and a third time by winter storms, the ship, Isambard Kingdom Brunel's iron-hulled *Great Britain*, arrived in New York harbor on 19 March 1889, Eleanor's twenty-second birthday. The crossing had made both women ill, and as soon as they disembarked and collected their luggage, they hired a cab to the Fifth Avenue Hotel, on Madison Square, thankful that Isaac had secured their accommodations in advance. At the hotel, they went immediately to bed.

The next day was the first of spring; outside their window a tree burst with early blossoms, its roots branching under a cab stand and fed by piles of horse dung. Dr. Scott, a handsome man of forty-odd years, received them in his well-appointed office. He served them tea; he fondled his fobs and his waistcoat buttons; he handed Eleanor a card on which fifty words were printed.

"Read them aloud," he said. "If you please."

And she began: *Adept. Ancillary. Bastion. Bakery. Celebrated. Candelabra.* She lisped through the entire alphabet.

"Ah," said Dr. Scott, pouring tea. He listened with his left ear cocked toward the young woman. "You see," he said, "so many speech problems are caused by teeth. Cured by their removal and replacement."

Eleanor looked at him. Unconsciously, she ran her tongue over the smooth surface of her incisors. Apart from a tendency to squint, she was a pretty enough young woman, her hair a dull blond, her features regular, if a bit small.

"My partner, Dr. Albert Boylan, is an expert in the science of dentistry." He stood and withdrew a card from the drawer in his desk. It was thick, creamy, the words it bore engraved. Under the name *Dr. Albert Boylan* was an address, 846 Broadway, New York.

"Yes, just one door down." Dr. Scott smiled. "He'll see you tomorrow, at two in the afternoon."

Eleanor and her aunt thanked him. They left his office and walked along Broadway through Ladies' Mile, where they purchased gloves and hats from a milliner by the name of Miss Marcy. They didn't speak of the consultation. They bought two black umbrellas with carved bone handles and a memorably good supper of spring lamb served with apple jelly, roast potatoes, and peas.

Eleanor's aunt spooned up the tiny green orbs. "Where do they get them so early?" she asked, and she ordered an extra portion from the obsequious waiter.

Back in the hotel, both women slept well. The next morning, neither could remember her dreams.

· · ·

DR. BOYLAN'S OFFICES were filled with the most modern American equipment. He pointed out the cast-metal chair with a reclining back that he could raise and lower by means of an ivory-handled crank, its red plush neck support, the red-and-turquoise pillow that padded the footrest. Eleanor looked at the silk fringes on the pillow. She ignored all the rest: the Whitcomb fountain spittoon that dispensed drinking water through the beak of a tiny brass swan perched over the basin, the foot-treadle drill, the complex arrangement of mirrors that reflected lamplight into the mouth of anyone lying in the chair. None of these impressed her. Eleanor looked at the fringes and told herself that nothing very terrible could happen to a person whose feet were resting on a red-and-turquoise silk cushion.

"Your lisp," Dr. Boylan said, "is caused by your front teeth. To cure it, we extract them. We teach you to speak without front teeth." He pressed his hands together, as if about to lead the women in prayer. "Then, when your new speech has been established—it ought not to take more than two months—we replace them with these." He opened a cabinet filled with little drawers, one of which held, on a blue velvet pad, two shining white porcelain teeth with gold posts.

Dr. Boylan pulled the drawer all the way out and offered it to Eleanor as if it were a gift. The teeth looked like jewels, like studs or cufflinks or earrings. When Eleanor hesitated to take the drawer, the dentist selected one of the false teeth and placed it in her palm.

"It's beautiful," she said softly. *Ith beautiful.*

"Yes," he agreed. From another, larger, drawer, contents jumbled, no velvet pad, he produced a handful of quite different teeth. "These are the natural ones I've replaced. Not so beautiful."

"No," she said, her voice a little faint. She and her aunt nodded silently over his album of testimonial letters from satisfied clients, many accompanied by smiling tintypes.

Eleanor looked up. "How much will it hurt?" she asked.

"Oh, my dear." Dr. Boylan's voice was unctuous, a melting pat of butter. "Not at all." He showed the women his ether inhaler, a glass globe with wadded cotton inside, a mouthpiece designed to hold the lips in a cold kiss. "We have both ether and a newer anesthesia, nitrous oxide. My colleague, Dr. Thomas Evans of Philadelphia—you've heard of him?"

Eleanor shook her head.

"No?" he said. "I *am* surprised. He's Napoleon's dentist. Charles, I mean. Charles Napoleon. Not the one who was exiled. Dr. Evans has emigrated to Paris and treats most of the royal families on the continent. It was he who pioneered the use of nitrous oxide, which has all the advantages of ether, but not so many of the disadvantages. No nausea. No headaches."

Dr. Boylan showed Eleanor a small pedal compressor attached to a rubber hose and mask. With his foot he pumped the pedal, put the mask over his nose and inhaled. When he spoke, his voice came out high, not so much like a woman's as like that of a music-hall actor impersonating a woman. "Affects the vocal cords," he explained. "Only temporarily," he added, noting Eleanor's look of alarm. He released a weird trill of laughter. "Wears off quickly!" He shook his head. "No longer use chloroform. Too dangerous. Colleague of mine. Most unfortunate. Had a young man succumb." Apparently, the gas had the effect of reducing a person's speech to fragments.

"Succumb?" Eleanor asked. *Thuckum?*

"Succumb?" her aunt echoed.

"Entirely." Dr. Boylan giggled.

Eleanor nodded. She squinted as though she'd gotten dust in her eyes.

"How do you make sure the new teeth stay in?" her aunt asked.

"Vulcanite plate. Very comfortable. Holds the posts." Dr. Boylan reached out and put his hand on Eleanor's chin. "Open, please," he said, and she did as she was told.

"Four teeth at most!" he proclaimed. "Maybe only two."

"Do you draw them all at once?" Eleanor managed to ask.

"No. By no means. One. Then another. Prevent shock."

ELEANOR AND HER aunt left Dr. Boylan's office and walked slowly to their hotel on Madison Square. En route they spoke little. Eleanor bought a copy of the *Evening Telegram*; they ordered dinner in their rooms. Over a meal of roast duck she read at table, a bad habit, but her aunt had pushed aside her plate and was writing letters. The front page included an inauspicious article about a jeweler who, having strangled two prostitutes, his housekeeper and her cat, now awaited his own end by means of an extermination device invented by a dentist. The dentist had tested it on horses and sheep. It was called an electric chair, but the horses hadn't sat in the chair, of course. The dentist put electrodes in their mouths and anuses.

Eleanor turned quickly to a feature on page three. An ornithologist had penetrated the aerie of an eagle and discovered its nest to be twenty-five feet in diameter. "Why," she said, standing and pacing the distance diagonally across the room, one corner to its opposite. "Why, that's almost as large as this room."

"Imagine," said her aunt.

THE NEXT MORNING, Dr. Boylan extracted Eleanor's right incisor while she lay in the clammy embrace of ether. Worried that nitrous oxide's tendency to trim a person's sentences might predict a similar abridgment of one's thoughts—or worse, one's capacity for thinking—she had refused the newer drug.

During the procedure Eleanor had a vision of herself plucked from the fancy dental chair by an eagle larger than she. Before the bird took her away, he measured her from head to foot with a gold tape he kept under his wing, and then he grasped her neck with his talons so that one curved claw penetrated her ear. She held the pretty cushion as the eagle carried her off, flying over wild and unfamiliar landscapes. As her legs swung beneath her, she saw rivers in the dodging space between her feet.

High above creation, Eleanor discovered the aerie's sticks were woven together in mysterious and unexpected patterns, like lace. In her new home she wore an apron and a nightcap with a tassel. Now a devoted bird wife, she cut up the rabbits and lambs the eagle carried home. Together Eleanor and the great bird of prey sat on the silk cushion in the round nest of black sticks and ate meat dripping with blood. Then they slept together, she under his black wing.

Suddenly, Eleanor was miserably awake, still holding the cushion. Dr. Boylan was shaking his head. "Most astonishing. Never happened before. I hadn't even begun when you picked it right up from under your feet." He shook his finger, as if at a naughty child, and gently withdrew the cushion from Eleanor's hands, plumped it briskly and replaced it on the footrest.

BEFORE ELEANOR REACHED the hotel, pain struck her abruptly in the face like a blow from a cudgel. She collapsed against her aunt in the cab and had to be carried from the street into the lobby, too faint to hold herself upright.

Taken to her room on the second floor, Eleanor lay on a couch, the hole in her mouth plugged with gauze: Laudanum did nothing. The torment she endured was so intense that it effected a revolution in her perception, such that all that had been true, real, and present before the extraction was now rendered false, unreal—banished by the black talons that now held her face tight. The one true thing in the world was pain.

Her aunt paced among the chairs and moaned with fear, while inside Eleanor's mouth the drop of arsenic routinely used by dentists to prevent infection seeped from the cotton gauze into the empty socket of her lost tooth. It reached upwards, into what Dr. Boylan could have identified as the *myrtiform fossa* of the *superior maxillary*. As it traveled, it killed bacteria, and bone cells as well. The death of the germs caused no discomfort to Eleanor. The death of part of her jaw inspired a baroque series of hallucinations in which the great black-feathered bird, once her affectionate husband, became enraged and slowly tore her face to bits.

Eleanor lay on the couch, panting slightly. Her aunt paced, paced, paced. Through the clerk downstairs she sent messages to Drs. Scott and Boylan, who replied that they made no calls; they saw patients in their offices only.

Eleanor's first sentence, a week later, was "I won't go back." Her second, that same day, "Pay them, and go to a booking agent to arrange our passage home."

The word *passage* revealed that the lisp, at least, was intact. *Pathage*.

Under the care of her aunt, Eleanor Clusburtson returned to England and, after a year's delay, to university, to a life of kind, elegant numbers, companions who required no conversation. If her fellow students thought of her at all it was not as stupid but as mute. Silently she attended lectures; mouth shut, she submitted her pages of proofs. She kept her head bent over equations; she kept house for her father.

In response to a letter from her father's solicitor, threatening a suit, she received from Dr. Boylan a single porcelain tooth on a gold post—nothing to hold it in place, as impressions had not been made. With her aunt she took the tooth to a London dentist, who fitted her for a vulcanite plate of a livid gingival red.

She never married; she had no children. After her father's bankruptcy (the result of answering, alas, another notice placed by a businessman no more scrupulous than Drs. Scott and Boylan), she accepted a position at Robeson Academy. There she willed herself deaf to insult, to hearing "Thmellinor" whispered after her in the halls. When Isaac Clusburtson died, she inherited nothing, as their house was owned by creditors; so she moved to the school, into a room half the size of Ma Robey's.

# DISCIPLINE FOR GIRLS

"**T**HERE'S THAT SOMEONE HERE TO VISIT YOU," said the nurse. "That very peculiar crippled female someone being pushed in a bath chair. And it's yellow trousers on her this time. You should see the looks she gets in the corridor."

"Who?" Alice asked. But of course she knew. So it hadn't been a dream. Her aunt *was* here, in London.

"I've told her she can only look through the glass, no sneaking past like yesterday, but she says she absolutely will come in. She's with the director of the hospital, and what he'll think of her I couldn't say."

And then, suddenly, May was there, in the isolation ward with her lacquered hair, her jade bracelets, and her silk jacket decorated all over with birds. And she was wearing silk trousers, beautiful, shiny, slippery, yellow silk trousers, and all of her smelled strongly of jasmine. Her tiny embroidered slippers were propped on the footrest of a bath chair. And Boy's brother was pushing her.

"Aunt May?" Alice reached out to touch the apparition.

"Alice," May said, smiling her red, red smile and getting out of the chair to kiss her.

"Oh!" Alice held tight to May's neck. "You're like a nice dream instead of a nasty one. Except I knew it wasn't a dream. You were here before. And you look so beautiful!" she added, rapturous. "Your hair is new. It's all up like a present in fancy paper."

May laughed. "Oh, dear, Alice. How we miss you! And Cecily, too, of course. It's terribly dull at home. No constables calling. No one running off with old soldiers."

Alice sat up. "Are you here, really?" she asked. "Are you real? What are you doing in that chair? You're not ill, are you, Aunt May?"

"Lie down," said the nurse, and Alice did. "Is this person a . . . a . . . I didn't think it was possible, when she said so yesterday. Surely you are not the relation of a Chinese!"

"Yes," said Alice. "I am. This is my aunt, Mrs. Arthur Cohen."

"I am absolutely well," said May, ignoring the nurse, whose mouth remained open in astonishment. "But London is a wasteland of no sedan chairs, not one truly, so I am having one assembled. Not so nice as home, but I won't be here forever, and meanwhile Boy or Brother Boy must push me on wheels. Nice for them as one can rest while the other works."

"You brought both boys with you? Are Mother and Daddy here, too?" Alice asked. "Where is Uncle Arthur?"

"Everyone is home in Shanghai. Arthur has given up on the wheelbarrow tax and is now attempting to prevent the transport of chickens by their wings." May rolled her eyes and flipped open a red silk fan. "A cook was had up last month in the mixed court for cruelly mistreating chickens—you smile but it is true. It was observed that the fowl were greatly distressed by inhumane transportation, and so now Arthur is afoot with chicken petitions. He means to re-educate all the cooks in China.

"Now, let me see if I can remember." May looked at the ceiling. "A chicken going to market must have its legs tied together, not too tightly, and be carried under the arm." She mimed the correct hold and laughed. "So now you know how to carry a chicken, Alice. I can't think why your father sends you to school when he could just set up Arthur with a pointer and a slate.

"I only just arrived and got settled in the hotel when up comes a boy with a tray and an envelope and inside a cable from your father saying you are ill and wouldn't I please see that you were convalescing properly. You can imagine the hysterics at home. They've probably had to pack poor Dolly in smelling salts.

"How are you? And who has made off with your hair, Alice? They say this fever is something to which children are subject."

"All right," Alice said. "They thought I might die but I haven't. I am bored, though."

"What? No mischief? You *must* be ill." May kissed Alice's hot forehead.

"Having you here, I feel fine. Do say you'll stay for a long visit!"

"A month at least," said May. "Your father gave me ship's passage to Europe, as I have never seen it." She looked at Alice and leaned forward, whispered conspiratorially. "I think he and Arthur think that away from home I will stop smoking." She laughed at the apparent absurdity of this; and even to Alice's stuffed nose she smelled as muskily of stale opium as ever. Although now, in the morning, her eyes were bright and mischievous. She must have gone back to taking only a bowl after dinner.

IN SHANGHAI, WHERE it was a challenge to find work for the abundance of servants, May kept an amah whose sole function was to procure and prepare her opium, to stoke her pipe with its long, ivory stem, to light it—to do everything in fact except smoke the drug and feel its effects, not all of which were pleasant. May suffered headaches and palpitations, irritability, nausea. She had a cough and was constipated and was in daily consultation with a Chinese apothecary, who supplied her with mysterious powders folded into colored papers, all of which May unfolded, sniffed at, and discarded without testing their efficacy.

In fact, after discussing the matter with Arthur, Dick Benjamin had booked May a first-class passage to London, but this was not to curb her use of opium. Having received word from Miss Robeson that Alice was ill, he didn't share the news with Dolly. Why, that was just the kind of thing to drive her mad. May would go to London in Dolly's stead, and perhaps the trip would do her good. Rescuing Alice might rouse her from the depression into which she had fallen: refusing food, lying curled on her chaise in her perpetually twilit sitting room, the drapes drawn until evening, sighing and sighing until he thought he'd go mad. Since his daughters' departure, Dick could hear May sigh through a brick wall. Two brick walls. It made no sense, but there it was, and to get her out of the house for a while would relieve his nerves of the sight of her moving through the halls with wan, arrested steps, and he'd get a break from the smell of her pipe. He wished he'd been able to send his brother-in-law, as well, but Arthur had himself been exhausted and bewildered by May's collapse. He worried that he was the cause of it—she'd been so impatient with him, and those clandestine trips to the solicitor. Dick had taken him aside; he had informed him—regretfully, he said—that May was looking for a child she had lost. He'd said this as if it might change things. Alter Arthur's feelings. But how? Why? May had a past. Dick might think him a fool, but of course Arthur knew his wife had a past. She never spoke of it, and he never asked. This was their tacit and affectionate, their respectful, understanding. Not that the news hadn't alarmed him—it had. Alarmed and injured. But that was him—not his feelings for May. His love remained intact, unassailable. Arthur thought the best thing for May might be to travel on her own. Surely he could survive two or three months of loneliness. They could write each other; they could cable.

Without his wife, however (this their first separation in all the years of their marriage), Arthur discovered he was useless: to himself, to chickens, to whatever or whomever he might think to rescue. If only he could think. But he couldn't concentrate on anything. Desperate for the cheap comfort of association, Arthur carried a pair of May's sleeping shoes with him. He kept an unlaundered binding cloth in his pocket so that he could bring it to his face like an immensely long handkerchief and inhale the smell of her.

"*Please,*" Dolly would moan. "Must you?"

Dick would wave his hand as he would to disperse fumes. "Get hold of yourself. You look so disreputable, like a squalid conjurer, with that . . . that dirty thing coming endlessly out of your coat!"

"OH, I DO miss everyone," Alice said. "It's wretched here! I want to go home!"

"Perhaps I shall take you back with me," May said, her voice placating. "I don't see the purpose of a school one detests, although your sister seems less miserable than you. You know, Alice, they are still worrying at home about the bad reports. I'm afraid your adventure on the train—well, *off* the train, to be more accurate—has thrown you under suspicion as a wild and unnatural child. And bad reports don't help."

Alice's eyebrows came together in one recalcitrant black line. "*They* worry, but you don't."

"Not at all." May smiled. "Quite the contrary. I'd worry if you liked boarding school. And of course, a bit of money does seem to have solved everything. Money is not the root of all evil. The English are so ridiculous in saying so. It fixes any number of unpleasantnesses."

ILLOGICAL. GARRULOUS. IMMODEST. *Clumsy. Giddy. Disruptive. Slovenly. Excitable. Unladylike. Unpunctual. Forgetful. Vulgar. Unreliable. Rude. Lazy. Impertinent. Careless. Dishonest. Nonsensical.*

The placards were kept in a box in Miss Robeson's study, each one clearly lettered in black and attached to a loop of string. Every Saturday, after tea, as the forty-six girls stood at attention, Miss Robeson reviewed the week's misbehaviors recorded in the black-bound book. On her left sat her mother, Ma Robey; on her right, Lovebird, her flatulent Pekingese, who accompanied her everywhere.

"Miss Benjamin."

"Yes, Miss Robeson."

"Immodest. Careless. Excitable. Disobedient. Disruptive. Giddy. Impertinent." Alice came forward and the headmistress hung the seven cards around her neck. "Most of our girls are specialists, Miss Benjamin. You seem to be a generalist. In the history of Robeson Academy no one has simultaneously cultivated so many forms of misconduct." The headmistress paused to stare.

"No, Miss Robeson," Alice said. Had Claire not been expelled so speedily, she might have accompanied Alice in disgrace. As it was, only her trunk remained, waiting in the hall for the address of the next school to which it would be shipped.

"Do you have nothing to say for yourself, Miss Benjamin?"

"No, Miss Robeson."

"An explanation, perhaps, for this unprecedented bestowing of placards?"

"I imagine, Miss Robeson, that it—that they all must have to do with the cast courts, ma'am."

"Do you, Miss Benjamin? What happened there? Tell us all, so that the few who missed out on the fun can share in it now."

"I left the group of girls, Miss Robeson."

"Why did you, Miss Benjamin?"

"To visit the water closet."

"Don't all the girls have that opportunity before leaving the school?"

"Yes, Miss Robeson."

"Were you taken suddenly ill, Miss Benjamin?"

"Uh, not exactly. I was . . . I was . . . It was a matter of laws of hygiene. Lower ab-dome-in-al." At the laughter of the other girls, Miss Robeson brought her hand down bang on the desk. Lovebird startled and farted.

The one thing Alice was learning at school was that her popularity increased in direct relation to her sins.

"Thank you, Miss Benjamin. That will be sufficient. You know your misbehavior has endangered the security of a person less fortunate than you. A person alone in the world, without a rich father."

"Yes, Miss Robeson." Alice flushed. She hadn't seen Miss Clusburtson since the museum trip, and this was because she had been suspended from her teaching position, demoted until the end of the term to tidying the schoolrooms and erasing equations chalked up by Mr. Samuels, who was teaching maths now, as well as music. It was he who'd come to the cast courts to collect the girls after they had been rounded up by a guard.

Miss Clusburtson retained her room and board but received no wages. As for the proof she said Miss Robeson would require, she'd been wrong; the question had never come up.

"Well, Miss Benjamin," Miss Robeson demanded, "what are you doing to reform your conduct?"

"I am wearing the placards my failings have earned me, and while I am wearing them I am thinking of ways to improve myself."

"And what might those ways be, Miss Benjamin?"

"I . . . I need more time to think, Miss Robeson."

"Well, Miss Benjamin, you shall have it."

Alice curtsied and stepped back from Miss Robeson's desk. "Thank you, ma'am."

All the following week, Alice wore the placards. All through breakfast, lessons, tea, and supper their cords chafed at her skin, and by the time she bent her head over her desk to write her weekly letter home—a missive both mandatory and censored, offering no chance to complain—the nape of her neck was raw and burning.

Ma Robey dictated sentences to include at the end of the letter: *I am afraid that I ran away this week, causing my headmistress much anxiety and trouble. I came to breakfast with a hole in my stocking and a stained collar. I lost my French text. I was rude to Mr. Samuels. But I will improve. Love, Alice.*

"OH," MAY SAID. "Before I forget, did you get your baths? Your father asked me to inquire about that as well."

Alice nodded. A warm bath every evening, for which Dick Benjamin had paid a surcharge, to ensure not only that she and Cecily got hot water, but that they shared it with no one but each other. The rest of the girls used the same cold water, and for the unlucky last girl it had turned gray and was scummed with soap and hairs. However, having been warmed by the bodies it had held, it was no longer so frigid.

May put her cool hands on Alice's hot cheeks. "Dearest, dearest," she said, "you're just not well. But you'll be better."

Alice slid half out of bed and onto May's lap. "What difference will that make! I'll always be myself! I'll always be restless and I'll always hate school! Everlasting rules and bells. I hate being told what to do every minute!"

May laughed. "You? You're going to be fine." She tried to pull Alice off her silk knees. "Now do as *I* say—you've never minded that. Lie down, and get stronger. I'll come back tomorrow with something nice from Fortnum and Mason. I saw towers of sweets in the window, a mountain of brown buns stuck together with gold syrup, little marzipan birds perched all over. Boy rolled me right past, but I was on my way here, so we had no time to stop." She stroked Alice's head, wound what remained of one curl around her white finger. "Do you know how I know you'll be fine?"

"How?"

"Because of your adventures."

Alice looked at her. "Getting off the train, you mean? The cast court?"

May nodded. Gently, she pulled her finger from the abbreviated corkscrew of hair, and it fell against Alice's cheek. She patted the ringlet. "How unlike Dolly you are," she said softly. "You're not your mother's daughter, you know. There's nothing of her in you." May began another curl, this one from the damp hair over Alice's forehead. "I think you're *mine*. You're the girl Rose would have been."

Alice looked at her aunt. Under the blanket she had Litovsky's coin, the little icon with her enigmatic, disappearing features. Alice had spent bored feverish hours rubbing her fingers over its surface, trying to discern the tiny convexities of the Virgin's face.

"Say the words," May said. "Say the words, *I'm yours*."

Alice hesitated. Then, "I'm yours," she whispered.

"As if you meant it."

"I'm yours," she said, more firmly.

May kissed her forehead, leaving the print of her painted red lips. "Of course you are, darling one. And not to worry—no one's feelings will be hurt. It's our secret, and no one will tell Dolly." She looked at Alice's overly bright eyes. "Why are you about to cry?"

Alice shook her head. "Nothing. Tired," she managed to say. Was she always going to be someone's dead daughter? But this was different, wasn't it? May was different. Different from the captain. From anyone. Still, a prickle of hurt indignation rubbed up against Alice's pleasure at being so wanted, and deflated it, a little.

"PLEASE COME BACK soon," said Alice, as May prepared to leave. "Promise you will."

"Yes," May said. "Tomorrow."

But as it happened, May did not return the next day or the one after that. Every hour Alice asked, "Has she come? Has my aunt come to see me? Did she leave word?"

And each time the nurse said, "No." She shook her head and pursed her lips. "She's the flighty type, that one. I could see right away. By the hair. The fingernails. And those trousers!"

Alice had fretted herself into a relapse before Miss Clusburtson came to deliver a note written in May's spiky, black, calligraphic hand. It was short, it said only that Alice shouldn't worry. Everything would be all right in a matter of days and then she would return.

"What does she mean?" Alice wrote on the reverse side of the page, and the nurse grudgingly took it to Miss Clusburtson waiting on the other side of the glass.

"A bit of trouble with the courts," Miss Clusburtson wrote back. "Your aunt is not familiar with London."

INSIDE FORTNUM AND Mason's, from the vantage of her newly built temporary London sedan chair, May had been selecting sweets to bring to Alice. The transportation was not so elegant as that to which she was accustomed; it was a walnut desk chair nailed to a ladder. The boys had constructed it themselves in the hotel, removing rungs from either end of the ladder to provide makeshift shafts for carrying the chair.

May had amassed three pounds of assorted sweets: marrons glacés, pralines, and nonpareils; marzipan in various shapes and colors, blue birds, yellow bunnies, pink flowers; toffees and brittles and divinities; Italian nougat with pistachios. Absorbed in picking out the candy, May had been oblivious to the crowd that had gathered around the shocking spectacle of an extravagantly dressed and exotically coifed Chinese woman perched on an astonishing conveyance carried by two small men wearing blue jackets and long pigtails. Now what was the world coming to when such a creature could be found in London's finest store!

"Hey!" called out a man in a black homburg.

May looked up from the glass display cases of sweets. "I beg your pardon?" she said.

"She's—She speaks English," spluttered a woman, and dropped her packages.

"Yes!" someone else cried, as if her fluency was not only unexpected but criminal.

The crowd, only momentarily curious and inclined toward indulgence, turned nasty and indignant. Why, wasn't May's face itself a kind of insolence? How dare she be so much more beautiful than English ladies!

"What d'you think you're doing!" demanded the man in the homburg.

"I am buying some sweets for my niece, who is in hospital. But I can't see that it's any business of yours."

"Have you ever heard such cheek!"

"Preposterous!"

"Get down off of there!"

"I don't know what heathen hell you've come from, but you can't go about on a contraption like that with, with slaves to carry you!"

"No, she cannot! She certainly cannot!"

In the midst of the growing discord, someone jostled Brother Boy, who stumbled sideways into a display of Walker's shortbread. The pyramid of red tins went over with a clatter.

"Call a constable, someone!"

"Quick! Don't let her escape!"

"Now that's enough!" the shopgirl wailed. "Every last piece will be crumbs!"

"Well, whose fault is that! Carried into a respectable establishment on a ladder!"

Then, someone pushed Boy, a tower of jars of lemon curd went over, a shard of glass stuck in Boy's shin, and a constable did come. He took May, her chair, and both boys away.

"She's not in any trouble, is she?" Alice wrote to Miss Clusburtson.

"Not exactly," Miss Clusburtson replied. "But she's having a bit of inconvenience. Her chair's been impounded and she's not allowed to have her boys carry her. She's not allowed to leave her hotel."

# TEN-IN-ONE

ONE HUNDRED THOUSAND AND SIXTEEN PEOple read the *Daily Mail* on 10 February 1914, and had she cared, May would have had the satisfaction of knowing that after only a week in the most important city in the world she was already famous to many of its inhabitants as an "exotic singsong girl," and a "celestial slave-owner." As it happened, though, Alice's aunt did not buy the paper, and as the staff of Claridge's was professionally uninterested in all of the hotel's guests, only two representatives of May's new public announced themselves to her.

The first was an American named Terrence Lown, whose outsized calling card included the title Theatrical Producer. He left this card with the hotel concierge, along with an invitation for May to meet him that afternoon at four in the hotel's ground-floor tearoom.

"Where are the boys?" he asked, looking disappointed as May approached the table alone and slowly, on her own feet.

"I beg your pardon?" she answered, standing, waiting for him to pull out her chair. It took a moment before he understood, and then he jumped quickly to his feet.

"I guess they're just for outdoors? Shopping, et cetera." He pushed in her chair, a little too tightly, she had to wriggle it backwards from the table.

"Ah, the Fortnum Mason *débâcle*," May said.

"Do you speak French?"

"*Naturellement.*" May felt that already she disliked this man. Well, what can you have been thinking, she chided herself, *theatrical producer*, and an American! "How did you hear about the riot?" she asked coolly.

Mr. Lown looked astonished. "Didn't you see the papers?"

"No."

Mr. Lown moved aside the tiered tray of sandwiches so that he could look directly into May's eyes as he offered to take her back with him to the United States. In New York she would complete his Ten-in-One, comprising (1) a fat lady, (2) a bearded lady, (3) the Living Skeleton, (4) Hortence, the three-legged, fifteen-toed woman, (5) Alligator Boy, (6) a midget, (7) Celine, the sword swallower, (8) a snake charmer, and (9) Jaganathan, an Indian Hindu born without hands or feet and aged thirty-five years who spoke and wrote seventeen foreign languages. Lown wanted both May and her boys; he would build a golden chair for them to carry her in.

"I'll give you a title. Royalty, whatever you like. Princess. Queen. Queen Consort—is that one? Empress of Asia—"

"But what do I want with snake charmers and handless polyglots?" May interrupted. "I have a home. I have a husband."

"What's he like?" Lown asked.

"I beg your pardon. What can you mean?"

"Is he like you? Are his feet like yours?"

"Certainly not. He's . . . He has big feet."

"He's not Caucasian, is he?" said Lown.

"Yes," May said. "He is."

"Oh." Mr. Lown sighed. "We don't need that. People won't like that."

"No," May agreed. "They often don't. But, truly, Mr. Lown, this is not the sort of offer I'd be likely to—"

"Will you excuse me a moment?" Mr. Lown said, and he retreated in the direction of the water closet.

After twenty minutes, during which he had not returned and May had overseen the replacement of the sandwiches by a platter of petits fours, she asked the waiter to please charge the tea to her account and to be so kind as to provide her with pen and paper. He peered with suspicion at the black characters flowing up and down from the nib, then picked up the missive gingerly, as if it might be instructions for assembling explosives.

"Please." May smiled. "If you would ask the concierge to deliver this to my suite of rooms."

He bowed, the concierge complied, and within minutes Boy and his sweet-toothed brother had come down for cake, their long braids swaying behind them, reaching to the backs of their blue-trousered knees.

THE OTHER READER of the *Daily Mail* was Miss Robeson, who, alerted to the article by a complaint from a parent, discussed the matter of the Benjamin girls with her mother. She paced five times around her parlor, her Pekingese trotting nervously after, getting underfoot and tearing the lace on her petticoat.

The Fortnum and Mason incident, it was the last straw, it confirmed every fear she had about the Benjamin sisters, especially the younger one. Hot baths, Alice's inability to remain in her own bed— these had proved rather lucrative concessions, occasions for delicate extortion—but riots caused by foreign women dressed as courtesans were another matter entirely. If other parents heard of the wanton Oriental aunt (and they would, they would, it was not a matter of *if* but *when*), they would withdraw their daughters from Robeson Academy. Miss Robeson and her aging mother would be left in the lurch: high, dry, and penniless.

She promised the distraught parent that the situation would be rectified immediately and instructed Miss Clusburtson to pack the sisters' belongings back into their two blue steamer trunks and deliver them, along with Cecily, to the impossible aunt at Claridge's, where both of them could await Alice's convalescence. Or they could go up hill and down dale in a wheelbarrow, for all she cared.

She wrote a diplomatic letter (such communications were one of her talents) to Mr. Dick Benjamin, who received it two and a half weeks later in Shanghai and held his head in his hands.

"Now, I ask you, who besides Arthur's wife could cause such a scandal!" He refolded the newspaper clipping that accompanied his daughters' expulsion from Robeson Academy and passed it across the table to Dolly, who read it and lapsed into a long silence.

"Well," she said at last, "you had better cable May to bring the girls home posthaste. It's a shame she can't be trusted to engage a good governess as long as she's there."

## JUSTICE SERVED

THE JUDGE, IN HIS SWEEPING BLACK ROBE AND
white wig, looked as exotic to the defendant as she did to
him. It was cold in the London courthouse. May had unfastened but not removed her fuchsia coat lined with
white fur. Beneath it she wore a silk jacket and trousers
of emerald green. Jeweled combs glinted from her shining black hair. Standing in the somber room, she gave
the impression of a riotous flower that had magically
sprung up between paving stones.

Mr. Justice Burns-Barrow cleared his throat. "This is
a country, Madame May—"

"My name is Mrs. Arthur Cohen."

"—a country, Mrs. Arthur Cohen, in which there is no
enforced servitude."

May nodded soberly. "I think that is well," she said.

"How, then, do you explain these young men?"

Boy and Brother Boy, their braids hanging limp below
the hems of their jackets like the tails of reprimanded

dogs, stood before the bench. One on either side of May, they sneezed: first Boy, then Brother Boy, back and forth with a regularity that seemed suspect, intentionally disrespectful.

"They carry my chair," May said.

"Why? Why do they carry you?"

"Because I cannot walk on feet like these." May slid one toe forward and lifted her trouser leg enough to reveal a pointed, fuchsia silk shoe. "My feet are—well, they are quite impractical for walking. Especially in so big a city as London."

"But you don't pay them," the judge said. "According to the report of the constable, Mr. Barrington, they are not hired but *owned*. Beyond that offense, with the help of these slaves you incited a brawl in Fortnum and Mason's department store on Knightsbridge Road—"

"I did no such thing." May's voice took on a falsely sweet, unmistakable edge of anger. "I was shopping when a crowd of rude, staring, uncivilized louts converged on my chair. They shoved the boys. They toppled a tower of biscuits and preserves, and I've had to pay the bill. As well as seek medical attention for Boy, whose leg was lacerated by a shard of jam pot. It all came to seventy-three pounds, two shillings, and some pence."

"But you don't pay your, your *bearers*. Is that what they are?"

"I beg your pardon," May said haughtily. "I am keeping my sedan chair boys at Claridge's Hotel in a well-appointed room—nothing so vulgar as a bridal suite but accommodations whose tariff, I can assure you, is not inconsiderable. Two beds and two desks they won't use. Boy sleeps in the bath tub and Brother Boy on the floor beside the heating contraption. And I feed them, of course, whatever they like. Breakfast, lunch, tea, dinner, and I'm sure you'd be astonished by the quantities of ginger biscuits and toffees between times.

"I'd come straight to Fortnum and Mason's from Liberty's, where I'd purchased wadding and wool. It is very cold here; the boys aren't used to this weather and if they get ill, I am immobilized. You hear for yourself what the chill does to them." She paused. The sneezing continued. The judge's mouth remained open, as if he might suffer from adenoids and have trouble drawing air in through his nostrils.

"I thought about marten and went to a furrier on Bond Street, but

I discussed the matter with another lady shopping there, a Mrs. Tidwell or Tidbit, something to that effect. She was very kind and said fur was not in the best of taste for servants. It is awfully dear and maybe not appropriate. Claridge's has been helpful in recommending a seamstress to make up the wadding and wool into heavy jackets. This trip is turning out to be much more costly than I anticipated and my brother-in-law—"

"All of this is entirely beside the point!" The judge felt for his gavel, lost under papers, and, impatient, ended by pounding his fist on the bench.

"Excuse me," May said, managing to look genuinely contrite. "I'm not sure what the point is." She smiled with an innocence so dazzling, so seemingly genuine and absolute, it couldn't have failed to strike the judge as practiced, insolent.

"None of this has to do with your enslaving two men!"

"Of course it doesn't," May said. "And that is because I am doing no such thing."

"They are carrying you in a chair and all of you are going about inciting unrest and outrage. And this"—the judge had grown quite red under his white wig—"*is because England has no slave class.*"

"There are many failings of which I may be justly accused." May paused here; she frowned a slightly theatrical frown that suggested she might be privately tallying her past crimes. "But slave owning is not one of those. I am a woman with feet too small to walk about on. And"—May drew a deep breath. Was this to be a long speech?—"let me say that England may have no slave class, but I have lived in her treaty port of Shanghai for all of my life as a grown woman, and slavery would be far more kind than—"

"Mrs. Cohen! You have been brought before the court of assizes, the Crown against Mrs. Arthur Cohen, because—"

"So it isn't only the populace that is against me but the Crown as well? I have to say—"

But the judge had risen, he was shaking his head, he was waving his gavel, he was holding his side as if he had a sudden pain. "Case dismissed," he bellowed.

. . .

"I FEEL RATHER sorry for that Miss Cuthburtson," May said to Cecily and Alice, all of them living at Claridge's in the remaining weeks before they embarked on the passage home. "Clus—, Cuth—, what is her name?"

"Clus-burt-son," Cecily said. "But she can't pronounce it."

"I do, too," Alice said. "Feel sorry. She's sad. And she hasn't any family at all."

"And so ugly." Cecily shook her head.

"She can't help her looks," said May. "A new hairstyle would help."

"Not enough."

"Cecily," May said. "Your challenge in life will be to learn charity."

"What about me?" Alice asked. "What's mine?"

"To sit still," May answered. "Thirteen is too old to fidget. Why don't we take her home with us?" she said, returning to the subject of Miss Clusburtson.

"What? To Shanghai?" Cecily, sitting cross-legged on the vanity to get as close as she could to the mirror, stopped what she was doing—applying cream bleach to the almost invisible down over her pretty lip—and turned around to stare at May.

"Why not? I know you don't want to go back to the Shanghai Jewish school, and all the girls from the public school are such prigs. I can manage languages and history. Piano and dance from that ridiculous woman around the corner, on Weihaiwei, and there are always advertisements for instruction in deportment and elocution. But you will need a teacher of mathematics. No one except your father is any good with sums, and he works all day." May smiled. She clasped her hands together in a gesture of self-congratulation. "Yes," she said, "I think I'll invite her. If I come home with a teacher, then Dick won't be so angry. Don't you think?"

Alice and Cecily said nothing. The idea of Miss Clusburtson in China was too revolutionary to respond to as anything other than a joke. The sisters began to laugh, one's mirth inciting the other's, until even Cecily was gasping and rolling on the bed.

"Stop! Stop!" Alice panted. "Look what you've done!" For there were white spots on her blue jumper, and on the coverlet as well, where the usually immaculate Cecily had splattered bleach from the open jar still clutched in her hand.

The next day, a Sunday, May left the sisters with Boy and Brother Boy and went to see Miss Clusburtson, in her little room at the top of the school. The ceiling sloped steeply, and the window looked out on broken chimney pots.

"Tea?" Miss Clusburtson offered. She wrung her hands in anxiety at the idea of having so inopportune a guest. Miss Robeson didn't allow teachers to entertain, except on Saturday afternoons, and only downstairs in the parlor. And no one had ever had a visitor of such a criminally colorful and exotic demeanor.

May looked around the dingy, dispiriting room and at its pale occupant. Eleanor's hair was down, her collar unfastened. She looked a good deal less unattractive than usual. "So," May began. "I am taking the girls home to China, and I'm thinking that perhaps you will come with us."

"I'm sorry?" Miss Clusburtson said. "I don't understand."

"Are you happy?" May asked.

"Am I— I don't— I must have misheard you."

"Are you happy? Here, I mean, at this, this school."

"Well, I am— I'm afraid I still don't understand." Eleanor Clusburtson sat suddenly down on her tightly tucked bed, her eyes brimming.

May shook her head. "I don't think you are," she said.

"I'm not . . . I've never put too high a premium on happiness." Eleanor held her head straight to prevent what happened anyway, the spill of tears.

"That's wise, of course. In the Orient you could smoke opium."

"Oh, no. I don't think so." Miss Clusburtson wiped her cheek with the back of her hand.

"Certainly you could. I do." May reached out and patted Eleanor's shoulder. "It doesn't make one happy, but it makes unhappiness irrelevant. How old are you?" she asked.

"I . . . I was born in eighteen sixty-seven."

"Oh, dear. Forty-seven. You've wasted far too much time already."

"I . . . I . . ." Eleanor didn't finish, alarmed by a sudden knocking. The door knob rattled.

"Miss Clusburtson!" came an angry voice. "Have you—I cannot believe you have the impertinence to lock your door!"

"Dear God," Eleanor gasped. "Miss Robeson."

"Really?" May said. "I am curious to see her."

"If she catches you here, she'll dismiss me. I'm already in trouble with her." Eleanor clasped her thin hands before her chest as if in supplication.

"Do you think she would?"

Eleanor nodded vehemently. "Without pay," she whispered.

The door rattled violently against the jamb. "Miss Clusburtson!" boomed the voice of Miss Robeson.

"Yes?" Eleanor said, weakly.

"I want a word with you."

"Now?"

"Immediately! If it's not *too* inconvenient." The voice exuded ominous sarcasm, and the door shook again in its frame. "You know that locking the rooms is not allowed!"

Eleanor opened the door and stepped back.

"Well!" said Miss Robeson, staring at May. "I am shocked, I am dismayed. I am, I am very nearly speechless." And Lovebird, his watery, protuberant eyes rolling in sympathetic astonishment, whined and trolled around the indignantly swaying circumference of his mistress's long skirt.

# DOLLY CLEANS HOUSE

THE FIRST OF ITS KIND IN SHANGHAI, HAVING been installed in 1915, the Otis escalator in Weeks and Company had become not so much a means of getting from one floor to another as a destination in itself. It was so crowded with onlookers, mostly foreigners or wealthy Chinese, that the department store had been forced to cordon off a path for those who wanted to actually step onto or dismount from the gnashing wood stairs.

Though she usually despised anything popular, May couldn't help being fascinated by the escalator. The promise of anything modern that might deliver her swiftly, without her having to move her useless feet, beckoned; and like the superstitious rickshaw men, as she passed, she stroked her fingers over the brass nameplate on its paneled side. At dinner she entertained the family with stories about the Otis. On the third day after its installation, as the last stair disappeared into the floor, it drew the long hem of a woman's dress down into the grinding machinery below. The woman's skirt and even her petticoat had been torn from her body before store personnel could turn off the escalator. She'd fainted, of course, and now fainting was a routine occurrence on the ride from the street level up to the first floor, a kind of litmus test for feminine delicacy.

Then, even as ladies swooned, one of the city's innumerable religious zealots seized upon the endless cycle of stairs as a perfect illustration for his hybrid creed of Taoist reincarnation. He stood on Nanking Road distributing pamphlets that included meticulous, annotated illustrations of the escalator, its illusory hierarchy of stairs going tirelessly around and around as the perfect representation of the karmic cycle of destiny. "The way that can be walked is not the eternal way!" he cried until he was hoarse. He was arrested routinely but always returned.

Alice and May stood in Comestibles and watched the stream of brave enthusiasts ascend to Millinery. "Let's give it a go," Alice said.

May clapped her hands together. And so they rode up and up and up, fourteen times from bonbons and lemon curd to spring hats trimmed with ribbons, descending each time in the old elevator, its rope pulleys manned by Chinese dressed like organ grinders' monkeys, in red jackets and red pillbox hats. When at last they'd had enough, they joined Cecily and the sisters' mother on the third floor, where they were shopping for a runner for the upstairs hallway.

It was late spring and everything in the house—everything except the windows and the mirrors—had been host to a delicate lilac-colored bloom of mildew. For days the amahs and coolies had been scrubbing. They'd pulled up the carpets, beat them and soaked the stains in lemon juice; they'd scrubbed the floors and all the woodwork with vinegar; they'd bleached the curtains and poured lye down the drains. Only the upstairs runner had stubbornly refused to come clean. In fact, immersed in lemon juice, the spots turned from lavender to purple to black.

"Why not a darker color?" May said, as the carpet salesman brought another stack of cream samples. "Much less trouble." She fanned herself, perspiring from the excitement of the escalator rides.

"But, May, dear, how would I know if it was dirty?" Dolly protested.

"Exactly," May said.

The two women looked at each other and, in a rare moment of sympathy, laughed. Cecily leaned against a stack of rolled Persian rugs and languidly turned the pages of her book.

"Let's go," Alice said, pacing among broadlooms and moquettes, rugs hooked, woven, and tapestried. "Can't we go? It's teatime."

OUTSIDE, ON THE sidewalk, Alice had been looking at the leper for some time before she recognized him as a person. She wasn't staring; she was too well-brought-up for that. Like all Shanghailanders, she'd long ago learned not to see bodies in the street. She was pondering what she thought was a heap of old carpets. Why, everyone in Shanghai must be house cleaning, she was thinking, when the ragged bundle suddenly stretched and stood and looked straight at her mother.

Quickly, Alice looked away, but then the leper was before her eyes again; he was lurching toward them, toward her mother. "Dollars," he said, using a word that even the most illiterate Chinese knew. Her mother looked away. "No can do?" he said. "Touchee!" And he reached his terrible hand out from under the stained rug he had pulled around him. He had three lumpy fingers, no thumb. Dolly Benjamin walked backwards, silent, white-faced, fumbling with the catch of her purse. The leper advanced.

"Touchee," he promised. "Touchee." His voice—either it was very low or it was weak, almost a whisper.

"How dare you!" May stepped between the leper and Alice's mother. "I'll call a constable. You'll be arrested immediately." Her Chinese, which she translated for them afterward, was louder than her English. Alice rarely heard May speak her native tongue. Loud and hard and heavy, like a heap of stones falling off the back of a wheelbarrow, the words seemed to come from a source other than her delicate, silk-clad aunt. The leper dropped his hand.

"How dare you!" she said again, and she threw a handful of coins onto the pavement, so that he was forced to crawl in order to pick them up.

Alice held her breath, waiting for her mother's hysterics, and saw with surprise that Dolly, smiling pleasantly, had turned to the white-gloved doorman of Weeks and Company to ask him to hail a rickshaw. On the ride home she said nothing of the incident, but returned to the subject of the hall carpet. "You don't think it was rather too yellow a beige?" she asked.

"Not at all," May said.

"No." Alice and her aunt looked at each other, raised their eyebrows, shrugged.

"Well, I suppose the wallpaper does have some yellow in it. I wish I'd had a bit of it to take and compare, though. I can't imagine what did happen to that extra roll." Dolly fidgeted against the seat back.

Once they were home, the evening proceeded smoothly, without any mention of the afternoon's incidents.

The following night, however, during dinner, Dolly asked, "What is that dreadful smell?"

"What smell?" Cecily said.

"Surely you smell it?" her mother asked.

"No."

Dolly looked at the rest of them sitting around the table: Dick, Alice, Arthur, May, Eleanor. "I've smelled it all day," she said.

"What's it like?" Alice pulled the steamy, moist middle out of a second roll, ate it, and left the husk on the edge of her plate.

"Nasty. Like something rotting, but not exactly. More like something . . . I don't know."

"Dead mouse in the heat duct?" said Arthur.

"Much nastier than that."

"Oh, how shall I put this? . . . A plumbing smell?" May tried.

"No."

"Dolly." Dick sighed as he buttered Alice's discarded crusts.

"I'm telling you!" Dolly stood. "I've smelled it all day. It's worse in certain spots—the upstairs library and the hall outside the water closet, but not the closet itself," she added, looking at May. "The telephone room, quite distinctly. And it was strongest at teatime, but then it got better, and now it's worse. You must have noticed it, all of you? One of you!"

She picked up the bell and rang for Number Four, who came in expecting to clear the table. "No," she said, and Number Four put down the plate he had picked up.

"Big Missy?" he said.

"Number Four, do you smell a bad smell?"

He looked at her silently, then said, "Big Missy smell bad?"

"Yes," she said. "Don't you?"

"Yes," he said, nodding in relief, having discovered the right answer.

"Obviously he's only saying so because he thinks he's supposed to!" said Dick. "Aren't you?"

The man looked uncertainly back and forth between his employers.

"Get Amah and Dah Su. Get all the boys and all the amahs," Dolly said.

By dessert, the whole staff was crowded around the table, Dah Su and Cook Boy and Second Cook Boy, houseboys numbers one, two, three, four, five, six, seven, amahs and under-amahs, even the little nightsoil boy, whose job it was to empty the chamber pots from the servants' quarters, separate from the main house. Dick and Arthur drank their port, Eleanor folded her blue-veined hands in front of her coffee, which was growing cold, and May held her head as if she couldn't wait a minute longer to have her pipe. Cecily and Alice watched their mother.

Dolly went from servant to servant. "Do you smell a bad smell?" she asked, pantomiming a deep intake of breath through her nose, followed by a grimace of disgust. And each of them, once he or she understood that she wanted them to agree, nodded. "Yes, Big Missy. Yes."

"See!" she said.

The next day, Dolly began her campaign to eradicate the smell. She forbade May to smoke, saying that the smell of opium confused matters; it masked "the offending—" She stopped midsentence, searching for a word.

"Effluvia?" May suggested.

"Yes. The, the whatever it is. It stinks like a *kong*. It's getting worse every hour."

"But, Dolly—" May said.

"Don't tell me there is no smell! How can you, when your nose is ruined with drugs!"

"Dear, my nose is not ruined. Now—"

"I'm telling you, May. If you want to smoke, you'll have to go out."

"She's wild on the topic!" May complained to Arthur that night. "She told me, well, what she said—she might as well have—was that I should smoke in a den! Can you believe it? Throwing me out into the street!"

"Darling," said Arthur. "She didn't throw you out. She asked that you stop smoking in the house, just until the smell is cured."

"Arthur! There is no smell! Have you left your sense as well?"

"Taken leave of."

"What!" May's usually faultless grammar broke down, as it did only during moments of extreme agitation.

"The expression is to take leave of one's senses."

"I'm not having one of your syntax lessons. Your sister has lost her tiles."

"Marbles."

"Arthur!"

"Be logical, love." Arthur came up behind May and put his arms around her; he pressed his lips into the nape of her neck as he spoke. "Why would an English idiom make reference to mah-jongg? Dolly has always been like this. She'll get over it."

"I'm sure she will, but what about us!" May pulled out of his embrace, refusing to be cajoled out of her temper.

Happy to be elsewhere, Dick moved himself to the Astor House, just three blocks from his office. Alice and Cecily went to stay with friends in the neighborhood. And as for Arthur, May, and Eleanor, they were left at home with Dolly and the servants, unwillingly drafted into the war against the smell.

"Did you know," said Arthur, sitting in the garden in his overcoat and drinking tea, "that the drivers of *kongs* from the Settlement charge farmers twice as much for their, uh, cargo?"

"Why?" asked Alice, who had come to see what progress had been made in her absence.

On the damp lawn, which was spread with oilcloths, stood the contents of the house. Seventeen rooms' worth of furniture, all being rubbed with lemon oil and buffed with flannel. Stacks of dishes, trays of glassware, racks of dresses, pairs of shoes set side by side, as if a chorus line, invisible except for its footwear, stood waiting to perform.

Inside, carpets, newly washed, were taken up and washed again. Scrubbed floors were being swabbed with cologne, cabinets scoured with soda, washed walls repapered.

"Because farmers consider that our waste makes for premium fertilizer. Owing to our rich diet."

"Arthur, please!" Dolly bustled out onto the lawn with a line of amahs in her wake. She directed them as they stacked books from the empty library shelves.

"Well, it's all this talk of sewer gases and muddy river smells that puts me in mind of such things," said Arthur. "I was speaking with a gentleman who works for the—"

"Once a smell gets inside a book, can it be aired out, do you think?" Dolly asked, fanning the leaves of a collection of essays under her nose. "This one decidedly stinks." She looked at Arthur, who didn't answer, and at Alice, who shrugged. "Oh, well." She set the book apart from the rest and sat down to preside over tea, laid on the displaced dining table.

"We'll throw away the ones that won't air out. Or donate them to the library at the club. Eventually all those cigars will fumigate them."

"So, Mother," said Alice, opening a cress sandwich to see how thickly the butter had been spread, "is it gone now, do you think?"

Dolly looked up from the sugar bowl. She held a pair of silver sugar tongs in her hand; they gleamed dully in the cloudy afternoon's light. Over her head, the wisteria was in full bloom. "No," she said. "It isn't. But do you know, I dined with your father and Eleanor at the hotel and I couldn't eat, I smelled it so clearly. And it was in Weeks and Company, and yesterday I noticed it's in the synagogue as well."

Alice looked away from her mother. With her fingers she withdrew one lump of sugar from the bowl and held it just at the surface of her tea, watching as the liquid reached up into the cube and dissolved it.

· · ·

"IT'S SHANGHAI," DOLLY said at last, defeated.

The family were all assembled in the parlor of the disinfected house, a room that smelled to everyone but Dolly of soaps and lemon oil and cologne. "It's Shanghai that smells. The city or the earth underneath it. The river. I can't think why I never noticed before, it's so strong." No one said anything. Dolly fell heavily into her chair.

"Australia is clean. And dry. Everything is lovely and dry. Australia smells of eucalyptus." She began to weep. "A eucalyptus would never grow in a dirty place like this. They don't like dirty, damp places. This—Shanghai is nothing but a moldy, wet, filthy marsh. A swamp. And the floors are all crooked! Slanted, I mean. The house is sinking into the ground. I dropped my ring and it rolled and rolled. In the kitchen an egg will gather enough speed to break against the opposite wall." She looked around at all of them.

"But, Mrs. Benjamin, think of the laundry," Eleanor said encouragingly.

"Yes, Mother," Cecily said. "Smell your dress!"

Dolly pressed her nose into her sleeve. "That does help a little."

In the midst of the cleaning and recarpeting, the scrubbing and whitewashing and repainting, all of which had taken a month, Dolly had consulted a number of local authorities, one of whom had suggested the Kobe-Shanghai laundry boat. A small steamer picked up soiled clothes and linen on a Monday and returned them the following week. It took eight days, but it was worth it. The tailor sewed Benjamin labels to every item, to every sock and vest, to knickers and bust bodices, even to May's binding cloths. It all went off and the next week came back white as white, and folded with merciless precision.

# CIRCUMNAVIGATION

W HAT ENDED AS HABIT HAD BEGUN BY CHANCE. Alice and Evlanoff had returned to his flat in the midst of their first quarrel, a stupid one: looking for the restaurant where they'd planned to have dinner, they'd lost their way.

"You never get addresses right," he'd said. "You never do. You don't bother."

"Yes, I do."

"No. Obviously you don't."

"Is it hunger that's making you so cross?" Alice had stopped walking to face him. She was talking loudly, her hands on her hips. She didn't care about making scenes; in fact, the presence of a potential audience encouraged her to raise her voice.

"No." Evlanoff cared very much about avoiding scenes, and the even, low tone of his voice was a measure of his irritation. "I'm just saying that details like street numbers are the sort of thing you can't be bothered about. It's part of your slapdash relationship to life."

"Slapdash?"

"Yes. Careless, if you prefer."

They returned to his room without having eaten. He stood at the window, arms folded, staring out. After Alice tired of sitting on his bed, fidgeting and sighing and rattling the pages of a magazine, she got up and stood behind him. Saying nothing, she rested her cheek between his shoulder blades. When he stepped back from the window and turned, she stepped back with him, her arms around his waist. He walked to the bookcase to lay his wristwatch and cufflinks on its top; she followed, arms still locked around his ribs; then together to the closet where he used the toe of one shoe to push down the heel of the other and kicked them both in.

They kept walking. "Why is it like this, anyway?" Alice asked on the first lap around the big, unmade bed.

"Like what?" Evlanoff said.

"Bed in the middle." Her voice was muffled against his back.

"It's as it was when I moved in."

"You never thought of moving it so that the headboard was against a wall?" The apartment was an almost perfect square and had a sink and mirror but no private bath or water closet. It was furnished with bed, bookcase, desk, two chairs and a wobbly drop-leaf table. Of these, all except the bed were pushed tightly against the wall. The bed sat in the center of the room, a margin of five or six feet on all sides.

Evlanoff walked, she followed, moving her feet in step with his, the occasional stumble, breasts and stomach tight against his back. "No," he said.

"Really not?"

"Is that so odd?"

Alice shifted from walking with her feet apart, outside of his, to short quick steps following his longer stride. Too awkward; she switched back. They'd circled the bed a half dozen times and still hadn't found a rhythm. "Most people," she said, "I think they'd want to, you know, take possession of a place by moving things around."

"What are we doing?" Evlanoff asked.

Alice squeezed him. "I'm not letting go until we make up." She closed her eyes, and rubbed her forehead up and down against his spine. "Besides, you like it, don't you? Being in step?" Alice tripped as she made this observation, stubbed her toe on a chair leg.

He laughed. "Except you never seem to be, quite."

"I like the clumsiness, too. Element of suspense. And your back. It's . . . I don't know. Big. Warm."

"Well, then," he said, his voice no longer cold. "It must have been for you that I didn't move the bed."

Alice looked around the room; she walked on her toes to see over his shoulder. "You don't think it might be that if you moved it against a wall it would block the door or the window, or be too close to the radiator, or keep you from opening your closet?"

He shook his head, bumping hers. "No. Not for those reasons."

"Maybe you really are a romantic. Rather than a pragmatist."

"Oh, I think so. I am Russian, after all."

"Well, then, why be so mean and curmudgeonly about addresses? Why, when one restaurant disappears, not be charming and romantic and find a charming romantic bistro? Instead you invent character flaws for me. Carelessness. Slapdashery." Alice nipped the tender crease between his arm and shoulder blade, pressed her groin suggestively into his buttocks.

"Not fair," he said. "To use my own lust against me."

"All right," she said. "I'll stop." And she stepped away, separating their bodies. He reached around, pulled her back against him. She let one hand drop to the front of his trousers, felt how hard he was. "Very effective strategy," she said. When he took her hand she thought he was going to move it away, but instead he guided her fingers up and down the shaft of his penis.

"It's not that restaurants disappear," he said. "But that spoiled little girls don't bother to check addresses."

Alice had undone all but the top button of his trousers and was trying to find her way past his underclothes. "I'm lost again. If you rescue me, perhaps you'll find that spoiled girls have desirable qualities, as well. Abilities more important than those used to locate restaurants." Evlanoff took her hand and pushed it past the waistband of his drawers, curled her fingers around the taut smooth skin of his penis.

They continued in a slow rocking gait, tilting left, tilting right. Around and around the big bed, some laps silent, others bantering, his stride more even than hers. "It's difficult for me to stay in step," she said defending her stumbles. "Your legs are longer, you have the advantage of being in front."

"Take the lead," he offered.

With her hand Alice directed the shaft of his penis right, left, up, down. "No. Instead, I'll use this for a tiller."

"You can be in front and still use your tiller. They are at the back of boats, you know."

Alice shook her head against his back.

"Why not?"

"I like it like this. I like how big you are in front of me, pulling me along. And I like not looking where I'm going. Walking with my eyes shut."

"Ahh."

"What do you mean, 'Ahh'?"

"I mean that at last we have the answer to the puzzle of Alice."

Alice's hand stopped moving. "What is the puzzle of me?" she asked. Evlanoff put his hand over hers in order to guide it back into motion.

"The historic question of why the little girl got off the train. It's the inevitable fate of a personality who wants to be pulled along with her eyes shut."

"You don't think you're making a bit much of this?" Alice said.

"Of what we're doing now, or of the train?"

"Well, I meant now, but either, I suppose. Besides, haven't you ever done a thing you can't explain?"

Evlanoff, attending to questions posed by fingers rather than lips, didn't answer.

"Haven't you?" Alice asked again.

He nodded, eyes closed, his whole body rocking forward with his head. Forward and backward, Throwing her off balance once again.

"What?" Alice persisted.

"It's, it's a thing of a different order. It's not to do with going off with anyone."

Alice waited through a few laps of his silence. Then, "Won't you tell me?" she asked, and she gave his penis a little shake.

"Yes. All right. My father bought me a microscope when I was ten. Not a child's toy but a real one—he got it from a jeweler. A power of magnification of eight hundred and fifty." Evlanoff stopped for a moment, then continued. "The body was brass. It had an oak case lined with velvet. Little indentations to hold the eyepieces that weren't being used. It wasn't new, but it was magnificent."

"Go on," Alice prompted when he paused, using the same method as before.

"If it's a story you want, you'll have to stop squeezing. Otherwise you'll get something else."

Alice withdrew her hand from his trousers. "Story first."

Evlanoff replaced the hand. "I didn't say stop *touching*."

Around the room again, Alice sighing with impatience. "I loved it more than any gift I'd ever received," he finally said. "I was in awe of it. Truthfully, such a microscope seemed too good a thing for a boy to have. When I was apart from it, at school, I thought of what might happen to it, how the case could be knocked from the shelf in my room, how a thief might steal it. And when I was home, when I wanted to use it, I imagined myself dropping the eyepieces. Breaking one of the lenses."

"What did you use it for?" Alice asked. "What did you look at?"

"Insect wings. Blood from a scrape. Feathers. Hair. Bits of plants. Dirty water from the fishbowl. That sort of thing. No great science, no revelations. Except to me."

"And? What happened?"

"I put the microscope, case and all, into my knapsack, and I took it far from our house, to a field, and with a hammer I smashed it. I broke the case, the lenses, bent the body. Everything."

"But why?"

"I don't know. That was the point of my telling you this story, remember? It was to be a thing I'd done and couldn't explain."

Alice was silent. Then, "Were you angry about something?" she suggested. "Were you angry at your father?"

"I told you, I don't know why."

"Were you sorry after?"

"I was. I wished for it back."

"Your father, did he find out?"

"No. I lied and said it had been stolen. And I was sorry about that, as well, because suspicion fell on one of the servants. She'd done a few other things my mother hadn't liked, so I suppose her position was not secure anyway, but she was let go because of the microscope. I used to think I saw her in the street, following me."

They had stopped walking. "Do you think you broke it because you loved it so much, that it was a way of, I don't know, escaping from worry over it?"

"If that were true, then wouldn't you be in danger?" he asked. Alice pulled away, intending to punish him with a little pinch or a slap, but he caught one of her arms and pulled her back. He pushed her onto the bed. "At last," he said, "we've arrived. He used one knee to keep her down as he pulled off her skirt. "I'd thought of it myself, that breaking the microscope was a way to end its tyranny, but I don't know that it was as simple as that."

Alice nodded up at him. "So we're even."

"A good match. Two authors of inexplicable acts."

"Don't you think everyone must be?"

"Do you?" Evlanoff was heavy on top of her. He'd pinned her arms, her legs, and she squirmed under his weight, claustrophobia intensifying lust, compounding the need for release.

"Well, everyone except Eleanor Clusburtson," she said, struggling to breathe, freeing one leg for no more than a moment before his stronger one recaptured it.

"Is she supremely rational, your Miss Clusburtson?"

Alice's eyes were closed. Under her lids, the color changed each time he thrust. It went from red to purple. "I think so," she said, finally. "Did you get another?"

"Microscope?"

"Yes."

"No. My father offered . . . He offered to replace it. But I said no."

"Didn't he . . . He didn't . . ."

Evlanoff stopped moving. "No more talking," he said, and he released her to reach for a pillow.

"He didn't want to know why?" Alice folded the pillow in half; she put it under her head, plumped and shoved and pushed her fists into it until her mouth was at just the right height.

"Why what?"

"Why you didn't want another."

"He," Evlanoff said, straddling her face, sucking in his breath as she bit down, very gently, just teasing, moving her teeth against the smooth, smooth skin, grazing it, reminding him: yes, there were teeth to consider; it wasn't that she was at his mercy; no, he was at hers.

# HEROES OF THE
# GREAT WAR

"LISTEN TO THIS." ARTHUR WAS READING FROM the editorial page. "Never will a horse forget any place where previously he had been wounded. When, for instance, he is taking ammunition up to a battery, he will shiver and tremble and hurry past at a gallop any exposed spot or dangerous crossroads where, perhaps months before, he stopped a bit of shrapnel."

May set her cup down. "Which animals are those?"

"I'm off," Dick Benjamin said. He rose from the table. "Before Arthur has me saving the warhorses of Flanders."

Eleanor Clusburtson stood with him. "Just let me get my coat." She hurried out of the breakfast room and up the stairs.

"Call the boy! That's what he's for!" Dick yelled after her. "Dashed peculiar woman!"

But Eleanor had already run up both flights. Since arriving in Shanghai, she had taught Cecily and Alice nothing—"Not a simple sum!" as their father said—but her presence had made it unlikely that the Benjamin sisters would ever be troubled by the kinds of trivial calculations a girl might do in her head, figuring the cost of four yards of silk satin against that of the same length of crepe, subtracting that from ... But what difference? Because of Eleanor Clusburtson—more accurately, because of her false tooth—the Benjamin family was no longer well-to-do. They had become fabulously, ridiculously rich.

It happened this way:

In 1914, when Alice and Cecily returned to Shanghai with their aunt and their maths teacher, Dick Benjamin was too excited about rubber to be worried about whether or not his daughters were growing up ignorant. Europe was going to war, and fortunes were going to be made, one of them by himself. He planned to invest all his capital in rubber. Armies needed a great deal of rubber: rubber for gaskets and rubber for tires and rubber for boots and hoses and the linings of greatcoats and heaven knew what else. The market was strong; it hadn't yet surged.

One evening, trolling past trays of canapés vanishing and crudités wilting under the pressure of false pleasantries at the French Embassy's annual Bastille Day open house (not one wedge of Stilton to go with a drop of dry sherry), he'd overheard a drunk military attaché drawling an interesting word. *Blockade*. Especially interesting was this word when attached to a port like Maracaibo, through which most of the world's natural rubber passed. He forgot his search for Stilton; he hurried Dolly into her wrap.

That very night, he made calls, he cabled Hong Kong and London, and yes, *yes*: it was confirmed, the Allies were blockading rubber. The following morning, as soon as the market opened, Dick Benjamin quietly bought up all the rubber he could and nervously watched the price per share climb and climb again. When the strain of his multiplying fortune grew so intense that he began to see auguries everywhere—in the trash floating on the river, the drift of leaves across his path—he sold. Then, a month after he'd unloaded the shares, a month during which he asked himself each day why he had waited, came word of a fantastic new substance. Dimethyl butadiene. A polymer, a magic polymer, $C_6H_{10}$ was going to make natural rubber obsolete—that was what was being said by the privileged few who knew about it, one of whom owed Dick Benjamin a favor. Dick liked doing people good turns; it always worked out well for him. What was once the limited product of a single small factory in Manchester—the formula invented by a Russian, smuggled by the Germans, and captured by the English—would change the course of the war and of history. Just before the inevitable rubber crash, Dick reinvested all the money he had made in dimethyl butadiene, getting in at the bottom of the market, just beginning its own volatile rise when Eleanor Clusburtson arrived.

"Pass the sugar, would you be so kind?" he asked one morning, a few days after the girls had returned from London. He spoke without looking up from the *North China Daily News*. The maths teacher—What could his sister-in-law have been thinking in bringing such a creature back to China?—said something unintelligible. Dick stopped reading. "I beg your pardon?" His hand dangled expectantly, waiting for the sugar.

The woman flushed a deep crimson and shook her head. She ducked her face into her napkin. When she looked up at him she was smiling with her lips pressed tightly together, not a happy smile but a miserable sort of sociable grimace. May pushed the sugar bowl toward Dick.

"Thank you," he said. He folded the paper, stirred sugar into his coffee, still looking at the peculiar new governess, or whatever she was.

"Miss Clusburtson has had a bit of trouble with her teeth," May explained.

Dick raised his eyebrows. "What sort is that?" he said, not really interested, but not wanting to appear unkind either.

"I have a plate," Eleanor said slowly, enunciating more clearly now that the subject of concern was hidden in her napkin. "But it i*thn't* . . . it ha*thn't* . . ."

May sighed. "Before we sailed I took Eleanor to a London dentist, who replaced her plate. She's too polite to complain, but it's proved quite inadequate. It's falling apart in her mouth."

"Not at all your fault," Eleanor said, looking into her lap. "You were being kind."

"I had hoped I was being kind," May clarified.

"I have a plate," Dick said. "Rotted two of my molars with toffee."

"It's my front tooth," Eleanor said.

"Mmm," Dick said absently. "What's wrong with the plate?"

"I*th*'s made with a new *thubthanth*. The old one wa*th* vulcanite, thi*th* i*th* dimethyl *tho*mthing. And it wa*th* fine for a month, but now i*th* cracked, i*th* falling apart."

"It was supposed to be a wonder," May complained, "a—"

"Diethyl, did you say? Or dimethyl?" Dick interrupted, his voice suddenly avid. "Dimethyl *what*?"

"Buta, buta *tho*mething," Eleanor said.

Dick stood up, jarring the table. Coffee slopped from their cups into their saucers. "May I see it?"

"I beg your pardon?" Eleanor held the balled napkin tightly in her lap.

"I want to see your plate."

"Dick!" May said.

"Give it to me!" He held out his empty hand, impatient. He'd used up whatever reserves of pleasantries he possessed.

"I haven't got it in," Eleanor said.

"I know that. It's in your lap. You've spat it in your napkin. Give it to me."

"But why!" May said. "Why on earth would—"

"Look." Dick ignored May. He put both his hands on the table and bore down on Eleanor. "I'm happy to have you as a . . . a guest in my home. For as long as you wish to remain. But there's one condition. You must give me your plate."

"Really, Dick!" May said.

"What's all the— Why, what is happening?" Dolly asked, arriving late for breakfast, an amah following with fresh coffee.

"Your husband is attempting to impound Miss Clusburtson's tooth," May said.

"Her tooth?" Dolly looked at Dick, bewildered.

"Her *false* tooth," Dick said. "The plate, to be specific. Now will you give it to me, or won't you?" He walked over to Eleanor's side of the table, and she curled protectively over the balled napkin in her lap. He put his hand on her shoulder. "I'll send you to my own dentist this afternoon," he promised. "I just want to see the plate. I need to." He squeezed the bony shoulder, a little too tightly. A bit menacingly. After an agonizingly long minute during which Eleanor, her eyes shut, told herself that of late her life had taken many peculiar turns and asked herself what was the harm, really, in showing a gentleman a false tooth? An etiquette book would certainly proscribe this as an act of un-wonted intimacy, but it was also true that an etiquette book would never acknowledge the transaction as one a polite person was likely to encounter. Oh, well, perhaps Eleanor wasn't polite. Perhaps she'd be-come the very type of person against whom her father's sister had al-ways warned her: a vulgarian.

Hunched over and hiding her face, she held up the napkin like a crumpled white flag of surrender. Dick seized it and, hurrying to un-wrap the plate, dropped it on the floor, where it cracked a little further, freeing the tooth, which bounced under the sideboard, to be retrieved by the silent amah.

"Brittle," said Dick, holding the grayish-pink arch, molded to fit Eleanor's palate.

Miss Clusburtson nodded, her face crimson.

"Was it always?" he asked.

She shook her head.

May and Dolly stared on in silence.

"What— I want you to tell me all about it," he said.

"Dick, what is this nonsense!" Dolly exclaimed.

"It's not nonsense! It's of the greatest importance!" And he sent Dolly and May away, mystified, and sat with Eleanor at the breakfast table, and she told him that, yes, it had been good for a few weeks, maybe more, it tasted funny but it was comfortable, slightly flexible, but then it had begun to crumble in her mouth, it had cracked, it was not nearly as satisfactory as the old vulcanite one had been.

"Everything to do with this tooth," she lamented, "has been very unfortunate."

But Dick was smiling at the plate in his hand. "No," he said. "I think perhaps it's going to prove to be a most astonishing instance of serendipity. Lucky for you, lucky for us all. I'll need to take it with me." He stood from the table and left, patting the pocket that held the plate and humming what sounded like the syllables of the words he'd just spoken. *As-ton-ish-ing, as-ton-ish-ing, ser-en-dip-i-ty!*

Chemical analyses confirmed that the plate was of $C_6H_{10}$, the same polymer that was to win the war. That was supposed to win . . . But $C_6H_{10}$ was unstable; it broke down. The question being *when*, and under what conditions? Did saliva make it less stable? And what about temperature? Would it crack in freezing weather? Dick brought a fragment home and hid it in the icebox.

The biggest question of all was this: How long before everyone knew what Eleanor had discovered? Shares were still climbing. When, *when* should he sell? Dick said nothing to anyone. For a week, two weeks, three, he whistled, he walked, he fiddled, hummed, drummed his fingers on the table, and tapped cigar ash onto the rug.

"What *is* the matter with you?" Dolly complained, but he just shook his head. He owned three hundred thousand shares and had borrowed five hundred thousand more against the promise to return them in two months, with interest. After twenty-nine days he sold out—value quadrupled—and then paced and smoked as the price of dimethyl butadiene continued to climb. In the icebox, the fragment of Eleanor's plate crumbled at his touch.

Then, at last, on the thirty-fourth day, on a field in Düsseldorf, the air temperature negative two degrees Celsius, the tires of twenty-eight German trucks burst. One hundred and twelve tires: all flat. The market in dimethyl butadiene began its precipitous plunge. By the sixtieth day, when, as stipulated by his loan agreement, Dick Benjamin had to buy back and return the five hundred thousand shares he'd borrowed, they were worth only 11 percent of their value at the time when he'd acquired them, a mere 3 percent of what he'd sold them for. Nothing illegal had transpired, and yet the profit, it was criminal. What might it have been if he'd had the nerve to wait just a few more days before the tires burst? But he wasn't going to calculate it—well, he was, he'd succumb to hindsight. He knew that he'd had to err in the direction of prudence, responsibility; still, he'd succumb. But not today.

Dick Benjamin almost skipped down the Bund as he left the meeting with his private banker. Came home with Swiss chocolates, Italian silk stockings, French perfumes, smoked North Sea salmon, a magnum of champagne. No one at home cared for truffles or caviar or Camembert, but he bought these as well. He emptied shop shelves of every item that the war had made scarce and even more expensive than usual, and when he arrived home, he erupted into the foyer like a holiday firework, discharging tissue and ribbon.

"My dear dear *dear* Miss Clusburtson," he said to Eleanor, who had come downstairs to see what all the noise was about. He embraced her; he kissed each of her pale cheeks and watched them turn red. "What can I do for you? Only say the word. Travel. Furs. Jewels. Anything!"

Eleanor blinked. "W-well," she stammered. "I . . . I . . ." She looked at May, who nodded in encouragement. "I am a bit bored. Perhap*th*, would you con*th*ider . . ."

"*Say it,*" May hissed.

"What I'd like i*th* to work at your offi*the*."

Now, FOUR YEARS later, she was a partner, and Benjamin, Kelly, Potts, and Clusburtson was the only hong in Shanghai to include a woman. Eleanor, they discovered, enjoyed nothing so much as work. She didn't smoke or drink or play cards or have any bad habits to divert her from her labors. And the money she'd made the family—about which she cared little—was more than enough to compensate for the extravagances of Arthur. A thousand times over enough.

"Dear May," Dick toasted his sister-in-law, on the night they celebrated Eleanor's partnership. "By bringing us Miss Eleanor Clusburtson, you have, against all odds, redeemed your ridiculous husband."

The family raised glasses of Pommery to Eleanor, her face flushed with pleasure and embarrassment.

"Dick!" Dolly said.

"Thank you." May executed a rare little bow to Dick.

"Yes, thank you," Arthur said to Eleanor. "I think."

Every morning, Dick Benjamin and Eleanor Clusburtson set out together in the pony trap to work all day on Jinkee Road, and every night they returned in it. At first Dolly was jealous, but "Dearest," cried her husband, "you know how I feel about clever women! And, why, compared to you, Eleanor looks like, well, like a wet brown paper parcel! How could I possibly!"

"Dick!" Dolly said, mollified, smiling in spite of herself. "How can you be so mean!"

"I'm not mean. Eleanor is perfection, and so are you. But Eleanor might just as well be a man, and you are my wife."

In Shanghai, where the ability to make money was valued above any other, Eleanor had become quite famous. Not that anyone knew the connection between her lisp and Dick Benjamin's fortunes, but there must have been something to induce him to make her a partner. Perhaps he'd simply been overwhelmed by her peculiar genius. Add, subtract, multiply, divide: Eleanor could do unlimited calculations in her head faster than a team of Chinese with abacuses; she never made a mistake. It wasn't advanced mathematics, but it was complex—mentally juggling the fluctuations of ten or more commodities at once, playing the numbers of the Hong Kong market off those in Shanghai. Not that the work she accomplished was what she'd aspired to at Oxford; it wasn't an elegant, acrobatic leap of theorem but a nervous choreography of numbers—like the New Year celebration she'd seen her first year in China, a great dragon of numbers reeling below fireworks of facts, winding over a hundred black-trousered legs, shaking its big head and twisting through hers. And much more absorbing than a classroom of rude, bored girls who would graduate without giving another thought to mathematics beyond whatever might be required to venture out, Dutch treat, for tea.

Ignoring her protests, May had taken Eleanor to the dressmaker, to the milliner, to the Siberian Fur Shop on Avenue Edouard VII. She had taken away all her hair pins and accompanied her to Monsieur Joseph to get her marcelled, and now, despite her advanced age, Eleanor received proposals almost weekly, from men of every description, native and foreign. She refused them all, just as she refused to ride in a rickshaw or to let the servants pick up after her or hold her towel as she stepped from the bath or shake out her serviette and lay it on her lap.

So, when Dick Benjamin said *Dashed peculiar woman*, it was this that he meant.

"Good-bye darling," he called to Dolly as Eleanor came down the stairs, pulling on her overcoat, and he kissed his daughters and raised his hat to May.

"What's he so happy about?" Arthur asked.

May pushed the paper toward him. "Revolutionaries tore up the track in Fukien."

"Again?"

She nodded. "No freight for a fortnight at least."

"Rice doubled?"

"Tea. Now what about the horses? Tell me."

"They are not from Flanders. They're from Australia. Each one cost six hundred pounds to transport to France and now they're dropping from battle fatigue. I mean literally. They shake, they fall, they go down begging on their knees when they hear a loud noise, the poor loves."

Alice sensed diversion. "So what's to be done?" she prodded. But Arthur was thinking too hard to answer. Before he'd finished rereading the article, he had a plan.

Arthur collected pledges from forty-seven rich, sentimental women in Shanghai, cornering them at dinner parties and tea dances, and especially at the race club, after a frisky pony had fattened their purses. The next day he'd send his boy to collect on the chits they'd signed. With the money, he chartered a mail boat out of Marseilles and paid an agent to oversee the building of makeshift stalls onboard, the collection of the horses, and the hire of a seaworthy groom to tend to them en route. For any horse strong enough to return to battle, Arthur provided an equine mask to protect it from nerve gas—a mask designed and manufactured by the company who fashioned them for humans.

As soon as the agent, a M. Arrete, cabled that the boat had finally left and would arrive in Shanghai in three weeks, Arthur went to inspect the old stable he'd rented from the Shanghai Horse Bazaar. Abandoned for years, the drafty building on Connaught Road was overrun with little native deer, which he regretfully chased off the premises. (Kindhearted to a fault, he provided them with the compensation of a salt lick some miles away, just outside Chang-su-ho's garden—far enough from the stable but not, as it transpired, from the country club, where, emboldened by a little salt and compassion, the deer attacked the rose garden en masse. Unnaturally aggressive—was there something in the lick? He'd bought it from a native apothecary—the deer ate every rose. They bit the blooms off and left the thorny stems, slaking their thirst in the fishpond.)

When at last the horses arrived, they presented a sorry spectacle, with dull coats rubbed raw in places, torn ears, tattered tails, every rib showing. Even the wharf coolies, a hardened, downtrodden lot, handled them gently. They stroked the great trembling noses that stuck out from under the blindfolds they wore to be led down the gangplanks.

Installed in the repaired stable, with *mah foos* to care for them around the clock, the warhorses were treated not only by veterinarians from the race club but by doctors from the London Mission hospital, whom Arthur paid to make stable calls. In addition, he dosed them with patent medicines: Vetarzo's Blood Medicine, as well as Clark's Blood Mixture, Chamberlain's pain balm, Petromiel, Chlorodyne, Dover's Powder, and especially Sanaphos's reconstructive nerve food, a case of which he'd wheedled out of a French chemist on Avenue Edouard VII.

"You'll kill the poor bastards," Dick said at dinner, "Pouring all that rubbish down them. Don't you know a horse's digestive system can't take such assaults?"

"But they're doing splendidly, Dick," said May, defending her husband. "You should come see them."

And, oddly, the horses were thriving. On bright afternoons, Arthur, May, and Alice picnicked out at the stable, with Number Four to serve.

"You have found yourself, Arthur," his wife said, teasing, half-serious, standing up as tall as she could to kiss his chin. "You are a rehabilitator of sad, sick cavalry animals."

The horses nickered at Arthur. They frisked and danced and checked his pockets for sugar lumps. They lipped his ears and nipped off his hat. With their hot, gusting breath, they blew the tinnitus right out of his head. The mere sight of their hugely warm and whiskered noses made him relax, and he offered his ringing ears to them, once going so far as to introduce a pinch of snuff into a cavernous, trembling pink nostril, laced with crimson veins. Quite a trick to align his ear to the rearing head. But the *relief*—the release of that deafening sneeze, and the silence that ensued. It wasn't as good as sex, but almost.

Arthur had thought to send his horses back home, but Australia was so far away, another long journey, so instead he sold them to rich Settlement families, who took great pleasure and absurd pride in veteran warhorses pulling their traps. What could be better, more fashionable, in the midst of wartime's social whirl, ladies off to bandage rolling and marathons of sock knitting? Arthur had the family tailor sew up military-looking decorations, affixing his approximation of a Victoria Cross with Palm to the horses' bridles.

"You know, Arthur," Eleanor said, reviewing his rumpled receipts. "You've actually made money!"

HE WAS EXPECTING the arrival of a second shipment of horses to fill his now-empty stable when the epidemic began. At first influenza was mistaken for cholera, because it struck so swiftly. Eleanor, for example, was sitting at her desk at the brokerage. The runner had just returned from the cable office with the latest numbers from Hong Kong. He placed them silently before her. She'd been waiting: in her head, ready to receive the prices, were eight towers of numbers. Like a city on a hill, she thought, surprised at herself for being so fanciful. Mathematics was austere and holy, a music sung unto itself, uncontaminated by sentiment or desire or any of what Eleanor would judge, if not foolish, then separate from her spartan life of the mind. She closed her eyes and saw that sunlight gilded the number towers; it sparkled off the corners of fours and sevens, slid in syrupy waves from eights and threes. She was so dizzy she put her forehead down on her blotter, right on top of the white slips of paper the boy had brought.

"Eleanor?" Dick asked. "Are you all right?"

"I'm not, I'm afraid."

"What's the matter? Shall I call for the trap?"

"Please," Eleanor said, although the idea of riding through the streets of Shanghai behind the jogging pony seemed dangerously ambitious. If she could move, she'd lie down on the floor.

"Will you—Eleanor dear, could you please pick your head up?" Dick asked. "I don't like to see you like that."

"I will in a minute," she said faintly. "Do you think you could ask them to stop the abacuses, just for a little while? The clatter is—"

"But they have. It's quiet in here." Dick leaned over and put his face near Eleanor's. "You're not crying are you?"

"It's just that I have the most terrible headache."

"But you're crying. I wish you wouldn't."

"I'll stop. Give me a moment."

Around Eleanor's desk collected a small, silent audience composed of Dick Benjamin and the other partners, Kelly stroking his mustache and Potts fiddling with the coins in his pocket, and the six Chinese bookkeepers, standing absolutely still.

"Too much thinking," Potts said at last. He was the one partner who had opposed Eleanor's inclusion in the business. "Women's brains aren't built for it."

Eleanor summoned her will and sat up. She looked at Potts. "You are a low and despicable man." Her voice shook. The office, which usually seemed dim, struck her as cruelly bright. "And I know for a fact that you do not understand how to predict futures with logarithms. Not really."

"Eleanor!" Dick said. "She's ill!" he said to Potts. "You can see for yourself that she's not . . . not herself."

"You can't!" Mr. Potts advanced on Eleanor's desk. "Logarithms have nothing to do with it."

"See!" she said. "What did I tell you!" Eleanor closed her eyes. She wasn't herself. Or rather, she was, but she'd been crammed into the skin of someone smaller, sewn in tight so that every nerve danced with pain. The golden towers of the number city were gone, and now, scribbled on the red inside of her eyelids, were hundreds, thousands, of prices, rising and falling in a seasick wave.

# SYNTAX AND SYMMETRY

THE EXIGENCIES OF EARNING WHAT SHE MUST to keep hold of the very room of which she despaired— the single room in which she slept and bathed and cooked and ate, in which she sat at a table under a bare lightbulb, laboriously translating texts from Russian to French and from French to Russian—had, since the Revolution, inspired Suzanne Petrovna to supplement her inadequate income with tutoring and piecework that came not from publishers but from refugees. By 1926, her steadiest employment had for years been the translation of letters whose object was to secure jobs or information, the whereabouts of lost relatives and strayed fiancées. She wrote complaints to magistrates and protestations of innocence to officials of the court, explaining injustices too complex to render in elementary, refugee French.

The cost of a simple grammatical mistake or a misspelling could be a man's credibility, a woman's honor—at least this was what Suzanne told herself, now that her texts had become human lives and she parsed not only documents but hearts. For her efforts she was paid modestly, sometimes offered food instead of money, but she grew used to—dependent upon—the emotional sustenance such employment offered. If it was not her honor that was threatened, if it was not she who had lost the woman she had planned to marry, the son she had nursed and bathed, at least it was she who chose the words to bring them back. Chose between *devastated* and *bereft*, between *implore* and *insist*, *hope* and *pray*.

An organized person, she liked to lay out her papers and pens and dictionaries the same way each time. She placed the text to be translated before her, reference materials to the left, scratch paper for rough drafts to the right, pens within reach in their tray.

She was filling the bladder of her new black fountain pen—a gift from a grateful client—when she heard the tread of feet on the stairs. A large person, she concluded, because the fifth stair creaked as it did when the neighbor to her left ascended, a man of substantial height and girth. Whoever it was moved slowly down the corridor, paused regularly as if looking for names or numbers on the doors. Most tenants of the building, which had no concierge, were too transient to bother to identify their rooms for callers—either that or too likely to be hiding from creditors. Only Suzanne had written her name on a card, with the words *Translation of Correspondence and Documents*, and pinned it to her door. The sound of feet stopped, as if the visitor was considering this information, and she stood, eager at the thought of unanticipated work. She tidied her hair in the mirror over the sink and looked to see that her dress was properly fastened, for sometimes, while bent over her papers, she opened the button at her neck.

*"Oui,"* she answered the knock, her hand on the latch but not yet opening the door. The voice from the other side was deep, and spoke French with a heavy Russian accent, inspiring the unlikely image of someone spitting out lumps of undercooked dough. Suzanne didn't recognize it.

"I want . . . I have a piece of business to discuss."

As most of Suzanne's work came to her by word of mouth, she asked for the referral: "Who was it that sent you to me?"

"No one," said the voice, and made no attempt to explain itself further. Suzanne found something familiar in its unapologetic terseness; what, she couldn't think. She drew in her breath, unlatched the door, nodded at the man before her.

He had what she considered a typically Russian face, melancholic and stubborn, eyes that believed in fate and a mouth that mocked it. His clothes were worn and grimy; his hands hung empty from too-short sleeves. He wasn't carrying the usual frayed envelope or rumpled sheaf of papers, but perhaps these were folded inside his coat. Suzanne stood back to let the stranger enter. He nodded, smiled, not with good humor but a sardonic stretch of his lips. He sat in her chair and dropped his hands in his lap, fingers laced.

Only after Suzanne had really searched his face feature by feature did she remember it. What she recognized was the peculiarly dark-pigmented skin under his eyes: brown, purple, blue, gray—it partook of all but was none of these, a strange color echoed in his dark but somehow bloodless lips. The rest of him was very changed; he was stooped, his hair thin. Deep vertical lines creased his cheeks, as if he'd lost too much weight too quickly. Defensively, Suzanne folded her arms; she didn't close her door but left it open to the public corridor.

"Go away?" she said, intending the imperative, but her voice lilted with nerves, and the words formed a question.

He shook his head, and his easy arrogance rekindled such a store of old resentments that she was forced to steady her voice.

"You must, though."

"Your mother. Is she dead?"

Suzanne nodded.

"When?"

"Years ago. Fifteen years. During the summer. The twenty-seventh of August."

"No one told me."

"No."

He nodded, glanced over the small, sparse room, noted the papers on the table, the two washed glasses on the shelf by the sink. "You have room for me for a night or two," he said. She shook her head, and he smiled, again without pleasure. He switched from French to Russian. "It wasn't a request."

Suzanne continued to speak in French. "This is my home. I ask that you leave it." Now he looked around, very slowly, allowing his eyes to rest on each object, conveying to Suzanne how shabby were her surroundings: the cracked enamel of the sink, the obviously mended chair, the flat and faded coverlet on the couch that served her as a bed. The Bokhara rug and mahogany armoire, the malachite lamps and the silver cup—all she had managed to retrieve from her dead brother's apartments had long ago been sold. Beneath the window frame, the wallpaper had been scratched until it peeled off the plaster below: the work of her sometimes cat, jumping up onto the high sill to quit the apartment.

"You turn me away? What life you have"—he paused as if to underscore that life's meanness—"I gave you."

"I will call a gendarme. I will—" Suzanne broke off, realizing from his impassive expression that her father knew how unlikely it was that any plea for help might be answered in such a neighborhood. At three in the afternoon no police were on patrol; any man sober enough to stand was at work. Down the hall was a consumptive laundress, upstairs the mother of two young children. There were no others.

"I need a place until the end of the week. Then I leave for—"

"Where?"

"Lyons. A job."

"Leave now, then. You can't stay here." Suzanne's voice surprised her with its sureness. She could see that her father, despite his quick arguments, was taken aback as well. Still, he challenged her.

"Why, when I have a daughter with a roof?" he asked. He was tipping the chair back as he spoke, an old habit, she'd forgotten. She watched as he balanced on the two back legs, steadying himself with one hand on the table.

Without thinking—it wasn't something she planned, not even for an instant, it was more reflexive than that—Suzanne reached her foot forward and gave the edge of the seat a hard push, enough to tip it over backward. She covered her eyes as her father grabbed at the table's edge, and kept them covered for a few seconds after she heard his head hit the tiled floor. She was frozen, just as when she was a child and he'd beaten her, or the night he'd stood on her brother's fingers. She was waiting for the blow and comforting herself with the thought that he'd grown too old, too weak, to actually kill her with his bare hands; and she, too, she was no longer a child, she was a woman now, fully grown and long past the time when he could have easily accomplished it, the end of her.

Suzanne was waiting, but she was waiting for nothing; there was no sound after the thump of his head, like the noise of a melon that had rolled off the tabletop. She opened her eyes, squatted by his chest to see that he was breathing. How odd that she'd never before looked at him so closely, her father. As it turned out, he wasn't ugly. She was surprised by the graceful curve of cheekbone under his closed eye, the straight narrow nose, nothing like the lumpy potato nose of the peasant she had come to think him. He was dirty, but the skin above his lip was freshly shaven, his chin and cheeks as well, as if he'd conceded this small measure of hygiene in preparation for coming to her room. Seeing this, she remembered the feel of his cleanly shaven face. Hadn't there been, long ago, lost in childhood, a holiday afternoon when he'd walked into the sea with her riding on his shoulders? She had put her hands on his face, just shaved, to steady herself.

Now what, Suzanne thought, still squatting. She was surprised to have done something she would have judged herself incapable of doing, surprised also that she felt neither guilt nor satisfaction in her violence. She was strangely unburdened of emotion. Early memories, even, had no power to move her. Did this indicate a disordered moral faculty, she wondered, an unbalanced mind?

She walked down the hall as far as the stairwell, to be sure it was empty. She could get him that far, anyway. But when she pulled at his boots, intending to drag him out the door by the feet, they came off easily—so big they must have been borrowed, or stolen—and she fell backwards onto her tailbone. He was wearing no socks, and his feet were as white as a corpse's beneath the grime, so she took hold of him by his trousered ankles and dragged him into the hall, his head bumping over the saddle. He was heavier than he looked; by the time she rolled him around the corner and into the stairwell, she was panting.

Suzanne's father fell only a few steps and then came to a stop, but his head struck each tread, so hard that she cringed. Perhaps this would grant her a few more minutes of his unconsciousness, safe-guard a chance for her to think. She set the boots neatly on the land-ing, returned to her room, and locked the door. It would be best to leave, she thought, to pack a bag and go—she didn't know where, but once she was outside she would think more clearly. Outside she could breathe again. She had a few francs; she'd go out the back way. But then from down the hall she heard a moaning, a French and Russian cursing, a tripping and stumbling, followed by one and then another stamp, the kind required to put on buckleless boots, even overly large ones. Suzanne looked at her door once more, to check that the bolt was secured; then she backed up until she was on the other side of her room. Under the bed, she could see two red reflections: the cat's eyes, round with surprise. She hadn't even known the animal was in the room.

Suzanne listened to her father pound on the door, counting the times, only four, and this, too, was unexpected—she thought he'd throw his shoulder against it until the lock gave. He didn't yell, he didn't call her any names, he didn't say anything at all. He walked away, and she listened to the sound of his boots descending the stairs. Sitting on the floor with her eyes closed, she heard the cat jump onto the sill, back legs scrabbling for purchase, the thud as he landed on roof tiles.

For eight days, Suzanne stayed in. She didn't open the door to any inquiries, and thereby she lost two pieces of translation from potential clients who didn't know her well enough to push valuable papers under a locked door, let alone money. She sat at the window and drank tea with sugar, then tea without sugar, and when the wet, reused leaves wouldn't produce even a hint of color or flavor she drank hot water.

She ate a tin of smoked herring—actually smiling that this had turned out to be the occasion for which she'd saved it—a stale half loaf, and two packets of biscuits, meted out three per meal. Then, after two days of eating nothing and feeling queasy, then faint, she went out, her auburn hair pinned under her hat, a dark scarf pulled up to her nose.

*He said he was leaving in a week, he said he was leaving in a week,* she recited as she stepped tentatively around corners, peering out from under her low felt brim. *I waited eight days, and he said he was leaving in a week.*

After a month, Suzanne forced herself to put away the scarf and hat, but her bravery was an act, and at night she lay in bed listening for a vengeful tread on the stairs. When she slept, her dreams were nightmares, and often she woke standing at her door, checking the lock to see, was it secure? Weeks passed, one after another; she didn't relax but grew only more and more nervous. She lost the ability to work efficiently and, worn down by poverty and apprehension, fell ill, recovered poorly. Even a short walk brought back her fever; she coughed until her eyes watered; she was obliged to seek a cure in the southern sun—in Nice, where, hoping to elude consumption, she lost what money remained to her and sat for hours on a bench overlooking the sea, calculating not only her poverty (for that math was simple enough: first she had very little, and then she had even less), but how, in the course of her life, one reversal had mysteriously precipitated the next, until there she was, discovering as if for the first time that the shoes she wore were not serviceable but ugly, her life was not one of simplicity but of privation.

As Suzanne followed the gendarme along the Promenade des Anglais—the mistral now whipping over the beach and threatening to tear the awning right off the tobacconist's stall—she crossed her arms over her chest to keep her coat closed. Into what new mess was she allowing her father to push her?

On the other hand, could anything be worse than spending a night outdoors, listening to the relentless washing and worrying of the tide? The Oriental woman in the litter: she had materialized like some mandarin fairy queen, held aloft by those two silent, braided acolytes, the severity of their dress emphasizing the opulence of hers. Suzanne hurried after the gendarme, coughing, panting. Perhaps there *were* witches and genies and ... She shook her head. No, what there were, were fevers, and when fevers didn't improve, deliriums.

# SPANISH INFLUENZA

ALICE OPENED THE WINDOW. FROM THE STREET came two sounds: the knock of a hammer and the clang of a bell. The hammer belonged to an itinerant casket maker, employed in the neighborhood for a week now. The bell was that in the Old City's joss house.

"God, what a racket," she said. She sat down at the breakfast table just as a hammer blow and bell strike converged into a single, sharp assault. The mirror over the sideboard hummed in its frame; the teacups whined over their saucers.

"You're in for it if Mother catches you with the window open," Cecily said.

"Pour me a cup, will you?" Alice answered. She indicated the teapot at her sister's elbow, but Cecily didn't look up from the paper, so Alice stood again and reached for the tea herself. "Isn't she up?" she asked. "It's nearly eleven."

"No," Cecily said, still not raising her eyes.

Alice sighed loudly, sat heavily, sprawled dramatically, and clattered the lid of the sugar bowl. "So, is she going to get up, do you think?"

Cecily raised her eyebrows, a gesture that echoed rather than answered the question.

"Well, I don't care what she does."

"Don't you?" Cecily asked.

"I'm going out."

At that, Cecily did look up. "Where?"

"Dulcie's having a party tonight."

Cecily smiled, and of all that a smile might convey—humor, joy, satisfaction—only the last of these was evident, and in its most bitter form. "Is Tsung going to be there?" she asked.

Alice didn't answer.

"I asked if—"

"I heard you."

"May will kill you if she finds out. When."

"How would she? How, unless you told?"

"I'm not going to say a thing. I want nothing to do with it. You. Just the idea makes me ill."

Now it was Alice's turn to smile nastily. "Good," she said. "I'm glad it makes you ill." She reached over and dug her spoon into the butter dish and then the jam pot, eating butter and marmalade together, without bread. "Making you ill is a measure of my—" She paused.

"Your what?"

"Pleasure."

"It's not safe."

Alice leaned back in her chair. "I don't care."

Cecily crossed her arms. "There is the curfew to consider. When Daddy gets back, he'll have a stroke."

"He won't be home any time soon. They've closed the Hong Kong port, and I . . ." Alice spoke slowly, stretched her arms over her head with conscious languor. "I . . . am . . . going . . . out."

In response, Cecily pushed the *North China Daily News* toward Alice, who turned it right side up to read the headlines.

6 March 1919. The city was suffering a shortage of coffin nails. The Shanghai death toll had reached 3,017, and with so many workers ill,

the forge had closed until further notice. Amoy, Tsingtao, and Canton were now infected. The municipal council had voted to require all tram drivers, rickshaw men, constables, and wharf coolies to wear protective linen masks saturated with formalin. Hospital tents had been pitched on the race club lawn; and, as a means of controlling panic in the Old City, ratepayers were insisting that the armed forces bury unclaimed native dead at night, in mass graves.

Despite the fact that native workers in the silk filatures and cotton mills were succumbing faster than any other subset of the population, rumors of revolutionary conspiracy multiplied. It was suggested that Sun Yat-sen had poisoned the water supply. On this matter the British consul could not be reached for comment.

"You'll never get a car or even a rickshaw," Cecily said. "Boy is sick and so is Brother Boy and all the nephews."

"I'll take Uncle's electric," Alice said. "He won't miss it."

"The electric! You might as well walk. You won't get as far as Shangtung. And how will you keep Mother from finding out?" Cecily looked at her sister with narrowed eyes. "Why hasn't Daddy cabled, if they've closed the port?"

"The wires are tied up. The line from the cable office goes on down the Bund for blocks. I sent Number Three first thing this morning and he's still not back. He'll be there all day." Alice stood and walked around the breakfast table, around and around, rapping her knuckles on its white cloth. "One more night in this prison and I'll slit my wrists."

"They'll shut Dulcie down," Cecily said. "With no one to chaperone, someone will call. The police will come."

"Let them call." Alice picked up the paper. "Didn't you read this? The police are all stationed at the race club."

"Push Mother too far," Cecily warned, "and she'll go right round the bend."

Alice snorted. "Too late," she said. "She has already." Alice withdrew a piece of stationery from under the lid of a lacquer box on the sideboard. "See?" At the top of the page were their mother's embossed initials; the rest was covered with black hatch marks.

"What's that?" Cecily asked.

"Calculations," Alice said. "Opportunities for infection that Daddy might conceivably encounter each day he spends in Hong Kong. Doorknobs. Coins. Sneezes at meetings. Cutlery."

Cecily took the paper from her sister. At the bottom, the number 119 was circled. She looked at it without speaking, handed it back. "What was that burning smell last night, around ten?" she asked. "I thought Aunt May must have caught the drapes again with her pipe."

"Galsworthy, the whole set. Swann in Love. The Scarlet Pimpernel—first edition. And Hugo, those nice ones with the gold leaf."

"But those were mine! She gave me those herself!"

"Well," Alice said, "they're gone now. She had Amah pour sulfur on the embers. Hence the smell."

As if summoned, the small, blue-coated woman came silently into the breakfast room, followed by Number Six carrying a toast rack filled with browned slices. "Piecee?" she said.

"My no wanchee." Alice licked marmalade from the spoon. "No likee."

"Yes, likee! Likee fine!" Amah snatched the spoon from Alice's hand. "That no belong good." She pulled the butter dish out of her reach.

"Come upstairs," Alice said to Cecily. "Help me with my costume. It has to be something Spanish."

"What, for Spanish influenza! Isn't that's just like Dulcie."

As the girls left the breakfast room they heard the amah close the window with a bang.

Smoke darkened the sky over the city, the smoke of thousands of fires: coal fires in furnaces, wood fires on hearths, the fires of hospital incinerators. And temple fires, too—the burning of spirit money to pay the way of the dead through the next world. New Year celebrations had given way to funeral parades, to black lacquer coffins carried swinging on bamboo poles.

In the joss house, under the clanging bell, priests bludgeoned the infected in an attempt to drive out fever demons. The line of supplicants awaiting their attention was hundreds long. At the Old City gate, a celestial in red robes charged a dollar to consult a mystical text. His book was upside down and dusty if not, as he claimed, ancient. The recent employer of the red-robed man, had he passed, could have identified the volume as V.K.W. Koo's 1912 work, *The Status of Aliens in China,* not significantly out of date by 1919, and missing for the past week from his library shelf. But Dick Benjamin was far away, in Hong Kong, and the Hong Kong port was closed.

THE HOUSE ON Bubbling Well Road, enclosed by a low wall behind which was a high boxwood hedge, was laid out in the shape of an E, two separate wings embracing small courtyards. When the epidemic began, it had been a simple matter to quarantine the east-side bedrooms in which the infected lay, exhaling germs. Dolly had divided the entire household—not only the sleeping quarters, but the kitchen, the laundry, the staff. Half for herself and her daughters, half to serve the afflicted: to boil the dishes, burn the linens, to make broth and run to the apothecary to leave messages in Dr. Bellamy's pigeonhole.

Since Dick had left for Hong Kong, May had been the only member of the family to travel between firm and infirm, sullenly wearing a mask soaked in disinfectant.

"Really, Dolly," she said. "I feel foolish in this getup."

"Better foolish than dead."

"Well, you don't think I wear this with poor Arthur! Only for you." May pulled the mask down in irritation. Dolly turned on her.

"Put it on," she said.

"I won't."

Dolly looked at her sister-in-law, the defiance in her black eyes. "In my house," she said, "you'll abide by my wishes." But May stood silently, not moving to replace the mask on her face.

"You infected us!" Dolly said. "You brought it here, into this house."

"I?" May said. "What about Eleanor? Or that Mr. Whoever-he-was who touched the books?"

"Not influenza! I'm not talking about that."

May raised her eyebrows. "Of what *are* you speaking?"

"Death. Misfortune. Poor little David. Rose. Now this."

May, expressionless, looked at Dolly. She betrayed no surprise at so irrational an attack; she said nothing in response.

"It's true. I know it." Dolly stepped forward aggressively, and then backed up, as if abruptly reminding herself of the contagion she'd blamed on the silent woman before her. "You . . . You tracked it in with your feet. With your poisonous, unnatural feet. You might fool Arthur. Arthur is a fool, he always has been! But I'm not. I have dreams about you—nightmares—I can't stand any more. I won't. As soon as Arthur can be moved, you'll have to go. Both of you." May moved toward the window. Dolly followed her. "In the dreams your legs are covered in scales. Like a . . . a serpent. Fangs and . . . and . . . We'll all die if you stay!"

"Would you like to see what they are like, really?" May bent down as if to unfasten a shoe.

"No!" Alice's mother recoiled.

"Dolly," May said, her voice smooth, soothing. "Your nerves have got the best of you. Don't say things for which you'll be sorry." She tried to guide her toward the door. "Why don't we have tea. Something to eat."

But Dolly pulled her elbow from May's hand, she ran back into the sitting room. "Don't touch me!"

"Why, Dolly," May said, and her mouth curled with what looked like genuine amusement. "You're more primitive than a Chinese. Everything that happens in this family, everything that goes wrong— it's my fault? Is that it?"

Dolly didn't answer. She pushed past May, left her standing alone in the parlor, the mask hanging loose around her neck.

THE INABILITY TO sleep or to rest, this made its contribution to Dolly's agitation, her irrationality. Each night she stayed up later. After the others had retired, she stood in her dry bathtub, its taps sealed against what might be carried by the suspect Shanghai pipes, and poured Aquarius carbonated table water over her body. She scrubbed every part of herself with carbolic soap, using a washcloth to reach between her shoulder blades, and then rinsed again with Aquarius. Carbonation foamed up like her husband's shaving soap; it stung her elbows and knees and mortified the red cracks between her long, white toes.

At night, after her daughters were asleep, while amahs and house-boys in the servants' quarters shoved garlic paste into their ears and noses, peppers into their mouths, Dolly paced in the library and frowned at the books. Which one was it that Mr. Connolly had touched? He'd come to retrieve a file of bank papers. Number Three had shown him into the library and given him a glass of sherry. And as Dolly came in with the papers, she'd seen Mr. Connolly lick his index finger and use that wet finger to turn a page. The book was bound in blue leather. She had been sure it was blue, but now that all the blue books were gone, it seemed as if it might have been a red one, or a brown.

She'd never feel safe until all of them were burned, even those on the high shelf. Although he probably hadn't climbed the ladder to re-trieve the one he held in his hands—the blue one, the red one, what-ever it was. But then, she hadn't seen him take it from the shelf, or replace it, for that matter. All she had was the distinct picture, framed by the door to the library, of Mr. Connolly standing with a book in his hands and licking his finger to turn the pages. And now he was dead.

It was past midnight. On top of logs that had fallen into embers Dolly laid *The House of Mirth* by Edith Wharton, and next to it Dr. Fan-shaw's *Introduction to the Knowledge of Nature*, an edition that included color plates, which burned with colored flames. She watched this, mo-mentarily distracted, before she piled on Plutarch's *Lives*, *Clarissa*, a set of Kelly and Walsh monographs on Daumier, Corot, Constable, Turner, and Millet. *An Englishman's Introduction to Eastern Religion and Philosophy*. *Essays of Elia* and *More Essays of Elia*.

She'd expected them to be damp—how could books be anything other than damp in this wretched climate?—and they were, but with added fuel they burned. Flames reached up into the chimney, she couldn't see how high, so bright they overpowered the ceiling lamp. Dolly sat in her husband's green leather chair to watch. Already it was nearly eleven o'clock. She wanted to finish them all off tonight. She'd have to use more kerosene to hurry them along.

Dolly unscrewed the lid from the bottle, slippery from previous unscrewings, from where its contents had spilled down the neck and discolored the paper label. Too dangerous to splash kerosene onto live flames—she'd have to pour it over the remaining books and, when the volatile liquid had soaked into their pages, throw them carefully onto the fire. She filled the empty coal scuttle with as many volumes as it would hold and poured the clear fuel over them, not bothering to hold her breath. Kerosene fumes were a smell she liked. As she worked, a few drops fell on the hot stones of the hearth and began to smoke. Dolly watched one and then another spontaneously catch fire. Little circles of flame, they burned brightly for a few seconds and then went out. They gave no warning of what would happen next, when drops landed on the shining, waxed parquet, on cabinets and bookshelves burnished with lemon oil, on the hem of her Kobe-laundered dress.

# DRINK THE WATER

"DON'T GO OUT OF THE ROOM. PROMISE ME you'll stay right here. I'm afraid when you go out."

"Oh, you really are a baby." May sat next to Arthur.

"Tell me about the horses."

"They're wearing cashmere sweaters and drinking port from your sister's cut crystal."

"That's good. I like that. Tell me something else."

May looked at her husband. To die of influenza, the doctor said, was a slow drowning. Arthur's lips and cheeks were mottled, purple, and he was panting, but no worse than Eleanor, and Eleanor was pulling through.

Still, seeing his cracked lips open for breath, May suffered the familiar confusion of trying to sort out apprehension from premonition. Had all his selfless crusades, his campaigns for hygiene, for rehabilitating tubercular rickshaw men and sick horses—had they all proceeded from a shadow cast backward over his life, a shadow cast by this illness? It was the same with Rose: impossible to think of the child without remembering how she hated baths, screamed if the water came up over her legs.

"Won't you try to sleep?" she asked Arthur.

"Talk to me. Please just talk to me. Tell me about the horses. I'll close my eyes."

"I've taught them to play mah-jongg. They're clumsy—their hooves are useless—so they each need a boy to handle the tiles. But we spend very pleasant afternoons together. Everyone disapproves, of course. Dick wants them to learn proper trades. He thinks they should go to mechanic's school now that the age of the automobile is phasing them out. He says they could open a garage."

Arthur said nothing. He didn't smile.

"Wasn't that good?" May put her hand on Arthur's forehead, as if to test for fever, left it there as he spoke. "Wasn't that at all amusing?"

"Do you know?" Arthur said. "I expected that the years would help. That it wouldn't be so sad for us after ten or fifteen years. But it doesn't make a difference, does it?"

May was silent.

"It seems so unkind that she would vanish when everything was perfect. When the day was so lovely, and I was thinking, just a minute before, that I was so happy. Ever since that day, happiness frightens me. I catch myself thinking how much I love you, and I'm afraid. Inside, I correct myself. I say no, she's not that lovely, she's not perfect. She doesn't make you perfectly happy. As if to fool the gods into letting me keep you."

"Because you love me, I'll be taken away?" May asked. "Surely you don't think that's why Rose died."

She was lying, of course, and he knew it. How could she not think the same as he: the magpie of fate—its prey is always someone or something that beckons. That shines with light or with love.

"Yes. No. I don't know what I mean." He was speaking quickly; fevers did that to Arthur. With a fever he was talkative, expansive. Brilliant. His thoughts moved with such speed, his mind leapt, it jumped sideways, he could barely speak fast enough to keep up. Sometimes his childhood stutter returned; and often, as now, the tinnitus grew worse: it got louder, and he had to outtalk it.

He grasped her hand. "That trip on the boat," he said. "It has such a strange, paradoxical quality. It was just a day that we had together, one day measured against thousands, and yet it's as if it has broken out of time, out of the measure of time, and spread into years. But it also seems an instant, a knife blade dividing one age from another. And it's so familiar, I've looked at it from every angle in my mind so often.

"Do you remember the tree? The one on the bank? I know just what we all looked like from the boughs of that tree, from the low bough versus the high one, versus the one in between. And from the vantage of a bird overhead. A bird watching us from so high and seeing the shape of the boat on the water, the way the boat sat in the water, ripples coming out from around it. Ripples of contentment. No, more than that. Exultation. The bird saw them and I see them, too, through the bird's bright eye. There was an unnaturally green bloom of algae in the water that day—you remember, I know you do. The water was an emerald mirror around the boat. The whole of creation glistened. Everything I saw was . . . it sparkled with life.

"I've gone over every part a thousand thousand times. Each stone in the temple—even at that distance I could make out the individual stones, the lines of mortar separating them. And the worms in the riverbank. Those odd, red worms that looked like threads of blood, like veins—as if the very earth were flesh. The eels, and that animal we saw but couldn't identify. Muskrat. Something. Every last creature.

"At night in bed beside you, in the dark as I hear you breathe, sleep, I lie awake and with every second that passes the scene takes on more intense color and life. It's . . . it's fantastic, revelatory, it sickens me. Because it's never over. It unfolds and unfolds. The night trembles and chatters around the boat, around our bed. Inside me, the sound in my head, it's like the gods are laughing at us. Your silhouette on the prow. The teapot beside you. You lifted the teapot—I loved it when you did that. You could do that now."

Arthur dropped May's hand and reached for her leg. "You could make tea, you—you could drink it from the spout. It's so . . . it . . . it makes me want . . ." He squeezed her thigh.

"You think of me taking you in my mouth." May's voice was low.

"Yes! God. I've never been happier, May. I never expected to be as happy as we've been together, as happy and alive. Or as miserable. Like being killed."

Tears ran from Arthur's eyes. "I remember the sound of the turtle's shell as the boy broke it. I know what he was thinking as he prepared dinner. And I know what the turtle thought—Yes! the dead turtle wishing for his life again, fearing the pot. I know what the water was thinking. And the mud below the boat—its secret dark observations. Its desires. I know each rice shoot. I know, I know—" He struggled up, sobbing; he held his arms out wide, empty. "May! I don't know what happened! What? What did happen? How did she drown? Why?" His voice keened and cracked, sounding as it must have when he was thirteen.

"Arthur. Please. Please."

"No! Don't stop me! Don't! You think these things, too! Don't tell me you don't. What do you dream about when you're smoking? Aren't you thinking about Rose?"

May put her hands before her mouth and shook her head. "No." When she spoke her voice was a whisper. Arthur couldn't hear; she had to repeat the words. "Sometimes. Not often."

"Why? Why!"

"Because. I can't stand to. That's what opium is for. Not thinking."

Arthur fell back on his elbows, panting. "So she's just one of a list of those you don't think about? Your mother. Your grandmother. Your father. Your first husband. The men you . . . the ones you entertained—"

"Arthur," May said. "Please. Please."

"—your first daughter. The one you had with someone else." He nodded, jerked his head violently up and down. "Except you do—you do think of her. You've found her. Seen her."

"No!" May reached forward as if to cover his mouth, keep him from saying any more, but then she dropped her hand onto his chest. "How?" she said, after a silence.

"It doesn't matter." Arthur was still nodding his head, but slowly now, his lips pressed together. When he opened them, he drew a breath and held it, as if preparing for exertion, or pain, something that required fortitude. He let the breath out. "I was . . . wounded. It felt . . ." He stopped speaking, looked down at her hand, her fingers worrying the button of his night shirt. "I felt it like a, a . . . I don't know," he said. "A wound, that's all. A . . . an accident. Something broken. Knocked out of place.

"In the days just after I found out, when I moved, I held my body carefully. As if I were afraid of . . ." He closed his eyes and let his head fall back. When he opened them, he was looking at the ceiling. Arthur breathed, sighed. "I wanted . . . I always wanted to share everything with you. But . . . but you didn't allow me everything." He looked back at May, her dry eyes, smooth forehead. "I would have helped you to . . . to find her. I would have . . ."

"How?" May asked again. "How did you find out? When?"

Arthur smiled at her, not sadly—he looked genuinely amused. "Years ago. When you began searching. You didn't imagine—did you, darling? My supposedly worldly darling—that a Shanghai solicitor could resist gossip?"

May pursed her lips as she did when catching herself in one of her infrequent grammatical mistakes. "And people say," she said, "that of the two of us, you are the fool."

"Have you seen her?" Arthur asked, after a moment.

She shook her head no.

"But you know where she lives?"

May dipped her head in the slightest tremor of acknowledgment. Only a person who knew her well could read such an admission. "I didn't . . ." She lowered her eyes, then looked back up, into his, began again. "I didn't do what you said. I didn't have her with someone else. I had her alone. I had her by myself."

Arthur let himself fall the rest of the way back onto his pillow. "Sometimes," he said when he had caught his breath, "I wonder, if I understood you better, would I love you less?" He held his hand back out to her. His fingertips were blue. "No," he answered himself. "It wouldn't make any difference."

"Please," May said.

"I'm going to die. I haven't the strength not to."

"Arthur. Please."

"Stop it!" Arthur cried. "You keep saying the same thing."

"I can't help it. Myself."

Arthur stopped talking, gave himself over to the task of breathing. A week ago, his collarbones were not so prominent. Now, when he struggled to inhale, the hollow between them deepened; it collected a little pool of shadow. Seeing this, May was frightened. Without meaning to, without knowing what she was doing, she touched the same place on her own body.

"Come," he said, after a minute. "Sit by the bed and wash your feet like you do."

"Now? Not now."

"Yes, now! Do it!" Arthur, suddenly flushed, wild, his red hair like a flame over his face, picked at the edge of the sheet, kicked fretfully at the blankets.

"All right," she said. "Yes."

May got the big bowl she used and filled it in the bathroom. She spread a linen towel on the floor beside the bed and sat before the bowl, unwrapping her feet. Arthur held his hand out, and she put the old bindings in his palm. She bathed her feet, left and right. He watched as she gingerly soaped and rinsed each folded toe.

"Give me the water," he said when she had finished. "Hold the bowl for me."

"What for?" May was wrapping her feet in fresh cloths.

"I want. It."

"Why?" she said, and she asked him again. "What for? For what?"

"I'm going to drink it. Then I'll. Know who you are."

May looked at Arthur. She saw he wasn't teasing. To herself she was the least mysterious of women. Who was she? She was still that woman, that girl, that desirable girl about whom it was possible to say to a suitor: *She never cried out.*

May picked up the blue porcelain bowl, its lip decorated with a thin line of vermilion.

"Give it to me," Arthur said. He reached his arms out. "Hold it for me. So I can drink from it. So I can know."

The water spilled over his chin; it wet the bedclothes. Ran trickling through his beard and into his ringing red ears. A few swallows more and he began coughing. May pulled the basin out of his grasp.

"Well?" she said, when he had caught his breath. "Have you figured it all out? Me?"

Eyes closed, he shook his head.

"Nothing?" she asked.

He inhaled, coughed. "No," he said when he could speak. "But," he reached out for her, caught her smallest finger and gave it a little shake. "I think you'll. Be very rich and famous. Your foot water, dearest, it cures tinnitus." He smiled with his eyes closed. "I can't hear. A thing." He brought the finger to his lips, kissed it. "Wonderful. A nice blue bottle, I think." He paused to breathe. "A ringing in the ears? Try May's. Magic. Water . . ."

# The Pipe Dreams

## of a Rat

"Where is everyone?" Alice asked, enter-
ing the shadowy foyer of Dulcie's home. "Too frightened
to come?"

Dulcie said nothing.

"They can't all be ill." Alice looked into the dining
room. There were glasses on the table. A bottle of claret,
a bowl of white peaches.

"You look beautiful," Dulcie said. "I knew you'd
choose flamenco." Alice twirled around so that her full
skirt swung out. Her makeshift mantilla caught on the
arm of a chair, and she freed it and draped it around her
shoulders.

"I had the tailor cut one of Mother's lace tablecloths
in half and dye it black," she said.

The house was dark, silent. Behind Dulcie the empty
salon, like the dining room and hallway, was lighted only
with candles. Dulcie unfastened her cape. "I have some-

thing to confess," she said. She was wearing a toreador's costume, complete with flat black shoes and tight knee pants.

"What's that?"

"I didn't invite any others."

"What do you mean?" Alice asked.

"I didn't invite anyone except you. Not that I meant to deceive you." Dulcie touched Alice's arm as she spoke. "Just that, well, after I talked with you, Tsung asked me not to ring anyone else."

Alice felt for the high comb holding her mantilla. "Well," she said awkwardly. "I imagine you're always in the position of owing him a favor. Aren't you?" Because it was Tsung who got Dulcie her opium.

"Please don't be angry."

Alice looked at her friend. "I'm not. Not much." She adjusted her headdress in the hall mirror. "Where is he, anyway?"

"Bathing." Dulcie was in the salon, putting a record on the phonograph. She'd wound it too tight, though; the music's tempo was accelerated.

"Where's your father?" Alice raised her voice to be heard over the music.

"Don't know," Dulcie called back. "Singapore?"

"What? Does he leave you alone? No chaperone? No amah?"

"I sent them away. I paid them to leave. All of them. Dah Su, cook boy, houseboys. Every last one of them." Dulcie wandered into the dining room, looked at the long table, the twelve empty chairs pushed as far as they would go under its surface. She stroked the table's gleaming finish. "By now they must be miles away. Fleeing from the fever." She poured claret into the three glasses she'd set on the table.

"How do you eat?" Alice asked.

Dulcie laughed. "I go through the pantry," she said. "We still have a lot of biscuits. Tins of things. Water. Wine." She lifted her shoulders, hunched them in a way that made her look younger, a naughty child.

"What about the peaches?" Alice said. "It's much too early for any from Kobe."

"I don't know where they're from." Dulcie picked up a peach and held it under Alice's nose. "There isn't anything, not anything, like that scent. Tsung got them. Somehow. Didn't you?" she asked, turning around. He'd come in without speaking, announced by his reflection in the mirror over the sideboard. Barefoot, he wore a long shirt, half buttoned, nothing more.

"Hello," Alice said. "All dressed up for me?"

Tsung took the peach from Dulcie's hand, brushed his pale lips over its furred skin, replaced it in the bowl without biting it. "This mine?" he asked, picking up the fullest glass. It spilled a little, wine dripping down over his long pale fingers. Tsung was tall for a Chinese, long-boned and slender, with a languid, disappointed air, only half cultivated. His artistic looks were misleading in that the only art he'd ever pursued was satisfying his desires. "I'm hot," he said, explaining his attire. "The bath made me hot." He spoke English with an American accent, picked up in a Massachusetts boarding school, along with a gonorrheal infection of his rectum that he endured for eleven months before coming home to consult with family bone-setters and apothecaries. "Apparently, my roommate had never seen a Chinese before and mistook me for a female of the species," he had said, betraying no bitterness.

Alice put her glass down, and Tsung slid his hand down the front of her skirt. "Carpe diem," he said. He kissed her on the mouth. "Do you know what I saw today? On the river? A coffin barge. Too many to count. I imagined they had bodies inside, but then I saw that the barge was floating high on the water, that the coffins must be . . ." He paused to lick the spilled wine from the back of his hand. "Empty." He drifted toward the kitchen, the long tail of his white shirt floating after him in the dark hallway.

"Father never checks on anything," Dulcie said. "He hasn't been back here since Mother left."

"Where is she?"

"I don't know. Singapore? She has a lover."

"Does she?" Alice tried to imagine such a situation.

"Haven't you heard? An industrialist from Bonn. Herr Groeder or Grouper. Something unappetizing like that. He has much more money than Father and he's buying up all the tungsten in the world, I can't remember what for. The way Shanghai talks, I thought everyone knew."

Alice shook her head. "I wish my mother would run off," she said.

"It is best like this," Dulcie agreed. "It's when they're home that I feel lonely."

Alice didn't answer.

"Tsung's laid a fire." Dulcie swung her cape through the door, in parody of trying to incite a bull to charge. "Come in," she said.

Alice followed her from the dining room to the salon, where the dark velvet drapes were drawn, no light save that from a candelabra dripping wax on the piano lid. Then Dulcie got the fire going, and the room was filled with a shuddering orange glow.

They sat on cushions before the hearth, held their glasses self-consciously. "Do you like this?" Dulcie asked. "There's other things, if you'd rather. There's brandy."

"This is fine." A pocket of gas popped in one of the logs and threw a cinder onto the rug. Neither girl moved to brush it off, and as it burned the wool it made an acrid smell. Alice took a deep swallow from her glass. She'd never had more than a sip before. "Guess what *my* mother's doing," she said.

"What?"

"She has an absolute *idée fixe* that someone's infected our books. Last week, when one of Daddy's associates came to pick up some papers, Number Three put him to wait in the library, and Mother's sure she saw him lick his finger and turn a page." Alice took another swallow of wine. Firelight lit the contents of her glass so that it seemed to be holding embers.

"And now she's found out he's dead, she's sure the library is contaminated. She doesn't know which book, so she's burning them all. She lies in bed during the day, awake, and throws books into the fire at night."

"What about your father? Can't he usually talk sense into her?"

"Stuck in Hong Kong."

"Your aunt?"

"Sealed off in another part of the house with Eleanor and Arthur. They're both ill, that's the incredible part of it. There's influenza in the house already. But Mother's sure it's the books that will kill us."

"She's mad," Dulcie said matter-of-factly.

Alice drained her glass. Her tongue felt spongy against the roof of her mouth. "Well, she's always been highly strung. And after David . . ." She turned her glass upside down, watched the progress of a red drop as it moved slowly toward the lip. "When David died, we all became more ourselves. Mother more nervous, Daddy harder-working, Cecily withdrawn. I fled them all. Divorced them for my aunt."

"Are you seeing Lawrence?" Dulcie asked.

"Who wants to know, you or Tsung?"

"I do."

"We play tennis, that's all." Alice lay back and balanced her empty glass on her stomach, holding its stem so it wouldn't fall.

Dulcie unfastened the buttons of her tight jacket and took it off. She got up to retrieve the claret from the dining room, returned with the bowl of peaches as well. She took Alice's glass and refilled it.

"Here," Dulcie said, and Alice sat up.

"Drink it," Dulcie said.

The two girls leaned back against the cushions, saying nothing, watching the fire. Dulcie used a piece of kindling to poke the coals. Its end caught, and she threw it in with the rest, set a new log on top. Two beetles emerged from under the bark and ran back and forth, trying to escape the sudden heat. "Poor things." Alice watched them. "Here's a question," she said.

"What?"

"May told me that once when she was smoking opium—"

"If only I'd had an aunt who smoked," Dulcie interrupted. "It would have made all the difference, really."

"—she looked up and saw rats. Rats on the rafters. And they weren't moving. They lay on the beams with their eyes open. She could see the glitter. They were intoxicated, inhaling opium. And what I wonder is, what are the pipe dreams of a rat?"

"Cheese," Dulcie said. "And bacon. Not attached to traps."

"No," said Alice. "That's too easy. That's obvious. And pipe dreams never are. Obvious."

"Oh, I don't know," Dulcie said. "A rat wants what a rat wants." She stood up. "Speaking of which . . ."

Alice looked up as Tsung came in.

HIS MUSCULAR TONGUE tasted of wine. "Don't push so hard," Alice complained. "You get the whole of yours in and I can't even move mine."

"Sorry. Overeager, is all."

The phone rang eleven times and stopped.

"Who would call now?" Alice said. "It's the middle of the night. It's—oh, God—it's after three."

"One of Mother's friends." Dulcie put on another record, sat on the piano bench and watched as Tsung, shirt unbuttoned, straddled Alice's chest. He used his hands to force her breasts together around his penis, wet with his own saliva, and moved it back and forth, eyes shut in concentration. Alice, eyes open, tried but couldn't get her arm around him to touch herself. When he came, semen landed on her throat, her face, and in her hair.

"And to think"—Tsung opened his eyes—"your virtue is still intact."

"My hymen, anyway."

He wiped her chin with his hand. "You know that's all that counts." Tsung offered Alice his index finger. "Taste it," he said. "Me."

Alice sat up, arms around her knees. "Why?"

"Education. Besides, you are fond of me, aren't you?" Tsung smiled, his usually pale lips flushed and full from his exertions.

But before Alice could answer, there was a knocking on the front door, and the two of them jumped up from the hearth. Before they could gather their clothes, the door opened, followed by steps in the hall.

"My . . . my aunt," Alice said, as she recognized the sound of the jade cane; and May walked into the room.

"Goddess of Mercy." May looked at Alice standing naked by the mantel, Tsung sitting naked on the divan, his legs insolently open. There was a pillow beside him, but he didn't use it to cover himself. May stared at both of them with undisguised contempt. Alice looked at the floor, but Tsung returned May's gaze. He said a few words in Chinese, his voice low, drawling, and she answered in English.

"A whore, am I? And what about you?" May's voice was slow, as if she'd been smoking. "The spoiled, lazy, sixth son of a Green Gang underling?" She was sober, Alice could see that she was. Still, it was as if she and the Victrola were winding down together. "Alice," she said. "Dress yourself. So we can go." Alice remained motionless, and May stepped forward. She raised her hand as if to slap Alice's face, let it remain there, frozen in the space between them. "How dare you. Is this— This is how you repay me?"

"But Aunt—"

"With a Chinese. A Chinese." May's hand wavered. Her voice— how strange it was. Unfamiliar—no, not unfamiliar, but somehow wrong. It sounded angry, and yet it lacked emotion, inflection. Its pitch was constant, unprecedentedly regular. It didn't rise; it didn't fall. Alice caught her aunt's hand and forced it down by her side.

"What can you be saying? What can you mean when—when you married Uncle Arthur? When you've encouraged me to . . ." *To disregard rules,* she had been going to say, but she could see May wasn't even listening. She'd sat down on the piano bench. Her cheeks were white, and she bent over suddenly, she hid her face in her arms. "What *is* the matter?" Alice asked. From her mother she would expect hysterics, catatonia—anything. After all, staying out all night was no minor crime, notwithstanding influenza, the curfew. But her aunt? May was different.

"Arthur," May said at last.

"What's happened? Has he—"

But May just shook her head.

Dulcie came forward with Alice's Spanish shawl. She put it around her shoulders. "What has happened?" she said. "Has something happened?"

May sat up. She rose from the bench, leaning on her cane, looked around the room as if slowly taking into account the fire, the bowl of discarded peach pits, the mantel clock's black hands approaching the hour of four, the candles dripping on the piano lid. At last her eyes came back to Alice. "Your mother has burned down the house," she said, her voice still slow, uninflected.

Alice covered her mouth. "Is—"

"She's dead. And Arthur. Arthur is dead. They didn't get out."

## THE HEAD OF
## THE FAMILY

INSTALLED ONCE AGAIN IN THE ASTOR HOUSE
Hotel, May found it difficult not to think of her first stay
there, a time when, like now, there was no Arthur, and
the past lay silent, obliterated. She remembered ruin-
ing the contents of the drawer in her grandmother's bedroom. Now Dolly had done the same. Not intentionally,
perhaps. But she had destroyed what she could not
bear. May felt an unanticipated sympathy for her sister-
in-law. The heat of the fire had been so intense that it
melted the ice on the drive. From the road, it looked to
May like the one brave thing her sister-in-law had ever
done.

Smoke had accomplished Arthur's suffocation a little
more quickly, that was all. The doctor said as much; she
couldn't blame Dolly. Hadn't she always expected to lose
him? Now, at last, circumstances had aligned to return
her to the self she had been before she met Arthur: a
woman who had endured humiliations and hardships

and who would, if fate required it, continue to endure. May, too, could be a locked drawer. And besides, perhaps there was comfort to be drawn from the hopelessness of the situation. What loss, she wondered, could be more painful than this?

In the weeks that had elapsed since the fire, Alice had not yet cried. She slept many hours each day, rising at eleven, going to bed by nine. "I can't be bothered," she said to every suggestion. "It's odd," she told May, "but I feel nothing. Absolutely not anything." They were sitting together on the small, unyielding sofa in the suite of rooms they had taken on the north side of the hotel, where the windows overlooked treetops rather than the river. "I worry that I'm wronging Mother. As if I can't give her what I want to, some evidence of . . . of grief. But when I look for it, it's not there." She sighed, a deep, yawning sigh. "No, that's not right," she said. "It's that she left me—us—so long ago, so very long ago. When David died."

Alice sighed and May kissed her cheek. "I'm leaving you here at the hotel this afternoon. I have a piece of business to address before we sail. You'll look in on Cecily and Eleanor, won't you?"

"What about Daddy? Is he going out, too?"

"Yes. Your father and I are going out together. Just a little tying up of . . ."

"What?"

"Nothing. Business. I'll bring you back some books, shall I?"

May went into her room. She took off her yellow cheongsam and put on a blue. Then she took that off and tried the mauve, the gray, the red, and finally settled on a plain black silk tunic and matching trousers. She considered herself in the mirror. She was forty-three years old, and in black she looked it. It didn't bother her that her face was aging. Her vanity, she'd discovered, was invested in her neck. Just under her jaw the skin had slackened; it made a little dimple when she swallowed, and two haggard cords stood out. Could it be possible that already her once smooth neck was beginning to look as her grandmother's had, the last time she'd seen Yu-ying?

May scrubbed off the red lipstick she'd carefully applied; she washed the rouge from her cheeks, the powder from her nose and chin and forehead. Watching her reflection, she removed the pins from her elaborately arranged hair, combed it out and pulled it back in a plain, tight chignon.

"You're not going out like that!" Alice said when she emerged. "I've never seen you look like that in my life. Even at Uncle . . . Why, even at Mother's and Uncle Arthur's funeral you didn't look like, like that!"

"No," May said. "But today I am not dressing for Arthur."

Alice followed her to the door. "Who? Who then?"

"No one," May said. "Myself."

"But—"

"Your father is waiting downstairs. We'll be back before tea."

Alice watched May as she walked down the hall to the lift, then went to her sister's door and knocked. When there was no answer, she pushed it open slowly. "Ces?" she said.

"What do you want?" Cecily was sitting on the floor, leaning against the unmade bed, arms hugging her bent legs.

"You can't cry all day," Alice said. "Not day after day."

"I didn't think so, either."

Alice felt a mean relief in seeing that Cecily could not grieve picturesquely, without red-rimmed eyes and a shiny, swollen red nose.

"It's unfair of me," Alice confessed, sitting down on the bed, "but I feel angry with you, as if you've stolen my feelings. As if you're showing off, one person's tears inadequate to your misery." She sighed, stood, and walked to the window, looking at but not seeing the street, the traffic. "May has gone out wearing a severe costume, all black, without any paint on."

"Has she." Cecily sounded entirely uninterested.

"Yes. Do you know why?"

Cecily shook her head.

"She said she was going somewhere with Daddy. That they had some business to settle."

Her sister said nothing.

"Well, don't you think it's odd?" Alice asked. "What business could it be? The brokerage has never involved May. They've never had . . . business."

Cecily looked at Alice. "I wish anyone had died except Mother. I wish May had. Or you. Why didn't you?"

Alice stood before Cecily, unmoving.

"To think of you having intercourse— Yes! How can you think I don't know!—with a . . . Chinese, while she—"

"But—" Alice interrupted.

"Will you get out of my room?" Cecily scrambled to her feet with uncharacteristic haste. "Get out! You make me ill."

DOWNSTAIRS, IN THE cool lobby, Dick sat in a leather armchair. He was drinking a cup of coffee when May joined him, walking slowly as she always did.

"Why, May," he said, startled by the austerity of her dress. He set his cup in its saucer. May sat on the edge of the leather sofa opposite his chair.

For the first time since its construction, footsteps echoed in the empty halls of the Astor House, announcing infrequent visitors to the hair salon, the tea room and bar attended by silent Chinese, uneasy in idleness, standing at attention as if it might be the Fever God himself arriving in his noisy shoes.

"You'll come?" Dick asked, as he had already several times before. "You'll come with the girls? With me?"

May put her hand out, patted his knee as she might a child's. "Yes," she said, "I've told you I will."

She hadn't spoken to Alice about Tsung. Whenever she considered what needed to be understood—that such an adventure could never be repeated—and how she might illustrate this injunction against entanglements with natives, May found herself overcome by anger. What further illustration could be necessary? What had been the point of the stories she'd already told Alice, stories about her first husband, her father? Alice was headstrong, she was curious, she enjoyed transgressing; and May was too livid for any delicate, considered examination of the topic of Chinese men. The family would leave Shanghai, and that would be the end of it.

"I can't handle them myself," Dick was saying, as if eavesdropping on May's thoughts. Especially— Well, especially Alice. She's ... I ... It was Dolly who knew the girls, really."

The waiter came with a little tray bearing the coffee chit and set it silently on the table beside Dick's chair. "You promise you'll come," he said again. All his bluster, his humor, had died with his wife.

"Yes," she said. Understanding that now it was she who was head of the family. "Yes."

Dick looked at his shoes. With an elderly sounding grunt, he bent down to polish the toe of one with his napkin. "Coffee before we go?" he asked.

"No, Dick. You know I don't like it."

"Oh. Right." He looked around the room vaguely. Frowned as if trying to understand how he'd come to be there. "Tea?" he said, after a moment.

"No. Thank you. Is the car waiting?"

Dick blinked. "I don't know," he said.

"I thought you'd asked for one."

"Oh. Yes, of course. I must have." He went to the concierge's desk, moving stiffly, as though suddenly arthritic. Watching him, May was distracted by the abrupt appearance of Alice, coming down the stairs two at a time, awake as she hadn't been in weeks. She'd brushed her hair; she was pulling on her coat.

"Are you going out as well?" May said to her. "Where?"

"With you. You said you were shopping for books."

May reached into her bag; she took out a jade bracelet, put it on her wrist, considered it, and then took it off and replaced it in her purse. "What I said was that I had a piece of business to address." She turned back to check on Dick, still standing meekly at the desk. A woman in a blue dress stepped between him and the concierge and began talking rapidly. Dick did nothing; he made no attempt to redirect the concierge's attention. Perhaps he hadn't even ordered the car.

"Please!" Alice said.

"All right," May said, and sighed. "Your father could use a quiet afternoon."

. . .

"TELL ME," ALICE said, when they were finally en route. "Why? Why haven't you mentioned her before?" She tugged on her aunt's sleeve, jealous at the revelation that May had a child, a secret daughter, all grown up.

"Why are you crying?" May said, not asking the more pointed, pertinent question: Why, when the death of her mother and uncle and the destruction of her home had left her dry-eyed, was Alice crying over this news?

"I . . . It's a bit of a shock, that's all."

"I can see how it might be." May revealed no more emotion than she might if discussing dinner plans that had gone awry. "I didn't mention her because I never knew where she was. She . . . as it turns out, she went to Siccawei."

Alice tried to put the information together. "She lives in the convent? She's a nun?"

"No, a . . . an orphan."

"So you had her before? Before . . . She's not Arthur's?"

"No."

"Just one, right? Not more?"

May gave Alice an aggrieved look.

"Well, I never know with you. You could do anything." Alice nuzzled her aunt's cheek. "You know I don't mean that unkindly. How did you find her? Or did she find you?"

May drew a deep breath, as if preparing for a dive, a lengthy submersion. "She—she wasn't looking for me. And there are a limited number of places that take such children."

"But she's . . . you said she was . . . Twenty-four is too old to be an orphan. Why is she still at Siccawei? Why hasn't she left?"

May closed her eyes; she leaned her head against the seat cushion. "She didn't want to live outside. The nuns allow her to remain."

"So she did convert? Profess, I mean."

"No," May said. "She did not."

"Why?"

May opened her eyes and looked at Alice. "She refused. She's an atheist. Doesn't believe any of it. That's what the nuns told the solicitor."

"Really," Alice said. "Well." The two were silent as the car proceeded slowly through the empty streets and then came to a stop before the tram tracks.

May had imagined, in the weeks after Arthur's death, that she might remain in Shanghai. After Dolly burned down the house, she fantasized about reunion with her lost daughter, her *found* daughter, one in which May would—she didn't know how but somehow—make the girl understand that she'd been young, little more than a girl herself when she'd given her child up. When her child was taken from her.

The two of them could live together; they wouldn't need a man. No, they'd be better off without one. She imagined the businesses with which they might occupy and support themselves. According to the missionaries, her daughter was a skilled seamstress, and May pictured them in one of the shops on Ningpo Road, yards of unblemished silk spread under their hands. Or they could start a language school. Apparently, Agnes had inherited May's ability. They could teach French, English, German. A future could be written in other tongues.

But twice May had come to the mission and the girl—*the girl? her daughter*—had refused to see her. Just the previous week, on May's second visit, she'd sent the message that she considered her mother lower than a turtle. She'd written the words in English on a clean white page, each letter formed with savage perfection. Formed with what May's eye recognized as controlled rage: a cold impossible anger, not a hot one that offered hope. The nun who'd handed her the note looked embarrassed.

"Seven years older than I," Alice mused and was silent, calculating further. "So it was some time before you were married that . . ." She didn't finish, and May, absorbed in her own thoughts, didn't answer. A laundry room as a nursery, a laundress for a nurse. May remembered the baby sleeping on bundles of sheets waiting to be washed.

"Why do they keep her at that age?" Alice asked. "Especially if she refuses to be religious."

May looked out the window at the shops sliding past. Used as she was to a sedan chair, she felt sick riding in an automobile. Unmoored and disoriented without the slapping of feet on pavement, the jog of human steps.

Fear of contagion had emptied the streets. The few pedestrians wore masks tied over their noses and mouths. They hurried on their errands, heads bent down. May pulled a small looking glass from her bag, considered her neck in the daylight before answering Alice's question.

"She works hard, they say. She's a member of their community. Acts in charity to others. Since the influenza epidemic she's helped care for the sick." May paused. "What's the expression? Actions count louder than words? Sound louder?"

"Speak."

"Yes. The sisters pray for her. For her to . . . They pray for her happiness, is how the nun put it."

The car rolled to a halt on the corner of Kiangse and Tientsin, just a few blocks from Madame Grace's, where one wet spring night May's first daughter had been born. Outside, in the street, a tiny native woman sat with a child next to her, a child of three or four in blue jacket and pants and still nursing, the woman's nipple clamped in his mouth, her brown breast pulled as long and flat as Arthur's razor strop.

"Why has he taken this route? It's not at all direct." May closed her eyes. "Another minute and I am going to be ill."

Alice looked out the window, thankful for any reason the driver might have avoided Bubbling Well Road and the ruined husk of her home, a few wet, charred furnishings on the same lawn where they'd been stacked for the great housecleaning. Now scavengers instead of amahs would preside over the display. "I think Ningpo has been cordoned off by the Red Cross," Alice offered. "I've heard you feel better if you look forward, out the windscreen."

May sat up straight. "No good," she said after a minute. "Doesn't help a bit."

"Does she speak English?" Alice asked. "Does she understand what the meeting's about?"

"She's literate. As well-spoken as you or I."

The car came to a slow stop. "We're here," Alice said. "A good thing, too. You've gone quite green." The driver came around to help them out.

"What's her name?" Alice asked.

"She's taken a western name," May said. "A name she chose."

"What is it?"

"Agnes."

Alice frowned and smiled, both at once. "How odd. Sounds so Irish."

"Catholic, you mean."

"I suppose." She slipped her hand into her aunt's. "Come on then. We'll get it over with. Aren't you glad of my company?"

May kissed Alice's cheek. "Of course I am!" she said. But her voice was brittle, drained of its usual melody.

THE SOLICITOR'S OFFICE was furnished in heavy walnut furniture, the legs of the tables and chairs pressing down into the thick crimson carpet with what looked like uncomfortable force. When May tried to move her chair she found she couldn't. The solicitor, Mr. Barrett, came in rubbing his hands as if they were cold. "They're in the back room," he said. "I'll just bring them in, shall I?"

Alice looked at May, who nodded. "Please," May said, icily. Though she had decided not to confront the solicitor for having betrayed what she had had every right to consider a confidence, she had changed in her manner toward him. She treated him with a punitive courtesy. But Mr. Barrett made no move toward the door.

"There's no point in waiting, is there?" Alice asked.

"No," the solicitor said. He sat in a chair opposite theirs, crossed his legs, uncrossed them, leaned forward with elbows on knees. "She's . . . Miss Agnes is not willing to accept your offer," he said to May.

May sucked her lips in, making her mouth into a taut line. She held them in that expression for a moment, then, slowly, she nodded. "She doesn't have to have anything to do with me. Does she know that?

Does she know I'm leaving? That I'll be far from here, in another country?"

"Yes."

"But," Alice interrupted. "If she's not willing, why did she agree to come here? To come to this meeting?"

"It seems," Mr. Barrett said. Again he attempted a relaxed posture and failed. "It seems she decided she'd like to have a . . . a chance to see Mrs. Cohen."

"Well," said May, drawing herself up in her chair. She smoothed the slick black fabric of her trousers over her knees, folded her hands in her lap. "Here I am. We can proceed as planned. You outline the offer while we . . . while she looks at me."

"Yes," Mr. Barrett said. "Right. I'll just bring them in then."

He was gone for a few minutes. In his absence, neither May nor Alice spoke. The mantel clock ticked with surprising volume. When Mr. Barrett returned, he was followed by an old Chinese Catholic nun in a white habit that hung just to the tops of her tightly laced shoes.

"I'm Sister Elizabeth," she said. "And this is Agnes." She pulled the elbow of the young woman accompanying her, and Agnes stepped forward an inch.

Despite what May had said about her daughter's atheism, Alice had formed the comforting expectation of a dowdy girl dressed as a postulant, a plump and possibly ugly, certainly very plain and downcast, young woman. But Agnes, wearing a long mauve skirt and blue blouse, was startlingly beautiful, as beautiful as her mother—or would have been if she had smiled or even scowled. As it was, she bore the look of a milliner's window model. Her pale forehead seemed empty of thoughts, her bloodless cheeks erased of desire. She held her head at an angle that suggested arrogance; and, as if she were in fact above them, on a pedestal or dais, it was possible to see the delicate symmetry of her nostrils. Alice found herself thinking of the cast court, dragging Eleanor through aisles of serenely frozen white-lipped saints.

Her father must have been quite fair, Alice decided, for Agnes's hair was not black but brown, her long eyes green. She was tall, too, taller than Sister Elizabeth, taller than the solicitor. Without success,

Alice tried to connect the yo... woman...
mother's small frame, her wa...

May dipped her head, sligh...
mained motionless. At the solic...
tened as he explained the trust N...

"It will pay a quarterly dividen...
income as you see fit. Certainly, it ...
pendence indefinitely. Your indeper...
for receipt. You may remain in the ...
the income, donate it to the mission, ... pacing off his little speech, hands in pock... ...ween desk and
mantel, but now he stood still; he stopp... ...peaking.

Agnes had risen from her seat and was walking across the carpet
toward May. It was apparent, as it had not been before, that she
limped; her left foot found its stride with a hesitation that suggested
pain. She stopped just inches from her mother's knees and looked
May up and down, carefully, thoroughly, as if having been given the
chance to observe an alien form of life. An opportunity at once distasteful and irresistible.

"What has—" May began by addressing the question to her daughter, then turned to Sister Elizabeth. "Was she—was Agnes hurt?"

"When she came to us, Agnes had been injured. Her left foot was
infected. Gangrenous, actually. The doctor couldn't save—she lost
three toes." The nun spoke in a low, disciplined voice, the voice of the
early canonical hours, of matins or lauds, a voice that betrayed ex-
haustion. "It appeared as though she'd been bitten," she added, as if
this were an afterthought. A minute passed, and another, before anyone responded.

Then, "Bitten?" Alice asked. "Mauled, you mean? By an animal?"
Sister Elizabeth didn't answer.

May looked at Alice, at the nun, the solicitor, Agnes. As her eyes
passed over each face, her lips moved, soundlessly. She seemed to be
saying a secret spell or prayer over them all.

Sister Elizabeth kept her eyes on her hands, which lay folded in her
lap. "Agnes was bitten all over," she said, her tone abruptly vehement,
shocking for its contrast to her previously calm report. "But only her

finish the sentence. She looked up at all of
the solicitor; her expression appealed to Mr. Barrett
ed justice, the laws he had studied. When she contin-
d her hands out, beseeching.

e never played with the other children. She couldn't run. She
n't speak until she was four."

While the nun talked, May watched Agnes, who remained standing before her. May searched every feature of Agnes's lovely face and then, at last, she lingered on her daughter's long green eyes. Alice watched her aunt watching and couldn't help but feel that what May was looking for was a chance, a reason to hope.

May had already concluded there was none; she understood that what she was doing was memorizing this young woman, whom she would never see again, when Agnes spat. The saliva arced out of her mouth and left a trembling strand, still fixed to her lower lip, which broke only after the rest had landed on May's breast.

"Agnes!" Sister Elizabeth jumped up from her chair. "I'm terribly sorry. This is most unlike her. It's, oh, dear . . . it's testimony, I'm afraid, to the strain this whole, this development has—I'm so sorry—introduced."

"No." May pushed away the nun's hand with its white handkerchief. "Please. Don't apologize for Agnes."

"We have to go," Alice said, and she stood up. "We have another appointment," she lied.

"No." May turned back to Sister Elizabeth. "I'm giving my daughter the money. It doesn't make up for anything, but I'm leaving, you understand, and I have money. It's for her. There isn't—I don't have anyone else. As Mr. Barrett explained, Agnes doesn't have to take the money. She can give it to you. To the mission, I mean. Or she can leave it in the bank. It's . . . you see, it belongs to her."

Sister Elizabeth nodded.

"Please." May looked at Agnes. "Feel free to leave." The girl stared back. Her eyes were as hard and dry as glass; they betrayed no remorse, no embarrassment. Nothing. Saliva still glistened on her lip.

. . .

"I'M SORRY," THE solicitor said, as he saw the women to their automobile. He didn't look at May's face or at the stain on her black silk tunic but at his own shoes.

"Why are you sorry?" May said brusquely. "What have you done?"

"What I meant—"

"What I have, I deserve." Oddly—and this was something Alice had never seen before—May began to bow, but then she caught herself, she held out her hand, Western style. The solicitor took it.

"I'll forward my address," she said.

It was dull outside the somber office, the sky a gray-yellow. A storm was arriving, and clouds blew quickly past. Looking up, Alice had the impression that the sun was in transit, hurrying backward, toward the east. She fell into the car's wide back seat and immediately doubled over, as if ill. "What a horrible, horrible girl!" she said into her lap. "I don't care if she is yours—She's not! She's a . . . a . . . No wonder something bit her!"

"Shut up!" May said. Alice, astonished, sat up and stared at her aunt. May sat with her eyes closed, her hands in fists at her sides. "Please," May said. "Please. Just please don't say any more."

# HOSPITALITY

THE GENDARME ESCORTED SUZANNE PETROVNA to a villa whose pink stuccoed walls and orange-tiled roof were flooded with light, its source hidden by the foliage of grand and trembling acacia trees. It was increasingly windy; the mistral gathered force at night, blowing dry leaves and dust through the street.

Suzanne looked at the black iron bars of the locked gate. She matched the number to that on the card in her hand.

### May-li Cohen
AVENUE DES FLEURS, 72

The name of the street was well chosen: cineraria, lavender, jasmine, salvia, convolvulus, bougainvillea, espaliered apples in blossom—a confusion of colors and scents.

"*Ici? C'est là?*" Suzanne said to the gendarme. *This is the place?*

"*Oui.*" He set her bag down on the ground and pointed his finger—a surprisingly slender and white finger, more like a magician's than a police officer's—at a black button in a ring of highly polished brass: the bell. "Shall I ring?" he asked.

"It's so late. Won't we disturb them?"

"Oh, they're up all night here." The gendarme waved his arm in an expansive gesture at the villa, all its brightly lit windows. Suzanne watched as two slender silhouettes passed from one second floor window to another. The glass panes, curtained with fabric as sheer as a silk stocking, extended from floor to ceiling. She could see the outline of the women's high-heeled feet as they walked though one luminous badge of light and into the next. As she stared—she was tired, the scene before her transfixing—the wind moved through the acacia leaves; they made an eager sound like that of dry hands chafing together, one palm stroking its mate.

"*Alors?*" said the gendarme. *Well?*

Suzanne nodded. With thirty-seven francs in her pocket, all that remained of what she'd received when she pawned her mother's necklace, what choice did she have?

The gendarme reached forward and pushed the black button. A Chinese houseboy, dressed in blue and wearing black felt slippers, emerged from the front door and walked briskly down the path to the gate. "*Bon soir,*" he said, bowing. His jacket was so perfectly pressed, the trousers bore such precise creases, Suzanne found herself wondering if he ever sat down.

"*Une amie de Madame Cohen,*" the gendarme explained, and in hopes of furnishing what might be understood as an invitation, Suzanne held out May's calling card.

"*Oui,*" the houseboy said, and he bowed again. From his pocket he withdrew a key to the black iron gate.

"*Bon,*" said the gendarme. *All right, then.* He tipped his hat to Suzanne, who gave him an anguished, panicked look.

He smiled. "Oh," he said, "you've nothing to worry about now. That"—he gestured at the calling card in Suzanne's clenched hand—

"that's money in the bank." He tipped his hat again, tapped his heels together in a jaunty military farewell.

"*Merci,*" she said, and again the gendarme threw his arm open in a gesture that seemed to sweep Suzanne forward through the gate. The houseboy picked up her battered, grimy tapestry bag. "*Merci,*" she said again, nodding, her mouth so dry that it was difficult to say even the one word. And the officer left; she followed the houseboy up the path, noting how neatly the crushed white quartz had been raked around the trunk of each rose tree that formed its border.

When they reached the front door, Suzanne saw that the villa was, in fact, filled with people who were not only up late on an unremarkable Tuesday in April but dressed as if for a holiday party, in evening clothes and jewels, talking animatedly, some dancing, others dining, and still others, given sounds of water splashing, swimming. Through the crowded salon's windows Suzanne saw flashes of blue from a long, illuminated pool in the back garden.

"*Restez ici, s'il vous plaît,*" said the houseboy, and Suzanne sat where directed, on a Chinese red lacquer chair in the hall.

When the houseboy returned, he was followed by the extraordinary Oriental who earlier that day had leaned out of a sedan chair to give Suzanne her calling card—or was that yesterday? Surely it was past midnight.

How slowly—with what mesmerizing, hypnotically slow grace— the woman moved. She walked, yes, but not like anyone else Suzanne had ever seen, the smallest slowest steps. Beyond regal. Otherworldly. A lifetime elapsed between hall and front door: trains arrived and departed; storms broke, the pavement dried; wedding bouquets wilted and were discarded, a few were pressed as mementos; children were born, old people died.

And the voice—musical, lilting, not at all slow. A current of nervous excitability, but modulated, graceful.

Suzanne stood and, catching herself in the ridiculous urge to curtsy, was relieved to have gotten only as far as twitching the hem of her skirt.

"I am glad you've come!" May said in impeccable French, and she seemed not only to remember Suzanne from their encounter that afternoon but to be genuinely pleased to see her. She held her hand out, a narrow, smooth, boneless-looking hand, perfumed, manicured. Suzanne took it with some embarrassment, her own fingers roughened and cracked, her nails unkempt.

"What would you like?" May asked. "You can stay up, have dinner with the rest. We're having a bit of a party tonight. It's Dick's sixtieth birthday. But we're not sitting at table, it's buffet. Boy will make you a plate. Or you can have dinner in your room. You could have a swim. Or sleep." She counted off possibilities on her fingers.

Suzanne, bewildered by what seemed the assumption of familiarity—her hostess spoke as if it were obvious who Dick was—looked at the white skin of May's hands, how intensely it contrasted with the dark blue silk of her gown, the red varnish on her nails. Impossible to look at a hand like that without thinking of fairy tales, of blood on snow, on sheets. She raised her eyes to the face of their owner, who smiled and lifted her eyebrows in a gentle prod of inquiry, at which point Suzanne, for the second time that day, began to cry.

"Oh, dear." May's face reflected sorrow as immediately as a looking glass, but with warmth, not a mirror's cold mimicry. She turned to the houseboy. "Please show Madame . . ." She paused, waiting for a name.

"Mademoiselle," Suzanne said, after a moment and in a low, embarrassed voice. How unfortunate to have to announce oneself as a spinster. "Mademoiselle Petrovna."

"Please show Mademoiselle Petrovna to her room. And after you've settled her in, a bit of dinner. *Consommé*, I think. *Toast. Thé— camomille. Non, gingembre.*" She turned and looked assessingly at Suzanne. "You're wheezing," she said. "Have you a chest complaint?"

Suzanne stared at her, her cheeks wet, so unexpected was the pain occasioned by a stranger's solicitude. Before the enchanted progress of the past hours—her afternoon encounter with May on the promenade, her rescue by the policeman, and her arrival at Avenue des Fleurs, 72—it had been a very long time since anyone had shown her so much as a flicker of kindness. Even the cat, whom for years Suzanne had considered her own, had recently forsaken her for a neighbor with a better larder.

"Well," May said, "I've asked for ginger tea. It will help if you do, and if you don't it can't hurt you."

Suzanne, still weeping, was led away, up a long, carpeted stairway to a room with a blue-and-crimson Persian rug, a high four-poster bed, a chaise upholstered in slippery chintz, a writing desk with a blue blotter and, standing on it, a clock and a lamp with a cut-glass base; there was also a round table with a lace cloth and a tall vase of tuberoses, and two chairs. The houseboy opened the wardrobe, put her bag inside, and withdrew silently.

"Oh," Suzanne said aloud, and she sank to her knees before the bed as if at an altar. She laid her cheek on the blue counterpane. How was it that she had never before recognized, never really admitted, her terrible tiredness? She was still kneeling with eyes closed when the houseboy returned with a tray, which he set soundlessly on the table. She wasn't asleep but was watching a series of lacquered, jeweled boxes opening up against a black backdrop. The sides of each came apart at the seams to reveal another that was both smaller and more complex and ornate. "Chinese boxes. Of course, Chinese boxes," Suzanne was commenting to herself, in an attempt to explain the curious, almost hallucinatory quality of her vision, when the houseboy, having unfolded her napkin and pulled out her chair, cleared his throat. She started and struggled to her feet, bowing awkwardly in response to his bow. It wasn't until she was sitting at the table, drinking ginger tea, that she realized a fire was burning beneath the white marble mantle. What dissolute madness could explain a fire burning in April, on the warm sunny coast of the Riviera? Suzanne watched the flames. She sipped her tea, chewed one triangle of toast, swallowed two spoonfuls of soup, and when her eyes began to close, went to bed, sleeping, as usual, on her side, with knees bent, arms folded.

When she woke, her room was filled with light, and she sat up suddenly in apprehension and looked around her. On the table was her dinner, almost untouched. Outside, beyond the pool, she could see citrus trees, their trunks painted white with lime. She sat in the chair by the glass door to the balcony—the room's private balcony—and drank the cold tea left in her cup.

Now what, she thought. The house was silent. The hands of the desk clock pointed to twenty minutes past noon. Still wearing the clothes she had worn the day before, and the day before that, Suzanne sat for an hour sipping cold ginger tea, her mind empty, as silent as the hall beyond her door. Her only thought was to note with surprise that she was thinking of nothing. A square of sunlight slid slowly across the blue-and-crimson carpet.

At half past one there was a knock at the door, a fast delicate rapping, so light that for a moment Suzanne thought the sound came from within her, a palpitation of the heart, perhaps. She stood from her chair by the balcony. *"Oui,"* she said, not very audibly.

The door opened. It was the Oriental woman, in silk again, red silk. Her hair was again dressed high, but differently from the previous evening. *"Bonjour,* Mademoiselle Petrovna," May said. "Did you sleep?"

"Yes. Yes." Suzanne nodded. She made an embarrassed, clumsy gesture with her hands, something between wringing them and indicating the rumpled bedclothes, but May didn't give any appearance of having noticed her awkwardness.

"I thought perhaps you'd like to join us at table?"

"Ah. Oh," Suzanne faltered. "Yes, of course."

May nodded. "When you're ready, just come down the stairs. Turn left at the big pot of flowers." She withdrew from the threshold of the room and closed the door softly.

Suzanne washed her face in the blue-tiled bathroom adjoining her room. Then, deciding that even if she would be late, she must take the time to bathe thoroughly, she filled the tub and sat in the warm water, regretting that she had no really clean clothes and would have to choose among her few wrinkled blouses. But when she went to her closet and opened it, she found the clothes that had been packed in her bag hanging freshly laundered and ironed.

*Please,* she thought, *oh, please just let me enjoy this without growing accustomed to it. Without learning to expect it.*

As a person whose optimistic periods were marked by a shift from atheism to agnosticism, Suzanne couldn't have said to whom, other than her own force of will, such a plea might be addressed. She knew only that all of her life thus far had been a grinding effort, and that from this light-filled, fragrant house of servants and soft mattresses she would inevitably have to return to her gray room in Paris's gray fifteenth arrondissement.

Suzanne looked in the mirror and twisted her hair into a tight, tidy knot at the nape of her neck. She put on her best blouse, with buttons that matched and a placket and collar that were not yet frayed, slipped her feet into her shoes and laced them with attention, finishing with neat bows whose loops were of equal length. From the pocket of her bag she withdrew a pair of gold-and-amethyst earrings (they matched the necklace she had pawned) and clipped them to her earlobes, wincing at the pinch. Then she stepped back from the full-length mirror on the back of the bathroom door. All of her appeared ready, except for her face, wearing its customary expression of anxious woe. Suzanne practiced a few smiles.

The staircase she descended seemed impossibly long, the flowerpot at which she turned obscenely large. A geranium of immense, almost rude, proportion held up blooms of the same vivid, bloody hue that colored her mysterious hostess's fingernails. Suzanne hesitated at the door to the dining room and looked at the long lacquer table it contained, an expanse so shining and so red, set with the whitest plates and napkins, that her eyes were drawn first to it and only then strayed to the people assembled around it.

"*Entrez.*" May was sitting at its head. "Do come in."

Suzanne took an empty chair at the far end. Like the others, it was of red lacquer with a white cushion. Next to the Oriental sat a man with dark skin and nearly white hair, beside him a young woman, not yet thirty, who resembled him, except that she was beautiful and he was quite ugly, although not at all mean- or unpleasant-looking. Across from the man, next to the Oriental woman, one place remained empty, as if waiting for a latecomer.

"That's the family," said a nervous-looking man on Suzanne's left. "The rest of us are just, um, visiting." He reached for his coffee cup, revealing a hand that shook. "Who are you?" he said.

"I . . . well, I suppose I am a visitor, too."

"I know *that*," the man said. "But where did she find you?"

"She? You mean Madame—"

"May. Yes, Madame May. How did you get here?"

"A gendarme brought me."

"What did you do?" The man put down his cup and looked interested. His cravat, she noted, was pinned with a gold stud fashioned like a tiny roulette wheel.

"Nothing."

"Neither did I. Don't worry. *Elle a des bons avocats.*"

"But why should I need a lawyer?"

"Well, you just said you hadn't done it."

"Done what?"

"Whatever the police said you did." He cleared his throat. "Me, I had trouble with the casino," he said.

Suzanne nodded, lacking the energy to correct the misunderstanding. Perhaps all of Madame May's guests were in trouble of some kind, lost in some way. On the other side of the man with the shaking hands was a big-boned woman with dramatically made-up eyes, rings on all her large fingers, and on her thumbs as well. Suzanne sipped water from her glass. A houseboy, dressed just like the one who had served her the previous night, was making his way down the table with a platter of poached salmon. Another followed with asparagus and another with a gravy boat filled with thick cream sauce.

The man next to Suzanne patted her shoulder. "It will all come out all right," he said. "I've actually stopped worrying." He picked up his spoon with his trembling hand and lifted a mouthful of soup from the plate before him. Suzanne watched as a drop of it fell from the spoon's wavering tip before he could put it in his mouth. As her neighbor, M. Fantoni, would explain during the leisurely course of the meal, he had just the previous month been employed as a croupier in one of the Hôtel de Paris's famed *salles privées*, not far from where he had lived, in a luxurious apartment in Monte Carlo.

"Rue Bel Respiro," he said, sighing. But, as fate would have it, one night he fell under an unjust accusation. The casino director (a man hired for his suspicious nature—he tracked the outdoor movements of his croupiers by means of spies and telescopes set up on the hotel roof) observed M. Fantoni in a behavior not tolerated by the management. At five in the evening of August the eighteenth, on the corner of

Boulevard de Suisse and Avenue de Roqueville he exchanged words with one of the guests of the Hôtel de Paris, a German who won that very night a hundred and thirteen thousand francs at M. Fantoni's roulette table.

Despite his protests that the German had only asked directions to a certain restaurant, and despite a complete lack of proof—the wheel was examined by house detectives and found to be quite in balance—Fantoni, accused of conspiring to swindle the casino, was summarily fired. This turn of events damaged his already taxed nerves (the life of a croupier is one of unnatural strain), so that an incipient and occasional tremor in his hands became constant. On subsequent interviews he couldn't handle a wheel without trembling all over.

"There wasn't much point to being interviewed anyway. Once your reputation is tainted, not even the Kitchen will have you."

"Are you a chef then, as well?"

"Not at all. You are ignorant, aren't you? *The* Kitchen isn't *a* kitchen, it's the big public gaming hall."

Suzanne smiled in embarrassment. While telling his story, Fantoni had interrupted his own travails to apprise her of those of their tablemates. The thin man with no hair, not even an eyelash, was a naturalist who had become suddenly and violently allergic to certain medicinal plants he had been trying to cultivate. The blonde was a Finnish opera singer—she'd lost her voice from fright when she debuted at Garnier's. To her left was a perspiring man with a cad's mustache. He'd lost all his money and taken an amount of chloral insufficient to kill himself but enough to induce his wife to go back to America without him. Sweat darkened the collar of his blue shirt. The woman with the rings on her thumbs was, naturally, a gypsy. "We were acquaintances," Fantoni said. "In Monte Carlo. She made her living as a fortune-teller, and they ran her out of town when one of the numbers she suggested turned out to be genuinely lucky."

"But what about Madame May? Who is she?"

"Oh, that's a story more complicated than anyone knows. She came from Shanghai with her two nieces and their widowed father, as well as that woman with the dreadful lisp. You see her there, next to the opera singer?" Fantoni pointed discreetly. "She's a retired spy, if you can believe it. Came from her post at a London boarding school from which the sisters were expelled. She'd been posing as a scholar and was ensnared in some peculiar contretemps. It had to do with smuggling Old Masters, I think, or sculptures on the black market. Something. At any rate, she finagled her way to China and followed them here. She has a real impediment; no one can understand her French. But, don't laugh, she made a fortune during the war. It had to do with a market crash, blockades. She had privileged information, a stolen formula for chemical weapons." Clearly flummoxed, Fantoni stared at Eleanor Clusburtson. "Perhaps it isn't a real lisp at all," he said. "Could be a disguise."

"But what about the woman?" Suzanne persisted. "The Chinese woman?"

Fantoni was finished, however, with any story but his own. "Dreadful, isn't it?" he said for perhaps the tenth time. He held his shaking hands out before him and considered their tremor. "I mean really just impossible." As he was frowning and muttering, a young woman joined them, walking with what seemed to Suzanne self-consciously long strides. She took the empty seat beside Madame May.

"That's the younger daughter," Fantoni whispered.

"Well!" exclaimed the three seated at the head of the table. They spoke almost in unison, and Mr. Dick, the father, the one who'd just celebrated his birthday, stood up so suddenly that he bumped the table's edge and upset his water glass. May rang a bell to the left of her plate, and a houseboy appeared with a cloth to mop the spill up from the table's gleaming top.

"Explain yourself!" Mr. Dick said to the young woman, whose name, Fantoni said, was Alice.

"Dick, dear." May put her hand on his sleeve. The other sister, Cecily, leaned, whispering, toward the slight, fierce-looking person on her left—"They call her Fräulein." She had a liverish complexion, severe cheekbones, and deep-set eyes heavily rimmed in kohl. Apparently, the two shared an unusual sympathy: they ate from one plate placed between them; they drank from a single cup of coffee, neither using its handle but each in turn holding it by the rim, first and fourth fingers extended with arch, almost satirical, delicacy. In that Cecily was apparently left-handed and Fräulein right-, the two seemed formed for symbiosis—at table anyway, where their elbows never crowded or clashed, and they could lean into each other without being clumsy.

The sister called Alice sat down and smiled brightly. "Coffee my," she said to the houseboy, who had finished mopping. "Wanchee all same. Piecee fish, soup." She shook open her napkin with a crack. Her cheeks had the kind of proud and mischievous blush that can be acquired only in a paramour's bedroom.

"Alice, dear, no pidgin. You know how many times I've asked you to speak in French."

"Sorry, Aunt." But Alice looked anything but.

"Where in heaven have you been!" Mr. Dick pounded the table so that everyone's water glass trembled.

"Dick, shall we talk after lunch?" May suggested, and Cecily leaned a little farther into Fräulein, her whispering lips almost inside the sallow curve of the woman's surprisingly large ear.

"Out," Alice said.

"All night!" her father bellowed.

"And on the old fellow's birthday, too." Fantoni sucked his teeth disapprovingly.

Suzanne looked at her lap. She didn't see May stand, indicating that lunch was over.

# A FACILITY WITH
# LANGUAGE

FOR MAY, WHO HAD ALWAYS HAD A FACILITY, AN impossible nimbleness, with languages—was it being otherwise hobbled that inspired this?—the movements of swimming seemed letters of a sublime new alphabet. It took months to develop the required strength, to learn to eat instead of smoke, and to use rather than ignore her body, but after initial falters and founderings she made almost inhumanly swift progress. As if assisted by angels, or demons—some unseen force—a keen, secret joy shook May. Her first unassisted laps reminded her of when she had at last mastered English and could hear herself speak sentences, whole paragraphs, without hesitation. Now each stroke was formed as surely, every kick produced an exultant spray; the skin on her face tightened with pleasure.

She conquered the pool quickly, and then it bored her. She said good-bye to the instructor; she had her driver take her to the shore. "Don't wait," she told him. "Come back in two hours."

She couldn't hobble over the pebbles, but at the far end of the beach one of the sanitariums had built a stair to make sea bathing possible for invalids, and with her cane May could slowly navigate its steps. It took as much as a quarter of an hour, but she got there. And seawater—how alive it was, how strong; its salt buoyancy did half the work. Nothing less than a revelation to move unhindered by her feet, to travel without help, as fast and as gracefully as any other person, and now unconstricted by the tiled barrier of a pool wall. How easily she moved, her body sufficiently occupied to set her mind free, to allow her thoughts to choose their own direction. Nonsense sometimes, disjointed images, scattered fragments.

A low table in a blue room, a table set with white cups, porcelain so thin the sun shone through them. Translucent, they glowed like candles. May snorted into the water. What pitiably small hopes the cups had represented! How surprising to remember a self, *herself*, who might hope for the happiness shed by such meager light. Though wouldn't it be good—better—to be that person again? Could it be true that she'd once possessed a soul that thrived on bright morsels?

To forget the cups she conjugated an irregular Italian verb, she listed the principal rivers of Africa, she recited from Defoe's *Journal of the Plague Year,* a book she'd first consumed during her years of feverish reading. In the passage she'd committed to memory, a man had swum the Thames. Infected, he'd outswum the plague, he'd outwitted and escaped his own illness.

May stroked; she breathed in deeply, exhaled lines of poetry, reviewed the rules of contract bridge and how they differed from duplicate. Strategies for chess, mah-jongg. Hangchow-Soochow binding style versus Canton versus the so-called Tientsin Trick for making the foot seem even narrower. Finger positions for the flute. Scruples, drams, and ounces; gills, pints, quarts. A quart was 2 pints, 8 gills, 32 ounces, 256 drams, 512 scruples.

Her mother, Chu'en, had liked to cook but Yu-ying wouldn't allow it. Vulgar for a lady to be caught in the kitchen. Tiny feet on a hot clay floor. Chu'en could fill dumplings with bean paste so pink and so sweet, it made marzipan a disappointment.

Too strong, too big to resist, the tide carried May backward. Returned her to a time she wanted to forget. To stories her grandmother had told her, trying to distract May as she bound her feet. In the town where she was born, Yu-ying said, it used to be that each spring a girl was selected for marriage to the sea dragon. Clothed in rich gowns and placed on a bed, she floated out on the tide, approaching the depthless pit that lay far to the east, the pit into which all the waters of the world poured—even the celestial waters, the great rivers of stars. At last the girl disappeared, they could see her no more.

"But that was a long time ago," May said, before her name was May.

"Yes, Chao-tsing," her grandmother agreed, sewing the white cloths tight. "Many, many years ago. A century."

"And I am not marrying the sea dragon."

May used to picture the girl on her bed. She'd give her an oar with which to paddle, turn sheets into sails bellying out in the wind. She'd save her.

"No," agreed Yu-ying, and she told May of the mythic island kingdom, a place no boat could reach. The water surrounding the island supported nothing heavier than a solitary swimmer, and only a woman who could swim as lightly as a feather drifting on the tide. All the women on this island lived peaceably together. Each month when they bled, they bled jewels, they bled rubies, and they used those rubies for money. As there were no men, they opened their legs to the south wind. Impregnated, they bore only daughters.

May could swim lightly. If there was any woman who could navigate treacherous water, it was she, accustomed to an undertow that returned her not only to her mother and grandmother, but to the daughters she'd lost.

Rose died too young for May to picture her as a woman, but May had seen Agnes as an adult, she'd seen her face clearly. She had made the mistake of memorizing it. What would life hold for a daughter who lived in a convent and yet turned her back on its promises, the consolations of heaven and God, mystery and glory? Sometimes when

May thought of Agnes she couldn't help but adjust things, endowing her daughter with fantastic gifts, like those granted in the old stories of the immortals. She'd make Agnes an archer and give her Shen I's divine bow. Then May would kowtow to her daughter, she'd rend her clothes to expose her breast, she'd hold her head still so Agnes could put out her eyes. Unnecessary, as Shen I's arrows always found their mark.

May swam quickly out past the breaking waves and swells. She let Agnes chase her, and now Agnes was Agnes with the nostrils of Heng. Nostrils that beamed deadly light and annihilated all in their path.

MAY SWAM AT all hours and in all weather, but there was nothing she preferred to the beach at night, when the stairs leading to the water were damp and cool. When there was no moon, and clouds obscured the stars. When the water was black, so black. She entered without hesitation, excited, her heart beating quickly. It was like meeting a lover. No—it was more like meeting a lover than meeting a lover could ever be.

May, who knew the sound of girls drowning, swam. They'd drowned in ponds, in streams, in rivers and lakes. They'd drowned in vinegar barrels. But she swam.

Soft-hearted mothers put a heavy stone in their daughters' diapers to prevent the brief but piteous cries. And the next year it wasn't difficult to guess who had scrambled through the dark with a kicking, muffled bundle. They were the ones who spread their porridge thickly, who emptied whole basins at the gates to the graveyard. Lakes of sticky gruel, their guilt soiled everyone's shoes. They burned wads of spirit money, and the light it cast on their faces betrayed them.

Some had been cowardly—or were they brave?—and drowned themselves along with their daughters. Vindictive, they jumped into wells and poisoned the town's water supply.

*Li-kuei.* Hungry, wandering. Unable to tell night from day. Even hell denied such a ghost her place. Once a year, a bellyful of porridge licked from the dirt, a fistful of burning money. She could never reincarnate. The only escape would come when another woman drowned, when another drowned and agreed to take her place.

Still, until that time, a suicide had power she hadn't had in life. Brave, cowardly—did it matter?—she had made herself fearsome now.

May swam far out, stroking evenly. Even when she realized she should be frightened, when she heard a boat whose pilot couldn't possibly see her black, bobbing head in time to stop, even then she felt no fear. She was a good enough swimmer to take risks.

"There is no such thing!" Alice had argued, frightened when she discovered May leaving for the beach after dark.

May shrugged.

"Not at night. Not when there's no one to see."

"See what?"

"See if you get into trouble."

May turned on her, eyes wild, hair long and unbound, flying out around her. "Who are you!" she'd cried, "to tell me what I can or cannot do! Do you listen to me? Do you!"

Alice said nothing.

The two of them stared at one another.

# THE SUNNY COAST

## OF FRANCE

"THANK GOD FOR SUZANNE," ALICE SAID.

"I suppose." Cecily turned from her stomach onto her back.

"What? You don't think she's nice?"

"*Nice?*"

"Stupid word. What I mean is, she's made life possible. You must have noticed that May is . . . well, not as impossible. Don't you think?"

"Yes," Cecily said. "It's just. I don't know. Why her, of all May's projects?" She winced, either at the sun or at a thought she didn't share. "There's something—she seems both odd and familiar. It . . . I can't explain. She reminds me of someone, I can't think who."

"Well, I don't care. I'm just glad she appeared."

"Yes. May is happy. Less unhappy."

The two sisters were lying on chaises by the pool. It was a hot day, and the bougainvillea blazed in the sun, the magenta of their blooms so intense that they quivered before the eye, rendered the darting hummingbirds as dull as sparrows.

"Do you think she misses Shanghai?" Alice asked.

"I don't know," Cecily said. "In all the years we've been in Nice— what is it now? Seven?—She's never spoken of going back. And the passage to China, it's not so long as it was."

"For a visit, you mean? She's not the visiting type. Not once she's turned her back on a place."

"No, I know. It's just that she's so . . . She reveals little of herself. Never talks of the past. Arthur. Rose."

"But," Alice said, "she never did speak about Rose." Alice didn't mention the other daughter. Agnes. She never had.

"No," agreed Cecily. She stood and stretched, walked slowly down the steps of the pool's shallow end, dogged by Fräulein. The two wore identical bathing costumes and swam in unison once up and down the length of the pool.

"Daddy doesn't care for her," said Alice, as Cecily emerged dripping from the pool. The water coursed down her sister's smooth legs.

"Who? Suzanne?" Cecily asked. "Well, what does that matter?"

"It doesn't. I was just—" Alice turned over on her back, closed her eyes against the bright sun. "Do you think they're . . . you know?"

"What?"

"Are they . . . You know what I'm talking about. They share a bedroom. It has one bed."

"How should I know?" Cecily reached for the comb she'd left on the table by her chaise and inadvertently knocked it to the ground. Alice watched as Fräulein picked it up and handed it to her sister.

Was it the result of so unusual an upbringing, the ever-present silent and obliging staff of boys and amahs? Though it hadn't affected Alice in this way, Cecily never would pick anything up from the ground. Never, not for all the rest of her life: not a shoe, not a spoon, not a letter, a stocking, an earring, a pen. And, as if in sympathy with her sense of entitlement, the world complied. Just as Fräulein had retrieved the comb, so did Alice, her father, Eleanor, or even May pick up and place in Cecily's languid white hand whatever she had dropped.

Alice looked at the narrow body tucked snugly next to Fräulein's.

"Well," she said, "you might know better than I whether or not they're lovers."

Fräulein smiled one of her small, cryptic smiles, sat forward on the chaise, and unscrewed the cap on a bottle of lotion. "If you want to know what I think," Cecily said. "I think you're too involved with her moods. Her private life."

"Involved? I'm not *involved*. Involved how?"

"Just that. What do you care what they are?"

"I'm curious. That's all."

"And she," Cecily said. "She's just as . . . The two of you have . . . I don't know. It's as if she's jealous of Evlanoff. You can't imagine what she's like when you spend the night with him."

"What *is* she like?"

"Violent. Raging. That glass door—what did she tell you, that the wind slammed it shut? She threw one of those heavy brass bowls through it."

"Because I went out?"

"Because she can't control you anymore. You've stopped being her . . . hers. Her girl. Her daughter. Whatever she thinks you are. Were. And the only thing she has, the only thing she thinks she might hold onto you with, is . . ."

"Money," Alice finished.

Cecily held out her other arm for Fräulein to rub with lotion. "Convincing Daddy to cut you out. If you insist on seeing him. If you were to marry him. The problem is, she's afraid you don't care enough."

"About the will, you mean."

"Money. Her. Any of it. You know, you've always chosen to ignore— or maybe you really never understood—that May only cares for people who are weak. People she can manipulate."

Alice said nothing. She looked up at the villa, a pile of wealth painted optimistically pink, the hue of perfect ripeness, and all—most, anyway—thanks to Eleanor's tooth, the plate May had bought for her. "Everything we have," Alice said, adjusting the umbrella over her chaise, "comes from her caring for a, a person she could manipulate, to use your word. What would there be without Miss C. and her tooth?"

...

AFTER THE RIGORS of transferring their household (what of it remained after the fire) from Shanghai to the Riviera, May had fallen into depression. Not that she spoke of it, and months passed before the rest of the family understood that something was wrong. Something other than fatigue, grief.

As for what May felt, the changes were subtle, at first they were. As if while she was walking through a garden the color had slowly, furtively drained from the flowers, the sky, the grass, and left her in a gray place. Alone, and without the capacity to feel desire. Everything she saw was the color of dust. Not that this was unbearable. It was possible to persevere without joy; she told herself it was. But then, suddenly—or was it her awareness that was sudden?—after pleasure had departed, then the conceit that life had meaning, this also abandoned her. Why such struggle? To what end?

Easy enough not to ask such questions while immersed in the details of setting up house, a process complicated by the family's having moved into a less than completely prime location before an ideal villa on a more desirable street went up for sale. As May had never before experienced this prosaically female pursuit, she made the mistake of assuming that decor would provide satisfaction, even solace. She imagined that the discovery of, say, the perfect vase for the niche in the foyer might offer a vicarious sense of harmony. That she herself might feel as if she were at last in the right spot. Why else would the best draper be booked for months in advance? For what other reason was the upholsterer's showroom crowded with avid, bright-eyed women eagerly fingering textiles and signing bank drafts?

May fussed over carpets and cabinetry; she oversaw plastering, painting, and stenciling, the installation of a new kitchen, the hiring of a chef and sommelier from Provence. She bought beds; she bought blankets; she bought teapots, champagne glasses, and punch bowls. Divans. Desks. Club chairs, armchairs, and hassocks. Coffee tables. Clocks. Candlesticks. Silverware. Dessert plates. Fifty white linen napkins, monogrammed in red.

She interviewed a score of gardeners, hired three, fired two, had the

274 · Kathryn Harrison

grounds torn up and relandscaped, presided over the digging of each hole for each shrub.

And then, when she was done, when there was nothing left to do, she despaired. What had any of it been for?

Each morning she flinched when through the open curtains she saw the sea crawl toward the shore, its glittering blue surface a cloak over evil intent. Dark, seething omens. Above the beach, wind shook the palms, it hissed through the umbrella pines and filled her with foreboding. Cypress on the hillsides rubbed together, gnashing and black, like dragons' teeth. Lemons hung malignly from the trees. Pine cones split open in the dry heat and made a noise like ill-fitting dentures, chattering, clacking. Mocking her.

Worse, hers was a misery that had no company. What tormented May seemed to delight others. Was that Milton's vision of hell? Dante's? Or was it that heaven consisted in observing from on high the torments of the damned below? Her memory, her ability to think: it wasn't just her feet anymore; now everything was failing her. Sleep. Appetite.

The pink insides of a fig, cut open and laid on a plate, metamorphosed into a medical drawing of a dissected ovary, a repugnant swarm of life. She shuddered and pushed it away. The houseboy who served it to her, the maids, they all filled her with loathing and terror. What more were they—what more she?—than bags of entrails, wet mouths at one end, sticky anuses at the other. Life was . . . there was no way to defend it. She looked up to the charming ruins of Roquebrune and saw a lair for angry dragons. The white light blinded her; it set a halo of bright pain around her head.

She quarreled with Alice, often apropos nothing. "You've become judgmental of me," she accused her on the afternoon they visited Roquebrune. The two of them were sitting in a picturesque café; their untouched water glasses sparkled like diamonds.

Alice laid her fork down on her plate. "Oh come—"

"It's true," May said before she could protest. "I feel it, your disapproval." She drew a breath, held it, let it go. "It's not unnatural. When I was twenty-five I was just as critical. It's because you're young that you refuse to see that every person does his or her best. . . . We're all imperfect. Broken. But one has to grow older to admit such disappointment. If you allowed me my failings . . . you'd have to allow the possibility of your own." As May spoke, her voice changed, softened. She punctuated her sentences with sighs. "And that wouldn't be right. Because you are young, and you must feel as you do. That the world is open to you." She put her hand across the table to Alice. "It's the way I want you to feel."

Alice stared at May. What an odd little speech from her aunt. Unprecedented. She'd begun by sounding angry and ended sad. May usually traveled in the opposite direction. Alice couldn't think what to say in response.

May looked out past the rocks to the sea. It lay flat under a wrinkled skin, ancient and alive, timeless. She'd been wrong in finding China overburdened by tragedy. She had no desire to return there, but China at least was honest, its streets unashamed of humanity's squalid soul. This rocky coast, this blue sea, this pristine land—Nice, what a ridiculous name for the city where Paganini put down his violin and died in a pinched room on the Rue de la Préfecture, his curtains drawn, his body curled tight as a starved tick's, hiding from the merciless sun—this meretricious place lied about life. It was trying to trick her.

WHEN SLEEP WAS possible, May was plagued by nightmares. Arthur appeared with Rose in his arms. He stood in the garden, the trees shuddering around him. *I found her!* he called. *I found her!* And she tried to go outside. She had to get to them to see if Rose was dead or just asleep. She was confused, and even in the dream she asked herself, was she about to die? Could she be dead already and join them? *Come! Our new home awaits us!* Arthur sang, and May walked to him in her sleep, she stumbled and fell on the stairs.

Alice came after her, running down three at a time, thanking God she was at home. She picked her aunt up and spoke to her, but May wasn't awake.

She was walking up a hill, up a long winding path to reach a mulberry tree—for the dream had changed; now it was like a story she'd heard as a child, the story of the mother of one of the immortals. May reached the hilltop and there was the hollow mulberry tree, but inside, instead of a baby, she found the corpse of her daughter Agnes.

May prepared Agnes's body for its passage through the next world. According to custom—traditions which for so long she had ignored—she took a rice bowl and she broke it. Then she washed her daughter's long body with care, she dressed it in new robes. At Agnes's shoulder May placed a lamp, that its light might guide her on her dark journey. In her left hand she put rice balls, with which to placate the dogs of the underworld, and she curled the fingers of her right around a stick—in case the rice didn't work.

To pay the dragon who guarded the precarious gates to Nai Ho Bridge, May filled Agnes's mouth with gold and jewels. She tried to. Because this was the part of the dream that always went wrong: the coins and the rubies, the pearls and jade pieces all spilled out. It was as if Agnes were spitting the riches back at her. No matter how many times she replaced them, not one would stay in. Alone on the windy hill, the mulberry yawning open before her, a womb transformed to a grave, May would panic. She'd shove the pearls back in, she'd force her daughter's lips closed around them, but nothing worked. The pearls got dirty, bloody. The new robes tore, and the two of them fought each other, entangled in long wet dirty bandages.

May woke, her hair heavy and lank with sweat, arms and legs slicked with it, her nightdress, too, wet and cold. She grabbed for Arthur and found herself in Alice's arms.

SHE WAS FORTY-SEVEN years old. She drank green tea with sugar, drank jasmine tea with milk and sugar, drank chamomile without, ate nothing. Without opium, she could not sleep. If it wore off, if she woke and could not fall back to sleep immediately: this was unbearable. Her heart beat so insistently, so fast and so hard, that if she lay on her stomach or her side, she felt it against the mattress. If she turned onto her back, she felt it in her neck and her wrists; she couldn't bear the touch of the collar and cuffs of her nightdress.

A Dr. Michael Evlanoff, whom Alice met the morning May suffered a spell of dizziness and vomiting (streaks of blood in the basin, her nose bleeding as well), examined her and said she would die. She was killing herself.

"My luck," May retorted, parchment-faced, horizontal, venom-tongued. "To be ill on a holiday, when only Russians pay house calls."

Evlanoff snapped his bag shut. When Alice gave him a check, he tore it up. "There isn't any cure," he said. "And I won't take her money."

The curt diagnosis, however, had the salubrious effect of making May angry. She sat up and had Evlanoff thrown out of the house; she ranted about Western quackery; she would have paced had her feet allowed such expression of agitation. Instead, she lay smoldering on her chaise, tapping her long fingernails against the side of a porcelain teapot growing cold on a tray.

The next week, she made a few investigative forays into town, up and down and back up and down the Promenade des Anglais, the Boulevard Gambetta, the Rue Dante. A rug over her knees, she was carried in a sedan chair by Boy and Brother Boy—both gone gray—and attracted much attention. But May was accustomed to stares and oblivious to all but the first of her projects: an organ-grinder whose monkey had died.

# SHOES FOR WALKING

Artificial Limbs and Braces read the sign over the door. The words were formed with small, discreet, almost ashamed letters.

"Well, I don't need one of those." May's tone was more than indignant. She stabbed the tip of her cane into the bed of begonias on the street corner.

"I know." Already Alice had employed every means she had of containing her temper. Counting to ten—that she was immune to. Deep breaths—they'd worked for the car ride. Now she was trying to avoid seeing May's face, to look whenever possible at her broken feet instead of at her perfected, icy disdain. "I know. I know. But they make shoes here, as well. This is the place." She pulled at May's arm. "Come on," she said. "It's hot."

"Why are you standing with your neck at that absurd angle? Surely you don't want to be taken for one of those dowdy little down-at-heel ladies who creep along streets with their eyes on the pavement."

Alice snapped her head up, scowled. The Mediterranean sun was shining too brightly. At midday, it was the kind of light that picked out every flaw in a face, every disappointment in a life.

Someone had decorated the office window with false arms and legs arranged among houseplants. A tendril of ivy crept through the grommet of a lace-up truss. "That," May said, "is a grotesque display. A person capable of such window dressing is not a person whose services I need."

"May, please. It's an hour, and then we're through. We have the X rays. Everything's been arranged."

Alice and her aunt stood on the corner of Rue Rossini and Avenue Auber, neither speaking. May leaned on the jade knob of her cane; Alice watched the cars heading south, trying not to cry. Why was it that the accomplishment of this simple goal, to get a pair of shoes—real shoes, in which a person could walk, shoes that would help a person to walk—why did May respond as if Alice had devised a sly means of torturing her? It was almost as if she resented Alice's attempt to relieve her pain. As if she felt Alice were stealing something from her. Something of value.

And the more strident May became, the more stubbornly insistent Alice felt. It had turned into a contest of wills. A voice inside Alice suggested that backing down would be wiser, that May would never use the shoes, that some disaster, even, would result from Alice's obstinacy. But she couldn't let go of the idea of getting her aunt into orthopedic shoes, and this was because suddenly she had become irritated—wildly, uncharitably, and unreasonably irritated—with May's slow steps. The pace that had once seemed enchanted, evidence that her aunt inhabited a different world, a realm of grace and ease, now struck her as impossible, recalcitrant. Abruptly, her lovely aunt seemed to her not only crippled, but willfully and perversely so. And Alice was going to be the one to change this. She'd nagged; the two of them had fought.

*"They cannot cannot cannot be fixed!"* May had yelled at her the night before. And then this morning she'd apologized. "I'm sorry," she said, sounding frostily insincere.

Alice didn't answer but dipped her spoon into her coffee, communicating insult with her studied, careful, silent stirring, her resolutely avoiding—as she never did—the touch of metal on china.

"You can't make me like other people."

"Of course not. Who would want to? I'm just trying to make life a little easier for you." Alice didn't admit her increasingly violent impatience with May's insufferable pace. Of course she didn't. But she felt she was going to shake her aunt. Push her. Scream. The rest of the family wanted nothing to do with this conflict. As soon as Alice said the word *shoes*, Cecily, their father, Suzanne, Eleanor: all of them disappeared.

Alice put the spoon quietly on the saucer. "I never said we were fixing them. Or that anyone could."

May nodded, as if in compliance, and they'd left for the appointment in good time. But now here they were, stuck outside the door. Alice watched the traffic, cars piloted by bright young people who looked happy and purposeful, heading determinedly into the future. Shanghai, Nice—neither was a place people actually came from.

A hand reached into the window display from inside the office. It pulled a string, and the slats of a jalousie blind came together to form a white backdrop to the ugly devices.

"Well?" Alice said.

"All right," May said, "I surrender." Like a hostage, she put up her arms and glared not so much at Alice as at Alice's chest, as if devising a way to stab her. "What choice do I have when you torment me so?"

Alice kept her mouth shut and held the door open. May went in. She sat on a blue chair while Alice silently offered the big envelope holding the X rays of her aunt's feet to the blond woman at the desk. "You have an appointment?" the woman asked.

Alice nodded. "Two-thirty," she said.

The woman got up and went through a door framed by two jade plants, brushing past their fat waxy leaves. In a minute she returned with a bearded man wearing a red apron. "Come in, Mrs. Cohen," he said.

"Would you like me to go with you?" Alice asked. May didn't answer. Alice watched as her aunt followed the man in the apron, moving slowly, even for her, maintaining an imperious pace. Her beautifully contemptuous nostrils flared wide, and the skin around her lips was pale, drained white: two unmistakable indications of rage. Alice sighed and fanned herself with the magazine she'd brought, stared out the window.

THROUGH THE NARROW door was a room outfitted with a reclining chair, like that in a dentist's office. "So," said the man with the apron, "I'm Dr. Dumonteil." He held out his hand and, after a moment's hesitation, long enough to convey distaste, May took it.

"You've never had orthopedic shoes before? Am I correct?"

"Yes." May sat sideways on the seat of the reclining chair. She kept both hands on the cool jade knob of her cane.

"The process is simple. I make impressions of your feet, and from them I make positives. What I mean is that I use the impressions as molds to create a replica of each foot: a plaster cast. And around these I build shoes." As he spoke, seemingly oblivious to the bad temper of his patient, Dumonteil opened the envelope and took out the X rays, set them carefully under the clip of a lightboard. He studied them with his back to May, who also looked at the films. She'd seen them before, in the bone doctor's office. To illustrate their deformity, the bone doctor had hung them next to X rays of normal feet. In comparison with those, May's looked like the extremities of another species.

Dumonteil stroked the hair on the back of his head. "Do you have much pain with this, mmm, condition?" he asked.

"That depends," May said.

"On what?"

"On how much attention I am paying it."

Dumonteil turned around, his expression mild. Either he was immune to the moods of others, or he was ignoring the acidity of her responses.

"You are fifty?" he asked, and May nodded.

"There are some arthritic complications," he said. "According to your doctor."

"Apparently."

"But you're not aware of them?"

May drew a deep breath. "Dr. Dumonteil," she said, "I am here because my niece has undertaken the rehabilitation of her Chinese aunt with the sort of missionary fervor she reserves for those few projects about which she is unwilling to compromise. She believes that new shoes will improve me. I have agreed to go along with . . . with *this*." The last word was pronounced with disgust.

The orthopedist sat on a wheeled stool. He rolled slowly forward until his eyes were level with the handle of May's cane, her white, ringed fingers. "May I examine you?" he asked.

She shrugged.

"Perhaps you'll remove your shoes. I've never seen any quite like them," he added, and now he sounded solicitous, gingerly, as restrained in tone and gesture as if preparing to dismantle and defuse an explosive.

May untied the narrow black ribbons over the arch of each foot. Silently she unwrapped the bindings. Left, then right.

Dumonteil contemplated what he saw. Beneath the layers of cloth, as much as a third of the skin on each of May's feet was ulcerated. The sides of her big toes were swollen, blistered, the knuckles of the remaining toes, curled under unnaturally to bear her weight, were thick with calluses and scabs.

"Dr. Guerin did call me," he said, as if to himself. "So I knew the history. But I've never actually had occasion to address this particular kind of . . . injury."

"No," May said. "Why would you?"

He took her left foot in his hand, gently, trying to avoid raw spots. "I don't know how you walk at all." He used a caliper to measure the distance from the joint of her big toe to that of the smallest.

"I must say," he said.

"What?" May asked, when he didn't continue. "What must you say?"

The orthopedist looked at her. "I'm in the business of correcting for natural mishaps. Accidents, sometimes. But mostly organic or developmental failures. Birth defects." Dumonteil turned May's foot. "This is just a bit . . ."

"What?"

The doctor traced his index finger along the areas of unbroken skin. "Disturbing," he said, finally.

"I should imagine." The idea of Dumonteil's trying to straighten bent backs and replace missing limbs reminded May of Arthur, and she found herself unjustly angry with him. She looked at the doctor's thick, curling hair as he bent his head over her feet.

"In China," she said, "parents forcibly bow the spines of their infants to create a scholarly stoop. In this way, their children—I'm speaking of boys, of course—are assured the respect due to men of letters."

Dumonteil said nothing.

"I suppose I am telling you that I come from another world. Your pity is misplaced."

He looked at her as if she'd slapped him. "I didn't say I pitied you," he said.

"Didn't you?"

"No."

Dumonteil stood and retrieved a shallow white enamel basin. "I use this to make the impressions," he said, and his voice was business-like.

May nodded. Her arms were folded, her legs were crossed; her jade-headed cane leaned by her side. She watched as he poured white powder from a stainless steel canister into a measuring cup. He added water and mixed it into a paste, spread it with a spatula into the basin. Over it he placed a layer of gauze, another of paste, then another of each. He looked into the basin, considering, looked back at May's right foot—not tucked away beneath her, but hanging, unbound, from her crossed leg—and added one more layer.

Watching him, May suffered the memory of her mother bending over a dish of clay, preparing the surface on which she was to record the outline of her daughter's small feet before May was led away to the binding chair.

As she stood on the clammy surface of the compound, her feet sinking slowly down, May moaned, a low noise, almost inaudible. Involuntary.

"Painful?" the doctor asked.

May didn't answer immediately. When she spoke her voice was low, composed. "My feet," she began. "My feet bother me when they are unbound. I need the binding for support." She allowed herself to close her eyes.

*We will tell your suitors,* her grandmother had promised, *that you never cried out. Tell me how you never cried out. Say the words, I never cried out.*

Dumonteil looked at his wristwatch, following the sweep of the second hand. "Half a minute more," he said. When it was up he took her elbow and lowered her onto the stool. Then he bent and lifted each foot away from the white cast, examined his work in the light from the window. "That should do it," he said. "I think you'll be surprised how much support the new shoes will give you."

May said nothing.

"What color would you prefer?" Dumonteil asked. "I can make them black, or brown. Navy blue. White."

"Oh," she said. "The color doesn't matter. Not white, though," she said, reconsidering. "And not brown. Or blue."

"Then it will have to be black."

She shrugged.

# PROPOSAL

AT THREE IN THE MORNING, ALL THE GUESTS had retired, the servants as well. There was no sound from the kitchen. The wind had picked up after midnight, as it did every night, and the white curtains gusted in through the open French doors. Suzanne coughed.

May felt the side of the teapot to test its warmth. She poured a cup, unbuttoned the frogs on her long turquoise and green jacket.

"You allow me to stay out of pity," Suzanne said, and May sighed loudly.

"Not this again."

"Why else? You know the facts of my life. You know I'm alone. And poor." Suzanne touched the button at her neck nervously. May set the teacup down in its saucer.

"I know a lot of solitary, impoverished people," she said.

"So why? Why, then?"

May pulled the pins from her hair slowly. She lined

them up on the tea tray. "I've never shared my bed, let alone my life, out of generosity. Not once. Much less pity. The guests you've met in my home—who eat here and sleep here because they have nowhere else—they are . . . they keep me from thinking too much."

"About what?"

"The past."

Suzanne coughed again, more from a need to make noise than to clear her throat. "What about me?" she asked. "What am I for?"

"Suzanne," May said. "I am entirely selfish. Can't you understand that?" She put her hands over her mouth, as if to warm them with her breath, left them there as she looked at Suzanne. Dropped them to her sides. "What am I?" she asked. "A displaced Chinese. Forty-nine years old. Widowed. My daughters lost. Who shall be my—" She paused to rephrase the question. "Who will keep me company?

"And," she said, smiling, teasing. Trying to change the mood of the conversation. "You've gotten very good at mah-jongg. After all my hours of tutelage, I don't want to start over with anyone new."

But Suzanne refused to be cajoled. "You have your family," she said.

"They don't need me anymore. Cecily never wanted a thing from anyone, with the exception of her mother. As for Alice." She snorted. "Alice has her . . . her doctor." *Doc-teur.* May pronounced the two syllables as if they were as bitter as medicines in his bag. "She's with him now. In his bed."

Suzanne stopped pacing and sat on the hassock. She drew up her knees and hugged them. May watched her, noting, not for the first time, the girlish awkwardness of her gestures. "It's remarkable," she said, "how young you look. Dressed as you are, as if for school, those ridiculous, sensible pleats. But even more when you take off your clothes. Is it because no one's touched you? I'm younger and look much older."

Suzanne said nothing. She put her feet back on the floor.

"Silly," May said, "I never thought such things mattered to me, but I am—I find myself drawn . . . *portée* . . . Is that the right word?"

"Drawn to what?" Suzanne asked.

"Compelled? Moved?" May shook her head. "Not exactly right."

"To what?" Suzanne asked again.

May lifted her eyes from a loose thread she had found hanging from a seam in her sleeve. "Your virginity," she said, pulling the thread, snapping it.

At the word, Suzanne cringed with embarrassment. She curled up, face in her lap.

May shrugged out of the jacket, pulled on a silk robe. She tied the sash, looked sharply at Suzanne. "It's not as if you like men," she said. "Mother of lightning! You told me the story of your father beating your brother and vomited in my sink. An incident that took place forty years ago!"

Suzanne spoke into her lap. "It wasn't the story," she said. "You know I hadn't been well."

"Yes, yes," May said impatiently. "I don't know why night after night we must pursue this pointless discussion."

"*C'est parce que . . .*" Suzanne said, beginning to cry. "It's because I'm very confused."

"Why? Because someone is being kind to you?"

"No. Well, yes, perhaps. I don't know."

May stood at the glass doors that overlooked the garden from her balcony. It was growing cool, but she didn't close them. Outside, the lamps were still lit; they made halos of light through the thin fabric of the blowing curtain.

"I'm not a . . ." Suzanne hesitated. "It's not that a virgin is what I set out to be," she said.

"No?" May turned, and Suzanne stood up from the hassock.

"No." Suzanne unbuttoned her blouse, her skirt. "Of course it isn't." Her voice was unnaturally high, almost shrill. In a minute she was naked, her skin faintly blue, like milk from which all the fat had been skimmed. The fullness of her breasts always came as a surprise, such amplitude heaped on her bony chest.

May looked at her, smiled. "What are you doing?" she asked.

IN BED, THE lights out, the doors open and the curtains still blowing, ghostly under a quarter moon, May lay next to Suzanne; when she reached for her hand she felt the quick tripping of pulse in Suzanne's wrist. "How?" May asked. "How am I to do it?"

"However you like," Suzanne said. Her words were sharp, formed with precision; but even had she remained silent, May would have known her anger. Beside her, in the dark, she could feel the pressure of imminent outburst. The two of them lay without moving. In the street tires skidded, and the women tensed, but then the automobile recovered, it continued around the bend. May turned her pillow over, plumped it, and lay back against it.

"Why not use your fingernail?" Suzanne said. "What else could be the purpose of such long, red nails? Or, here." She sat up and groped for a teaspoon left on the nightstand. "How about this?"

May accepted the spoon, saying nothing, feeling the cool weight of metal in her hand, how quickly it took on warmth from her touch. Abruptly, Suzanne swung her legs over the side of the bed, turned the light back on. Her usually pale cheeks were flushed, her eyes glittered.

"How about this? Or these?" Up now and stalking around the room, she gathered things from shelves and countertops, she dropped them on the bed. A letter knife and a fistful of pens. A button hook. Hair combs. Opera glasses. Nail scissors, buffer, and file. Family photographs in silver frames. A dish filled with jewelry—it hit the headboard, and rings, bracelets, earrings spun off it and fell around May like hailstones. An ivory-handled hairbrush and matching hand mirror; the bright circle of glass popped out, rolled off the bed, and, oddly, didn't break. "What a relief," Suzanne said, sarcastic. "No bad luck for us."

She was moving more and more quickly, sweeping things up carelessly, throwing them toward May, if not exactly at her. A set of cloisonné boxes. Five little horses carved from pink jade. The empty teapot, the cups with their residue of wet leaves, the hairpins May had aligned beside them. Books. Papers. Perfumes. An antique brass carriage clock. May's smoking tray complete with spirit lamp and tapers, the long ivory and silver pipe, her companion of so many years. The bellows hanging on their hook by the fireplace, and—"Yes! Why not!"—the poker, too. Suzanne hurled it like a spear; its tip streaked the bedclothes with soot.

May pulled her feet out of the way of the growing pile. With her legs drawn under her she sat, arms crossed, taking up no more room than her pillow, and occupying its usual place. "Are you finished?" Her voice betrayed nothing, neither censure nor amusement.

"No! No, I'm not!" Suzanne tore through the room, she heaped everything she could find onto the bed, as if preparing a bonfire. Yanked at the white curtains so that the rods came down with a muffled clang, and kicked the whole mess toward May. Hurled a vase of cut flowers, water soaking into the bedclothes, running dripping off the foot. From the bathroom flew soaps and towels, a box of scented powder that burst open in a choking cloud. Lotions, suppositories headache powders. A clutch of patent medicines in blue and brown glass bottles. Out from the closet: evening bags and shoes, May's collection of canes, more than a dozen, all with ornately carved heads and metal-covered tips. Suzanne held them like kindling, dropped them with a clatter.

At last, when there was nothing left, when shelves were bare, the desk and the tables as well, Suzanne removed a set of four framed miniatures from their hooks over May's vanity table. She put them on top of the pile. One slid off onto the floor, and she bent to pick it up.

Then she lay across what narrow space was left at the top of the bed, her head hanging off one side, her left foot between May and the towering heap, the right on the headboard. Her thighs were parted, her genitals exposed, held open for May to see. Suzanne lifted her head, the cords of her neck straining, to look at May, who remained expressionless, impassive.

"Now!" Suzanne said. "Go ahead! Now you can do it! Put it all in—everything!" She pulled a fistful of her own pubic hair, stretching the flesh so that her vulva narrowed into a tight mauve line, the color of an old scar. "Go ahead!" she screamed. Her voice was ragged, and the cry provoked a fit of coughing, but she wasn't through.

"You! You who've been everywhere and seen all there is to see! Slept with everyone and had what you wanted and what you didn't, and lost it and found it and, and . . . Go ahead! Force all of it in—your whole life! Souvenirs! Photographs! The things you've collected! The people! Your pipe! And here—" She sat up, seized something from the pile. "What about one of your shoes, your little red shoes? Don't neglect those! Blood won't stain a shoe like this." With a chopping gesture, she forced its toe inside her.

Still May said nothing.

"Go on!" Suzanne screamed, and she reached out and slapped May. She struck her across the face. "Make it up to me! All I've missed! What else—what else besides my *virginity*—my, my emptiness—have I to offer you?"

# PROMENADE

ALICE HAD BELIEVED THAT SHOES WOULD HELP. She'd crusaded for them, she'd nagged; she'd badgered. And now she was discouraged because May didn't walk in them. Didn't walk in any of the ways Alice had hoped. Not with energy or enthusiasm. Not with relief. Certainly not with gratitude. New shoes hadn't changed May's life. Or, if they had, it wasn't that they'd made it easier, more comfortable.

She was wearing them when she came home from the final fitting, but as soon as she came in the door she unlaced them, she put them back in the box.

It took Alice a month to convince her aunt to wear them to the promenade, the setting Alice had chosen for the inaugural walk. The three of them went: Alice, May, Suzanne. It might have been a larger party, but Cecily and Fräulein were off touring in Italy, and Eleanor refused to accompany them.

"Alice, dear, I'm—I've little faith in rehabilitative devices. And you know I can't bear family quarrels."

"But Miss C., please! Shoes aren't the same as dentures, and no one's quarreling."

"Not yet." Eleanor, obdurate, held up a book in explanation of her afternoon's plans—it was *Villette*, for the eleventh or the twelfth or the seventeenth time: the Brontës were her weakness—and retreated to the conservatory. Aside from Eleanor and the servants, the villa was nearly empty. In the past months, May had grown bored with entertaining, bored with houseguests, bored with menus, meals, and the flattery of candlelight. She hadn't thrown a party all season, she seemed to care for nothing but swimming; and her only remaining project was a lingering Italian lieutenant suffering from battle fatigue. There was Alice's father, of course, who never left the property. He had an armchair under the wisteria arbor and sat in it for hours, looking toward the sea, newspapers folded in his lap. By teatime, Alice knew, he and Eleanor would be together in the library, with their new toy, a telegraphic stock ticker, almost pulling the tape from its metal lips while arguing companionably about investments, *Villette* face down on the desk and the newspapers lying discarded on the floor.

For the occasion of the walk Alice asked the kitchen to prepare an exceptional picnic: sandwiches, cold salads, cheese, biscuits, grapes, lemonade, a cake; and they would have champagne as well. They would have had, but May saw the bottle and removed it from the hamper. "Have a little mercy," she said. And Alice felt a wrench, one that she wouldn't understand until later.

On the sunny promenade, the three women sat on a wrought-iron bench and ate under a cloudless sky. Suzanne opened her sandwich and aligned the slices of roast beef more evenly. As if they were strangers thrown together in a waiting room, none of them spoke. With the nail of her smallest finger, Alice removed a shred of meat from between her eyetooth and its neighbor.

May sat with her legs crossed, the toes of her new black shoes pointed toward the blue sea. She raised her glass of lemonade. "To the foot tax."

"Now, that's not fair," Alice protested.

"I can't help it if they remind me." May turned to Suzanne. "My previous attempt at Western footwear," she explained. She stuck out her feet and tapped the toes of her new shoes together.

"These aren't *Western* exactly," Alice said, remembering the masquerade of the big shoes laced tight over three pairs of Arthur's wool socks. Surprising her aunt in the dressing room as she swayed toward her reflection in the mirror.

"No, not exactly." May folded her napkin. "They are—what is that depressing word?—orthopedic. Curative. They will straighten me out." The tone of her voice was one Alice didn't know how to interpret. So rarely had she heard the sound of May grieving.

"Well," May challenged, after no one had spoken for a few minutes. She used her cane to stand, and the others followed her lead. The three women silently circled the flowerbeds, blazing red and orange and pink. They did it twice, three times. They walked up and down the promenade, a mile or more, before they returned to their waiting car and went home.

Once inside the door, May took the shoes off. She left them on the end of the dining table, and no one removed them, not even at dinner time, when they sat at the far end like unwanted guests, tongues lolling.

"I'm not very hungry this evening," Suzanne said, and she coughed. "Such a big lunch." She excused herself in the middle of the meal. At its conclusion, Eleanor and Dick preferred cognac to dessert, the library to the dining room; after all, the library had the ticker spitting forth its endless and endlessly fascinating sentence of numbers. Then, as the shell-shocked Italian ate alone in his room, Alice and May were left alone, looking at each other across the uncleared table. Neither of them stood, and Alice wondered if they were about to have a fight.

"So," she began, feeling for a topic that was neutral without appearing too obviously diplomatic. Not swimming, not shoes. Not the past, nor the future. Not books. And no new guests about whom to speculate. No gossip. "We could—" play mah-jongg, she was going to say, when May interrupted her.

"Do you know me?" she asked.

"What?"

"I asked, *Do you know me?* Do you think you know who I am?"

Alice hesitated. She drew her dark eyebrows together. "Yes," she said, after looking into her lap for a minute.

"Why haven't you ever asked me about Agnes?"

"I . . ." Alice was too startled to think. "I'm not sure. I don't know." It was a topic they hadn't approached for many years, not since they'd left Shanghai.

"Why?" May asked again. She folded her hands on the table.

"I suppose I didn't want to. And I . . ." Alice surprised herself by blushing. "There was no reason to think you'd want to speak of her."

The houseboy came through the dining room's swinging door, but before he had even reached the table, May stopped him. "Go away," she ordered in Chinese, and he bowed silently and backed out of the room. May turned back to Alice.

"It's been so long." Alice stood from the table. The boy having retreated, she began to collect the silverware that hadn't been used. "It's been . . . it seems a lifetime since that afternoon at the solicitor's. Can't we—"

"No!" May said, and Alice looked up from the table, the dishes of half-eaten food. Surprised by the anger on May's face, she dropped a spoon, bent down to retrieve it.

"I didn't want to know any more than . . . than what I knew already," she said. She stood up, her face even redder.

"Because you preferred to go on loving me?"

Alice blew the air out of her nose in an exasperated gust. "I've never been able to help loving you," she said. "Not then any more than now."

May crossed her arms. "You don't seem to. Lately."

"That's because you insist on making it a contest. Between you and Ev. As if I were incapable of loving two people at once."

May ignored this. "Admit something," she said. "I shouldn't have taken you with me to the solicitor's. I should never . . . I should . . ." She shook her head. "It . . . it must have been Arthur's death that did it."

"Did what?"

"Unbalanced my—I usually have a good sense of what can be shared. Of what I could share with you." She pressed her lips together, paused. Then: "I gave in to loneliness. I don't usually, but on that day I did."

"Uncle Arthur," Alice asked. "Did he know?"

"What do you think?" May said.

"I think he didn't."

May shook her head. "You're wrong."

"Well, he would have—"

"Forgiven me? Yes. Of course. He forgave everything. But I didn't—I don't—want absolution." Alice remained standing. She held the silverware before her in both hands, a bright, awkward bouquet. "Do you understand me?" May asked. "Do you understand what I'm saying?"

"That you're not expecting—asking—forgiveness?"

"Yes."

"I do. Yes." Alice transferred the cutlery to one hand, wiped the other sweat-slippery palm on her skirt.

"All that crying," May said. "Back at the hotel, when we returned. It wasn't, as you said, pent-up tears, your finally breaking down about your mother. Was it?"

Alice shook her head. "No. I don't know. It was all—so much happened. All at once." Her voice was low. She dropped another spoon but didn't bother to retrieve it.

"It was what you'd seen at the solicitor's. What you'd understood. About me. Am I right?"

Alice didn't answer. May took her wrists. She emptied Alice's hands of forks and knives and spoons and pulled her back down into the chair next to her own. For a moment she was still, then she picked up a handful of silverware and threw it so it hit the opposite wall. A knife struck a framed picture, a triangle of glass dropped to the floor.

"*I* bit the child," May said. "*I* crippled her."

"No!" Alice put her hands over her ears, but it didn't work, it didn't prevent her from hearing what May said.

"She was in the laundress's quarters, in the basement, four flights down. Clutter. Broken furniture. I would go there at night. Because I wanted . . . I had to touch her. I was going to . . ." The words came slowly, as if May had forgotten the language she knew so well.

"I was going to kiss her, and I went down the stairs slowly to avoid making noise." May snorted. "Because I can't walk any way other than slowly," she corrected. A single fork remained on the table, and she snatched it up, hurled it against the wall. It hummed after it dropped, like a tuning fork.

"Each time," May said, "I thought—I was sure—it would turn out differently. The last clients had left. Laundress asleep. Baby quiet." May paused. She looked around the dining room, its walls and ceiling, all the elegant appointments she had chosen. Were a stranger to see her, that person might conclude that May wasn't in her own home, that this was an unfamiliar house. A place, perhaps, whose purchase she was considering.

When she continued, her voice was no longer halting. "As soon as I touched the baby, she cried, the laundress woke. But I'd threatened her before." May laughed, a mirthless noise. "I'd told her I'd killed my own grandmother. After that, she lay still on her pallet, she let me do what I would."

"You, you didn't, did you?" Alice stammered, her hands still uselessly clapped over her ears.

"Didn't what?"

"Kill your—"

"No." May smiled. She closed her eyes, just for a moment, then opened them. "I bit Agnes's arms and feet until she screamed," she said.

"No. No, you didn't!" Alice shook her head. "You didn't ever—"

"Yes!" May slapped her open palm on the table. She did it over and over, ten times or more before she stopped.

"As soon as I . . . as soon as I held the baby I felt the claim she had on me. That having escaped one kind of servitude, here was another." May stopped speaking. After a minute, Alice took her hands from her ears.

"The most terrible feeling," May murmured. "I can't begin to reconcile myself to it. Her feet were . . . They were soft. Like butter against my lips. Teeth. Afterwards, I'd push Agnes into the laundress's arms, then hurry upstairs." Alice stared at May.

"Her feet. Her *feet*. I keep asking myself—does that make it better or worse? More understandable, or less?" May shook her head. "Less shameful, or more?" She kept shaking her head.

"If I gave her what I owed her—everything—then . . . Then it would all be ruined. All my . . . my . . . plans." May looked at her palm, red where it had repeatedly struck the table. "In the basement, I'd hold my breath, I'd try to think. Hadn't I, by force of will, invented a future different from the one for which I was made? Denied my fate? The baby was a mistake, a miscalculation. She was an error in timing. The daughter of my dead self.

"So," May's voice was even now, calm. "They took her away.

"No one spoke to me," May went on, having given Alice the chance to respond. But Alice sat silently. She ran her tongue over her teeth, said nothing. "*About* me, yes. I overheard Madame Grace speaking with the doctor. I'd had . . . I was pregnant once before, and a doctor had come, they called a doctor and he—" May shook her head, shut her eyes. "I couldn't bear for that to happen again."

"What?" Alice prompted, when she didn't say. "You don't mean a . . ."

"He ended it. So the next time I. I ignored it. Pretended I wasn't. Pregnant. Until it was too late to do anything. Then, after, when Agnes was . . . she was downstairs, and I overheard Grace talking to him, the same doctor. I was on the landing outside Grace's sitting room, I was eavesdropping. 'Do you think the Chinese girl might be dangerous?' Grace said to the doctor. And he laughed. 'If she bites your clients,' he said, 'you can charge them more.' "

May made a noise, a noise like a moan. "Strange words to have heard inside my head so many times: *If she bites your clients, you can charge them more.*" May looked at Alice. "When I was having the shoes made—the impressions, and then later when I returned for fittings, adjustments—the same words would repeat, over and over. *If she bites your clients, you can charge them more.*" She continued to search Alice's face. "I don't know why," she said, as if expecting Alice to explain it.

"Both," Alice said.

"Both?"

"Both more and less shameful. Understandable."

"Her feet? That I hurt her feet?"

"Yes."

May dropped her head. She let the silence grow before she spoke. "I went down one night, the baby was gone. I looked through the basement, among piles of rubbish, broken things. No one. The missionary ladies had come, they had taken her to Siccawei.

"The next day I woke at noon, the light shining bright on my face. I got up. Sat at my table, drank my tea. Opened my books to study. The previous night, the dark stairs—I put it out of my head. I could do that. I could do it then, but not now." She looked at Alice. "Why is that, do you think?"

Alice shook her head.

"Because I was young?" May shrugged. "My body carried no mark to remind me. Having a child was—it was something I could put away. As if in a drawer I never opened, a place out of sight. It interrupted work for no more than a season. And I suppose if Grace hadn't been a, a Christian, then Agnes would have been . . ."

"Just one more discarded native girl." Alice reached forward, as if to touch May, but then dropped her hand back into her lap. "And what has happened now?" she asked. "So many years later? What has changed to make you think of it—her—now?"

May lifted her shoulders. "I don't know. New shoes?" She laughed, looked at Alice, frowned. "You cry," she said. "I don't. Why is that?"

Alice got out of her chair and onto her knees. "You don't want forgiveness, but I do. Why, *why* won't you give it to me?" She put her arms around May's waist and lay her head in her lap.

"Forgiveness for what?"

"Evlanoff."

May put her hand under Alice's chin; she lifted it to look into her face. "I can't. Don't you see? You promised me you were mine."

Alice shook her head. "Even real daughters fall in love. They marry."

"Ah, well, *real* daughters, *real* mothers." May raised her eyebrows.

A person who didn't know her might have mistaken the look for one of amusement. "Perhaps they can afford it."

The word *real*, the way May had pronounced it: Alice found she couldn't answer such bitterness. She buried her face in May's silk trousers, thinking again of that afternoon, years before, when she surprised May in her dressing room. May standing for whole minutes, watching her reflection as it moved in the mirror.

"Did you mean it?" Alice asked. "About the shoes? About the shoes changing . . . anything?" She sat back on her heels. "Forgive me that. At least forgive me the shoes."

"What about them?"

"Thinking they could help. They . . . They were a mistake."

"Were they?" May leaned forward. Feature by feature she touched Alice's face, all of it. Traced the orbit of each eye, its brow. Nose. Lips. "It's odd, I couldn't have predicted it. But I'm not sorry to have told you what I did."

May straightened up, she brushed her palms together, a gesture, consciously ironic, of dusting them off after a dirty job. "As for the shoes." She smiled brightly, a little too widely. "I'm not going to wear them. I'm going to throw them into the sea."

# BIRTHDAY CELEBRATION

ROSE APPEARED TO MAY IN A DREAM, CALLING her not Mother and not May but Chao-tsing.

*My fourth birthday approaches,* the child said, speaking formally as she never had in life. *The occasion must be one that we will remember with joy and satisfaction. For, you know, it is to be my last.*

May nodded. She looked at her daughter and saw with shock that Rose was not a blending of Chinese and European but an awkward juxtaposing of differences. She had one round blue eye, one narrow black one.

Noticing how her mother stared, Rose smiled. Her expression was strangely melancholy and sophisticated for a little girl. *Yes,* she said, nodding, and she picked up her skirt to reveal one bound foot, one natural.

*But how do you get about?* May said, understanding the question to be useless, even stupid, and yet unable not to ask it. *How do you play?* she asked.

Rose laughed, a high peal, so mirthful, so blithe that May smiled even though she didn't find the sight of her daughter funny. *Oh, I manage*, Rose said. Her expression became serious.

*Now, here is who must attend the party.* She counted off names on her small fingers. *Your mother and your father and your father's mother, Yu-ying. My father and my cousins' Alice, Cecily, and David. And*, she said, *you must write the invitations yourself. In your own hand.*

May nodded. *Of course I will*, she promised.

Rose listed the foods she wanted served. Sticky dumplings filled with red bean paste, hot soup dumplings with bamboo straws through which to drink the broth, quail eggs, and sweet yellow pickles. Weren't these all the foods May had herself preferred as a child?

Rose told her mother what games she wanted to play: *Charades. Hide and seek. And that funny one, you know, where we build cities with mah-jongg tiles.*

*But that—that was I, Rose*, May argued. *Not you. That was a game I played with my mother.*

Rose stamped her foot in anger. *No!*

*What presents shall you have?* May said, to placate her.

*Side-button white kid shoes*, Rose said. *As soft as gloves. And both the same size, the size that fits the unbound one, so that in them I can hide my mismatched feet.*

*And toys?*

*Yes, but I'm not going to tell you everything. I want you to surprise me.*

Once more she reminded May that as this was to be her last birthday, all must be perfect. *You know you have just two days*, she warned, and she looked over her mother's shoulder as May wrote down lists of all she needed to accomplish.

When May looked up from the paper, Rose was gone.

In the markets, May went from stall to stall. On her own feet, without her cane or an amah, she searched the market for lanterns of the style Rose had requested—tall blue ones decorated with characters for luck and happiness—but she couldn't find one. When she pleaded with a vendor to allow her to order them—she promised to buy however many he asked, a dozen, two dozen, three—he refused, he said there wasn't enough time. And besides, didn't she know where she was? This was Nice. This was France, not China. If she wanted Chinese lanterns, she wouldn't find them here.

It was the same with the dumplings. She found soufflés and tarts and sausages, pots of caviar, trays of whelks and mussels, heaps of pastries, mountains of canapés, but there was not one sweet red bean dumpling to be had. There were no quail eggs or yellow pickles. And where was it that one could buy such things, the *boulanger* wanted to know. Surely not in the south of France.

No blue firecrackers. No red. No pink.

And not one pair of side-button white kid shoes in which Rose could hide her mismatched feet.

Then light was pouring through the open curtains, Suzanne was shaking May's shoulder. She was awake and sobbing in frustration.

# THE BAY OF ANGELS

SEPTEMBER THE TWENTIETH. ALREADY THE SEA-
son was over, the summer crowd had departed from
Nice, the cafés were no longer serving outdoors. Bad
weather was forecast, and the sky had darkened. The
palm trees were tousled by a sudden wind; the sound
made by their fronds rustling together was so like rain-
fall that, were she to close her eyes, May would have
sworn that already the storm had arrived. Her teeth chat-
tered, but perhaps this wasn't from cold. In any case,
she'd feel warmer in the sea. The previous day's water
temperature had been recorded as seventy-two degrees,
the tide had reached its high point at 4:44 P.M. Of late,
this was the only section of the paper May bothered to
read.

"Come on," she said to Suzanne. "We'll be brisk." She
used her cane to navigate the steps down to the water.

"I'm not brisk," Suzanne complained, hugging herself as she walked. "And neither are you."

"Not on land," May said. "In the water we're fine."

"You are."

The Promenade des Anglais was deserted, the sky an affronted, glowering purple. Thunder thudded over the bay; it made a noise that recalled fireworks discharged above the Whangpoo, a dull, shuddering report that mocked the celebratory showers of sparks. May looked back, over her shoulder. What light remained painted the hotels' white façades an unhealthy yellow, like jaundice. The black gaps of their shadowed doorways looked like lost teeth, and the pretty buildings with their windowpane eyes seemed like suddenly aged faces. Each day, dusk came earlier and with increasing menace. The light had shifted, it had changed; but what May saw was not an effect of the season. She recognized the return of despair.

As the tide receded, it left the beach wet, pebbles bright. Two gulls balanced on the back of a bench, and another rested on the rocks, the feathers on its breast puffed out to conserve warmth. Others floated on the water, barking at each other like curs. May laid her folded towel on the last dry stair and sat down to unlace her custom-made shoes. The only time she wore them, grudgingly, was when she came to swim; the shoes made it possible for her to descend the stairs to the water by herself. She pulled the pins from her hair and undid the long braid she'd made that morning.

"What? Aren't you wearing your bathing cap?" Suzanne winced as she pushed her hair under the tight rubber of her own. The sea lapped at the lower stairs, green and treacherous with algae.

"The cap makes my head ache. I'd rather leave my hair undone."

"You'll catch cold."

"No."

Suzanne sighed. "What's the point in trying to talk to you?" she said. "You'd argue a cat's hind leg off." She held her towel around her shoulders. "Come on, then. The sooner we're in and done with it, the sooner we'll be home and in a hot bath." Suzanne watched as May picked up one of her expensive orthopedic shoes and hurled it into the bay. She opened her mouth and left it open, too surprised to say anything. The shoe sank immediately, and May threw the other after it. Air trapped in the toe kept it afloat for a minute, before leaking out;

then that shoe, too, went down. As it disappeared, Suzanne recovered her speech.

"What are you doing! What can you be thinking!" She stamped one foot in agitation. "How are we going to get you back up the steps? You told the boy to go home. You told him we'd have the doorman at the Negresco hail a car!"

May shrugged. "We'll manage." She scooted forward in a sitting position, using her arms to transfer herself onto the last stair, submerged below the sea's surface.

The salt stung May's feet; there were always open blisters. But once in the water, she moved swiftly out into the bay, and Suzanne followed doggedly. As they approached, the gulls flapped and lifted themselves off the waves, keening as they flew. The two women were soon out past their depth. Having mastered the crawl as well as the breast-, side-, and backstroke, May had succeeded in teaching only the breaststroke to Suzanne, who became competent but never enthusiastic.

May found the impulse cruel—she couldn't explain it to herself as anything other than cruelty—but she enjoyed leading Suzanne out beyond the point where she felt comfortable. Without her glasses, Suzanne's eyesight was so poor that she could see almost nothing; it all melted into a wet gray-green fog. Absorbed with the task of breathing, she trailed farther and farther behind, she didn't speak. She couldn't tell in which direction she swam, couldn't tell where was the horizon, the shore.

May swam hard and ignored Suzanne's panting. A wind blew west, along the coast, licking the waves into spray. Gusts played over the surface of the sea, and water slapped May's face as she swam, stinging her eyes, forcing its way up her nose. It burned and dripped down the back of her throat, tasting like tears.

"I'm tired," she heard Suzanne gasp. "Please let's stop. Let's just float for a moment. I haven't—You know I haven't the breath for these fast swims."

"A little farther," May said, and Suzanne, too blind to return to shore by herself, followed.

The water heaved beneath them. Who knew what it contained? The sea emptied Suzanne's mind of everything but fear. Beneath her body she pictured gelid, black, oozing caves. Wet jaws. Pincers. Eels big enough to pull down a ship. She coughed her habitual, nervous, clattering cough. Everything that aggravated May was in its noise: everything that made her feel desperate, wild with aggravation. Usually when she heard the cough, filled as it was with the sound of catastrophe, May pictured herself falling down long staircases with trays of dishes. And yet now she felt composed, she felt calm, as she had for the past few days. A distance, even a dispassion, she hadn't known in years, deep and absolute. The agitation and jealousy to which she was prey evaporated, and every action—pouring tea, braiding her hair, paring her toenails—was suffused with peace.

As she swam steadily, rhythmically, suddenly May knew when it was she'd last felt this way. She was fifteen and recently married. She was pouring lamp oil into a teacup. Looking through her clothes for a sash strong enough to bear her weight. Having made a decision, she was no longer impeded by the usual friction of human ambivalence and distractions.

*Of course,* May thought, tasting the water, the salt of it. How obvious it was, how abruptly and almost laughably obvious. All along *this* had been the point of the lessons.

*Drowning was the reason for learning to swim.* A secret she'd been keeping from herself, one she'd glimpsed, barely, and just a few times during her more reckless swims, but never admitted.

In her bedroom, just an hour before, May had picked up a photograph of Alice taken on her seventeenth birthday. Looking at Alice: it had been a test of May's footing in the world, as well as an attempt to reattach herself. Not that she'd understood this while staring at the photograph. She knew it only now that she was in the water and far from shore, from home.

Except that she had no home. She could make a home for others, but not for herself.

May had held the silver frame, polished a faint smear from the surface of the glass. She'd recognized Alice; of course she had: Alice. The child who was to assuage her loss, who was to be a daughter, not a niece. And for a while—a long while, really—this had worked. Alice had been solace and affection. She'd been amusement. She'd been defiance; she'd been worry and argument and anguish. And she'd been a companion. She'd protected May from solitude. Sometimes, even, Alice had needed her.

But, holding the photograph, it was as if May were looking at a stranger. *Who is she?* she found herself asking, and she'd felt a quickening of pulse in her ears, a sensation she associated with fear. She even asked herself: *Am I afraid?* And answered: *No. Not afraid.*

Still, who was that young woman, a strand of pearls at her smooth throat, eyes tilting with mischief?

She was *na guo ning.* A foreigner. May turned the photograph face down on the bureau. She called down the hall to see if Suzanne was ready to leave for the beach.

IN THE WATER, May freed her right arm from her long hair that had tangled around it. Her eyes smarted with salt.

"Please," Suzanne said. "Can't we turn back?"

"We have," May lied. "It's hard to tell because the waves are high."

As May spoke, one caught Suzanne full in the face. She spluttered, gasped. "How much longer?" She was breathing hard. "I can't see the steps. The beach. I can't see anything."

"Not so long now. Five more minutes. Maybe ten."

Suzanne stopped swimming. She turned onto her back, breathing, coughing. The swells were big enough to disorient even a person with good eyesight.

"I don't know why I followed you," she said at last, when she'd caught her breath. She laughed, a short, wry choke of a laugh. "I don't know why, after I noticed that you'd left your cane uncovered."

Because May hadn't done what she usually did. She hadn't folded the polished jade knob into her towel in case a passing beachcomber were to see its gleam and think to steal it.

May didn't answer. She treaded water silently. They'd been in long enough to get chilled, and she felt the cold as an ache in her thighs and groin, an ache to which she was vulnerable.

"Poor Alice," Suzanne said.

"No." May shook her head. She spat to get the salt out of her mouth, wiped her stinging lips with the back of her hand.

The sun had set and it was dark enough now that the troughs between waves were filled with black shadows. Whenever either woman was in one, she was invisible.

"Why?" Suzanne asked. "Why not poor Alice?"

"Because she's free. I'm setting her free."

Suzanne snorted. "That's self-serving," she said. Her voice came as if from the water itself.

"But I am self-serving," May answered.

"What will she do?" Suzanne asked, after a silence.

"She'll stay with Evlanoff. Or she'll find someone else. Whomever she wants. She's an heiress, remember. Or will be. She can choose."

The water was increasingly rough, and it seemed colder in the sudden shadows.

"Do you think so?" Suzanne said. "Do you think anyone chooses?"

FROM THE WINDOW of Evlanoff's apartment, Alice was watching the light die on the surface of the sea. Wind moved across it, making silver scrawls. "Baie des Anges." She shivered, wearing only a slip. "Who named it that?"

"What?" Evlanoff said. They were dressing for dinner; he was looking for his cufflinks.

"Please," Alice turned and opened her arms to him. "I want to go back to bed."

"We've only just gotten up." He put his lips to her hair as he spoke, the words tickling. As she felt this, the gooseflesh on Alice's arms tightened, each bump tingled. On the windowsill behind her were pieces of sea glass, a few shells and pretty stones she'd collected. As they embraced, they knocked a few to the floor.

*"Please. Please let's."*

Evlanoff looked into Alice's eyes. He'd been about to laugh, but then, at her plaintive expression, he stopped. "All right," he said, and he began unbuttoning his shirt. "Three times in one afternoon is too much for an old man," he teased, as she pulled the blanket up.

Alice cupped his testicles in her palm, felt them draw away from her cold hand. "You're not old," she whispered.

"Compared to you."

"Besides, I'm not asking for that." She put her cold feet on his warm legs, tucked her hands under his side. She was still shivering. "I just want you to hold me."

Arms around her, he nuzzled his forehead down between her breasts. She felt the heat of breath on her skin, heard his words muffled by the blanket. "This is the only time I'm really happy. Not worried, not . . ." He trailed off, sighing. "The rest is just time in between," he finished. She kissed his head.

In the dim light from the window, books piled by the bed (thick, illustrated medical texts in Russian—Alice liked to open them, to shudder at the pictures) resolved into a dark staircase. Voices floated up from the sidewalk. From the Negresco, a few doors down, it was possible to hear strains of music. Alice closed her eyes.

" 'The Blue Danube,' isn't it?" Evlanoff asked. She didn't answer. She heard him, but she was hurrying toward sleep. Alice didn't know why, but she had to get there right away, and the *yes* she spoke was only a thought; no word came from her mouth.

Such pleasure in his arms, such warm comfort. His arms and the smell of him, cologne, tobacco. The feel of his beard prickling, she loved that, she squirmed down to put her mouth and nose against it. That funny cooked smell of hair. She saw Dah Su's kitchen, the shining pans, a long shelf of them. Scullery boys scrubbing. Odd what one thought of while falling asleep. She was safe in Ev's arms, she was inhaling the smell of him and suffused with that enviable feeling—once having felt it, Alice recognized it as the thing everyone wanted: the sheer luckiness of love, undeserved and therefore a little scary. It arrived with giddy speed; would it depart as quickly? But Evlanoff was right, it was hard to worry in love's arms, impossible, really. Love made everything else so . . . small, so much less than its object.

Alice was asleep, the landscape she'd traveled to get there familiar, though it had been years since she'd crossed it: a blue-white expanse, ice the color of sky, and a train running silently off its rails. Without a sound it penetrated a lake's frozen surface, it sank through dark water. An enchanted realm, it must be—how else to explain the warmth, the *heat*, of such depths?

And then came the dancing, Alice in the captain's arms, except the captain wasn't the captain, he was Evlanoff. Magically, he was both men: the alchemy of dreams made it possible.

May was there. She danced, as well. But May didn't dance with a man, she danced by herself, and her feet moved like anyone else's. May was dancing in her new shoes, the ones Alice had convinced her to wear.

In the dream, ice lay over warm water, and in the dream May liked the shoes, she loved them. They were her partners. They were all the partners she required. Alice and the captain—the captain who was Evlanoff—stepped aside, the piano played under unseen hands, and the drowned passengers cleared the center of the floor to watch May dance, an audience too awed, too breathless, to applaud.

In her sleep, Alice murmured. With her head tucked under Evlanoff's chin, her right hand found his left.

"You were waltzing last night," he'd tell her the next morning. "I was talking about a piece of music as you fell asleep. 'The Blue Danube.' They were playing it at the hotel, and it must have slipped into your dreams." Alice nodded against the pillow; she rolled toward him, her eyes still closed.

"A good dream," she said. "An old favorite."

OUT IN THE bay, in order to hear each other over the noise of the water, May and Suzanne were yelling things they'd never before whispered.

"I thought you were braver," Suzanne accused.

"You were wrong." May had stopped treading water and was on her back, her face barely above the surface. The swells picked the women up, and then put them down. Over and over. They hadn't felt it so much when they were swimming. "You saw I left my cane uncovered and followed me anyway," May said. "Why?"

"I have no life. Apart from. You. You know. That." Suzanne panted between clauses, between words.

"Yes." May raised one arm, began stroking again. "That's why I'm taking you with me."

Suzanne dog-paddled feebly after her. "How long. Have you. Planned. This."

"I didn't," May said. Her backstroke was fast. "I'm going to swim out farther," she warned.

But with a sudden, violent, clawing leap, Suzanne had climbed onto May. It was something, May realized, that she ought to have anticipated: a strength she knew well, that of desperation. Suzanne didn't speak, she keened.

*Here I am already,* May thought. *In the lake of blood, hearing the cries. What was it? One gasp in trade for each peal of the bell?*

She went under with Suzanne like a cat on her shoulders, battering her head. May let Suzanne push her down, she accepted her weight as assistance, remembering the young swimming instructor, entire days spent practicing holding her breath. Silver bubbles streaming from her nose past her open eyes.

Down. She had to stay down. Under. But in spite of herself she wriggled out of Suzanne's arms and legs and surfaced a few yards away, gasping. Then she swam, kicking as hard as she could—kicking both to propel herself and to obliterate the noise of Suzanne drowning. Even so, as she swam, it struck her that the sound of Suzanne dying was the same as that of her living: a clattering, choking cough.

May concentrated her will and forced the air from her lungs. She dove with her eyes closed, plunged downwards in a modified, underwater breaststroke. Six feet below the surface, seven. Now it must be ten, twelve. She felt the water pressing her all over. It stabbed into her ears, and she wondered for a moment if Arthur's tinnitus had caused him pain. Could it be that she'd never asked? Stones clacked together on the sea's floor. Or was she hearing the noise of her own pulse, erratic, panicked without oxygen?

Eyes shut tightly, May stroked, stroked. Swimming was hard now. She'd made it as hard as walking.

Where was the buck? The white buck with silver antlers, a bridle set with jewels, a saddle carved from jade. Just outside the city, the city of Shanghai, deer drank from the dirty Whangpoo. They left prints of their cloven hooves in the silt. Arthur had shown this to her. He'd stood on the bank, pointing. "Look," he said. "Your footprints are no bigger."

Where was her white buck? Wouldn't he arrive, as he had before, to rescue her, to carry her away? Without breath, May's chest burned. She was cold, so cold, but inside it was as if she'd inhaled fire, she saw not black but red. Swells of red before her eyes. Her blood was banging inside her head. Cymbals. A parade. The clanging of the firehouse bell.

A man jogged across the Garden Bridge, a gold harp on his back. Shanghai. Here was a city where anything was possible.

She was waiting. She could wait, she'd always excelled at it. Look how long she'd waited for this. A minute more, two at most. That would be all: her body would end it.

She opened her mouth and her heart to the water.

ACKNOWLEDGMENTS

The author wishes to thank Stella Dong, Dawn Drzal,
Janet Gibbs, Joan Gould, Nan Graham, Emily Hall, Colin
Harrison, George Hayim, Kate Medina, Aziza Mowlem,
Christopher Potter, Meaghan Rady, Joyce Ravid, Deborah
Rogers, and Amanda Urban.